Author's notes

The Hated is a work of fiction. Names of Characters and places apart from the obvious such as Belfast are from the author's imagination. Any resemblance to actual persons living or dead are entirely coincidental. Some incidents are based on the author's experiences and some from the author's imagination.

MICK COTTON

The Hated

For my Family: Audrey, Mike & Annie

Dedicated to Brummie, Doc, Stovie
and the rest who never made it.

I
BELFAST 1971

1

The night was pitch black, moonlight and stars shut off by a dark blanket of rain cloud. The rain fine, almost misty, could only be seen against the weak amber light of the only working street lamp.

The men came running, tall men and short men, crouched low as if against the rain. Twelve of them, six either side of the road in a purposeful trot, hardly a sound in the otherwise deserted street except for the rhythmic slap as twelve sets of feet struck the wet pavement in unison. Only when they neared the working street lamp did the pattern change when one of the files swerved to avoid the unfriendly glow.

They came to the end of the street where it joined the main road. The leader stopped and dropped flat under the overhanging hedgerow merging completely with the darkness. The rest immediately followed suit using gardens and pathways for concealment. The leader strained his eyes and ears reaching into the ink in front of him.

The main road was empty of traffic and looked like a gleaming black river, rain water gurgling down the gutter added to the effect. The leader cupped his ears and let his jaw slacken in concentration. Turning his head to the left and looking down the road he saw the glow of a fire inside the skeletal remains of a double decker bus. He then heard the unmistakable sound of human voices, the loud unrestrained voices of angry men and women.

The leader crawled forward for a better view his small sub machine gun clutched to his chest. He looked directly down the road, about three hundred yards away he saw in the flickering fire light a crowd of youths hurling debris at an unseen target. There must be at least twenty of them he thought.

The leader snapped his fingers two or three times and signalled with his hand, at all times his eyes staring left, right and forward but never back. The others emerged from their dark recesses and bunched behind him, tensing and flexing like athletes on their starting blocks, then the leader was up and running across the black gleaming river road, his followers hard on his heels. Within a couple of seconds they were all across. The leader vaulted the cemetery wall without breaking his stride.

Major Alan Briggs rested his elbows on the wing of his Landrover, raised his binoculars to his eyes and spoke softly to no-one in particular. "Its marvellous how these things greatly improve detail, even on a filthy black night."

He was looking intently at the area of the burning double decker bus, the fuel tank had long since gone up and now it was just the tyres and upholstery that blazed. To the front of this was a crowd, youths mostly, shouting and screaming at the single line of soldiers that separated them from the Major and his group.

Every so often one of the soldiers would jerk an arm to fend of a missile with his small metal shield, but in the main they stood still, almost rigid against the highly mobile, vociferous aggressors.

"Do you think we should retaliate now sir?" said a young, well spoken voice at his side.

Major Briggs lowered his glasses but still continued to look at the scene to his front. "No.. There's only a few of the buggers yet and I don't want 'em scared off...I want them to get closer, I want them more cocky and confident," he said briskly, turning to the direction of the voice.

He regarded the young man by his side and saw that even with his face heavily streaked in black camo cream he looked boyish, a little anxiety showed in the eyes but was countered with a forced grin. The boyish face looked back at the Major expecting him to carry on speaking and when he didn't, said awkwardly, "Anyway sir my gang's ready to go."

"Be sure of that Tony." said the Major softly, "Because when she blows it may get a little sticky and you'll need to be damn quick." He turned back to the scene and once more raised the binoculars to his eyes.

Lieutenant Tony Orchard grimaced, his hands gripping his rifle so tightly that the wooden stock began to make a cracking sound. He was just about to say something else when he was aware of a figure approaching out of the gloom, he saw the bright white dog collar and an almost as white face contrasting greatly with the black cammo cream that everyone else had plastered on.

The figure dressed in an ill fitting camouflage smock strode up close to Tony Orchard, nodded in feigned recognition and turned to Major Briggs. "Evening Alan." He said loudly. Briggs turned swiftly, startled by the resonance of the voice. Most soldiers naturally speak softly at night when training and even more so on operations like this. "Would recognise you anywhere with those bloody great binoculars." He boomed out heartily in his broad Yorkshire accent, completely oblivious of the tension around him.

Major Briggs' moment of surprise and anger passed quickly and he even managed a smile. "Good evening Padre." he said as he ushered him to the comparative safety by the side of the Landrover.

The Padre continued in his booming voice, "I were just saying tut CO, there's trouble in the air tonight Colonel, and you can bet your bloody life that old Alan Briggs will be out in it somewhere. An' I were right weren't I?" He beamed good naturedly at the Major. Before Briggs could respond the Padre continued with a mock theatrical voice, "And I come bearing gifts your majesty." He reached inside of his bulging camouflaged smock and produced some newspaper parcels. "Fish and chips for the hungry troops."

Alan Briggs was flabbergasted, partly embarrassed and partly amused, there they were, in the middle of a riot and up turns the Padre with fish and chips.

"Er...Thanks Padre, but things are a little awkward at the moment as you can see. I'll give them to my signaller and he'll give them to the platoon behind us. Damn good of you though." He pushed them on to a soldier with a radio on his back and told him to hurry.

The Padre looked a little crestfallen and said in a quieter tone, "Sorry Alan, I should have thought...I mean, with this riot and all..."

"Nonsense Jack, that was a fine gesture. Look, who else but Padre Jack Thorpe would think of bringing fish and chips up to the front line ?" Both men laughed.

"Is it bad ?" Jack's tone was now serious as if trying to make amends for his former brashness.

"It will be soon."

"Those lads look awfully lonely there Alan." Jack was staring out to the single line of soldiers receiving abuse and bricks in good measure.

"Yes I know Jack, but do you see those derelict houses just to the rear of them...There! On the left hand side of the road? Got another thirty chaps in there, ten snatch squads, when I slip their collars we'll see who looks lonely eh?' he turned to the Lieutenant at his side. "Yes, young Tony here, is in charge of them, he will join them in a minute and on the given signal, will rush out and arrest 'em."

"And what will that signal be?" said the Padre in a lower, more conspirital tone.

"Ah! We have a secret weapon abroad tonight Jack, in the shape of Sergeant Britton and a few of his lads. You see, every Saturday night it's the same....Bloody rent a riot. All the young chaps and er ..chapesses in this estate, egged on by the IRA, gather at some focal point, tonight it's there at Murphy's Bar." The Major waved in the direction of the burning bus and jeering crowd. "They block the road with hijacked vehicles, set 'em alight and taunt the soldiers. We attack, they withdraw into the estate and when we are in the open and paddy is safe the sniper or gunmen open up. So simple, yet very effective. We've been lucky, damn lucky this last couple of times. Pearce got it in the leg and young Thompson got a flesh wound, went straight through his flack jacket and plonked him on his back side."

"And so Alan, what's so different this time?" whispered the Padre who was really hooked by now.

Briggs raised his glasses again and surveyed the scene. He had gotten a little carried away and wanted to appear calm before he spoke again. "Britton and his men are at this moment sneaking up behind them, he'll attack swiftly and silently from their rear. They won't be expecting that."

Padre Jack looked a little puzzled, "But surely Alan, even with surprise on his side, it would need more than a hand full of blokes to face that lot..Eh?"

Even the patient Major was now starting to get a little irritated, "Yes, you're right and that's where Tony's gang hidden in the derelict house comes in. When Britton materialises out of the estate, Tony's snatch squads will attack, classic pincer Jack." The Major made a motion with both hands as if gripping a throat. "We'll nail the buggers tonight!?"

As if to punctuate the sentence, there was a huge 'Woomf', the whole area lit up in an orange light followed by a great cheer, as the fuel tank of another hijacked car went up. Lieutenant Tony Orchard gripped the stock of his rifle till it cracked.

2

Frank Britton lay with his back against the oblong slab of a headstone. His face was wet with a mixture of sweat and rain, he was breathing deep after the run through the streets. Most of his men were strung out in a circle around him facing outwards. A silhouette of a man, large, even though he was bent almost double, crawled his way up to Frank and gave a thumbs up signal just in front of his face.

"Cheers Norrie." whispered Frank. Norrie was the tail end Charlie, when he was in, they were all in.

"Okay, close in a bit.' Frank urged. The men gradually eased in to the centre and faced Frank. He knew them all well but it was hard to recognise any of them in the darkness. Black camo cream plastered on thickly all but obliterated their features, he could only recognise Norrie because of his huge frame.

"Is everyone alright?" asked Frank in a voice that was just above a whisper.

There was a moments silence so Frank continued, "This is it from here we go straight in, it's about 500 yards through the estate until we get to them. Don't forget when we move from here stay in your snatch squads, one with a rifle, one with the baton and one Grabber. When we get near them and we get seen all hell will break loose. Follow your Grabber let him decide who to get and then follow it through to the end. Come shit or high water get your victim back to the base line to the arrest teams then wait for further deployment. If the shit hits the fan and the shooting starts get into cover straight away, drag the bastard with you, use him as a shield but get the bastard back, do you understand?.... Good! Its going to be noisy, we'll be outnumbered maybe ten or fifteen to one but we have surprise. They've been on the piss all day, lucky bastards, that'll slow 'em up and don't forget as soon as we show up Lieutenant Orchard will appear with the Seventh Cavalry...Let's go!"

Lieutenant Tony Orchard made his way from the Major through the shadows to the derelict house. The base line was still holding firm under a steadily growing barrage of rocks and bottles. He entered the derelict where the rest of his platoon were waiting. One man was up at the gaping hole that was once a window some sat on the bare floor of the living room smoking and talking quietly in the gloom, others were in the back room doing much the same.

The mob up the road were chanting slogans and female voices were singing "If you hate the British soldiers clap your hands!" To the tune of: She'll be coming round the mountain when she comes.

Orchard could contain himself no longer, "Get away from that window! For God's sake man you'll be seen."

"I've got to be here sir, keepin' a look out for when Britton shows up, that's our signal to go." retaliated the sentry.

"I'm more than bloody aware what the bloody signal is now get away from that window!" hissed Orchard, his blackened face contorted with rage.

The small compact figure of Corporal Reece loomed into Orchard's path and said calmly, "I put him there Sir, he can't be seen, we need....."

Orchard cut him off mid sentence. "Get all those fucking cigarettes out now! And you, you get down from that window! Don't you people know there's a riot going on out there!"

A voice in the gloom full of sarcasm said, "A riot? Oh! That's what's keeping me awake!" There was an outbreak of sniggering.

"Who said that?" screamed Orchard whirling around in rage, "Corporal Reece I want that man put on a charge for gross insubordination." The sentry at the window turned to the group and shouted, It's all happening out there! Britton's arrived! Come on let's go, yahoo!"

"Don't anyone move!" screamed Orchard, "Now, I intend to get to the bottom of this, who made that remark?"

Frank Britton and his men trotted down the side of the cemetery wall until it gave way to railings. After ten yards they came to a part where there was a section missing without pausing they burst through it and on to the street along it and up into the blackness of the vast housing estate. They used the centre of the street now, two Columns of black faced men rhythmically pacing up the street, slightly leaning into the incline, silent apart from the slight slap on the wet surface and some heavy breathing.

They rounded a bend and at once they saw the towering flames and heard the shouting and chanting but still their view was blocked by rows of houses. Frank, who was slightly in front of the two columns quickened the pace, his heart pounded, he could feel the hand of fear in his gut growing, its fingers gripping and twisting.

They started to come across people walking in twos and threes silhouetted against the glow. There was about two hundred yards between them and the mob, they started to overtake these groups. The warning screams started too late to warn the main mob but the groups just ahead started turning around. One middle aged man tried to block the column Frank shouldered him out of the way and a baton flashed out of the column splitting the mans head open, he went down on his knees. A rifle butt finished him off.

One hundred yards to go, they rounded the last bend and there before them they saw the inferno, the blazing bus on the main road, two burning cars and a bonfire of burning tyres.

A mob of about one hundred and fifty were screaming, singing and chanting in the general direction of the soldiers on the base line. The more daring, about twenty in all moved in close enough to hurl bottles, paving slabs and anything else they could lay their hands on. These were the ones they were after, the hardcore.

Frank moved to one side in a pre arranged signal for Norrie the Grabber to take the lead and select his prey. The seemingly lumbering hulk of Norrie passed him then took off like a rocket straight through the crowd on the periphery in a direct line to the stone throwers. The crowd looked on in astonishment as the six foot two inch gorilla smashed through them as if unaware that they were there. His eyes fixed on the still unaware stone throwers. He made a bee line for a man who was stripped to the waist and rugby tackled him to the ground which he hit like a sack of potatoes dropped from a three storey building.

Frank and the baton man caught up with Norrie as he tried to yank his victim to his feet but the rag doll just kept collapsing back to the ground. A screaming banshee of a woman jumped on Norrie's back tearing of his maroon beret and hanging on to the collar of his smock. John the baton man closed in to take a swipe at the woman but was blocked by two raging youths, he swung the baton and caught one of them on the side of the head he faltered but kept coming. The other one had a piece of scaffolding tube and swung it like a crazy windmill while screaming at the top of his voice. Frank ran round behind him and jumped onto the back of his legs they both fell to the ground the rioter on top.

Norrie heaved his great frame forward and ducked down, the banshee arched over his head and landed heavily on her back. Norrie then swung round to where Frank and the man were writhing on the ground. He dragged the man off, Frank head butted him and threw him down on the ground with the rag doll. John in the meantime had finally felled the other youth with a rain of blows from his baton.

The three of them paused for a moment to get their breath, people and soldiers were running everywhere. The three other snatch groups instead of making arrests were now fighting for their lives. At first the sheer surprise and ferocity of the attack had panicked the rioters and they had headed swiftly for the safety of the blackened housing estate but they just as quickly realised that there were only a handful of soldiers and turned on them. This was the precise moment that Lieutenant Orchard and his men should have arrived but they were nowhere to be seen.

Frank could see that the situation was worsening as more and more youths and women started to pour back on the scene carrying bricks and pipes to lay into the soldiers with. He ran to the base line for help. "Come on! Come on!" He yelled at them. In an instant they dropped their shields and ran toward the melee, looks of sheer hatred on their faces. The looks that only men can give when they've stood for an hour impotent in front of a baying, snarling mob that had been taunting them, calling them cowards and wishing death upon them.

They closed with the rioters batons working up and down like pistons screaming and yelling. Now it was their turn, pent up fury replaced reason and order. They lashed out at all and any in range chasing if they had to, two, sometimes three on to one, not ceasing until the victim slumped to the ground.

As the tide finally started turning, a flaming object trailing sparks like a distant comet flew through the air and exploded amongst the screaming entangled mass of soldiers and rioters, a youth with his hair and jacket ablaze screamed, "God have mercy! God have mercy!" Over and over until another pulled him down to smother the flames.

A soldier lay on the ground his uniform smouldering, he too screamed for help the arm of his smock glowing like the embers in a fire. The mob turned once more in a final frenzy to subdue the soldiers. With more men and women pouring from the estate they started closing in armed now with iron bars, fencing posts, stones and bottles. They were now at fever pitch with staring eyes and mouths wide, hatred emanating from every pore.

Faced with this there was only one thing to do. Frank screamed at the top of his voice, "Come on! Lets go! Get the bastards!" They rushed the large crowd shouting and yelling. Norrie dropped his baton and picked up the four foot long scaffolding pole that had been used on him, he flailed it in a huge arc around him and split the mob in half. Just then the platoon from the derelict under command of Orchard burst in on the scene. The mob who had already had enough broke and ran. Orchard's men quickly caught up and laid into them without mercy.

A middle aged woman wandered slowly through the battleground screaming. Not the scream of a frightened or distressed woman but a deep, continuous, flesh crawling sound that originated and escaped from somewhere deep in her tormented soul. Her head was thrust back and froth oozed out of her mouth like lava from an erupting volcano.

Nobody went near her, she just walked stiff legged until she stumbled to the ground rolling and now whimpering into the still burning debris of the petrol bomb. She staggered back to her feet looking incredulously at her burning dress., the flames now starting to leap up her body and arms. She collapsed, a soldier and two of the former rioters ran to her aid beating out the flames, they raged at the soldier to leave her alone which he did and they dragged her stiff, moaning body toward the estate leaving only the soldiers and their muted prisoners on the road and waste ground.

Frank ran over to where Norrie had dumped his two prisoners. Norrie was sitting in the rubble nearby desperately clicking a lighter over and over in a vain bid to light the cigarette protruding from his mouth. "Come on let's get out of here," Frank urged, he then raised his voice and repeated the command to the others.

"Look at that bastard strutting around like Lord shit." sneered Norrie pointing to Lieutenant Orchard, "Where the fuck was he? We damn near got fucking slaughtered because of him arriving late."

"Come on Norrie, get moving! Get them prisoners back!" ordered Frank.

He looked towards Orchard confidently walking around where hardly a minute before men had been fighting for their lives. Orchard turned toward Frank and demanded, "Why are you ordering the men back Sergeant Britton? There are some snatch squads who haven't arrested anyone yet, we should get those bastards over there." He pointed to a small group at the very edge of the estate still ranting and raving.

"We've achieved our aim Sir, now let's get the fuck out of here before the gunmen open up, we're like sitting ducks in this light." Frank turned away from him and shouted to a few stragglers, "Come on! Move it!"

One of the soldiers ran up to them and spoke urgently to Frank. "Sarge, have we got any of our lads over in the estate? Because I just seen a soldier in the alley, didn't look one of our blokes but definitely a soldier."

Frank looked at Lieutenant Orchard who just made a Gallic gesture and said, "Not to my knowledge, let's get out of here." Frank's reminder about the gunmen had hit home.

"We have to check sir," stated Frank, "We can't take the risk and leave one of our blokes out in this situation." He started to run toward the alley that had been pointed out to him automatically expecting Orchard to follow him as a back up, he didn't. Orchard tried to turn Frank's decision around but nothing came out of his mouth.. Frank by now was committed and running toward the alley.

The waste ground was now empty as even the die hards on the edge of the estate had disappeared. There was just the flickering orange light reflecting on the soft rain and the crackle of the burning vehicles perfect for snipers. A stab of fear ran through Orchard's guts, he knew that he should be running toward the estate with his platoon sergeant providing vital cover but his mind could not make his legs work. He compensated by running back toward his own lines and shouting for some assistance, when nothing happened he hid behind some rubble, his mind on the edge of panic.

Frank reached the alley and immediately hit the deck just inside the darkness. He shot a backward glance to see where Orchard was and got alarmed when he realised he was by himself. He shouted down the alley, "Is anyone there?" All he could hear were the sounds of movement in the street to his left, the time was ripe for the gunmen to come out, he would wait no longer.

As he got up to make a dash for it a light went on in the backroom of the house on his left, he automatically looked in that direction and saw the outline of a man with a rifle in an instant he thumbed the safety catch of his sub machine gun and swung it in the direction of the figure.

"Don't shoot man! I'm 'B' Company." Shouted the figure. More lights went on in the house and Frank could now see the tall, well built man in uniform carrying an issue weapon his face and head still in silhouette.

"Who are you? Where's the rest of your patrol?" demanded Frank.

"They are back there, I need to get back to them." Ignoring everything else the soldier then brushed past Frank and ran off down into the blackness of the alley.

Frank was caught off balance, everything had happened very quickly and his mind was racing. What the hell was B Company doing on our turf? He had never seen this guy before and even his accent didn't sound right.

Before he could dwell on the matter any further the reality of the situation came rushing back to Frank and he made a sprint to the dark edges of the waste ground and back towards friendly forces. He was about to reach the road when the crack! Crack! Crack! of three high velocity bullets just missing his head sent him diving to the ground and crawling to the shell of a burnt out car.

Another bullet slammed into the car, went straight through it and sent dirt and tiny shards of metal into Frank's face, he crouched as low as he could.

The good book said that in these situations you had to try and locate the enemy by his gunfire thus enabling you to return it accurately, thereby winning the fire fight. Reality was a little different and if there had been an open sewer next to him Frank would have dived into it.

He heard the unmistakable sound of Norrie's voice some way behind him and now the continuous Kaboom! Kaboom! As he opened up onto the estate with his powerful SLR. Frank didn't need a text book to tell him what to do next, in an instant he was up and running for his life toward the friendly gunfire.

3

Major Alan Briggs sat behind his desk in the small room that served as his office. His unit occupied a school and the Major who was the Officer Commanding (OC) of the Company had naturally been allocated the Headmaster's office. The fact that it was one of the smallest rooms in the location and his second in command had the large airy Master's Common Room to himself didn't seem to matter to anyone least of all Alan Briggs.

Classrooms had become barrack rooms where the soldiers lived and slept. The playground once the lively domain of scores of kids was now a park for Landrovers and the large Humber armoured cars known to all as "Pigs". The original wall and fence around the school and outbuildings had been shored up with ten foot high sheets of silver corrugated iron or wriggly tin as it was generally known, topped off with rolls and rolls of barbed wire.

At each corner of the fence was a guard post known as a sangar with slits for the sentry to have maximum visibility without himself being seen. These sangars were raised on stilts of scaffolding to give a commanding view of the area outside. The large double gate was also made of wriggly tin and controlled by a ground level sangar. All windows in the school had been blacked out and like the walls sandbagged for extra protection.

Alan rummaged in his desk until he found his pipe then stuck it in his mouth and sucked it noisily for a few seconds. He remembered the promise he made to his wife to cut down, smiled and placed it on the desk. He checked his watch it was a few minutes to ten, he would see Lieutenant Orchard at ten o' clock as planned then do his rounds of the location with the Sergeant Major.

Compared with a few hours before he looked immaculate, his ruddy farmer's face freshly shaved and glowing. He wore an olive green shirt with sky blue parachute wings sewn neatly on the right arm. His once red hair had given away to grey except on his clipped moustache which was predominately ginger.

There was a soft knock on the door followed by a cough, Alan looked at his watch it was exactly Ten. "Come! Come in!" he commanded.

The door opened and Lieutenant Tony Orchard came hesitantly into the office. "Sir, you wanted to see me."

"Ah! Morning Tony, manage to get some shuteye? What! With all that excitement last night and it being your first operation it must have been damned hard. Take my advice, a tot of whisky or rum as you get into your sack does the trick, just a tot mind, wouldn't want a raving alcoholic at the end of the tour." The major finished his sentence with a good natured chuckle. Orchard laughed along with it although he felt anything but mirth.

He had hardly slept at all. The events surrounding the riot had kept racing around in his mind. It had indeed been his first operation, up until then it had all been training, realistic and thorough but training none-theless. This had been his first opportunity to test him-self 'under fire'. According to one part of his mind he had failed miserably and made himself out at best to be a fool and at worst a coward.

The survival part of his mind however told him that he had led a successful operation and that any small mistakes he may have made were down to the in-competence of his Platoon members from Sergeant Brit-ton downwards. The more he thought about it the more he convinced himself that *this* was the true version.

The Major picked up his pipe once more and ush-ered Orchard to a chair, after sucking at the stem for a few seconds he looked at Orchard and began.

"We were damn lucky again last night, the plan went well. We arrested fourteen of the buggers in the end and some had a hiding into the bargain, though I must say that some of the injuries looked excessive. The big Lance Corporal…Er.. Norris that's him, went bloody berserk at one stage, saved the show though. I've a feel-ing that if he and Britton and a couple more had not taken the initiative when they did it might have been a different story.. What? It could have been our soldiers seriously hurt or worse. Why were you late Tony? How come you didn't react quickly enough when Britton's men came onto the scene?"

The question jolted Orchard he had not been pre-pared for it. He knew that he could have been a little quicker off the mark but he had had the discipline prob-lem with Corporal Reece and the still unknown person who had made the insolent remark in the darkness. Yes, the incompetent Corporal Reece and all the rest of the lazy bastards just lying around in the derelict as if they were on some cushy exercise on Salisbury Plain and here he was taking the bloody rap for it...The bastards.

"Late sir? Yes, I must apologise, things were a little out of control when I got to my Platoon in the derelict. Half of them were asleep, asleep would you believe! By the time I'd got them to their feet, things had started to happen."

The Major arched his eyebrows, "It was corporal Reece in charge there wasn't it?"

"Yes indeed it was sir." Orchard thought quickly, he knew Reece, Britton and a good few others went back some way with the Major. They had done at least one other tour in Belfast with him, he would know their individual strengths and weaknesses well, he had to be careful. "And a fine Corporal sir, but they had been on the go all day, I blame myself, maybe I should have got there sooner or did more to make sure they had got more rest earlier, I..."

The Major cut him off, he waved his hand in a dismissive manner and said a little irritably, "No! For God's sake man it's not your fault, I'm not getting at you personally. You and your men were late maybe less than a minute but *late,* and we could have paid a price for it, a heavy price, we didn't but we must learn the lesson. Of course your men were knackered, so was I, so were the lads who stood on the base line taking all that bloody crap. Being knackered is half the game Tony that's where leadership comes to the fore, that's when it counts!" He finished his sentence by lightly hammering the desk with his fist.

The Major got up out of his chair, he changed the subject to signal an end to the interview. "Got to do my rounds old boy, a chore but a necessary one. Got to show the troops you care." he laughed and to take the sting out of his little lecture patted Orchard on the back as he ushered him out of the room.

As soon as the door shut the Major heard some voices outside in the corridor followed at once by a sharp rap on the door which opened almost immediately. In stepped a short figure of a man in his mid thirties with a square jaw, slightly crooked nose and two gleaming dark eyes hidden under an overhung forehead. A smile was spread across the weathered face showing a row of large, crooked, white teeth. "And a good morning to you sah!"

"Sergeant Major, good morning." replied the Major jovially, he was always pleased to see his right hand man, Company Sergeant Major (CSM) Reg Wallace.

Reg Wallace accompanied the Major down the passageway to the former school stationary office that now served as the 'Ops Room' the nerve centre of the Company. Reg was less than average height but broad. He walked with a strange rolling motion and this coupled with his longer than normal arms earned him the nick name of 'The Gorilla.' Despite his comic appearance and seemingly insulting nick name Sergeant Major Wallace was a very capable and fair minded person who commanded a lot of respect from the Officers and soldiers alike. He now pushed the door of the Ops room open and allowed the Major to enter first.

The windowless room was lit by three long strip lights which gave everything a bright and new looking appearance. On the right were a bank of radios that kept them in touch with patrols on the street, the other Companies that bordered their area and Battalion Headquarters in a police station about two miles away.

The walls were covered by maps, the biggest of which was the "tribal" map which portrayed the whole of Belfast. It was shaded in two main colours: orange for the Protestant or Loyalist estates and green for the Catholic or Republican estates. Other maps gave the Company area in great detail down to small alleyways and house numbers. A coloured knob pin had been inserted for all incidents that had occurred on the patch since they had got there. Red for a shooting, black for bomb, yellow for riot and so on, the map was already looking like a multi coloured hedgehog.

Along all walls like a border was a single line of black and white photographs of the most wanted men in the province. The line of photographs above the radios were the wanted men and women in the Company area.

A duty signaller sat in front of one of the radios a set of earphones clamped on his head. He was intently reading a JT Edson cowboy novel a cigarette burned in an ashtray that was brimming over with dog ends. He was completely oblivious to his new audience. The major walked over to a batch of signals that had piled up overnight, he picked them up and started reading them. They were mostly situation reports known simply as SI-

TREPS, updates on the security situation throughout the Province as a whole.

The signaller now aware of the visit straightened up and scooped the ashtray into the bin, at the same time trying to ease his book under a message pad. Neither the Major or the CSM took any notice, they were only too aware of the boredom that can envelope a soldier when he was on radio 'stag' just listening to the hissing white noise of the ether.

"All quiet Corporal Staveley?" enquired the Major without looking up from the SITREPs.

"Sir?" said the Corporal taking off one of the earphones so that he could hear properly.

"The OC," Reg repeated, with a look of mock disbelief on his face, "Would like to know if everything is quiet. You can answer, if you can tear yourself away from that book."

" Er.. Yeh, yes sir," replied the young signaller pushing the earphones off his ears, "But there's some info from the RUC that a body's been found near the scene of last nights riot."

The major shot a quizzical glance at the CSM and said, "Where is the Watch Officer?"

"He's just gone for a .. er...To the toilet sir" replied the signaller. At that moment the Ops room door swung open and in walked Captain Nick Summers the Officer of the Watch, a cheery grin on his handsome face. He had a mane of black hair that was too thick and too long even for an officer, It was scraped back in a vain effort to stop a lock of it constantly swinging in front of his eyes.

"Morning sir, Sarn't Major" he said heartily. This formality over he would now call the Major by his first name for the rest of the day.

"And morning to you Sah!" replied the Major, equally as hearty. He regarded Nick with great fondness. They went back years and had served together on a number of occasions. He had a great deal of respect for Nick's ability and coolness, especially when under pressure. Secretly Briggs was delighted when he had been posted in as his Second in Command just before the beginning of the tour.

Nick Summers should have been a Major himself commanding his own company but the problem was that he could not suffer bad decisions gladly and had fallen foul of too many more senior officers in the past. The rebel in him of course was recognised by the soldiers which made him very popular with them and another reason why he was mistrusted by the establishment.

Major Alan Briggs knew all this of course but to him it wasn't an issue. He knew that Summers would be good for the morale of the troops, a very important factor on a tour of duty in Ulster, a fact that was seldom taken into account by the leadership. He also knew that Nick had a deal of respect for him but equally would speak his mind if he thought things were not right.

Nick offered his mug of tea to Alan and sitting on one of the Ops room tables began automatically to give a debrief of all that happened since the riot folded and they had withdrawn to base.

Uncharacteristically, Nick had been in the Ops Room all through the big incident and not on the streets with the troops. Alan had wanted it that way for this operation, he had wanted a firm back up who could co-ordinate help quickly had things gone wrong on the ground.

"The RUC took the last arrested person from this location at 0410 hrs. We arrested twelve in the end. I decided not to proceed against a girl she was obviously pregnant, God knows what the hell she thought she was up to and a guy who is a known lunatic from the Estate, he was so chuffed to be arrested he offered to make everyone tea and cook breakfast. Out of the twelve arrested five were hospitalised, two expected to be released this morning...From hospital that is..."

"The injuries Nick, what were they?"

" Oh! The more serious were burns from that damn petrol bomb, the others, well, the normal bumps and bruises one can expect from a good nights rioting. Our man Pinky Watson had his arm burned but not seriously and good old Sergeant Britton had some small fragments embedded in his face and neck, he didn't go to hospital but got treated here."

Nick walked over to a small desk picked up the radio log and continued, "Now a report came in from the RUC just an hour or so ago to say that a body had been reported seen on our patch in the Estate, near to last nights riot. I gave them a patrol as cover and they found it, but we've heard nothing since."

"I wonder if we hit the gunman." suggested the Major.

"What a wonderful thought," replied Nick with a smirk, "We pumped nine rounds back at them courtesy

of Corporal Norrie Norris covering Britton's withdraw-
al, but he admitted that he hadn't exactly seen the gunman, just fired at the flashes, not exactly text book but
Britton was pinned down and isolated."

"Quite." said the Major softly.

He was about to continue when one of the several
phones rang, the signaller picked it up listened, spoke
a few words then handed the phone to Nick Summers,
"The RUC, Sir." he said.

Nick listened intently, said thanks and hung up.
" The body was of a male, seventeen years old and no
form, although he was living on the Estate."

"Well, had he been shot?" interjected the Major.

"No, as a matter of fact he wasn't, they're await-
ing confirmation but it looks like someone had taken
a knife to him, not stabbed as such....Rather slashed to
ribbons."

Reg Wallace, who had remained in the background
for most of the time stepped forward and threw in his
opinion.

"Bit of 'in fighting' that. Some bugger has decided to settle a score while riot were in progress, an ideal
time. Probably a punishment meted out or a woman involved, mark my words."

"Mmm, probably." said the Major deep in thought.

4

Frank sat on the edge of his bed still a little drowsy after his sleep. He had started to clean his rifle and the bits were all over his bed. They had got back to the base at something like four thirty that morning after escorting all the arrested rioters to the main Police Station about two miles down the road.

The aftermath of the riot had not gone well. The troops had been on the ground for most of that day before the riot had started. After the riot the 'adrenaline high' had worn off and everyone had started to get irritable, a few arguments had broke out in the back of the Pig when they were travelling back.

Lieutenant Orchard had chosen this time to bend Frank's ear about Corporal Reece and the conduct of the lads in the derelict. Frank had told him that it would be better if they talked after they'd had some kip, surprisingly Orchard had agreed and they'd left it at that.

Food in vast quantities had been waiting in the cookhouse when they got back and after filling their faces with bacon, rubber egg and fried potatoes they wandered off to their beds to crash out for hopefully a few hours. There had been no interruption until a general call went out for anyone wanting lunch. A few had responded but others like Frank just sat around and sorted out their kit, cleaned weapons and made light conversation.

Frank still felt drained, in situations like the riot you lived on a high, you ran faster, thought faster and yes, hit harder and you never felt a thing, not an ounce of fear, fatigue or regret. And then when it was all over, weariness crept in from the shadows and took its place in brain and muscle to demand repayment in food and sleep.

He stood up and for the tenth time since he woke, checked his face and neck for the little wounds caused by the minute flying shrapnel of earth and metal. They were now doused in dark brown disinfectant after the medical orderly had pulled out the bigger pieces with tweezers. He considered himself lucky, he could have very easily taken a couple of rounds, but mainly thanks to Norrie's intervention he had got out virtually unscathed. All he did when he saw Norrie back at the base was grab his shoulder and pat it, no words were needed.

Frank slid the working parts back into his SLR and snapped it shut, cocked it a couple of times and pulled the trigger, satisfied he hung it back on the wall next to his bed. Next to it was a shelf with three metal magazines on it, each one holding fifteen rounds. Although twenty could be crammed in, he and most of them just put either ten or fifteen, it took the pressure off the spring and the first round fed easier into the chamber when the rifle was cocked. When he went out of the location on patrol, his rifle and mags would accompany him.

Corporal Taff Reece walked into Frank's bunk area, his hair was damp and well scraped back as if he had just had a shower, but his face creased and white through lack of a good sleep. "Hi, Frank, how's the face? Christ, you weren't all that good lookin' in the first place, what's all that brown stuff? Is it the shit seeping out?" Both men laughed, Taff, the heartiest. He loved his own voice and thought himself a real comedian. Before Frank could make a reply Taff carried on his mood now more sombre and his tone quieter. Frank listened for a minute or so to Taff who stood at the end of his bed a mug of tea in his hand.

Frank started to feel a little irritated, it was something about his voice that was getting to him. It was high pitched and no matter what he said, it always sounded as if he was whining, or was it that Taff was reflecting his own unspoken thoughts? Now, for a second time Taff started to relate to Frank what happened in the derelicts.

"For Chrissake, Frank man, the lads were only lying down on the floor. Jesus, they were tired! We'd been on the fuckin' go all fuckin' day man! We were ready to go though, as soon as the word come, well you know we were, fuckin' hell it wasn't as if we'd never been in these situations before. All he was interested in was that some fucker had gobbed off at him. We heard you arrive, I said to him, *Come on sir! Lets go!* But no, he just went on and on about what a disgrace we were, you should have heard that shit...In the end we all burst out of there. I mean Frank, we were in the middle of a bastard riot man..."

"Yeh Taff, I know what you are saying, but you must remember, he's only a young sprog, he hasn't found his feet yet. Most of us have done what? Two, three tours now stretching back to the start in 69, two long years ago. Remember how we faced that first riot? Eight abreast and six deep, all marching in step and the officer, what was his name again? He actually tried to read out the Riot Act! What a farce, a couple of the paddies even started laughing! Yeh, we were all green then, didn't know our arses from our elbows as far as this place was concerned and we're still learning. It's the same for him, it's all new to him, so let's give him a chance eh?"

Taff grimaced and nodded his head, "Yeh, I suppose you're right but I still think..."

"Taff, one more thing," interrupted Frank, his voice a little sterner than before, "Don't go moaning to the blokes about this, it does no good.. okay? And who was it that gobbed off at Orchard in the derelict?"

"Digger Davis."

"I might have guessed." Frank watched Taff saunter away, he may have convinced him for now to be a bit more tolerant with Lieutenant Orchard but he couldn't kid himself as easily.

Frank got dressed in his green, cotton uniform trousers or "O.Gs" and shirt of the same material, boots and puttees. He walked down the passageway towards the Dining room commonly called the "Cookhouse". It was the largest room in the school and the busiest with differing groups of soldiers eating all through the day and night having just come off patrol or sentry duty.

Tables were pushed together to make three long dining tables with collapsible wooden chairs lining either side. Near the serving hatch were two urns, one for tea and one for coffee, which were regularly replenished. Meals were served at set times during the day but outside or between these times there was a vast stock of bread, eggs and margarine stacked next to an electric hot plate, so groups or individuals could make an egg "Banjo" without having to use the main kitchen. Frank helped himself to a mug of tea and joined a group of the lads who were in the middle of lunch.

The huge iron gates were swung open by the sentry and a Pig rumbled and revved into the former playground of the school. It was followed immediately by a Ford saloon that found a space and halted.

A thickset man in plain clothes got out of the passenger side of the car, he had yellowish wispy hair dragged across the top of his head in an effort to cover a bald patch. His face was fat and florid and he had the beginnings of a double chin. He retrieved a briefcase from the back seat and waited for the driver. A tall, thin, pale faced, rather serious looking younger man got out of the driver's seat and together they walked toward the main school building. The sentry wandered over to a couple of soldiers who were getting out of the back of the Pig.

"Who's them two?" he asked them.

"S. I. B. mate, we just escorted them up from Park Road Police station." stated one of the soldiers who spoke again when he saw a look of puzzlement on the sentry's face. "S.I.B.. The Special Investigation Branch of the army. Fuckin' Gestapo mate." he turned and spat.

The driver of the Pig, a Lance Corporal with too many years service came up and picked up on the conversation. "SIB? Shit Inside of Bastards, more like." he sneered. Some laughed some didn't.

Company Sergeant Major Reg Wallace having finished his rounds with the Major settled in his office and started on the crossword in a tabloid newspaper. He chuckled to himself as he solved a clue. It was his secret little ambition to complete a whole crossword in one day before the end of the tour. A couple of times he had come close but always two or three clues had evaded him.

His office was next to the Major's. It must have been the school secretary's because there was still a row of Lever Arch files on a shelf with a notice on it written in extremely neat crayon: "Do not remove" and a metal filing cabinet that was locked, with no apparent key.

He had five clues to go, this could be the one he thought. There was a sharp rap on the open door, Reg looked up and saw a strange flabby, red face staring at him. The figure stepped forward brandishing an ID card. "Staff Sergeant Stokes S.I.B, and you are the CSM?" he asked loudly in a South London accent. Before Reg could reply he parked his briefcase on the desk and continued, "I will need an interview room and a gofer, you know someone on hand to fetch people for interview when I need them. I've been 'ere a few times there's a room up the corridor what I've used before, it…"

Reg who up until now had just stared at Stokes, rose up from his chair and cut Stokes off mid sentence with a very loud, "YES, I AM THE COMPANY SER-

GEANT MAJOR, STAFF SERGEANT." His dark eyes glittered with hostility under the overhanging cliff of a forehead. Stokes immediately stopped in his tracks and for the first time took in the CSM's menacing look.

He spoke again, this time quieter with some respect in the tone. "Fing is Sir, I haven't got much time, my gaffer wants all this sortin' out today, an' I can't leave 'ere 'til it's sorted. That means interviewing all the soldiers involved in the riot last night. It's a fackin' nightmare....Sir."

Reg gave up his aggressive stance and said in a slightly mocking tone, "Well I hope you bought your bed with you, do you know how many were out on the friggin' ground last night? Almost the whole Company, about eighty at a guess...Anyway, what's this all about? Is it that body they found?"

Stokes relaxed, now he was more on *his own* terms, in that he knew something more than the other person. He took his time in answering, shuffling in his pockets for a cigarette, he offered the pack to Reg who refused. "Yep, they found a body alright." he glanced at the wall and saw the inevitable Tribal Map, walked over and stuck a nicotine stained finger on it, "Just 'ere, in this alleyway, that narrows it down a bit surely?"

"It does," replied Reg. " but your still talking about a lot of soldiers, what happened? Was he beaten? Or was he some alky who drowned in his own vomit?" Reg knew that he had been stabbed but he wanted Stokes' version.

Stokes stuck a fag in his mouth and took a deep drag. "Nah! Nothing like that, haven't seen the body m'self and we're still waiting for the autopsy report, but by all accounts he was sliced up. Fackin' 'orrible, not just stabbed and all that but...Gutted, real Jack the Ripper stuff apparently."

There was a cough in the corridor outside and Stokes' assistant came in to view. Stokes turned and introduced him, his cocksure manner returned. "This is Corporal Pugh, my assistant, he'll need an office too." Reg Wallace's eyes receded back under the cliff and glittered.

Frank sat in the cookhouse with a few lads from his platoon, all were busy maunching through plates piled high with food, a good riot always gave a good appetite. There was a variety of food to choose from and it all came with chips. Norrie had eaten the Shepherds Pie and had made a huge sandwich out of the remaining chips, it was so thick that even his shovel like hands could only just fit around the ends, chips bulged out everywhere and Norrie studied it like a predator studying a hedgehog, trying to find a way into it.

A voice boomed across the cookhouse, "Sergeant Britton!" Frank looked up and saw the anthropoid figure of the CSM staring at him, his eyes sunken and arms akimbo, a sure sign of trouble. Frank left his food, scraped his chair back and walked toward the waiting Sergeant Major.

As Frank approached, the Gorilla broke his stance and ushered him into the corridor away from eyes and ears. He stopped and stared at Frank, he looked like he was being forced to chew something scraped off a pavement.

"Frank, there's a great big obnoxious piece of shit, sitting in *my* office, on *my* chair. He is one Staff Sergeant Stokes from the SIB and he wants to talk to Lieutenant Orchard, you, Norris, Reece and the rest of the NCOs who were at the scene of the riot last night. His streak of piss oppo, is down the corridor in the old stock room and he wants to speak to the rest of the blokes. Lieutenant Orchard is in with Stokes at the moment and you are next."

"What's up Sir?" Frank's senses had sharpened. SIB, always meant trouble.

"Seemingly, they found a body last night near the riot scene. It had been carved up bad. I'm surprised you haven't heard about it yet. Lad of about seventeen, probably involved in the riot at some stage, looks like one of their own did it but we've got to be seen to do our part and get investigated this end. Frank, watch the bastard, he's as slimy as they come." Frank nodded and went to walk away but halted when Reg called him. "Frank," he looked and sounded a little sheepish, "Do you know the name of a lettuce? Three letters."

Stokes lit up his third fag since he'd been in the office, through the smoke he regarded the young nervous officer in front of him. He was in his element. A crime had been committed and that gave him power. He had seen over the years the look of loathing and even hatred for him on the faces of his fellow soldiers and countrymen when he was grilling them but he had also seen the look of fear on those same faces and that was compensation enough for him.

He didn't expect anything from this investigation. The murder he thought, must have been a revenge or punishment carried out by the victim's own kind, however, he would milk it for a while, an image of the CSM flashed into his mind and he reminded himself to be careful…. What a fucking ape man he thought and shuddered.

He took another pull from the fag and dusted imaginary ash from his tired suit. "You realise of course Sir, that this is an informal interview? If it was anything else you'd be seen by someone of appropriate rank. What I've gotta do, is get a picture of what 'appened last night, who was where, and at what time, that sorta fing. And when it's sorted we can all go home and put our feet up…Well at least, *I* can!" Stokes laughed out loud. Orchard forced a smile, the arrogance and sheer rudeness of the man was really getting to him.

"So, *you* were the commander last night? Well, well, they say you must be getting old when a policeman looks like your son, but what age are you?"

Orchard dropped the pretend smile and answered a little sharply. "Look, Staff Sergeant, I've been up all night and I've got lots to do…"

"Haven't we all Sir, haven't we all? Now, I'm going to draw a sketch map of the riot area and I want you to show me where you were." Stokes got a sheet of paper from his briefcase and a felt pen, he quickly drew the waste ground at the edge of the Estate and the main road. "Right, point out your locations." He made no attempt to pass the paper to Orchard instead he scraped his chair back, looked at his watch and lit up another cigarette.

Orchard leaned over the sketch and started to outline the positions of the soldiers.

Stokes was hungry, he listened with feigned interest his large stomach gurgling. He would give it a maximum of two hours here, that would be time to gather enough information to please his boss and the RUC. He got up, opened the door and shouted to a passing soldier, "Hey! Get me something from the hot plate and bring it here pronto son. I'm starving."

He went back in the office. Orchard was still recalling his actions of the previous evening. Suddenly his trained mind alerted him, "What? What was that you said? Who emerged from the Estate?"

Orchard looked up in surprise at the sharp interjection, "I said it was Sergeant Britton, he and his men sneaked around the back, came through the Estate and surprised them from the rear."

"What route did they take? Through the Estate I mean."

"Haven't got a clue actually, it was his show, you'll have to ask him."

"So you *can't* account for his actions then?" Orchard wriggled uncomfortably in his seat and remained silent.

Stokes pursued aggressively. "So, for all you know he could have been in the Estate for some time.. Well! Couldn't he?" shouted Stokes.

Orchard stood up his face contorted, he stammered in a high pitched voice, which over emphasised his public school accent. "Look, you'll bloody well have to ask Britton that yourself! Dammit man! I'm............ Trying to ask, I mean answer your questions.." he trailed off and sat down staring at the floor.

Stokes smiled, and when he spoke it was mockingly calm, in stark contrast to Orchard's outburst. "Now, now Sir. I've got my job to do. An answer to a few simple questions is not too much is it? Well, look at the time, thank you Mister......Orchard, that will be all." Stokes looked down at his note book and started scribbling.

Lieutenant Orchard slowly rose to his feet and stared at Stokes. He went to say something but changed his mind and turned to go to the door, as he was about to exit the room Stokes without looking up from his notes said in a loud voice, "Oh! Send in the Sergeant will you!" Orchard glared and slammed the door shut. Stokes chuckled to himself.

Frank was getting tired of Stokes' little mind games. He had been under interrogation now for about twenty minutes. Stokes had got him back in the alleyway with the stranger from B Company. In the confusion and hectic aftermath of the riot Frank had forgotten all about the encounter and subsequently had not reported it. It was only after Stokes had taken him back stage by stage, that he remembered it.

"That was the fackin spot near to where they found the body! Why didn't you report any of this?"

"Dunno, I was tired, there was a lot going on, it slipped my mind."

"Come off it!" yelled Stokes, "Some geezer gets ripped to fackin shreds, you practically stand on the corpse and it slips your mind? You're unbefackinlievable you are."

"No, you come off it." sneered Frank, "Do you really think, if I'd seen a body I could forget it, you're just wasting my time." Frank stood up to go, there was a knock on the door and a young soldier entered with a sandwich on a plate.

"Egg banjo for Staff Sergeant Stokes." he said.

"Oh! Good, just what the doctor ordered." Stokes took the plate and started wolfing the banjo, egg squirted out of the sides and ran down his fingers, he stopped and looked up at Frank as if he was surprised to see him there. "Tell yer Sergeant Major, I want to see him." He carried on wolfing as Frank walked out.

Frank saw the young lad, Pinky Watson, who had bought in the sandwich, he was in the corridor just outside of the interview office with a couple of his mates. By the look on their faces Frank knew that something was going on. "What gives" he said, a half smile on his face.

"Did the SIB man enjoy his egg banjo?" asked Pinky.

"Yeh. Why?"

"Well, Steve here has got a really heavy cold and he sorta used the top slice as a hanky just before I took it in." They all burst out laughing and were still chuckling when Stokes stuck his head out of the office with yoke running down the sides of his mouth, he looked suspiciously at the group, who burst out laughing again as they broke up and disappeared.

5

The old factory was relatively quiet for a building that housed over two hundred soldiers. The large floor space that used to house dozens of machines was now a dormitory full of metal framed beds some stacked three high. Men in various states of dress wandered around or just sat on their beds talking. Some slept, oblivious to the steady hum of voices that filled the huge hall.

Lance Corporal Paul Van Der Borgh lay naked in his iron cot the sheets and blankets pulled up to his eyes. He was lucky, he shared a small room off the main hall with just two others, it was quieter and a little more private even if the "door" was only a blanket hung on wire.

Van Der Borgh was wide awake, it was always the same after a "mission." He had to keep going over it in his mind again and again, hundreds perhaps thousands of times reliving the stalk, the pounce, the look of terror, the gurgling and screaming, the blood. He tried to imagine it from his prey's side coming face to face with death, seeing the knife.......The knife.

He tightened his fist on the ivory handle grips feeling the naked blade clamped between his upper thighs knowing that the slightest movement up or down would result in the honed edge slicing through his flesh.

He ventured a glance at his comrades, one bed was empty and he heard deep, soft snores emanating from the other. He let go of the knife and slowly reached out of the bed to his issue webbing belt, from one of the pouches he pulled a black plastic water bottle. Without taking his eyes off his sleeping comrades, he unscrewed the top and took two mouthfuls of the liquid inside. He held the second mouthful while he screwed the top back on and replaced it in his webbing then slowly released the liquid down his gullet, feeling the fire build up in his stomach.

Once again his thoughts turned to the previous night. He had been very lucky. He had been seen and could have been shot! What was that soldier doing on the wrong side of the riot? And by himself? A kindred spirit perhaps, he permitted himself to smile. Now *that* would really be something! He slid his hand back down to the knife and jiggled it oh so slowly, until he felt the burn of the biting blade. It had been the best yet, nearly getting caught had heightened the pleasure.

Paul Van Der Borgh had left his native South Africa five years previously and taking advantage of his dual nationality had joined the British Army. He had formerly been in the South African Army but he had left prematurely and hurriedly, to avoid a few years in gaol, or worse.

His first posting with the British Army was to Aden. The once bustling lively port on the tip of South Arabia was now a place of turmoil and death. Britain slow to hand over its Protectorate was desperately trying to maintain law and order, several rival factions fought with each other day and night, but they all had a common enemy, the British soldier, who, as usual gave his life while politicians wavered.

Life had been good in Aden for Van Der Borgh, patrolling the streets, a contact with the enemy every day, shootings, bombings, grenades and killing. Nobody had given a damn who was beaten or who was killed, as long as it was "one of them."

That's where it had first started with Van Der Borgh. After a drama filled day patrolling on the streets of the town, he had lain on his bunk under the mosquito net unable to sleep. He was boiling with frustration and rage.

They had been on foot patrol in the morning and had heard an explosion a couple of streets away, when they ran round the corner, they saw one of their Landrovers on fire, a grenade had been thrown into the back.

The two soldiers who had been in the back had jumped out of the moving vehicle before it exploded and had lain on the ground, more shocked than injured. The driver too, had made good his escape but the vehicle commander in the front had took some of the blast and lay slumped across the seats with flames licking around him.

Although Van Der Borgh was the newest member of the unit having only been flown out from the Depot a week earlier, he was the first to react. He had dropped to his knee and fired two shots at an Arab running off with one of the injured soldier's rifle, the impact of the heavy high velocity rounds had lifted the would be thief off the ground and had catapulted him ten yards forward.

This had dispersed the gathered crowd, next he had run to the Landrover and tried to drag the unconscious soldier out, in doing so he had dropped his own rifle automatically thinking that it would have been taken care of by someone else in the patrol.

As much as he had strained he could hardly budge the unconscious body. Flames were now intensifying and he was only too aware that there were two petrol tanks located beneath the seats, no one had come to help him. He looked around in desperation and saw the Corporal in charge, Peatly, cowering behind a corner then the injured soldier had regained consciousness and started screaming.

The flames by now had gripped. Van Der Borg made one last attempt. Reaching in over the flames, he had grabbed him by the hair and belt and yanked with all his might. The soldier started to move but in his agony, thrashed about and got tangled with the gear stick and hand brake.

With one final, tremendous yank, Van Der Borgh freed him and they both fell back onto the road. Instantly a tank went up in ball of flame and he had rolled and rolled dragging the smouldering heap with him to get away from the inferno. As they got clear, the other tank blew and he had sat there gulping in air while the inferno burned itself out.

Help had arrived and it was discovered that his rifle had been spirited away while he was trying to get the injured man out. One of the others in the patrol had seen a child of no more than seven or eight grab the weapon and drag it away.

Corporal Peatly who had cowered round the corner, had then tried to reassert his authority by yelling at Van Der Borg for losing his rifle, when they had got back to Base Camp he had been marched into the guardhouse and flung in a cell like a criminal.

He was released sometime later to get his burns treated and explain himself. The Company Commander had listened in silence. Van Der Borgh was well aware that Peatly had already spoken to the OC at length about the incident. The OC then summed up by reprimanding him for acting in a hasty manner thereby placing other members of the patrol in jeopardy.

No acknowledgement was made about his rescue, however, he had not been formally charged and he was released from custody. The injured man was recovering in hospital.

Corporal Peatly could not face Van Der Borgh, who then found out that Peatly had claimed the glory for himself and had also stated that Van Der Borgh had lost control, thereby losing his weapon. To top it all, just as he was turning in for the night the Company Orderly had told him that as of first thing in the morning he was posted to the Transport Platoon to drive the ration truck.

That had really stung Van Der Borgh, taking him from his beloved patrolling to what he considered a dead beat job, surrounded by blokes that couldn't hack anything tougher than changing a wheel. It was a message from the top that he was considered as being next to useless.

He had lain on his bed staring through the mosquito net, his guts churning with hatred and frustration, knowing that that bastard coward of a corporal was now probably propping up the NAAFI bar telling all his mates his version of events.

He had reached into his equipment, pulled out the Knife and clutched it to his chest with both hands as if praying. He had studied the blade as he thought about what he was going to do to the corporal, how he was going to confront him, force him to his knees to beg for forgiveness and then how he would slash his throat and walk away leaving him dying. The vision was comforting but not practical.

He would be suspected immediately, there would be no escape. No, he had thought, this must be done in the fullness of time, in the UK when everyone had forgotten about it. He could pick and choose the time.

But that thought had done little to cool the burning in his brain, he had to do something that very night.

That's when it really started, sneaking out under the wire at the dead of night, searching amongst the shacks and outbuildings on the edge of the town, evading his own patrols, getting a kick out of seeing without being seen but not really knowing what he was after. And then on the fifth night it had happened, he had trodden on an old man who had been sleeping rough, in the shadows.

The old Arab was shocked to see what was obviously a white man, stripped to the waist and covered in streaks of black cammo cream, he had started to shout. Van Der Borgh's reaction had been swift, without a seconds thought he had whipped out the knife and thrust it in to the scrawny figure, who immediately slumped to the ground, dead.

He had run back to the camp, his heart pounding, he was on a high, it was almost as if he had been born purely to fulfil that one act.

He had lain on his bunk going over and over it in his mind, a hundred, perhaps a thousand times.

Nothing was said, not a murmur, the killing it seemed meant nothing. Well, he thought, maybe the next one will, we'll see.

He had found the taxi driver asleep in his cab not far from the main gate of the camp. He had woken him with the point of the knife a fraction of an inch from his eye, he tried to get a reaction from him but the poor man just stared transfixed, so he began feigning jabs with the knife until the man snapped and started wailing, this was the signal for Van Der Borgh to go into a slashing frenzy.

This time, news of the killing did reach camp. The taxi driver had lived long enough to say that it had been a white man with demon eyes. Rumour abounded and only a half hearted internal enquiry was started. After all, how could one of our chaps have been involved in a thing like that? It just *wasn't done*.

Van Der Borgh basked in the conversations about it, throwing in his theories with the rest of them, adding that the guy must be brave and skilful to remain undetected for so long.

The missions had to stop after that, the publicity had now tightened things up too much. A few months later they were homeward bound to the UK and a couple of years of boredom for him in Crimea Barracks near Salisbury. He had craved for the right conditions to begin his "missions" again, but England was the wrong country to start that sort of thing.

They found a soldier, beaten half to death with his ears sliced off by the Bus station in Salisbury early one Sunday morning. Local gangs had been blamed for a "squaddy bashing" that had gone too far. No arrests were made mostly because the victim, Corporal (Now Sergeant) Peatly, could remember nothing.

He had started thinking about doing one of his disappearing acts, probably back to the African Continent when all of a sudden Ulster flared up and troops were deployed to help the RUC to swamp the civil unrest. He had stayed on, anxious to get out there. He was promoted to full Corporal and still he waited, but it was to be eighteen months before they jumped off the ferry in Belfast and transported to the large, dirty, stinking Factory that was to become their base and "Home" for the next six months.

He had got his own patrol now and had displayed outstanding leadership qualities, although he could never quite win over his men completely. There was just something about his dark brooding personality that didn't endear him to anyone, however, he was good at his job and was trusted by the senior staff in his unit.

He taught his patrol how to lie up, how just to melt in the shadows not moving, not making a sound for tens of minutes sometimes for an hour or so, just observing, giving the local baddies a false sense of security. It had paid off, his patrol had the highest arrest rate in the unit.

It also gave him a chance to sneak off on his own, he simply got them into a lie up position then secretly left them . He had started his "Missions" again, wandering around in the dark, observing, planning, getting high on the thrill of it.

The big riot in the Para's area had drawn him like a magnet and after lying his patrol up, he had moved in to observe at close quarters. He watched transfixed at the violence, the screams and turmoil.

Lots of people were passing the alleyway where he was hidden, they were in groups or in twos running to take part in the action. He was about to pull out when a youth had staggered into the alley and started urinating, he was laughing and shouting at his mates who had carried on up the road.

Van Der Borgh had closed in and grabbed the lad by his long hair, twisting his head round until he was almost kissing him, the blade of the knife held in front of his face.

At first the youth's terror had been complete, but when he saw the beret and the grinning face, he had become surly and abusive, after all the Brits *were* bastards, but not knife wielding murderers.

Van Der Borg had to watch it. He didn't want to have to explain any blood stains on his clothing, so with his first stab he had killed him and stood clear for a few moments, then carefully stepped in and vented the rest of his rage on the corpse.

As he left the alley, he thought that he had been seen by one of the Paras on the periphery of the riot, so he decided to dodge back in and wait a few moments. Then the other soldier appeared silhouetted in the mouth of the alley, he was calling someone. All Van Der Borgh had to do was wait a few seconds in the dark before this guy moved on, but the lights had gone on in a house and bathed him in light, he had been challenged immediately.

He had thought quickly, he knew that the Para's other Company that bordered on to them was B Company, so he had gambled and said he was part of them, running off before any deeper investigation could take place. It had worked...Just.

Lying on the Bunk in the old Factory Van Der Borgh was now sweating and slightly out of breath. He slowly looked across at his room mate who was still softly snoring, and reached for a towel to wipe his abdomen.

6

"Well the fing is sir, the facts are, we 'ave a body, well, what's left of it and a soldier or at least someone in uniform seen lurking around the alley where it was found. Your man er.. Sergeant whatsit er.. Britton, is in the clear, he didn't 'ave enough time.." Stokes, once more in his element with an audience outlined the facts to the OC, Major Alan Briggs, who sat in his small office with the Sergeant Major and Captain Summers.

He continued after lighting up another cigarette. " So if we go along with his story about the soldier he saw, who said he was from B Company, we, or at least I, have got to go across to your B Company and start all over again."

The Major interjected, "That's the strange thing about it, if you look on the map here you will see that B Company is to our east and yet this supposed patrol from them was seen here, well over to the South West of our area. We do have patrols wandering over into our area now and again, as no doubt our patrols wander into other areas for whatever reason, but this...This is.. It just doesn't seem right. It would seem logical if it was a patrol from the Princes Own Yeomanry who are housed in the old Factory here." He stabbed his finger on the map and traced it down the border of their area which came within three hundreds yards or so of the murder scene.

"But why would he say he was part of your unit?" mused Stokes

"Maybe if he belonged to Princes Own, he were worried that he might drop in the shit if we reported him," threw in the Sergeant Major. "Crossing into other unit's area is dangerous, patrols from either side are likely to come across each other unexpected like and start blasting away at each other, it 'as 'appened and soldiers have died."

"Yes all very mystifying indeed." said the Major standing up and looking at Stokes. "but if we're in the clear.." Stokes took the hint and stood up.

"Yes, well thank you Sir. I must get to it and visit B Company to try and wrap this up, I'm still convinced its some sort of gang vengeance...But we'll see. Goodbye sir." Stokes turned from the Major, gave a small nod to Sergeant Major Reg Wallace and left the room.

After a few seconds the Major spoke to Captain Summers. "Nick, phone the OC of the Princes Own in the Factory would you please, his name's Rory Macalpine, I'd like to speak to him...Thanks."

Paul Van Der Borgh pushed aside the blanket door of his room and made for the Ops room in the Factory. He was around 5' 11 but because of his short neck and broad build he looked smaller, his hair was always cropped close to his scull, this coupled with flat slav features and blue eyes set in a brooding face, gave him a menacing air.

To get to the Ops room he had to cross the main floor of the Factory that housed the majority of the unit.

It was nicknamed 'Bed City' because most of the area was taken up with them, some stacked three high. In a space at the side were six tables placed together, sat around these were half a dozen young soldiers of the Princes Own, swigging tea and chatting.

A freckled faced, ginger haired lad looked up and saw Van Der Borgh approaching, he turned to his comrades and said softly, "Watch it men, here comes mein fuhrer. Hitler has risen from his grave." After some sniggering the group fell silent as Van Der Borgh approached the table.

He sensed their hostility, it did not bother him, in fact it often made him feel good, after all it was fear and when people feared him it gave him power and sometimes he had to demonstrate this power.

He stopped at the table and looked at each man in turn slowly and deliberately. A couple got up and moved off immediately. When he spoke, he turned on his full South African accent, in a low but menacing manner. "You said something my little ginger friend? Perhaps you would like to tell me what it was.... No? Well, let me see if I can guess." He picked up the lad's mug of tea and sipped it. "Ah! I know, you said that the tea was fucking awful." With that, he dropped the mug into the ginger lad's lap.

Ginger at once jumped up and in his flash of temper squared up to Van Der Borgh who took one pace toward him and hissed, "Come on then sonny, hit me, take a fucking swing. I'll give you the first three...No?...Then sit down you freckle shit!" The lad sat down flushed with anger and humiliation, Van Der Borgh swaggered off laughing aloud.

"Bastard." said one of them.

"You don't see him picking' on anyone except those he knows he can beat." said another

Ginger watched the big frame disappear to the other side of the floor. "Fuckin' shirtlifter, I suppose he's off to see his boyfriend in the Ops Room." The remaining bunch started laughing as Ginger continued, "I hope his knob turns brown and drops off."

A black corporal approached the group and said urgently, "Come on lads, the OC is off over to the Para base in the school and we're doing escort, lets move it!"

Van Der Borgh entered the Ops Room, like any other the walls were covered in maps that were festooned in coloured pins. Radios were hissing static and telephones ringing. Four soldiers of various rank were working in the room. He looked across to a fair haired youth who was checking a wall map and scribbling something down on a note pad.

The youth looked across to Van Der Borgh, smiled then quickly checked himself and looked guiltily around to see if anyone had seen him, which they hadn't. Van Der Borgh gave a slight signal with his eyes and withdrew from the Ops Room.

He walked to a coffee machine and started to feed coins into it, the hot water had just finished pouring when the fair haired youth came up behind him. He spoke softly, almost a whisper tinged with anxiety, "Is something wrong Paul?"

"Just calm down a little," said Paul, his tone low and even. "Here, have this coffee." He passed the cup over and fed more coins into the machine watching intently as the cup dropped and started filling with foamy brown liquid. Once it was full he turned and said gently. "Is there anything happening Peter? Anything in the SI-TREPs I should know about?"

"Not much, a riot last night in the Para's area, a hijacked car burst through a VCP on the Falls Road, three bomb explosions in the city, troops shot at from a car, really that's it...A normal Saturday night. Do you want to read the SITREP? Its in the Ops Room, I can get it."

"No, no, it's okay, just heard the riot last night, wondered what was going on."

"Usual crap Paul, a load of pissed up bastards started.. Oh yes! There was a body found, looks like the Paras stiffened one of them in the riot. The Major is just leaving to talk to the Para Major about it now."

Van Der Borg became alert at that last statement. "Tell me Peter, why would our boss want to see them about it?"

"Don't know really, it was a request that came from *them*, about half an hour or so ago."

"Keep your ear to the ground on this one Peter." Van Der Borgh looked him squarely in the face, his eyes cold and stonelike. "If anything, anything at all comes up about this, give me the nod immediately....Do you understand?"

"You know I will Paul.... Is there something troubling you?"

"Stop your damn fussing!" forced Van Der Borgh through clenched teeth, "Just keep fucking alert!" He then smiled brightly at Peter, gave him a wink and walked away.

Peter Gant watched Paul go. He hated it when Paul was upset. Lord knows he was never the happiest of people at the best of times, he pondered for the nth time as to what demons drove him. Paul he thought, had been so good for the last couple of weeks but he had sensed the tension building in him. The last time this happened he had watched the tension grow and grow in him until it exploded when he was on a Vehicle check point on the Springfield Road.

A driver had refused to get out of his car. Paul had literally ripped the car door off its hinges and dragged the screaming man out repeatedly bashing him against a brick wall until dragged off by his comrades. Luckily the victim was a known violent offender, so the story they had concocted stuck and no action was taken.

Now it was happening again. Peter puzzled as to why the riot the previous night and the OC going over to speak to the Paras had caught Paul's attention. He went back to the Ops Room and started to scan all reports hoping he could find some answers.

Van Der Borgh walked through the parked vehicles at the side of the Factory. The park had been tarmac at one stage but constant use by heavy military vehicles had pockmarked the surface with dozens of craters that were now filled with water.

He took a sip of coffee and looked at the perimeter of the base. It was fairly typical of all the hastily utilised areas. Where the Factory wall was inadequate for protection, twenty foot high walls of silver corrugated iron took its place. The usual watchtowers or sangars were in place at each corner and a larger one situated at the double gates. The gates had two sentries, one who remained in the sangar with a rifle and the other with a pistol, searched the civilian cars that came in now and again.

Van Der Borgh slowly made his way through the Humber "Pig" armoured personnel carriers and Landrovers until he came to a blue civilian Ford Saloon looking very odd amongst its big, tough camouflaged cousins. He fished in his pocket for some keys, all the time casually scanning for anyone watching.

He slid the keys into the doorlock and heard the click of it unlocking. He took one more casual glance around then quickly got in the driver's seat. Moving fast he turned on the ignition, checked the fuel gauge then fired up the engine, as soon as it caught he turned it off and carefully got out of the car and re-locked it.

He carried on casually walking through the vehicles. He now felt a lot better, just a little less trapped, having those keys gripped in his palm gave him a rein on his destiny. He had made Peter steal the keys from the Ops Room some weeks before. There had been big trouble about it at first but the keys were replaced and the incident forgotten.

The car was for the Intelligence Officer and his small crew who used it only now and again, to visit or recce unobtrusively.

Van Der Borgh had got that weird feeling invading his skull again, the feeling that things were beginning to close in on him, the feeling that the base was his prison and he was waiting for the Warders to appear and bang him up in a cell within the Factory.

He had gotten this feeling before many times and it usually proved right. The last time was when he was in the South African Army, because of it he had gone on the run. He found out later that the police had arrived at the camp to arrest him just two hours after he had disappeared, and here was that feeling again.

He sat on the tailgate of a Landrover and sipped his coffee, the park was still quiet, he tried to concentrate his mind. Why was he anxious? It was certainly nothing to do with conscience, his brain didn't operate like that. He came to a conclusion. It was about the Major meeting up with the Para Major. It had to be something to do with the body.. Why? Because he had been seen? He could not be recognised, he knew that. He had been silhouetted and things had moved too fast, but they must have checked out B Company's patrol programme and come up with a blank, so now they will check out ours he thought and guess what? Corporal Paul Van Der Borgh was right in the middle of it. He stood up, crumpled the coffee cup and said out loud, "As of this moment I am on red alert."

It was five o'clock in the evening and all those in the school base started queuing for their evening meal. All were in uniform some with their camouflage para smocks on, some in brown pullovers or shirts. The ones in smocks would probably be eating just prior to going on patrol or on "stag" in one of the sangars that protected the base.

The hotplate was alive with white coated cooks clanging trays of hot food onto the counter. The cook Sergeant looked along the hotplate to satisfy himself that all was in order then nodded to the first man in the queue, who immediately shoved his plate out and got it half filled with chips.

In keeping with tradition the officers and senior NCOs kept back until the vast majority of soldiers had passed through. They then leisurely picked their way down the hotplate and over to a table specially set aside for them. These were the same type of Formica tables as the rest, except that they had cutlery for each place, preset around a maroon place mat bearing the Regimental insignia.

The Major normally sat in the centre of the table with Reg Wallace the CSM and Nick Summers his Second in Command flanking him, the rest of the officers and SNCOs filling in the other places in no set order.

This particular evening the Major was missing, as were Reg and Nick, they were in the Ops room waiting for the arrival of the Major from the Princes Own.

Frank sat with Vince Longthorne a fellow platoon Sergeant. Lieutenant Tony Orchard had come in after them but had chosen to sit at the other end of the table. Vince swallowed a mouthful of food and said to Frank, "So he was a bit of a twat then, this SIB bloke?"

"Yeh, he tried to come the heavy, just full of wind and piss, wouldn't like to come up against him if I was guilty of something though."

"Would you recognise that geezer again Frank? The one in the alley who said he was B Company."

"Not really it was dark, he was well built, that's about it."

"You say he spoke to you?"

"Yeh, funny accent, *I'm B Company, going to join them,* " mimicked Frank.

"Sounds like South African or Rhodie." replied Vince.

"He was definitely well out of his area then!" Both men laughed.

There was a commotion as half a dozen soldiers in flak jackets carrying rifles entered the dining room led by a tall man wearing spectacles striding confidently ahead toward the Ops room.

Lieutenant Orchard looked up and said to the two Sergeants, "That's the OC of the Princes Own, wonder what he's doing here."

"Probably trying to find his way to South Africa." said Vince dryly and both men laughed aloud once more, much to the puzzlement of Orchard.

The black Corporal from The Princes Own came over to their table and spoke to Frank in a strong Midlands accent, "Hey Sarge, any chance of a scoff? We missed ours at the Factory on account of us comin' here sudden like." He finished with a big grin showing a row of even white teeth. Frank waved him to the hotplate.

"Yeh, I'm sure there's not a problem, what are you doing here anyway?"

The Corporal stopped in his stride and turned to Frank. "Not too, sure but I think it's something to do with a Paddy that yow lot were supposed to 'ave stiffened last night...Sorry, I didn't mean..."

"That's ok, hopefully it'll be sorted out pretty soon, exactly who did it."

Frank shouted for the cook Sergeant who unhappily consented to finding the Corporal and his men some food. When they all got their plates full they sat around some tables and started eating, there was a clatter as an SLR that was leaning against an empty table slid and fell onto a chair.

The Corporal shouted, "For Christ's sake Ginger, get a friggin' grip! Always lay your bondook on the floor and it won't fall no further." Frank noticed the freckle faced lad sheepishly lay his rifle on the floor as if laying a dear friend to rest. He noted that the Corporal had used a name for the rifle that they had all picked up in the Middle East, he walked over to their table just prior to leaving the dining room. "What's your name?" he asked.

" Riffington, everyone calls me Riff."

" Did you get out to Aden? "

"Yeh, it were a dream compared to this place." he laughed.

Major Alan Briggs swung around at the large double knock on the Ops room door in time to see Major

Rory Macalpine of The Princes Own Yeomanry stride in.

" Alan ! Good to see you old boy !" said Macalpine in a loud and genuinely warm manner. "Must be big trouble for our Para friends to call on us for help." He held out his hand and Alan shook it warmly.

"Good to see you too, er.. Rory. And a big thank you for coming over. Things were a little too sensitive to talk on the old squawk box. Please come to my office, we should have this cleared up in no time.

Alan Briggs outlined the saga of the corpse to Rory then went into more depth in answer to specific questions. After a few seconds silence from Rory he wrapped up. "Well, er.. That's about it Rory, the facts are that there *was* a soldier seen on two different occasions, albeit within a few minutes, near to where the body was found. A fleeting glimpse by one of our soldiers then one of my Sergeants actually talked to him. Our B Company had no-one in the area at all, they were all tied up in a damn bomb incident. We need to sort this out...I mean it would be ideal if you could sort your end of the matter out before these SIB and RUC wallahs start getting their teeth into it."

Major Macalpine put down the empty cup he had been holding, he appeared to be deep in thought. He stood up still in silence and reached for the flak jacket draped over the back of the chair and started putting it on.

At last he spoke, "Indeed Alan, indeed. And you say that your B Company, er.. Harry thingimijib has accounted for *all* his men?"

" Harry Norton? Yes, they were no where near the interface of our area and his." They both looked at the enlarged map of Alan's area, which also showed a large chunk of both B Company's and The Princes Own area.

Rory ran his finger down a section of it , "You see here Alan, where our borders meet, its only a half dozen streets away from that damned alleyway." He seemed to have lost some of his former bounce, he sighed and said , "Ok Alan. I'll nip back and get Ops to sort out last nights patrol programme, maybe one of them saw something, one never knows…I'll keep you informed of course."

Both men walked down the corridor to the dining room. Alan was keeping up a buzz of small talk but something was eating at Rory's brain about this whole episode and he couldn't just focus his mind, to get to the bottom of it.

They came to the Dining room, his escort had just finished eating and Riff was in conversation with Frank and Vince. Rory had recovered his bounce and said. "Ah! Had time to fill your bellies I see."

"Just seein' what decent grub tastes like Sir." said Riff cheekily, with a broad grin on his ebony face.

Alan Briggs laughed, he always appreciated humour, he held out an arm to Frank and said, "Rory, this is Sergeant Britton, we talked about him." Rory smiled and shook Frank's hand.

"Good to meet you Sarn't Britton, quite an eventful night last night. I see you didn't manage to escape completely unscathed." observed Rory, glancing at the smudges of brown disinfectant dotted around Frank's face and neck.

He turned to his escort and said with mock anger, "Right come on you lot, off we go." He shepherded his men toward the exit and as they moved off he drew Frank to one side and asked quietly, "Did you get a good look at this man...The fellow last night in the alleyway?"

"Not really Sir," Frank answered, surprised by the urgency in Macalpine's voice, "He was around six foot, well built and he had a funny, well, colonial type accent, probably South African or Rhodesian, something like that."

The bubble of amnesia in Macalpine's head burst, he looked around quickly to see if anyone else had heard Frank. The ginger lad was nearest but he seemed too pre-occupied with untangling his rifle sling from a chair leg to have heard anything. Rory turned to Alan and said in his normal voice, "Alan, I'd like Sergeant Britton to accompany me to the Factory, won't keep him long, he might just be able to clear something up for me, do you mind?"

7

Major Rory Macalpine's stripped down Landrover followed by a Pig roared out of the school gates.

It was dark and the black cloud threatened rain once more, a few drops hit the windscreen of the rover as it sped through the quiet streets.

Two soldiers in the back of the Rover sat facing each other, their eyes searching the buildings and roof-tops, rifles at the ready, sights flicked up and set on minimum range of 200 yards, butt in the shoulder, ready. Whenever the vehicles slowed, their vigilance increased.

The Pig lumbered on behind, struggling to keep up with its more nimble cousin. The steel doors at the back wide open and like the Rover, two alert soldiers their wits sharpened and weapons at the ready.

Major Macalpine sat in the passenger seat of the Rover deep in thought. It had to be Van Der Borgh who was in that alleyway, of that he was certain. He knew without consulting his Ops, that Van Der Borgh was on patrol at that crucial time last night. But he had to be sure before he made any moves. He would get Britton to see him and hear him talk then he would question the rest of his patrol. He had to do this in a short space of time without arousing suspicion, a hard task indeed.

Rory had known Van Der Borgh for some years now since the days when he was a young subaltern in the Middle East. He knew him to be a loner, moody but very professional in the execution of his military duties. Always well turned out and never griped about any tasks he was given. A good leader and yet for all that, a misfit who could never get the absolute best from his men for long. To some he was a magnet, usually weaker people that needed the security of having a more powerful friend for protection.

Rory knew that he had been badly treated in his early years in the Regiment and had admired his fortitude in sticking it out and coming through. In his last report he had recommended him for promotion to Sergeant but the CO had wavered and in the end did not give his support.

The thought of those unsolved murders in Aden came flooding back to Rory and he felt a grip in his guts. It was always thought that a soldier had somehow been involved in those awful crimes but nothing had come of the investigation. He had to be careful this could well blow up in his face, he could lose the respect of a good NCO if he was wrong and be made to look a bloody fool into the bargain.

Frank sat in the back of the Pig. The Princes Own Major had told him to say nothing to anyone on the subject of the killing, if pressed he was to say he was on a liaison visit. He had a feeling that he was wanted for a lot more than that.

The Landrover swerved round a bend on the main road, the Major lurched over to one side, this snapped him out of his train of thought. "Slow down!" he ordered and then looked back for the Pig, it too rounded the bend its engine straining.

They turned into a housing estate on the last leg of their journey to the factory. Immediately a bottle bounced off the bonnet of the Landrover without breaking, followed by half a house brick, which hit the side of the vehicle. "Drive on!" the Major ordered, leaving the unseen attackers jeering in the darkness.

The housing estate comprised of the usual rows of terraced houses with gaps where some had been demolished, some were boarded up, others just open and abandoned. Every area of wall space was taken up with graffiti, some just daubed on hastily, others were near works of art. "PROVOS RULE STICKIES BEWARE" was a warning from the Provisionals to the Official IRA and a popular slogan. Others were: BRITS OUT! and TOUTS BEWARE!

Personal insults to Regiments who had long finished their tours of duty were plastered everywhere. Gable ends whitened with hooded silhouettes of figures, clutching Kalashnikov rifles stared balefully down at all who passed.

As they approached the factory down a blacked out street the huge gates swung open and the two vehicles swept in and stopped with a scrunch at the unloading bay. They all dismounted, pointed their weapons at the sandbagged wall and unloaded them.

The Major said a few words to Riff who then told his men to fall out until required. The Major came over to Frank and said politely, " Follow me would you, mind the potholes."

Paul Van Der Borgh looked at his watch, despite his frame of mind he felt tired. He was sitting at the small table in his room with his two other room mates playing seven card bragg for a heap of cash in the middle of the table.

They had just come back from their tea meal and had an hour or two to kill. He had caught Peter Gant's eye while at tea but by his reaction knew there was no new information forthcoming.

"That's it !" exclaimed one of the men who threw his hand down onto the table, "A prile of bitches and six, seven, eight on a bike, what a hand! And for what?.. Six bob !"

Paul stood up and stretched, "That's it for me."

"Aw, come on Paul, one more hand." pleaded the winner scraping a pile of coins off the table.

"Nah, you're on a streak you ugly bastard." he retorted in good humour and casually walked to his bed. He reached under, dragged out his suitcase and placed it on the bed between him and the other two so that when he opened the lid they couldn't see the contents.

He unlocked and carefully opened it and took out a neatly folded holdall, this he unfolded and placed on the bed.

He didn't look at the other two but relied on his periphery vision to ensure that they were keeping their distance. Into the holdall he placed a pair of jeans and a pair of walking boots, a shirt, a thin anorak, shaving gear and two tins of food.

Still ensuring that the other two were pre-occupied with their card game, he pulled apart a pair of smelly woollen socks that were in a ball, took out a roll of money that was held together with an elastic band and placed it in the holdall followed by the knife in its heavy leather sheath.

His two room mates finished the card game noisily and got up shouting good natured insults at each other. Paul suspended his actions until they flopped on their beds. Seeing that they were now settled he continued by pulling out a large diary with a small tinny lock on it, he opened the lock and thumbed back a few pages to uncover a passport resting in an exact size recess, he placed it between the clothes in the holdall. Lastly, he dug deep in the suitcase and came up with a thin cardboard box, he eased out a wig and after inspecting it gently laid it with the rest of the stuff.

Now came the dodgy bit, having stretched for his spare combat jacket he spread it open on the bed and put the bulging holdall in it, wrapped it up so that it looked like a laundry parcel and put the suitcase back under the bed. Without saying a word he casually lifted the bundle, walked out of the room through bed city to the vehicle park.

To all intents and purposes he was going to the "Dhobi" room, a small outhouse that contained several industrial washing and drying machines. Once outside in the dark he squeezed in and out of the Landrovers and Pigs until he was completely absorbed in the inkyness. There he stayed for several minutes, absolutely motionless so that even a curious observer would have lost interest.

When satisfied that he was alone and unobserved Paul moved to the dustbin area to a row of large paper sacks. This was classified rubbish from the Ops room which would be destroyed by burning at ten o'clock in the morning witnessed by an officer.

He carefully opened one of the sealed sacks, crammed down the loose shredded paper, placed the holdall in and folded the top back over. Finally, he placed the sack slightly apart from the rest. Carefully standing up he rechecked out the area of the park. If all went well he would retrieve the holdall first thing in the morning, if not….. He smiled grimly put on the combat jacket and worked his way back to the main building of the Factory.

The rain intensified making Paul feel better, it always did, the worse the weather the more it made people inefficient. Sentries bowed their heads and shrank back into shelter, the baddies got off the streets and into cover, they all shut it out and he alone embraced it.

Paul badly wanted a drink and desperately fought the idea of going back to his bunk and swallowing the strong pure vodka from his waterbottle. He *had* to remain sharp for at least the next twenty four hours. Remaining outwardly calm and forcing himself to act casually like playing cards was starting to take its toll, he could feel his anxiety building. Time to check with Peter.

He took a walk around the Factory probing the atmosphere, finding nothing out of the ordinary he made his way to the Ops room. Peter was not there, clenching his fists and cursing inwardly he made for Peter's bed space. It was empty. He eventually found him in the washroom alone, stripped to his waist cleaning his teeth. Paul checked the lavatory cubicles to make sure they were empty then came up behind Peter who jumped when he saw Paul's reflection in the mirror.

Paul's face twisted with rage and he hissed through grated teeth almost inaudibly, "You fucking shit! I've been searching high and low for you and where are you in my hour of need? You are here! Like some fucking whore tarting herself up!" He gave the terrified Peter a short but powerful jab in the buttock with his knotted fist. He fell against the sink snivelling and wimpering.

Paul swung him round and held him by the neck with one hand and drew back the other as if to punch him in the face. "You'd just love to see me swing wouldn't you, you bastard.. eh? Just like the rest of this fucking scum!" He let Peter go and continued to stare at him, breathing deeply.

"Paul, please stop! I've been stuck in that Ops room all day like you said keeping my ear to the ground, this is the first break I've had, honest to God, Paul please..."

"Stop your fucking wailing man." hissed Van Der Borgh.

"I'm sorry Paul, I'm sorry, but you're scaring me." he sobbed. "Nothing, absolutely nothing has happened since the OC left. I've scanned all the SITREPS, took all of the phone calls.. Nothing! Paul I don't even know *what* I'm supposed to be looking for, for God's sake Paul what's going on ?"

Paul came out of his trance like state, he relaxed his features took a deep breath and let it out. "Look," he said in a normal voice, "just go back to the Ops room and keep an eye on things. The Major must be due back soon, be on the spot, pick up what's going on and tell me straight away….Okay ? Come on man, buck up !" he smiled at Peter and gripped his arm reassuringly. Peter smiled back through his tears and blew his nose on the towel.

The door to the washroom swung open admitting a soldier. Paul immediately broke away, he looked the newcomer up and down then left slamming the door.

The soldier looked at Peter then back at the door, "Bastard." He said.

"Yeah," said Peter, "bastard."

Peter Gant entered the Ops room. He had taken some time to compose himself, Paul had shaken him. He had promised last time that he would never hit him again. On that occasion he had spent a week in Salisbury Hospital with broken ribs and nose. He hadn't shopped Paul, instead he said that it was a bunch of squaddie bashers that had cornered him in Town. He had even given detailed descriptions. Paul had never even thanked him for it, but did promise…

"You're bloody keen young Gant!" Peter turned to see the Intelligence Officer, Captain Hugh Perry in civilian clothes smiling at him. "You must have been in here all day."

"Just got to finish filing some patrol reports Sir." he said weakly.

"You alright lad? You look terrible."

"I.. I.." began Peter but was cut off by the signaller who shouted to Perry.

" Major's back Sir! Just arrived."

Paul Van Der Borgh stood at the entrance of the TV room watching the remnants of the local news, a burly corporal strode up to him and said. " Paul, Bald Eagle wants to speak to you, he's in his office."

"What's he want?" asked Paul without taking his eyes off the screen.

"Didn't say, didn't look too happy either, but then again, does he ever?"

Paul sauntered off through bed City, he noticed that Riff was back, that meant the Major was too. Riff was relaxed, flak jacket off and rifle stowed in the rack, he must have been back some time he reasoned, why hadn't Gant warned him?

Company Sergeant Major, Gerald Peachy known to everyone as Bald Eagle, sat behind his desk looking at some paperwork. He looked up as Paul entered.

"Ah ! Corporal Van Der Borgh." he said as if he had been searching a continent for him. Paul hated the way he pronounced Borgh to rhyme with forge and not Borg, but then there was a lot he despised about the squat being in front of him, with the flaring nostrils and shiny dome. By rumour a coward who was reluctant to go on the streets. A man they said who was even afraid of barking dogs.

Nevertheless, if nothing else Paul was a professional soldier. He came to attention and said in a confident manner, "Sir, you sent for me."

Bald Eagle, for a moment seemed a little flustered.
" Er.. Yeh, You are on patrol tonight yeh ?"

"That's correct Sir, eleven thirty."

"Good, when you go out....On patrol I mean, keep
an eye on the, er.. Yeh, keep an eye on the illegal drinking clubs...It's.. It's fucking illegal got it!" Before Paul
could react the door to the adjoining office, which was
the OC's opened and out stepped the Major in conversation with Frank.

They both went to pass by the CSM and Paul when
the Major stopped as if surprised to see the CSM, "Hello Sergeant Major, Corporal Van Der Borgh, do excuse
us." He went to pass by but had an after thought and
turned to Paul saying, "Ah! Glad you're here Corporal
Van Der Borgh, this is Sergeant Britton from the Para
Company next door, you may be seeing more of him
he's familiarising himself with our area in case we get
some combined Ops in the future, have you in fact been
out today?"

Paul cleared his throat and said a little hesitantly,
"As a matter of fact, no Sir, I am due out later if the sergeant would like to accompany us?" He studied Frank's
face, his own flat and expressionless. Frank, feigning
lack of interest agreed to but at a later date. He and the
Major then left. Bald Eagle dismissed Paul.

"Well?" asked the Major when they were well clear
of the office. He was quite relieved that his hastily
planned little playact to get Britton to see and hear Van
Der Borgh had worked.

"It's him, I'm ninety nine per cent sure, the build the accent, unless there's anyone else that could fit that description..."

"Okay Sergeant Britton, many thanks for coming, the CSM will get you speedily back to the school. By all means report to your OC...But no-one else please." Both men shook hands and went their separate ways.

Ginger held court, around him were a dozen or more of the Bed City gang, clinging on to his every word. At the urgent request of a couple of newcomers he began his version of recent events again. "There we were in the Para's camp, just had our grub and old Macalpine says to this Para bloke, they was as near to me as you lot are, he says, would you ever recognise this bloke that hacked the paddy up? And straight away the Para says, yes Sir, he was a Princes Own and he had a South African accent......Kind of narrows it down a bit don't it fellas?" Ginger finished with a huge smug look, staring each of his audience in the eye for a split second. Peter Gant lurched away from the periphery of the group almost vomiting.

Paul walked away from the CSM's office puzzled. What was that stupid twat on about? He always knew that Bald Eagle was barmy, now he must have flipped. *Illegal drinking clubs are illegal, so keep your eye on them!* What the fuck!

Then it struck him! The Para sergeant, he was the one in the alleyway last night! The realisation jolted him, he could feel panic starting to rise in his gut. He fought it down. Just then a figure jumped out in front of him, it was Peter.

"Paul!" he started to wail bordering on hysteria, "They're on to you, some Para saw you hack up a bloke last night and..." Paul pushed him through a door to a disused office.

"Stop shouting you hysterical bitch!"

"I can't help it Paul, what's going to happen? Please Paul what's going to happen? They'll take you away...Oh God!" Paul stood back and watched Peter fold into a sobbing heap, he then grabbed his chin and said urgently, "Stay here! Don't move from this room for two hours.. Do you understand? Two hours.. Do you?" Peter nodded and tried to reach for Paul who slapped him savagely away. "Two fucking hours.. don't forget." He went to the office window and forced it open, had a quick look, then jumped into the darkness.

Rory Macalpine sat alone in his office and rested his forehead on the tips of his fingers. He mulled over his next moves. Van Der Borgh had to be arrested and questioned. He would call and inform the CO first. He picked up the secure phone and dialled.

It was raining heavily now, making a din on the surfaces of the corrugated tin. Van Der Borg made his way to the dustbin area, rain was running down his face in streams. He found the sack and ripped out his hold-all, his heart pounding with excitement at the prospect of escape, evasion and the great unknown.

He found the Ford opened it and slung his holdall in the passenger seat, as he was about to get in, his eye caught a movement to his right and a curious voice demanded, "Who the devils that? What are you doing with that car?" Paul swung round to face the Intelligence Officer, Hugh Perry, dressed in a trench coat and a flat cap.

After the initial shock Paul could not believe his good fortune, maybe he didn't know they were after him, it didn't matter anyway, firstly he had to throw him off balance.

"Good evening Sir! The Majors orders I'm afraid. There's some kind of flap on, the car is needed, I'm to drive him to Battalion HQ." said Paul matter of factly.

"Oh! Its you Corporal Van...What's the flap?" Perry started to move closer to Van Der Borg, "Hey! How did you open the car ? I have the only set of keys." Van Der Borgh started to speak and in doing so closed in to Perry, he lashed out with his right foot landing a tremendously powerful kick in the pit of Perry's stomach, as he started to crumple forward, he took a measured step backward then booted Perry full in the face, he straightened up then collapsed without making a sound.

Working rapidly he felt under Perry's left arm and pulled out his Browning 9mm Pistol, checked that the magazine was full, then stuffed it in his map pocket, next, he took his wallet, then pushing and pulling he stripped the trench coat off him. Finally, with all his adrenaline fuelled strength, he lifted and dumped the still silent Perry in the boot of the car.

Van Der Borgh stood up panting heavily, the welcome rain streaming down his face. After a few seconds he donned the trench coat and flat cap, got in the car and fired up the engine.

The sentry ran to the gate at the last moment hunched against the downpour. Once it was open Van Der Borg drove through slowly, making sure that the sentry who was impatient to close the gate and get back inside saw 'Hugh Perry' driving out with his turned up collar and flat cap pulled down. Once through, Van Der Borgh gunned the car into the pitch blackness of the stormy night.

8

Major Alan Briggs waited patiently for the gathering in his office to sort themselves out. Chairs were passed over at head height and jammed into spaces around his desk, reacting to a gesture from the CSM they both moved the desk back a foot or so, only to discover that now he could not get back into his chair.

The CSM wondered for the nth time why they couldn't hold the Orders Group, known commonly as " O " groups, in a more spacious room. God knows he thought, there were plenty of them in the base. They moved the desk back slightly and the Major slid in, a slight grin on his ruddy face. The rest settled and went quiet.

As well as Major Briggs and CSM Reg Wallace, there were three Lieutenants including Tony Orchard, who were the platoon Commanders, three Platoon Sergeants: Frank, Vince Longthorne and a wee Glaswegian Tommy McGregor. Captain Nick Summers doubling as Second in Command and Ops Officer sat puffing on a King Edward cigar.

The seating arrangement looked haphazard but closer inspection would reveal a distinct pecking order. The Major sat on the "Throne." Nick Summers sat nearest to him in a leather lookalike armchair also facing the group, the most senior of the Platoon Commanders sat close to the desk, actually resting his note book on it

and the rest filled where they could on collapsible wood-
en chairs, apart from the CSM who, although could vie
for a place next to the OC, opted out and had his chair
at the back to control the door.

Lieutenant Tony Orchard sat three away from
Frank, he had been avoiding him since the riot. Frank
looked across to him and wandered what the hell was up
with him, was it embarrassment because he had turned
up late with his men to support him at the riot? Or because he failed to run with him to investigate the mystery soldier seen in the alley, leaving him exposed to the
gunman?

Frank himself, had put both incidents down to inexperience on Orchard's part and had dismissed any
other suggestions on the matter. He just wished that Orchard would talk to him about it so he could reassure
him. It was bad for the morale of the platoon to have
the two top men at loggerheads with each other but he
had avoided any such meeting and Frank had given up
hoping that he would come quickly out of his sulk.

The Major finally stopped rummaging around in
his drawer when he found his pipe and stuck it in his
mouth. He went through the blowing and sucking routine. The room fell silent in expectation.

"Gentlemen," he began in his quiet way, "shan't
keep you too long I hope. I know we're all fairly busy
people but there are one or two things that need to be
said and I'll say them in no particular order. Firstly, this
sad business up at the Princes Own." he paused and
looked round the group subconsciously conveying the
seriousness he felt.

He continued, "It seems that this er.. Van Der... What ever has slipped over the border to the South. The Garda of course are on to it but with all due respect to them I suspect it's without the pressure and impetus of our lot. Their Ops Officer, er.. Captain Perry is recovering in the Victoria Hospital but is still poorly.....Nick?"

Nick, who was in a slouch straightened up and spoke to the group. "Yes, was up the hospital this morning, he took a hell of a beating and being left by the roadside undiscovered for hours in that weather didn't help much .."

"Where exactly did they find him Sir?" enquired the CSM.

"Actually I couldn't pinpoint it on a map but it was on an unapproved road leading to the South near Forkhill, found by some locals who thought it was a dead body...A few more hours and it could have been." Nick sat back in his chair to signal the end of his report.

"Thanks for that Nick," continued the Major. "apparently the bugger was tipped off that arrest was imminent and drove out in the Op's Officers car with him inside it. Nobody knew this of course and it was some hours before they discovered what had happened. That Factory is like a bloody warren apparently, they had to search the whole damn lot...Bloody psychopath! It will take a court of law of course to convict him of that killing in the alley but off the record they're not looking for anyone else...And indeed at this juncture I will say a public well done to our intrepid Sergeant Britton who played no small part in identifying this madman...Well done!" The Major beamed at Frank who grimaced and squirmed a little.

"Now gentlemen, onto more mundane matters." Briggs stared down at his notes and started to cover some points that had come to his attention over the last few days such as the toilet areas being in bad order, mud getting dragged through the Dining room, the standard of dress slipping and so on and so forth.

The CSM, Reg Wallace then followed him up with his solutions to the problems, with threats as to what would happen if the general situation in the base continued to decline.

The O Group began to stir and fidget, everyone in the base was on an average workload of sixteen hours a day, therefore time, or rather time off, was a big issue. Being bottled up in a crowded little office for long began to make people restless, except for the one doing the talking of course.

The Major listened to the CSM and nodded in the right places but was anxious to get to his own main reason for calling the meeting. As soon as the CSM hesitated a mite too long Briggs cut in and with a warm thank you to him, began with his customary address. "Gentlemen, what I'm going to cover now is not, not to be related to anyone outside of this room." The general atmosphere in the room changed as people raised their heads and looked at the OC.

"There is a strong belief that some kind of initiative is soon going to be taken against the IRA, as to what exact form the initiative will take I..." the Major cleared his throat, "I've no idea..... And I don't want any speculation!" he said this last sentence in a louder slightly aggressive manner.

Reverting back to normal he continued, "The only reason I am telling you this, is so that you can discreetly start to sharpen up the men, get all the weapons checked out for serviceability, that our transport is roadworthy and most of all ensure that all your men and yourselves are getting enough shuteye. None o' this late night gamblin'. Oh yes! I know it goes on. But remember gentlemen, not a word about the initiative. The CO told me to use my discretion as to whom I informed, if indeed anyone. But because we're on the frontline here so to speak in the middle of a hard Republican area we need all the information and warning we can ruddy well get."

"Sir?" It was an interruption from the well manicured voice of Lieutenant Orchard holding up his pencil.

"Yes Tony?" replied the Major with a slight smile.

"This initiative Sir, could it be in the form of internment?"

The Major looked as if a red hot poker had touched a sensitive part of his anatomy. He shot a glance at Captain Nick Summers who had smothered an involuntary laugh by throwing a coughing fit on the cigar smoke, the Major then spoke sternly to Orchard.

"I did say young Sir, that I didn't want speculation and that's what I jolly well meant! Now where did you get that claptrap from? Bloody idle talk at Headquarters no doubt."

"Actually Sir," said the red faced Orchard meekly, " I just caught it on the local news before we came in here, they said more troops were being drafted in to cover the apprentice marches, but a reporter said that it could mean internment…"

" Bloody conjecture"! shouted the embarrassed Major, his ruddy face now glowing, but it was too late, the whole O Group broke out in hysterical laughter led by Nick Summers who had tears rolling down his cheeks. After a few seconds the Major also saw the funny side and allowed himself a grin while shaking his head from side to side.

When it started to subside, the CSM said in a loud voice, "Now come on gentlemen keep quiet…I SAID, QUIET!"

"Thank you Sergeant Major…I don't think I can top that," said Briggs good naturedly, "However, gentlemen it still stands, I want no speculating! And Nick," He turned toward him, "I want maps of all our adjoining areas, the ones that show all the house numbers, and all the latest information you can get on the baddies in our areas." Nick nodded. After winding up the meeting the OC dismissed the Group.

Nick Summers remained in the office with the OC. When they were alone, the OC said in a mock exasperated voice, "For God's sake Nick, the Colonel and I talked about this in his office only two hours ago, it has only just come down from HQ Northern Ireland.. a bloody secret!"

"No more Alan, it seems." replied Nick sympathetically but still with a smile on his lips.

Frank entered the classroom that served as the bunkhouse for his platoon. All thirty four of them had a bed space in it. Some were in beds double stacked and some triple, none had the luxury of a bed on its own. The large glass windows had been boarded up and sandbagged on the outside, a solitary extractor fan laboured non stop day and night and its noise, like the permanent fug of human flesh went unnoticed.

Personal kit was stacked everywhere, there was just enough space to form pathways between the beds. There was no privacy at all, no-one had secrets and if anyone made a mistake, big or small it was known to everyone and the unlucky person had to be prepared to take unmerciful 'slagging' until some other guy cocked up and took the pressure off.

The platoon had just come off a three day stint of patrolling, going immediately onto another three days of 'Standby'. Eight men were on 'Immediate' standby, fully dressed ready to jump in the Standby Pig the second they were called out. They waited in a specially designated room next to the Ops room to cut down on response times. A good crash out would see the Pig screaming through the gates thirty five seconds after the signal was given.

They would remain on this duty for eight hours then go on 'Back Up' for another eight, boots and flak jackets could be removed for this but little else. If the Immediate were crashed out they would automatically get fully dressed again and refill this position. The remainder of the Platoon were on 'Rest.' Rest meant that in theory at least they could strip and climb into their beds and get uninterrupted sleep but that never happened. If any jobs had to be done around the base it made them fair game.

At one end of the room nearest the door was a six foot wooden trestle table and a few chairs, most of the platoon had gathered round this area while others sat on beds nearby.

Frank stood there among them, he glanced at his watch, Lieutenant Orchard said that he would be there straight after the 'O' Group to brief the men. Fifteen minutes had now lapsed and some of the men were resentful of the fact that they had been woken up just to sit around.

Frank decided to crack on without him and shouted, "Okay, listen in! The boss will be here in a few minutes to give you the latest but firstly I've a few points to cover." He sat at the table and flicked open his notebook, as he did the comparative silence was broken by a loud voice with an Australian accent.

"What's all this internment crap we keep hearin' about Sarge?" drawled 'Digger' Davis.

"We're not supposed to discuss it." answered Frank honestly, "More info may come out later but as of this minute." Frank finished his sentence by putting his finger to his lips.

Digger persisted, even louder now and more confident, conscious of the sudden interest he had created in the hitherto bored assembly. "Yeh, but Sarge, why are we always the last bastards to know the fuck what's 'appening? It's bloody *Internment*! Lockin' people up without trial? I mean the bloody RUC know about it, the Taigs and bloody Prods know!"

The rest of the lads started a chorus of "Yeh! That's right."

Digger finished his rhetoric with a final, "Even Abdul, the Paki in our coffee shop knows, so what's the score Sarge?" At this Digger and the rest of the lads burst into laughter, it subsided and stopped when a grim faced Lieutenant Orchard entered the room.

He looked at Frank, made a beckoning gesture with his index finger and said sternly "A word!" and then walked back out of the room. Frank felt his hackles rise at the way Orchard had spoken to him in front of the platoon, he followed him out.

Orchard suddenly turned in the empty passage outside and rounded on Frank. "What the devil do you think you are doing Sergeant Britton? Not ten minutes ago, the Company Commander himself told us...Ordered us! To keep our bloody mouths shut about this internment thing and there you are openly discussing it, not with a fellow sergeant which would be understandable or with a corporal which would be forgivable but with that bloody bunch in there! The whole lot of them laughing, shouting and jeering! I tell you *Sergeant* Britton the whole damn discipline in this Platoon is going down the chute, what with their open defiance in that riot...And you, *you* are the one responsible ..If that is the right word to use."

"Have you finished Sir?" said Frank with a detached calmness. "Because if you have, I'll reply....Sir."

"Watch your step Sergeant Britton, I'm warning you!"

"Oh, don't you worry Sir, I'll watch my step alright. I'll be a tick tock soldier, watch my Ps and Qs, two kids and a mortgage. Yes Sir! No Sir! But you listen this once, just this once. That *bunch* in there regardless of what you think of me will see us through this tour. That *bunch* in there are good, well disciplined and loyal but what do they get in return? They get fucked around most of the time and treated like kids. Do you really know or even care what all that was about in there? It was about a group of hard working, intelligent people who put their lives on the line every hour of every day, wanting to know why they can't be trusted with something that's vitally important to their wellbeing. Something that apparently half of bloody Belfast knows about. And how do they react to this? Do they riot? Or do they fester and moan about it? No! They laugh, they laugh their fucking heads off…. That's discipline Sir! And the likes of you and me should be grateful and pray that they keep on laughing."

Orchard sneered, "Oh very touching Sergeant Britton, did you go on a course to RADA, or is this something you can you can just summon up when in a personal crisis?"

Frank snapped, words failed him, the tunnel vision, the electric current in his gut, he clenched his fists and moved toward Orchard with gritted teeth, somewhere in his brain he prayed Orchard would run.

"Oy! Tony old son, are you going to get your shapely arse to the Ops room? It's your stag." It was Nick Summer's voice booming down the corridor. "Come on old boy, you're keeping me away from my wanking sack!"

The confrontation broke off after Orchard hissed, "You haven't heard the last of this."

Frank stared after him until his eyes met with Nick Summers, they looked at each other for a second then Nick followed Orchard to the Ops room.

Frank slowly let out his breath, took a few seconds to compose himself then made his way back into the bunkhouse.

Big Norrie Norris filled his face with forkfull after forkfull of chips and when he could get no more in and could hardly chew, he decided to carry on his conversation with Digger Davis and Ronnie Gittins. "It's certain that, that bastard Orchard is going to get his lights punched out in the near future and I want to be around to see it happen." he stated in his strong Nottingham accent.

"Fing is," chimed in Ronnie Gittins, "whoever did it would be up to his neck in the brown and smelly. Court Martial for sure. And if you mean, who I fink you mean, he'd really get banjoed. Busted, nick, kicked out.. Everything finished, all because of a two pip twat like Orchard."

Norrie stopped chewing and looked at Ronnie, "You mean they'd do that to Frank!? Bust him and boot him out, after all he's fuckin' done for this Regiment?

"Naffink more certain Norrie."

"So why can't somebody do something about that twat then?"

Ronnie took a swig of tea and looked left and right furtively, the hum of conversation bouncing off the hard bare walls gave him a feeling of security from being overheard.

"What are they going to do Norrie? We have a keen young officer who's daddy was a fackin General, he's the apple...Forgive the pun, of the OC's eye, he can't do wrong and if 'e does it's because he's young and inexperienced and it's expected." Ronnie drew nearer to Norrie and said with finality. "And even if he fucked up big style on sammink, Frank would get the blame for allowing it to 'appen."

Norrie shook his head and shoved his cleaned plate to one side. Like most of the lads he respected Ronnie's broader non biased views on situations and couldn't find any real argument. "It ain't right, it just ain't right." he muttered.

"In Oz," snarled Digger, "we'd have strung the bastard up before now, officer or no officer."

"Oh, shut it Digger!" Both Norrie and Ronnie said in unison.

9

Captain Nick Summers took a stroll through the vehicle park to where Frank was talking to one of the platoon members. The soldier walked off as Nick approached. The sun was beginning to set in a blazing gold inferno, a fitting end to what had been a rare glorious day. Nick made it look like a chance encounter but in fact had waited for an opportunity to speak to Frank in relative privacy.

Frank winked at him and declined the offer of a cigar. Nick placed one in his mouth and carefully lit it up.

"How's things Frank?"

Frank didn't react to Nick using his first name usually a strict *No* between officers and other ranks. He had worked with Summers before and knew that he only rarely did that as a sign of genuine friendship and respect. He knew that he had always been an offbeat officer but had never been disloyal to his own kind or anyone else for that matter.

Frank though, suspected there was a deeper meaning to this apparently casual, chance conversation, so he answered a little guardedly. "Yeh! No probs, things are fine." he turned slightly away from Nick and looked at his watch.

He was just about to utter his excuses and go when Nick shot.

"Are things getting *you* down Frank? "

"What like?"

"Oh, things, you know…People."

"Huh! No more than they usually do and if they did…What then?" Frank took the edge of his statement by giving a grin.

"Well, you know where I am." Offered Nick.

"Yeh, cheers Sir." said Frank in a serious tone and walked off toward the main building. Nick Summers stared after him for a few seconds then followed suit.

Peter Gant lay on his bed in the Factory, it was around three in the morning. Even here in bed city it was quiet except for the sound of snoring and the occasional sound of someone talking in his sleep.

Peter lay awake as he had done for the few nights since Paul had absconded after beating the intelligence Officer half to death.

He had done as Paul had ordered and stayed in the unused office for an uncertain time after he had disappeared through the window. He had felt utterly dejected and lonely, he knew of course that he would be linked to the escape but this had hardly mattered to him. He was sure that he had lost Paul for ever and the prospect made him feel suicidal.

As things went he was only given a rudimentary grilling by the SIB, much the same in fact as everyone else. After a few days things had quietened down and everyone carried on as normal.

He'd got strange looks from the lads and nasty remarks thrown his way mainly by Ginger Tomlins and his crowd but he was used to that anyway. To him they were just a group of unfeeling morons, who couldn't think further than their next meal. Brutes, who night after night revelled in stories of how they'd beaten some civilian to pulp whilst out on patrol. They sickened him and he wished now that he had followed his original intention over a year ago to get out, back to the sanity of civilian life. But then Paul had come into his life.

Lance Corporal Paul Van Der Borgh had literally walked in on him one Saturday afternoon in the barracks by Salisbury Plain. The lads had all come back from the town the worse for drink and had started to tear the room up, tipping beds over and throwing water around.

Peter had tried to exit the room but was gripped by two of them who had called him a pansy and had tried to rip his clothes off much to the merriment of the jeering audience. Suddenly the door had opened and Van Der Borgh had walked in stripped to the waist, his arms swinging loose from his broad shoulders. He never said anything just stared, his hard cruel face uncompromising in front of six or more potential foes.

Peter had not long been in the unit and had never seen him before. There were a couple of NCOs among the crowd and after an awkward silence one of them shouted a greeting to Paul and offered a bottle.

Paul had just stared at him and after an embarrassing silence they all broke up and went their ways, shuffling past hung down and muttering. Not until they had all left did Paul turn to go. Peter had rushed up to him trying to get out a thank you message but he had got the same glare as the others and had shrunk back as Paul left the room to go back to his own across the corridor.

That had been the start of a fatal fascination for Peter. He learned that in the coming tour to Northern Ireland he had been assigned to Ops in Paul's Company. The prospect pleased him and he decided to make a determined effort to get to know him better.

He had found himself combing the bars in town until he found the one Paul was drinking in, usually alone. Trying to make it look like a casual encounter he would sidle up to him and attempt to engage him in conversation, for the most part a one sided effort which could end abruptly when Paul would empty his glass and walk off with a "See yuh." Leaving him feel awkward and hurt, wondering again why he was driving himself on this course of action, he suppressed the answer that loomed in the darker recesses of his mind.

Then one weekend it had happened, from making slow progress in their relationship it had gone to the speed of light leaving him an emotional wreck.

A Long weekend had been granted which meant that the vast majority of soldiers had bomb burst through the gates early on Thursday afternoon. Peter had enjoyed the luxury of being alone in the block, he had contemplated going home to his parents but had for no particular reason decided not to. On Friday night he had lain on his bed reading a book when he heard the door at the end of the corridor opening loudly as if being booted.

Fear momentarily gripped his stomach, expecting to hear the shouting and ribald laughter of returning drunks. Instead he heard the steady click of steel heel studs on concrete coming up the passage, they stopped in front of Peter's room. The door was pushed open forcefully, slamming it into the wall. There stood Paul Van Der Borgh, a smile on his face.

Peter had never seen him smile before but then again he had never seen him drunk either. He was pleased and excited to see him but could not drive the uneasiness from his mind.

Van Der Borgh had dragged him out of his bed then stood back studying his nakedness. Pushing him back on the bed he gripped him in a powerful embrace, the hot, foetid stench of his drink laden breath blasting into his face.

Peter remembered all the beginning, the passion, the secrecy and then for him it had turned into infatuation. This had alarmed Van Der Borgh who was well aware of the view the army had on such behaviour and had no intention of being discharged with disgrace... No, when he left it would be on his own terms.

He had warned Peter to keep his distance and when he hadn't, he had meted out a severe beating. Then they reached a compromise, no physical contact until after the tour in Ulster then he promised they would get out and set up together somewhere. Paul talked of South Africa and Rhodesia. Oh! The things they were going to do and the places they would visit. And now what? He was an alien in an environment he loathed. He was alone, despised, spat on. At the worst, detested, at the best, detested.

He had contemplated suicide, he would pick up his rifle, sit on the toilet and fit the flash hider in his mouth as far as it would go before retching, then pull the trigger and blow his brains out. He had even rehearsed it going as far as pulling the trigger on an empty chamber.

The postcard had changed everything. It was lying on his desk in the Ops room. It simply said, "ALLS WELL SEE YOU SOON. DAD" The card showed a view of the White Cliffs taken from the sea. Peter knew it was Paul. They had talked about waving their former life in England away from the deck of a ship on a world cruise many times, and as for "DAD", his father hardly knew or cared he existed. He was ecstatic and had started counting the days until the end of the tour. Paul would be waiting, he had to be.

Peter could feel the sleep coming over him. He deliberately put in around eighteen hours a day in the Ops Room, partly to be in a relatively friendlier place than bed city and partly to make time go quicker. Also there was a new Ops Officer, who being basically lazy, appreciated it very much. It was good to be appreciated.

A noise to his side, he turned and came face to face with two eyes staring through the slits of a black Balaclava, before he could utter a sound a hand from the other side of the bed clamped around his mouth. Others now pounced and cut his writhing down to a minimum. Ropes were wrapped around him and a masking tape wound round his mouth, finally a hood was placed over his head.

He was carried like a coffin through the quietness of bed city and across the vehicle park. He felt them stumble over the potholes. Now he was stood up and forced to shuffle down steps in an enclosed place. Down and down, now along a rubble filled narrow passageway into some subterranean room under the factory.

They stopped, he felt others shuffling in and around him, he heard the hiss of a kerosene fed pressure lamp and could feel some of its warmth through the hood.

A voice right next to his ear said in a deliberately distorted voice, "Make one fucking sound and it will be your last!" The masking tape was ripped from his mouth but the hood remained.

A muffled but audible voice, Peter guessed it was someone wearing an issue respirator, said in official tones. "Peter the Pufter Gant. You stand before this Court Martial accused of aiding and abetting the escape of your queer partner in crime, namely, Paul Van Der Bum Shafter. What do you plead, guilty or guilty?" He heard suppressed sniggering about him.

"Well?" boomed the voice, "Guilty or guilty?"

Peter had known deep down that it would come to something like this one day, he just hoped that he came out of it alive and not too badly injured. He had already crapped himself and involuntary urinated, but at this moment he didn't give a damn about dignity.

"Just get on with it you scum!" he screamed at the top of his lungs, "Do your damndest you scum! You scum!"

The first blow was no surprise, it came low and hard seeking the genital area but landed low in his gut. He crumpled and felt a rain of kicks going into his head and body, no pain just a disorientating effect. He felt something solid on his side, was it a wall or a floor? Still the kicks kept coming. Was he still on his feet or lying on the ground? Where was the blackness? It came.

Lieutenant Anthony Blake Orchard pushed his empty plate away and gently dabbed his mouth with his handkerchief. He listened to the Major talking to Nick Summers about some trivia that had been on the six o'clock news and after a few seconds excused himself from the table.

He could never quite get used to the loud hum of conversation that was always present in the crowded Dining Room. If he were able to get away with it he would eat alone in his room or at least with his fellow officers in a separate area.

He had been quite surprised when they had first arrived. The Major had scrapped the use of a separate mess for the Officers that was already up and running for the unit they were taking over from. None of the others seemed to mind and he got blank looks from them when he raised the subject. He took his plate to the wash up area but instead of dipping it in the hot soapy water, washing it and stowing it on the rack, he as usual just dropped it into the water and walked off.

There was not much that he could do while his Platoon were on Standby. Even if they crashed out to an incident it would be led by a Corporal unless it was something major. He felt a twinge in his gut and immediately fought off the feeling of dread at the thought of being in the middle of another riot. Things had been quiet lately, but he feared that this was just the lull.

The incident with Britton had shaken him. He felt sure that he was about to be struck by him if Nick hadn't appeared. He thought hard about reporting him but was unsure of his ground, would the OC support him? Would Nick Summers? He knew Nick was pally with Britton, he even talked about him using his first name! Britton would no doubt blab about his cowardice, ah! That word! You are not a coward! A little unsure maybe acting with no support from the platoon. Britton had seen to that he thought grimly, leading a propaganda campaign to highlight his inexperience and gain cheap popularity for himself.

He reached his small room and let himself in sitting down on his carefully made bed. He looked at the picture of himself and his father taken the day of his Pass Off parade at the Royal Military Academy at Sandhurst.

Major General Andrew Orchard, DSO OBE, had been retired for a few years now. He had been Second in Command of the Battalion that Tony was now serving in and had Commanded another one. The General had been proud and if the truth were known relieved when Tony got into the Regiment but it should have been his elder brother Charles.

Charles, five years his senior and mentor in most things had been a rare mixture of the academic, fine athlete and extremely popular person, especially with the ladies.

Charles had delighted the General when he announced that he had chosen to go for a commission in
the Regiment. He had wanted, he said, to get things out
of his system before joining the Bowler Hat Brigade in
the City. He was going to do it of course, because he
wanted to and because it would make Dad proud. The
General secretly hoped that he would make it his career.

The cruel hand of fate struck one sunny afternoon on a country road in Kent. He had been riding
his Matchless 650, not recklessly but a ' Touch fast' as
one witness put it. He had lost control after crossing a
small hump backed bridge. It had acted like a ramp and
he had flown. When he landed the front wheel couldn't
recover, he had slammed head on into an oncoming
truck.

The fortune that come out of misfortune was that
it happened outside of a Doctor's weekend cottage while
he was there on a rare midweek visit. He had without
doubt saved Charles' life...But for what? Thought Tony.
He was just a poor replica of his former self. Wheelchair
bound, incontinent, couldn't feed himself. Sometimes
he recognised the family, sometimes not, his speech reduced to grunts and moans.

The family of course had been devastated. The
General aged ten years immediately, and took early retirement to be closer to Charles and his wife.

Tony had bottled up his grief, for months he
couldn't function properly at school and was feared to
be on the verge of a breakdown but he got through it.

He had announced on his eighteenth birthday that
he would join the Regiment and was a little puzzled why

his father had initially tried to dissuade him. But now he was here, he looked fondly at the old chap smiling into the lens his arm around him.

Tony knew himself to be a little different from the others. At school or Sandhurst he could never assume that easy going relaxed attitude that many of his peers possessed. He had often been ragged about his serious view on all things. With Charles he had been different. Charles had plenty of character for both of them, he'd made light of everything and took the sting out of potentially bad situations. When Charles had been struck down he had taken a large chunk of Tony with him.

Tony looked at the photograph again, his face set grimly. He knew that at his Father's side just out of shot, Charles was slumped and dribbling in a wheelchair. He felt his throat go tight and his chest ache. With an effort he stood up and looked at the stern young face in the mirror. "I will Charles, I will!" he said firmly.

10

Lieutenant Colonel Quentin Harper MC, Commanding Officer, cast his eye over the group of officers that were assembling in the large conference room. He was receiving the latest Situation Reports from the Intelligence Officer, a tall bespectacled, hawk faced man who towered over him.

He had been through all the SITREPS himself an hour before so was listening in a relaxed mode, mentally counting the Company Commanders in the room. When all six were there and one or two other important persons, he would have them called to order and begin his O Group.

Under normal circumstances, say back in England or Germany, the O Group would have been called at a certain time and he would have walked in at that exact time or a little after, confident that all who should be, would be there waiting. However, times were not normal, they were in Belfast on operations. One of his soldiers had already been shot dead by a sniper, two others badly wounded by bomb shrapnel, a half dozen others burned or otherwise wounded. He called the O Group and then waited for his Company Commanders to get there in the best time they could make, incidents and traffic permitting.

He noticed Major Harry Norton talking to Alan Briggs, between them they held down the two most troublesome areas in the City. Hard uncompromising Republican areas, hot beds of IRA activity. He had deliberately chosen them for the job. Ironically they were contrasting characters. Alan Briggs of the old school, steady, reliable unflappable, he would get no further of course, having been passed over for promotion the last couple of times he was now out of the age bracket. He knew this but to his great credit still gave one hundred and ten percent.

Then there was Harry Norton, a small wiry man who always spoke quickly and to the point. A very capable but impulsive man with a demonic temper, a man who didn't suffer fools gladly but nevertheless was well liked and respected by his men. A man destined to go far in the Regiment.

The Quartermaster stood away from the main group talking to another of the Company Commanders, tall and slim with a ramrod straight back and waxed moustache. He had been a Regimental Sergeant Major the year before and had taken a commission.

Bill Macdonald, on taking the commission and being given the rank of Captain had thought he had arrived. He had still not settled in properly, he had an inferiority complex and strived too hard to please his Commanding Officer. To Bill, nobody else in the Battalion really mattered and he evaluated all others as to how much of a problem they would be to him. He was terrified of being found wanting and before every decision he made or order given, he ensured that he was fireproof, free of recrimination if things went badly.

The intelligence Officer finished his brief to the CO. Quentin thanked him, turned to the Adjutant and nodded. The adjutant cleared his throat and said in a voice just loud enough to cut through the hum, "Thank you gentlemen we are about to begin." The hum was replaced by the scraping of chairs and the clack of notebooks and diaries being placed on the long oak table.

The CO, when all else were seated and looking expectantly in his direction sat in his chair at the head of the table. He was flanked by his adjutant and Intelligence Officer. He smiled and spoke to a couple of the assembly, throwing in a couple of funny remarks which raised a smile from most and laughter from Bill Macdonald.

He then went serious to signify the start of the O group. Gesturing to the hawk featured Intelligence Officer, he asked him to give out the salient points from the SITREP. This over he looked at his watch and said simply, "Gentlemen, in ten hours time, at zero four hundred hours, Internment begins."

He waited for the gasps and exclamations to die down then said in the same even voice. "There is a lot to be done between now and then, so I will not detain you any more than I have to. You are not to brief your men until midnight but as of .." he looked at his watch. "As of eighteen forty five you are to suspend all operations and put your men on enforced rest, use any excuse you like, tomorrow will be a long day.. Yes Harry?" He had seen Harry Norton raise his finger.

"Thank you Colonel, what about the men in the sangars? We must keep the base protected."

The CO replied quickly, a smile on his face. "Thank you Harry but I was just coming to that," he turned to Bill Macdonald. "Bill , you are to release all your staff from normal duties, that includes your storemen, cooks not on duty, REME mechanics and so on. How many men roughly?" The swiftness of the moment knocked the Quartermaster off balance and he fumbled for the sheet of paper which listed all his staff.

"Er.. Give me a moment Sir I'll.."

"Right, all of them will be split amongst the locations to take over guard duties, there is to be only one cook on cooking duties per location and I strongly suggests he makes a ruddy great airborne stew that can be dished out quickly as and when it's needed. You are all to split your companies down into four man arrest teams. You will give each team an address or addresses and a name or names to be arrested. The person named, WILL be arrested, there are no exemptions, unless of course they are not there. Bill ," he turned again to the Quartermaster who was earnestly counting names and trying to listen at the same time, "you are to supply each location with six foot metal pickets, to enable doors to be forced if necessary."

"As good as done Sir!" he replied with fervour.

"And Bill , I want your spare bods to take over all guard duties as soon as possible."

"Absolutely no problem Sir!"

The Colonel gave out as much information as he possibly could to his Company Commanders and then handed the show over to his Second in Command who had just arrived from another meeting at Brigade Headquarters, he in turn handed out the lists of names and addresses of those to be arrested.

The meeting finally broke up and the group of excited leaders rushed to their Pigs and Landrovers to get back to their locations as speedily as possible. The tea, coffee and biscuits laid out using the mess crockery and silver was left untouched.

Sergeant Tommy McGregor who was always referred to as Wee Tom or Tam sat in his bunk room with his platoon Commander Lieutenant Donald Munro-Fraser. They were both Scotsmen but that's about as far as any likeness went.

Wee Tam as he nickname suggested was around five feet four inches tall and small boned. An incredibly hard man that had held his own on the tough streets of Glasgow since he could walk, an amateur boxer who had shown promise. Those few, that had mistaken his small stature as a measure of his softness had met with a swift and bloody surprise. He never bothered anyone unless they kicked his cage over and was a generally liked and respected soldier.

Lieutenant Munro-Fraser was also from Glasgow, North Kelvinside. A tall, blond, handsome youth with a long aquiline nose and a public school accent. He had joined the Regiment whilst it was in Belfast making him the newest man, not only in the Company but also in the Battalion. Surprising to some he and Wee Tam got on very well, he the willing pupil craving knowledge and experience and Tam the fatherly teacher and protector.

Tam rolled a cigarette using one hand on his knee, stuck it in his mouth and lit it expertly snapping his silver zippo lighter open and shut again with just one hand. He took a drag and concentrated his mind for a few seconds then said to Donald in his hard Glaswegian accent that years in the army had failed to soften, "Ye see Sor, command is a funny thing, *you* command the platoon an' that. What *you* says goes an' that, and that's where I come in. If you see what I mean. You say some-thin's gotta be done and I make sure the lads do it but at the same time, now here's the funny bit. At the same time as you being in command, *I'm* in charge...On ac-count o' my experience an' that." Donald nodded his understanding but his slightly open mouth gave away the fact that he didn't quite grasp it.

Wee Tam continued, "You see sor, if ye can picture a stagecoach in one of them Western filims, you know John Wayne an' all that racing across Texas with Geron-imo and his tribe chasin' and shootin' the fuck out o' them. Well if ye can picture that right, well you're the geezer sittin' inside the stagecoach tellin' me who's sat up top holding the shotgun, to get the fuck oot of it. So I shout the guy next to me who's got the reins and a big whip, now that would be in this case Corporal Garland. I'd shout tae him, okay lets go! And in turn he would thrash the fuck oot the horses who are? That's right, the lads in the Platoon! An' I'd sit there making sure that all they horses are pullin' in the same direction, if you see what I mean." A big smile lit up on Tam's battered face allowing a rare glimpse of his crooked teeth which were usually hidden behind his thick bushy moustache. Donald smiled too and nodded.

"Ye see Sor, it's really simple but if you for instance tried to get on my platform with me and Garland, there wouldn't be any room for any of us to operate properly. So the horses wouldn't know what the fuck was goin' on and stop, then Geronimo and all his tribe will catch up with us and scalp us."

Donald nodded sagely and said in his impeccable voice, "And presumably, Geronimo and his tribe are the IRA?"

"The IRA? No way sor! The IRA don't come into this! The desert, that the stagecoach is crossing is .. Is the .. It's Battalion life, if you know what I mean. Geronimo and his tribe is the RSM, the CSM, the Quartermaster, the adjutant and SIB, Military Police, and any other bastard that thinks he can get a knife into ye. They're the ones that's continually after ye. The IRA only have a pop when you come over *here*."

"Is it *that* bad Sergeant Mcgregor...Really?"

Tam saw the crestfallen look on his pupil's face and immediately set to work to rectify it. "Och no sor! Its no *that* bad, it's just that you've got to be aware, you being young an' new to this, an' aw that. You can do one hundred good things in this man's army and no one will say fuck all tae ye, not even a cheers pal, well done. But you fuck up just once, just once mind ye and it is never forgotten.... Mark my words."

Frank like a few others in the Company sensed that something out of the ordinary was going on. He had seen the Major arrive back from the Battalion "O" Group and in turn had been expecting a summons to go almost immediately to the Major's own 'O' Group which would have been the norm, but it had been an hour now and nothing. Then the patrol programme had been cancelled and all those not on duty were told to rest, including Frank's Platoon who were now on Stand By. The Guards on the gate and sangars had remained.

Reg Wallace was cruising around the location pouncing on anyone that was not on his bed resting. He came across Frank in the vehicle park.

"All your men resting Frank?"

"Yes Sir, what's going on?" The CSM smiled and tapped his nose.

"That good eh?" said Frank with a laugh.

"Well Frank, I don't really know. The boss is tight lipped but wants to speak to me in a minute." Any further conversation was muted when the big main gate swung open and three covered Landrovers came in.

The Quartermaster, Captain Bill Macdonald got out of the lead Rover, on spotting Reg and Frank strode across. He looked immaculate from his symmetrical waxed moustache down to his highly brush polished boots, he wore no flak jacket and didn't carry a rifle, he had however, a pistol on his belt held in a green canvass holster. Both men noticed that he did not bother to make it safe in the sanbagged bay as requested in Standing Orders.

He returned the salute from Reg Wallace and said briskly, "I can spare you three men, one cook, an armourer and my clerk, he's spasticated and can't stand for long but that's all your getting." The CSM was puzzled, had he missed something? What the hell was the QM on about? He knew him to be a very devious and sly person, he would have to tread carefully.

"These men Sir, I wasn't aware we were getting any extra bods."

The QM turned an irritated look on his face, "Well I suggest you bloody well get briefed Sergeant Major." He said curtly while striding back to his little convoy.

"Arsehole." growled Reg and went to find the OC.

The three men detailed by the QM walked slowly toward the main building loaded down with hastily packed kit that hung awkwardly off them. Frank recognised the bulky cook who had stopped to pick up a dropped sleeping bag. "What's going on Podge?" he asked using the cook's nickname.

Podge Hopkins recognised Frank and a smile split his fat face. "Huh! It's fackin' internment mate, startin' at four in the morning, didn't you know? Ha! Hah! It takes a fackin' slop jockey to know what's really going on!"

"Yeh, nothings changed." muttered Frank. As an afterthought said, "Watch who you're saying that to fat man, its obviously still meant to be a secret round here." He winked at Podge who continued struggling with his kit into the school. So that was it, internment! Frank felt a surge of electric.

"Well I'm afraid the QM has rather upset things," said Alan Briggs gravely. He was speaking to Reg Wallace. "I was on the verge of briefing you, Captain Summers and the Platoon Commanders in readiness for midnight. It's Internment of course, you can now replace the guard with the reinforcements the QM bought with him."

"He's only bought three men Sir." retorted Reg, his black eyes gleaming under the overhanging forehead. "With the best will in the world Sir, even if we put one of our own two cooks with them making four, they couldn't man the sangars and the gate. There would be no spare men to relieve them, inside of three hours they'd be knackered and totally useless, we need at the very least another four."

Alan Briggs was deep in thought, characteristically his hand supported his jaw and he stared at the floor. They were interrupted by the door being simultaneously knocked and opened, in the doorway, looking immaculate, his arms akimbo on his slim waste was the QM.

"Evening Alan, looks like tonights the night then." He had a broad smile on his mouth but his eyes were not committed.

"Indeed yes," said the major simply and continued staring at the floor. Just before the silence got embarrassing he shot to the QM, "Glad you're here actually er.. Bill . You left me only three men, it's not enough, I need at least another four to operate correctly."

"Impossible Alan, you're lucky to get those three, another four? Out of the question! The Commanding Officer stated and I quote…."

"Yes, very well Bill, I'll just have to phone the CO I suppose and tell him that I cannot complete my Company task because I'll have to pull off an arrest team to fulfil guard duties. He'll hit the roof of course, but still war is hell eh?" Alan reached for the phone and started dialling.

Bill Macdonald's antenna went up, if Alan involved the CO, there was a good chance the flak would end up being directed at himself. He had worked out that if he gave each location the minimum amount of his staff, he would still have enough men left to run the little empire that he'd set up in a Gymnasium outside of the City. If it was discovered that he had deliberately held men back it could mean recrimination, especially if things went wrong. "Just a moment Alan, if things are as bad as all that I'm sure we can dig some other bods up. Just give me an hour, see you."

Alan replaced the phone and listened to the QM's footsteps rapidly disappearing down the passageway, he turned and looked at Reg. "What on earth are you smirking at Sergeant Major?" He asked with mock astonishment.

The last few soldiers crowded into the dining room dressed as everyone else in patrol order consisting of camouflaged smock, green denims with puttees and boots, a web belt with a water bottle and two ammunition pouches and blackened faces under a maroon beret. Of course everyone carried their SLRs.

The hum of conversation was deafening, this was the first time the whole Company had been together under the same roof at the same time. Company policy meant that at least a quarter of the manpower was out on patrol at any one time.

The atmosphere was charged, only fifteen minutes before they had been ordered off enforced rest and into the dining room. When they got there each man had two egg banjos and a mug of coffee pushed into his hands.

Reg Wallace, with some difficulty got his three platoon sergeants to report to him and they told him that all their men were present. Reg then got hold of a ladle and banged it loudly on the metal hotplate, the room immediately went silent. Major Alan Briggs using a chair, climbed up on the hotplate and surveyed his waiting troops, who to a man were silent and waiting.

"Gentlemen, Internment is in!" The roar that followed made it impossible for the next thirty seconds or so to say anything, even Reg Wallace didn't attempt to stop them, he and the Major just smiled. The roar receded and a voice somewhere at the back started singing the unofficial Company song, followed immediately by the rest of the lads at the top of their voices, stamping their feet and banging empty mugs on tables in unison.

"IF I SHOULD DIE IN BATTLE
OR SINK TO THE BOTTOM OF THE SEA.
REMEMBER THIS MEIN FRAULEIN
I GAVE MY LIFE FOR THEE !
SO GIVE TO ME YOUR HAND FRAULEIN !
YOUR LILY WHITE HAND FRAULEIN
FARE THEE WELL, FARE THEE WELL
FOR TOMORROW WE MARCH AGAINST THE ENEMY...

And on it went for another verse until everyone broke out in a huge cheer.

"That's the first time anyone's ever serenaded me." beamed the Major.

"Men, we have a serious job ahead, act with all the professionalism that I know you possess. Once the arrests have been made, it will be like a hornet's nest has been kicked over and the real job will then begin. There will be no let up, you've all seen it before but this time I think it will be a real test. Captain Summers will now brief all the arrest team commanders in the passageway outside the Ops room.. Good luck." The Major could never quite understand why he was clapped and cheered as he left the dining room.

11

The cloud ensured that it was a dark morning. Around sixty men broken down into four man arrest teams sat noiselessly in the vehicle park. They had all been briefed and most had received two names to arrest. At the appointed time they would enter, arrest and take their 'name' to a central pick up point where Company Headquarters run by the OC and CSM would load them onto a fleet of three ton trucks. When full, the trucks would take them to a designated Police Holding Centre. This would continue until all those on the list were accounted for.

The arrest teams would use no vehicles, all approaches were to be made on foot, a pool of Landrovers would be at the central pick up point for use after the arrests if needed.

Wee Tam and his group sat around the back wheel of a truck. Tam and one of the others were having a crafty drag. A figure approached, stopped and in a well spoken whisper asked for Sergeant McGregor.

"Aye, it's me Sor." he rasped back.

Lieutenant Munro-Fraser knelt down beside Tam and spoke in a voice low enough to exclude those nearby. "Look, you know you told me that I would be working at the pick up point with the OC, well I've spoken to him and he is happy that I go as part of an arrest team."

Tam let out a sigh and stood up, he ushered the Officer out of earshot of the others and said slowly, in a pleasant but firm manner. "Ya see Sor, the reason I fixed it for ye to be up there was to keep ye oota the road, if you see what I mean. It's gonna get rough out there and it'll be bad enough for me an' the blokes who's done it all before.."

The well manicured voice interjected, too loudly at first then self consciously lowering but insistent all the same. "But Sergeant McGregor! Sergeant McGregor, I'm the only platoon commander that's not directly involved and I feel, well I feel bloody useless! If you see *what I mean*. I've got to start somewhere and.."

"Alright Sor! Alright. You'll go with Corporal Garland! Now mind ye Sor, yee'll do exactly what he tells ye…No matter what. Now is that understood…Sor?"

"Yes! Umm. Cheers Sergeant McGregor, I won't let you down."

Wee Tam watched the Lieutenant melt away in the darkness. "I dinna like it one bit." he muttered.

Frank and a few of his Platoon sat grouped around the unloading bay, like everyone else they just wanted to get on with it. For the first time in a few days Lieutenant Orchard had struck up a conversation with him. It was just after the briefing, he had come up to Frank smiling, a trace embarrassed perhaps. Together they had sat in Frank's bunk and worked out the composition of the arrest teams. When they had finished a little stiffness had gone and Frank had asked him if he was happy with all the arrangements. He had nodded given a tight smile and walked off. Digger Davis had come up later moaning that he was on Orchard's arrest team but had received short shrift off Frank.

Sergeant Vince Longthorne and his Platoon commander Lieutenant Rob Thomas both carefully lit up and took a drag. "Maybe the last one for a bit." whispered Rob as if to pardon his breaking of the OC's last order not to smoke while they were waiting.

"How long have we got now?"

Vince looked closely at his luminous dial. "Around fifteen minutes if all goes to plan."

"Can't bloody wait, if we can just get a half dozen of their top men it will have been worthwhile." said Bob enthusiastically.

"Can't see it m'self," answered Vince in his normal dry tones. "most likely been tipped off and legged it across the border by now, the top men that is. Most likely we'll pick up the dross, the ordinary volunteers and old has beens."

"God! Your cheerful for an old cynic." laughed Bob quietly.

"Aye, well you know what I mean, we've been out manoeuvred a hell of a lot of times now, maybe this time though...Just maybeez."

Lieutenant Colonel Quentin Harper MC, Commanding Officer, Roman Catholic, wearing full Patrol order knelt on one knee by the side of his bed and without removing his head dress prayed. First, for the well being of his men, then himself and finally, that some good would come out of it all. He then stood up, crossed himself, slid a magazine of twelve rounds into the grip of his pistol and walked out to his waiting Rover Group.

Padre Jack Thorpe having failed to get a ride with the CO stalked around the base looking to join up with some other patrol, he didn't want to miss anything.

At 0315 hours exactly the huge iron gateway of the school was swung quietly open. The first few teams that had the furthest to go trotted out, the others started to move toward the exit, tense like runners on a starting block. Every minute or so another team was released until all that was left at the base was the OC's group and the small ad hoc force that was guarding the place.

Frank's eight teams got to the roundabout. The morning was dark and still, a huge dark cloud hung over the Black Mountain being pushed gently by a soft breeze. This roundabout would transform itself into the Pick up Point at zero hour. From there each arrest team then made their separate ways to a place just short of the target house and lay up waiting for 0400 hrs.

Frank and his three men crouched in an alley at the end of the street where he would make his first arrest. He had two arrests to make as well as Norrie, Lieutenant Orchard and a couple of the others. The rest of the teams had one arrest only. He had taken two of the newer members of the platoon and one of the older hands. If it went to plan it would take he reckoned, five minutes to gain entry five minutes to arrest the target and three minutes to the Pick up Point, approximately thirteen minutes. The second arrest, he thought, would be a different story.

Wee Tam looked at his watch, 0350. He stood up in the garden where he had lain up and said in a normal voice, "Okay, lets go." His three men stood with him. Tam looked down to the far end of the street where Corporal Garland and the Lieutenant were hidden. "Who's got the toothpick?" he enquired.

"Me." said one of the lads holding a four feet long piece of angle iron.

"Come on, let's give someone an early call." One of the blokes peeled off and went round to the back of the target house to prevent escape, he would be let in once they gained entry. The rest walked with pace down the street counting the houses as they went, nobody believed house numbers in Belfast any more. "This is it," he said trying the door handle, "Smash the fucker down!"

The toothpick holder hesitated and said in a confused voice, "I thought we had to knock first for five minutes Sarge."

"You heard me, now get on wi' it man!" Two seconds later the angle iron started smashing into the wooden panels.

Frank heard the banging and smashing three streets away, there was still eight minutes to go. "Shit to it!" he said out loud, "Let's go!"

Norrie who had been hanging about right outside of his target house for ten minutes also heard the racket and immediately shoulder charged his door which caved straight in. He stumbled and fell onto the stairs that were directly behind the door but recovered quickly and bounded up the stairs followed by one other.

He kicked the first bedroom door in and with his torch saw there was two children in bed sleeping, he turned to go to the next bedroom and the landing lights come on, a man in his thirties stood there a look of fear and anger on his face. Norrie squared up and shouted, "Are you Thomas O'Neil?" The man nodded. "Well get some clothes on quick, your coming with us, you got two minutes either way!"

A woman appeared at his side. "What d'youse fuckers want!" she screamed.

"Four cuppsa tea love, two wi' out sugar." Was the immediate reply from Norrie, a big stupid grin on his face.

Wee Tam finally got what was left of the door to open, both he and the tooth pick man were sweating profusely having taken turns to bash in the portal. Tam went to climb the stairs but was met by a man coming down followed by a woman, they were both in their fifties. He came up to Tam and spoke. "It'll be me yer after, me name is Seamus Dolan, lets go!"

He turned to his wife, kissed her on the cheek and whispered something , she pulled him close and said with a sob, "Take care love."

Frank stood in the living room of the house. In front of him half dressed was a thirty something man, at his side his wife and two daughters the eldest of which was about fourteen. Frank read out the prepared arrest script from a card while the man's wife screamed abuse at him.

The younger daughter was crying hysterically and clutching her fathers legs, the elder daughter ran into the kitchen and came back with a long carving knife screaming that she was going to kill Frank. One of the young soldiers immediately cocked his rifle and aimed it at her. At once the Father hurled himself at the soldier dragging the other daughter with him, the three of them piled into the settee which toppled over sending them into a heap at the foot of the window, they were immediately covered in torn down curtains.

The daughter came at Frank with the knife and he swung the butt of his rifle catching her on the forearm, she screamed and dropped it, the mother meanwhile started choking and fell flat on the floor.

Frank and the other soldier who had been standing with his mouth open pulled the man off and pinned him to the wall. "If this is the way you want it!" Frank screamed. "Then this is the way you'll have it!" The room went silent apart from the sobs of the younger daughter.

The man then saw his wife on the floor, "Oh Jesus!" he sighed, broke free and knelt at her side,

"We never touched her Sarge!" said the open mouthed soldier.

The woman came to, and hugged her husband, "Oh Joe , Joe, Joe," she sobbed repeatedly. He helped her up and she picked up their crying daughter, "Why, why are ye takin' him? He's never hurt a soul in his life, he's a good man, all he's ever done is work for his family, he doesn't even take a drink, for God's sake soldier, why are ye takin' him?"

"It's orders, I'm sorry love, it's gotta be done." stated Frank, anxious to get away.

"The fucking SS took orders, and that's what youse fucking lot are, lousy stinking Gestapo, SS."

Digger Davis was at boiling point. They should have arrested the man and been out of the house at least ten minutes before, but Orchard had not acted. They had identified their target alright, a man in his late thirties. He had been co-operative enough keeping his wife calm and getting dressed quickly, he had then asked permission to say cheerio to his son which Orchard had granted and had accompanied him to the bedroom.

There, on the bed was a boy about twelve years old with Downs' Syndrome, confused and upset at the happenings around him. Every time the man went to leave the boy called him back loudly and the man had returned to comfort the boy.

Digger spoke to Orchard again. "Sir, we'd better clear outa this shit hole before it gets too lively out there, can't you hear it starting up?"

"Davis, get back to your post on the door! If you desert it again there will be big trouble!" Orchard hissed through clenched teeth.

"You'll be sorry." sang Digger as he went back down the stairs.

Lieutenant Orchard spoke to the man again, "Look, I'm sorry but we're going to have to leave."

"Have a heart," pleaded the man. "can't you see the wee man's upset, if we get him downstairs with the

Missus, he'll probably be alright...No! He won't let you near him, go and get the Missus and we can sort this out quickly." Orchard hesitated then ran down the stairs, Digger Davis was at the foot of it, "Davis get up there to the bedroom, I won't be a minute.."

"Sir, we need to get the fuck outa here.."

Orchard ignored him and strode into the living room, Digger climbed the stairs. Orchard confronted the woman who sat on the settee smoking and glaring at the soldier who had done a search of the room. "Your Husband needs you upstairs...To give him a hand to get your son down here, he's...He's a little upset."

"Aye! And can ye friggin' wonder why? Ye bastards! You come in the middle of the night, break the door down and arrest my man, and you say the boy's upset! Are you for fuckin' real!?"

"Sir!" Orchard turned to see Digger standing in the doorway, before he could react Digger stated with a smug look on his face, "Your little birdie has flown, right through the window." The woman shrieked with laughter.

Lieutenant Donald Munro-Fraser started getting a little anxious. Corporal Garland had placed him as ' Cut Off ' in the small yard at the backdoor of their target house. He had wanted to be on the team that had entered the house but Garland had insisted, so he had complied, after all as soon as they gained entry and identified their man they would let him in.

He had been in the small backyard for over ten minutes now and no-one had come to the door, he had tried it but found it locked. He could hear nothing in the house itself but the noises around him were getting louder and louder. People cursing and shouting. Noise of people running and now, a new sound, the rhythmic banging of metal on concrete, first a solitary noise and now growing.

Donald was no coward but the uncertainty of the situation was getting to him. Something had gone wrong and just standing around was not going to make it better. With some reluctance he decided to leave his post and see what was happening. After banging loudly on the door again and getting no response, he opened the door into the alley and made his way along it.

Dawn broke and the streets were in uproar, women with dustbin lids had come out in force banging the lids repeatedly on the concrete and tarmac. Youths and children shouted and screamed while hurling missiles at the arrest teams making their way through the labyrinth of streets to the Pick up Point.

The Sergeant Major counted the teams in and put the prisoners on the backs of the trucks. Major Alan Briggs and his signaller crossed names off a list. He had seen most of the teams return. If they didn't have a second arrest they were either deployed to help the Sergeant Major or sent back in to give cover for those that still had arrests to make.

Britton and Lance Corporal Norris had been through and had gone back for their second arrest along with several others, it all seemed to be going well.

Frank and his team ran to his second target house constantly diverting to miss marauding mobs of youths and women. He turned a corner and ran into Wee Tam with his prisoner, he immediately stopped him and blurted, "Frank we've lost the boss, he was supposed to be the cut off man for Garland but he wasna' there when he checked. I've been lookin' everywhere fer him man, have ye seen him?"

When Frank answered in the negative Tam let out a shout of anguish, just then another patrol crossed over to them. Frank didn't hesitate. "Tam give your prisoner to them, we'll help you find Fraser and then you can cover us for our arrest." Tam immediately complied, pointed back into the estate and said urgently, "Garland is still down there, we'll try and find him first!"

They set off at the double ignoring the screams, curses and rain of stones pelting down on them. Quite unexpectedly they came up behind a screaming mob focusing their attention on something they couldn't quite see. Did they divert or investigate? Wee Tam made the decision for everyone by immediately screaming at the top of his voice and attacking, they all followed.

Tam drove into the back of the mob by smashing his rifle butt into the head of the first person he came in contact with, then another. They all followed suit and the mob broke in panic and ran, leaving behind four blooded rioters and a couple more helping them.

They then saw the object of the mob's fury, it was Corporal Garland and his patrol wedged between a parked car and the wall of one of the terraced houses. Garland's face was white which made the blood pouring

down his face look scarlet, "Thank fuck you got 'ere!"
he shouted almost hysterically, Tam ignored him and
shouted back, "Did ye find him?" For a second Garland
looked bewildered then said excitedly, "Yeh! Yeh, he's
here, we got to him just in time, they were going to kill
'im.!"

Tam ran around to the space between the wall and
car and saw Lieutenant Munro-Fraser lying on the pavement with one of the patrol tying a shell dressing to his
neck, his white blonde hair drenched with blood. His
eyes were open but sleepy, he managed a smile when he
saw Tam, "They got 'im with a knife or a bottle." said
Garland anxiously.

"Why didn't you zap the bastards!" snarled Tam.

"We didn't realise what was 'appening at first, we
only saw him when we got right up close, he was here
in the doorway, damn near got his rifle they did." He
couldn't hold Tam's stare and looked away.

Tam became aware of the yelling and screaming
that had been going on all the time, he stood and saw
Frank's Patrol split in two and back to back holding the
ground in the middle where they were.

He saw the crowd surge forward, a chunk of concrete bounced off his shoulder. Tam got up and walked
past the two soldiers oblivious of the bottles and stones
that were directed at him, he cocked his rifle and slowly
bought it in the aim pointing to the middle of the rioters. They stopped then started running back around
the corner, he traversed his aim tracking a youth in
jeans and white T shirt, he pulled the trigger the rifle
punched back into his slender frame. The report ka-

boomed loudly bouncing off the brick walls. As the youth rounded the corner a huge chunk of masonry the size of a head disintegrated and disappeared off the corner of the wall, the brass cartridge ejected and arched until it hit the wall clinked onto the pavement and rolled in the gutter. For a few seconds there was silence and the streets were clear.

Frank ran up to Wee Tam, "Come on mate, we've got to get him out of here and back!" Tam relaxed his face and nodded, "We'll carry him, you watch out for us!"

As they were about to lift Munro-Fraser the unmistakable sound of a straining Landrover engine was heard and down the street came the two stripped down vehicles of the OC's Rover Group with Alan Briggs in the front vehicle. Briggs appreciated the situation immediately and they loaded Munro-Fraser on to the second vehicle with Reg Wallace. The rioters started to appear again, a flaming bottle exploded several feet from them.

The OC summoned Frank and Tam and asked what the shooting was, when Tam told him, they checked around the corner warily, it was still full of shouting people but no dead body, it confirmed that Tam's shot had missed.

The Rover Group started to come under a sustained attack from bottles and broken paving slabs. The Major calmly told Frank to try for his secondary target backed up by Wee Tam's patrol then he and his Rover Group set off straight through a crowd of about thirty frenzied youths and women. Simultaneously a battery of rubber bullet guns opened up from the two Landrovers as they sped through, using this as a diversion Frank smashed the butt of his rifle directly over the yale lock on the door of a house, it opened immediately and the two patrols ran through the house to the back alley.

Digger Davis despite his hard exterior was a worried man. It wasn't the crowds in the street outside ranting and raving, Lord knows he'd seen and heard it enough over the last couple of tours, no it was the fact that Orchard had completely lost it.

They should have gone straight for their secondary target when the first one had escaped, it was obvious to him and it was obvious to the others. Because Davis was the older soldier, the others had started to look to him for answers. Lieutenant Orchard it seemed had gone into shock when it was discovered that the man had jumped from the bedroom window and made good his escape. Only minutes before he had called in the cut off from the back yard. It was as if he could not believe what had happened, he ordered them to search the house twice, including the attic.

The mother sat on the bed with their son laughing and throwing out crude insults especially to Orchard whom she delighted in calling "Shitey Mouse".

When they had finished searching for the second time he told them that they would wait in the house for a while until things had died down a little outside. It had got steadily worse. The crowd had not known they were inside. The woman had gone downstairs to the door to "invite" them in and Digger had grabbed her and pushed his huge iron, Rubber Bullet gun in her face and promised to let her have it if she did, she sat down and reverted to her ranting insults.

Davis had attempted to rouse Orchard into some kind of action but with no effect, he continued to go to each room in the house in the apparent hope that his prisoner would re-appear.

They all heard the single rifle shot, it seemed to be in the next street.

"That's it!" shouted Digger. "We're outa here, whether you're comin' or not!"

With the two other soldiers behind him, he wrenched open the door and ran into the street. The crowd were running away from the direction of the rifle shot. Digger looked behind and saw that Orchard had not emerged. "Aw Jesus!" he shouted and went back into the house. Orchard stood there looking at him his mouth half open. "Come on Sir!...That shot has scared them, let's go quick!" He yanked Orchard and shouted again, "Come on Sir!" Orchard complied and they both went into the street with the other two.

The brick seem to come from nowhere and as Digger turned to run toward the direction of the gunfire, it hit him square in the face, he dropped to the ground immediately blood pouring from his mouth and nose.

"He's dead! He's fackin' dead!" shouted young Stevens staring at the spread-eagled body of Digger. Orchard stood with his back to the wall, several rioters were still running past. Orchard stared at Digger's body lying at his feet and then became aware of young Stevens still shouting, "Sir! They've fackin' killed Digger the bastards!" With that he cocked his rifle and took aim at a passing youth who immediately stopped and backed against the wall his hands stretched out as if to try and ward off the bullet.

"You murderin' bastard!" screamed Stevens, the rifle still in the aim with the end of the barrel almost touching the quivering youth. "I'm going to let you have it now, right between the fackin' eyes, you bastard! I'll splash your fackin brains all over the road!"

Orchard snapped out of whatever trance he was in and shouted to Stevens to stop what he was doing, just then they heard the salvo of rubber bullet guns being fired and at the end of the street saw the OC's Rover Group speeding past.

Orchard screamed after them "We're here damn you! We have a man down!" All they heard was the disappearing whine of the engines, he felt like a survivor on a raft in the middle of the ocean and surrounded by sharks when the search plane flies past, unseeing.

Orchard ran to Stevens who was still holding the cowering youth. "Let him go! Davis is not dead but we must get him out of here, come on!" They both ran to Digger who by now had started to stir, there was a pool of dark red blood where his head had lain on the pavement.

Slowly they stood him against the wall his arm around Orchard's neck, a bottle smashed against the wall above their heads from a gang of youths who were slowly advancing back down the street shouting and screaming. Digger slumped and became a dead weight.

It took a major effort from Orchard and Stevens to keep him up, the fourth member of the patrol a young soldier, kept between them and the advancing mob, he was inexperienced and bewildered. Should he shoot to protect his mates, or wait a bit longer to see if the situation changed?

Then, from the other end of the street they heard the gentle purring of Landrover engines, turned and saw two stripped down Landrovers festooned with antennae slowly advancing up the street toward them, the driver wearing goggles. At first Orchard thought that the OC's Rover Group had returned and almost sobbed with relief but then he realised that it was not Alan but the Commanding Officer, Lieutenant Quentin Harper MC.

The Landrover came slowly to a halt beside them and Orchard found that he was looking the CO in the eye. Colonel Harper saw the young Lieutenant splattered with blood holding up one of his soldiers, his free arm with his rifle at the ready, his back to the wall. He spoke to Orchard in a normal voice as if he had suddenly come across him at a mess function. "It's Tony isn't it? Look plonk your team on the back and we'll get you out, there's nothing to be gained here any more, that's Davis isn't it?"

"Yes Sir! He was hit by a stone." reported Orchard a little too loudly for his own liking.

"Well, it'll take more than that to keep him down for long, hop on, let's go!"

Frank and Wee Tam halted their combined patrols in an alleyway. Tam immediately lit a cigarette up and said "What now Frank?" They had gone to Frank's secondary target but it was too late, the place was empty apart from a sneering youth who was immediately beaten and kicked to the ground.

"We'll make back for the pick up point, there's no point in doing anything else." stated Frank. He turned and raised his voice to the rest of them, "Okay we're going to head back now, keep alert keep your eyes on the windows and roofs, don't hesitate, if you see someone with a weapon or petrol bomb, zap the bastard!" They shook out and walked down the street, the two tail end charlies walking backwards with practised ease.

Shouting and screaming filled the air, coming it seemed from every direction with the unique rhythmic sound of dustbin lids being hammered on the road and pavements. The odd shot was heard and now and then the "Woomf " of a petrol bomb followed by cheering.

The OC and Sergeant Major Wallace returned to the roundabout after their brief but eventful tour of the area and watched as the tailboard of the last truck was about to be raised and pinned. Inside the truck Reg saw a half dozen men with ages varying from mid twenties to early sixties lying on their backs, hands bound with plasticuffs and resting on their stomachs.

Reg looked toward the Company Commander and tapped his watch expectantly. They had just met an ambulance and transferred Lieutenant Munro-Fraser on to it. The situation, so it seemed to Reg, was rapidly getting out of control. Most arrests had been made but there were still three teams who had not yet returned. It had been almost two hours since the first arrests and the streets were now full of enraged rioters, he knew by experience that gunmen would appear next and that things were so chaotic on the streets it could easily turn into a bloodbath.

Major Briggs was also thinking along these lines and reacted at once to Reg's silent enquiry. "Okay Sarn't Major get that truck on its way we're finished here, we'll wait until the missing men turn up then withdraw back to the School."

Norrie, not normally given to panic had to quell another bout of it that had risen from his gut, he stared at the boot that was sticking through the bedroom ceiling and flailing about trying to retreat back up into the attic from where it came. "For fucks sake come on!" he roared. The muffled shout in reply was inaudible.

"Norrie! They know we're in here!" shouted one of his team members downstairs. As if to confirm the statement a house brick smashed through the bedroom window.

This was Norrie's second arrest and it had started badly, he had shouldered the door in and had immediately heard a commotion from the kitchen area. Investigation found a man struggling with the cut off he had placed at the rear of the house. "Caught the bastard Norrie!" he said triumphantly, "Trying to escape, but I got the bastard!"

The man looked calm and even had a slight smile, he looked Norrie full in the face and said half laughing, "For God's sake, I was going to feed the friggin' rabbits! What the hell is going on boys?"

Just at that moment Ronnie Gittins sidled up to Norrie tugged at his sleeve and whispered out the side of his mouth, "Norrie, we've got the wrong 'ouse mate, we should be next door."

Norrie was thrown for a couple of seconds then shouted to the other two members of his team, "Get next door and make an arrest!" They looked at each other a little confused but jumped to it when they saw Norrie was about to erupt in fury.

"Do youse want a cup of tea lads?" asked the man pleasantly, as he held out a kettle.

"Aye, get the fucker on, why not." said Norrie. "What's your name anyway?"

"What, my name? I'm Tommy Morgan....Is it internment.. All this racket I mean?"

Norrie paced the kitchen, "Yeh, and about friggin' time." he said aggressively.

"Too right," said the man, "there's too many bad bastards round here. Let's hope you get them all."

There was some noise as the door to the kitchen opened and the other two came back in with a man between them. "We got 'im Norrie, hidin' in the wardrobe."

"Well that's it then." said Norrie, after he had confirmed that the man was the one he was after. He turned to Tommy Morgan who was still busying himself with cups and kettles,

"Okay, you're un arrested and we don't need the tea now, let's go!"

"Norrie." It was the little cockney, Ronnie Gittins again.

"What?" said Norrie drawing closer to him.

"Arrest 'em both. Did you see the way that Tommy didn't even look who we'd bought in? And do you think he would allow himself to be seen by one of his neighbours making us tea, he'd be head jobbed within a week."

Norrie turned and barked, "Arrest 'em both."

"Oh, come on Soldier," said Tommy a look of disbelief on his still smiling face. "you've got your man, what d'ye need me for?"

"And search the rest of the house." was Norrie's reply.

After a few minutes one of the lads who had been detailed to search upstairs shouted to Norrie to come up. He and Ronnie shepherded the two prisoners up to the bedroom and saw the foot through the ceiling. Then the brick smashed through the window.

"Well get up there and help him for fuck's sake!" growled Norrie who was anxious to get away.

"I've tried man, but the attics full of all kinds of crap."

"Norrie." It was Ronnie Gittins again showing him his watch, "We're gonna have to get going mate, it's getting' shitty out there."

"For Chrissake shut ye nose Ronnie!...I know!" He turned to the other soldier and shouted, "Now get back up there and get him out!"

The two arrested men sat on the bed with Ronnie between them and the door. While Norrie was preoccupied with the situation Tommy spoke to him, "Can I smoke soldier?" Ronnie only just heard him above the noise of the crowd outside.

"What?.. Yeh!.. How can you? We took your smokes."

"I thought maybe you could spare one." came the gentle reply. Ronnie like the rest of the team was starting to get agitated because they were delayed in the house, it felt like they were trapped.

"Here!" he snapped and threw his own pack on the bed between the men, followed by a lighter. Both arrested men lit up. Norrie left the room and started shouting up through the trap door of the attic, the foot was still waggling around up on the ceiling.

"Thanks soldier," said Tommy showing Ronnie the cigarette. "You know I could get that crowd outside off your back, I'm well known to the community here, they'll listen to me, let me have a word with them."

Ronnie became alert and retorted, "What about your mate, don't he ever say nothing? How comes he's supposed to be the big man around 'ere and yet you act as though you are? And how comes you're makin' us tea and being ever so nicey nice, when every other fucker in this estate would dance on our dead bodies? .. Eh?.. Eh?.. answer me that, Mister Tommy nice man."

At that moment the complete ceiling fell through and the two soldiers in the attic came bursting through and landed on the bed. In a flash Tommy shoved Ronnie out the way, ran through the open door straight into Norrie who laid into him with his rifle butt. Tommy tried to break through but eventually went down under the vicious rein of blows.

Norrie surveyed the scene, the gaping hole in the ceiling and four people covered in dust and bits of plaster then he launched at Ronnie "You stupid bastard! You almost lost a prisoner!"

Ronnie, his face and shoulders still covered in thick grey dust boomed back. "You fackin' what? Half the bleedin' house caves in on me and you are worried about a geezer that you were going to fackin' let go, not ten minutes ago! For facksake Norrie wise up and let's get outa here!"

Frank and Wee Tam saw the large group outside of the terraced house smashing the windows and trying to batter the door in. Unsure of what was going on Frank nevertheless made a snap decision to find out.

"Let 'em have it with the rubber guns." he shouted and two members of the patrol whipped the heavy iron pieces off their shoulders, ran half the distance to the crowd, knelt and simultaneously fired the hard rubber missiles directly into them. At the same time the rest led by Frank rushed toward them yelling at the tops of their voices, the sudden noise and attack made them break up and withdraw immediately.

Frank got to the door that was all but smashed down, as he started to go through it he was astonished to hear Norrie and Ronnie arguing loudly. "Come on children!" Roared Frank up the stairs, "We're all tired little Teddy bears and need some kip."

Reg Wallace saw the teams of Frank, Tam and Norrie running up the road towards him with the two arrested men between them. He shouted to the OC, "That's it Sir! There's our last three teams coming in... And with two prisoners!"

"Okay Sergeant Major load the two detainees on our vehicles, the teams can make their way back on foot." He walked up to Reg and clapped him on the shoulder, "With Lieutenant Orchard and his men accounted for by the CO, that's us complete." stated Alan with a sigh of relief.

12

Podge Hopkins wiped down the hotplate in the dining room for what seemed like the hundredth time that day. It had he thought, seemed like a week since he had arrived at the school with the QM to help out. It had certainly been a long day.

He had watched the arrest teams go out well before dawn and a couple of hours later listened to the shootings and bomb blasts echoing continuously around Belfast. Sometime after that the teams had started to return in dribs and drabs wolfing down the huge fry ups that he was producing quickly and efficiently. "The grease is provided free to make it all slide down nicely." he had said with a smile on his jowls if anyone complained.

It was now 5pm and there was a lull in the day, for some reason it had all gone quiet. Most of the Company lay around the dining room dozing in chairs or on the floor still dressed in full kit clutching their rifles ready to be re-deployed onto the streets at a moments notice. Every few minutes one or two would rouse and help themselves to a mug of tea from one of the many urns scattered about.

It had been a hectic day, spontaneous rioting, shootings, general disorder and unrest had kept the Company on the streets. Everyone was dog tired and grabbed sleep at every opportunity possible, not the deep refreshing sleep that one was normally used to but cat naps, the state where one could instantly doze off and yet waken quickly and be ready for action.

Podge finished cleaning the hotplate, slumped into a chair in the kitchen and lit up. His cooks whites were covered in grease and food stains. Single handedly he had kept up a continuous supply of hot food and tea for the men over the last twelve hours. The other two cooks plus some of the QM's men had been on stag in the sangars around the camp all day. Taking a final drag, he too succumbed and nodded off.

Alan Briggs gently snored, he like the rest of his men was still fully dressed for the streets. He dozed in an old armchair in his office. His bed was only a few paces away but because he had ordered his Company to be on full alert and not to use their beds, he led by example.

He and his Rover group had been on the streets all day roaming the complete Company area, giving support and encouragement to the foot patrols. They had been stoned and bottled continuously. In one incident his driver had nodded off momentarily, the vehicle had mounted the pavement before he had woken. Alan took the wheel himself for an hour to give the lad a break. Only when the noise and trouble gradually decreased and all went quiet did he order most of the Company off the streets to rest.

His office door creaking slowly open bought Alan instantly awake. The Commanding Officer, Quentin Harper stood in the half open door.

"Ah! Colonel, must've dropped off." Alan stretched as he stood.

"Sorry Alan the last thing I wanted to do was to disturb you...Coffee?" The CO produced a flask and began pouring the contents into two plastic cups, he also had been on the go all day apart from a quick lunch at Headquarters.

"Well, in the main it's good news." he said putting the flask away and sitting down opposite Alan. "We got around eighty percent of our targets which is good, a lot better than I expected.... A few injured, mainly by nail bombs but as yet nothing serious."

"Er, how's young Munro—Fraser Colonel? Couldn't get an update."

"Oh! He's fine, nothing too serious but he may have a nasty scar, looks like they got him with a bottle on the chin and neck. Do you know why he was isolated from his patrol?" Alan grimaced, and replied cautiously. "Well Sir, Corporal Garland whose team Donald was with is still on patrol. I've not had much of a chance to speak to either of them yet.."

"Of course." nodded the CO.

"But I gather," continued Alan, "that Donald was sent as cut off at the rear of the target house and somehow went to the wrong house. Apparently, he decided to try and link up by going back around to the street but ran into a pack of them.. He's...Er.. inexperienced and.."

"Follow it up Alan please. I would like to know." The CO let it hang for a second then smiled and said. "I must say I was impressed with young Tony Orchard, he was having a hell of a time out there but showed amazing command and control, was he injured? I saw blood."

"Er.. No, he wasn't actually, well not to my knowledge any rate."

"Hmm, the blood must have come from young Digger Davis, he's recovering well, anyway must be off. Be on your guard Alan, it's far from over, as I'm sure you will appreciate."

The CO stood up and replaced the empty cups on his flask, "Oh! By the way, we caught a big fish today, one of *your* patrols bought him in. He was using a false name but one of the Special Branch boys recognised him to be Padraig Macree, Londonderry Brigade. What he was doing in Belfast is anyone's guess."

"But if he wasn't on our arrest list, I wonder how we got him?" said Alan a little puzzled.

"Well, whoever arrested a Thomas Morgan, got our man." beamed the CO. "See you Alan."

He closed the door and Alan listened to his footsteps disappearing down the corridor. His door opened once more and Reg Wallace with two steaming mugs entered. He smiled at Alan and offered a mug. Alan, having just finished off a cup of coffee still didn't have the heart to refuse so accepted it with a smile.

Reg looked white faced and had dark smudges under his eyes. He had felt himself nodding off in the Landrover following the OC around all day but ironically had not been able to sleep when the opportunity had arisen. He had been aware of the CO's recent visit and this spurred him to splash some water over his face, get some tea and investigate.

Alan yawned and was about to speak when Nick Summers came in fresh and beaming, his long thick hair brushed back apart from the unruly lock that always hung across his forehead.

"Ah! Nick." said Alan massaging some life back into his arms, "Sit down and here share my tea." Nick sat down and after some small talk with Reg fell silent and waited for Alan.

"Just had a visit from the Old Man, he's very pleased in the main and we got a big fish, Nick who arrested a Thomas.. er .. Thomas.."

"Thomas Morgan?" ventured Nick.

"Yes that's him." Shot back Alan

"I've just finished compiling the arrest reports and his name stood out because he wasn't on the arrest list. Lance Corporal Norris arrested him because he was suspicious…...Who is it Alan?"

"One of the top men in Londonderry apparently, good for old Norris eh!"

"Well, well," said Reg shaking his head in wonder, "big daft Norris comes up wit' goods." They all had a smile at that and then Alan went businesslike and spoke to Nick.

"Have you just come from the Ops room?.. Is there anything happening?"

"No it's all gone quiet, we have Rob Thomas and Sergeant Longthorne on the streets and the rest on Immediate Standby in and around the Dining area. I think it may be a good time to start reorganising, get some men on their beds and brace ourselves for the night.

It will be dark in a couple of hours." Nick finished and stood up to leave,

Alan spoke nodding his head enthusiastically. "Yes good idea, get as normal a routine as possible going, one platoon can get their boots off and the other Platoon may remove equipment and rest on their beds. How long has Rob's lot been on the streets Nick?"

"Around three hours now."

"Okay, well keep them out for another hour or so then swap them over so we have a fresh lot out at dusk."

With that, the small gathering broke up and Alan sat back in his chair and closed his eyes.

Sergeant Vince Longthorne walked warily up the back alley to where Lieutenant Rob Thomas was kneeling and peering out of the entrance onto a strip of road. They had agreed on the radio to meet and discuss some plans.

"Alright Boss?" asked Vince using the semi-familiar term that was acceptable on the streets. Nobody wanted to be identified as a "Sir".

"Yeh, no problem," said Rob breaking off his observation and smiling at Vince. "and that in itself is a problem.. It's so damn quiet, half an hour ago we couldn't move without getting stoned or bottled."

"I agree." said Vince lighting up and shielding the cigarette in his paw. "I've got me blokes deployed all around Shannon Street, they're bloody well knackered man, me too, I'm chin strapped."

Rob immediately took the hint and said, "I've radioed in and they say we'll be relieved just before dusk, 'fraid we're going to have to stick it out for an hour or so yet."   "Yep, I thought so, what do you want me to dee like? I can stay put in Shannon Street or continue to patrol the area." said Vince without any enthusiasm. "Keep patrolling and gradually make your way back to base through the cemetery. We'll do the same but come through the estate....Okay?" Vince nodded and moved off stealthily.

Podge Hopkins struggled up the enclosed ladder to the sangar. He was not in the best of moods. When his equipment snagged on something during his slow ascent he would let out a savage, "Bastard! Bastard!" No way he thought, should he be doing a stag. He'd worked in the hot stinking cookhouse all day dishing up slop to the ungrateful masses that came in at all hours.

That had been the deal with the other cooks, he would work all day and night alone and they would do sentry duties but what happened? The cook Sergeant gets pissed off staring at nothing all day through the slit of a sangar and when all the hard graft in the kitchen had virtually been done and he was having a well deserved rest, in he stomps and says *Okay Podge, time for swapsies*....The Bastard!

Podge was out of breath when he reached the door of the sangar, everything was enclosed and dark. It was unfamiliar territory to him, the smell of stale urine and walls of sandbags that he had to feel his way by. The door swung open, Podge could just make out the QM's clerk standing there in the gloom. "You took your fuckin' time you fat slob!" the clerk shouted. "I should have been relieved ten soddin' minutes ago!"

Podge reared up, he was not a fighting man but this was as close as it got for him, "Listen, you friggin' spastic." he yelled, "I've just about had enough of you and this whole fuckin' operation, so just do me a big favour and Fuck Off!" The clerk muttered something and pushed passed him.

Podge looked around him, he was still breathing heavily but felt more happier now that he had vented on the clerk. The only light came from the slit overlooking the waste ground that led to a housing estate a hundred or so yards away.

He found himself in a box about six feet long and four foot wide, there was no chair, but he notice that a couple of sandbags had been pulled out to allow the sentry to sit. After some more investigation he found some paper sticking out from a gap beneath the sill of the slit window, he pulled it out and saw to his delight that it was a porno magazine. He turned the pages excitedly and his thumb came in contact with a sticky substance, he recoiled in horror and started scraping his thumb furiously along the sandbags in a frantic effort to cleanse it. "You dirty friggin' wanker!" he shouted and flung the magazine against the wall.

Nick Summers dragged on a King Edward Cigar and placed his feet on the Ops room table, it had been a long day for him too co-ordinating the arrest operation and then after that he had sat in the Ops room listening to the various conversations and SITREPs on the air from all his patrols and arrest teams.

From these reports, he had tried to build up a picture of what was happening on their Company patch and then relay it to Alan and the patrols. As well as all this, there was also the bigger picture in the Battalion area to consider and analyse.

Nick realised the importance of his role. Despite his seemingly lethargic laid back character, he had acted with great professionalism and competence. Alan had known what he was doing when he placed him there for this operation. Nick himself, had felt alive for the last few hours, had felt as if he was really contributing and earning his pay.

For a year or so now he found that he had to make a huge effort to seem even slightly enthusiastic about anything. This he thought would change for the beat up training before going to Belfast and then of course for the tour itself, but it hadn't. His marriage was cracking up and the separation didn't help one bit.

He had been married to Anne for four years now. The problems seem to start when he realised that she was a career woman and wasn't interested in having children. It was Nick's second marriage and he had no children from the first. He hadn't realised his yearning to be a father had been so strong, he was getting no younger and desperately wanted to settle down with a family.

He knew that his Officer career was all but ended, he would get no further unless he was prepared to take some obscure job behind a desk somewhere getting fat and grumpy. So he had decided to quit and had handed in his resignation just before the tour began. When it was over he would be a "free" man and would make a real go at his marriage and a new career.

Anne had been impressed he thought when he had announced this on the eve of his departure. He felt sure that most of the problem was the separation. Anne wouldn't consider children until he was settled, so he would do his part and quit. He had told nobody accept Anne. The CO and Alan knew of course but it was not for general knowledge.

The sound of repeated shooting close by pulled Nick back to the conscious world, he had nodded off. The cigar had an inch of ash which fell off as he moved, he looked at the signaller the only other person in the Ops room, in unison they shouted "Jesus !"

Podge Hopkins stared out over the waste ground, he had simmered down considerably and typically had accepted his lot. The light was beginning to fade and he felt sure that he would be relieved soon. Something caught his eye at the far end of the estate, a movement. It was a figure of a man walking stealthily toward the base, then to his left another and yet another at *his* side.

Podge got excited, he knew they were not soldiers, they were in civilian clothes. Then he froze. He could see they were carrying weapons. He had to tell someone but how?! Nobody had told him. He thought about leaving the Sangar and telling the gate sentry but he couldn't move he stared transfixed at the gunmen who were moving closer by the second.   Finally the spell broke, he raised his rifle and tried to take aim but something was wrong? "Me Back Sight!" he rasped and flicked it up. Once again he bought the rifle in the aim, he closed his eyes and snatched at the trigger...Nothing happened.. "Oh! Lord 'elp us" he moaned frantically and grabbed the cocking handle, he ripped it back viciously, screaming, "This is it you bastards!" Took a rudimentary aim and just kept pulling the trigger. Boom! Boom! Boom! The noise was deafening and only stopped when the fifteen rounds in his magazine had all gone.

Vince Longthorne heard the gunfire and acted immediately by heading toward the sound and urging the other patrols to follow.

Podge coughed and choked on the stench of the cordite trapped in the sangar. He was slumped on the floor pouring with sweat, a metallic voice kept on repeating "Send Sitrep! Send Sitrep!" He located the source of the noise it was a square squawk box nailed to a plank in the corner of the Sangar.

He scrambled over to it reluctant to raise himself off the floor, as he pressed the red button to speak a bullet slammed into the side of the Sangar sending a shower of sand over him. "Help me!" he sobbed, "They're trying to fackin' kill me!"

Vince stopped his patrols at the edge of the waste ground, the light was fading fast. The radio told him that no 3 Sangar had done the shooting, he was now looking at it and the ground that was in its arc of fire. A figure jumped up and fired a shot at the Sangar then ran back toward the estate, he disappeared before Vince or anyone else could get a shot.

He heard some screaming coming from near to where the man had just fired from. As he and his patrol started to run toward the sound a machine gun opened up on them from the estate, they immediately dived for cover. Vince let out a shout and pitched forward, he felt as if he had been hit from behind by a car.

Nick Summers bounded up the ladder to No 3 Sangar. He had not wanted to leave the Ops room but decided that it was the only way to find out quickly what was going on. He opened the door and saw Podge hunched in the corner, "What happened!?" shouted Nick.

"I've only pissed me fackin' self." said Podge gloomily.

"Sergeant Longthorne's down Sir! He's been hit!" shouted the signaller to Rob Thomas.

"Fucking Bollocks!" exclaimed Rob, he grabbed the handset off the signaller, "Send SITREP!" He demanded urgently. He instantly recognised Alan's calm tones answering.

"Your Sunray Minor is down, we are handling that end. I want you to enter the estate and clear it. It seems that they were ambushed by a machine gun from that area. Move now....out!" Another burst of machine gun fire echoed around the now darkened streets. Rob gave a quick briefing to his patrols on the radio then moved speedily toward the estate.

The Company Medic, Seamus was guided by a member of Vince's patrol to where he lay. Two soldiers were bent over him, one looked up and recognised Seamus, "He's got it in the back." Seamus snapped on his torch and the other soldier yelled, "Put that out! Do you want us all killed?!"

Seamus yelled back in his thick brogue. "I'll do my fucken job and try to help him. You do yours and protect us!"

Podge came down the Sangar ladder after he had been replaced by the now terrified QM's clerk. As he emerged into the vehicle park one of the soldiers came over to him and clapped him on the back, "Well done Podge! You fucking zapped one of them.. He's dead!"

Podge felt his legs buckle, tears welled up and ran uncontrollably down his puffy cheeks. "I'm not a killer," he wailed. "I'm a cook, a fackin slop jockey, get me home and outa this fackin dump! Everyone hates everyone else. Get me out!"

By now the base was like a hornet's nest of activity, the shooting had steam hosed away all tiredness. Patrols hung around the gate raring to get out and do something but Alan held them back, too many on the streets would be too dangerous he reasoned. Still they bunched like coiled springs waiting to be released.

Rob kept all but his own patrol back. He made them go to ground then led his four men into the dark and still Estate. It had been around five minutes since they had heard the machine gun. Rob thought briefly about how badly Vince might have been hit then forced it out of his mind.

He calculated that he was about a street away from the firing point. The streets were quiet apart from a record player somewhere in the estate blasting out "Kevin Barry".

He now wished he had bought another patrol with him so that he could encircle the next street. He decided to call one forward, as he began to whisper into his radio, a long burst of green tracer rounds hammered just over his head.

"They've sucked us in to an ambush!" He yelled at a member of his patrol as they dived through hedges into gardens. An explosion a few feet away confirmed his thoughts, he heard shards of metal whining past him at the speed of sound and flattened himself to the ground.

As he raised himself another burst of rounds ricocheted of the paving slabs and wall, this time he managed to see the flashes coming from a hole in the wall at the end of the street.

He kneeled and fired five quick shots at the hole. As he finished he heard another gunman to the rear open up and then one of his patrol firing back at him. Something flew through the air sparking, "Grenade!" he yelled and flattened as he heard the thud of something landing by him he looked with horror and saw a cylindrical object with silver nails packed around it not two feet from him. Letting out a cry of anguish he scooped the package up and flung it over the hedge into the street, a second later it exploded, red hot fragments showering him after they bounced off the walls.

Rob loosed off another five shots at the hole in the wall then turned and shouted, "Have you located the gunman to the rear yet?!"

One of his patrol leopard crawled to him an said breathlessly, "He's one of ours, 'is patrol must've come forward to see what the shooting was and got us mixed up...The stupid twat."

When Rob got to the other side of the wall he found the firing point, piled high with empty cartridge cases, but no weapon or firers. The nail bomb thrower had also disappeared. Rob slumped against the wall, drained. Once more his thoughts turned to Vince.

"He's got an entry wound in his side Sir but I couldn't find the exit. He himself didn't seem in any pain and was going in and out of consciousness. I dares not move him until I got the proper kit when the ambulance came and that was the reason for the delay. He had to stay put. I left him at the Victoria just now." Seamus had given his report to Alan in a monotone. Alan nodded and thanked him, as Seamus turned to go Alan clapped him ion the shoulder and added a *"Thanks"*. He looked at his watch and turned to Nick.

"One fifteen a.m. Nick, did you send a Sitrep to Battalion?" Nick nodded. "Then get some shut eye and that's an order, be sharp for tomorrow morning." Nick got up, he was bleary eyed through lack of sleep. The shooting had stopped after Rob's contact. Nick had organised a follow up search programme and the houses of many suspects had been entered and searched to no avail.

One of the gunmen who had crossed the wasteland had been shot dead. Two patrols had returned fire on lone gunmen, the area had now gone quiet. Alan put five patrols on the streets and the rest of the Company dozed with their rifles handy and their boots on.

13

The Humber Pig pulled up in the car park of the Royal Victoria Hospital, Belfast. The sun was shining and it promised to be a beautiful sunny day.

Frank, Wee Tam and Lieutenant Rob Thomas jumped out of the back and walked toward the entrance. They were in uniform and instead of a rifle each carried a pistol in a canvas holster. They mingled with other men and women entering the hospital, some carried flowers and bags of fruit. Nobody seemed to take any notice of the three, it seemed that the hospital was some kind of neutral place where hatreds and pressures were left outside on the pavement and the only concerns were for the problems that lay inside.

They approached the secure ward. In the hallway outside sitting behind a desk was a soldier, he too carried a pistol. He looked up at them as they approached. Rob spoke, "Lieutenant Thomas to see Sergeant Longthorne and Lieutenant Munro Fraser." The soldier nodded and gestured them into the ward.

It was a long ward with nine beds either side. Down the left hand side were injured servicemen. Ironically, because there was only one secure ward in the hospital, the right hand was reserved for suspected IRA members. A row of tables divided the ward and the nurses flitted happily around the ward with smiling faces, indifferent to whom lay what side of the ward.

Donald Munro-Fraser turned stiffly around and smiled in surprise at their approach. Like all the other patients he was in a blue towel dressing gown. He had been sitting beside his bed talking to one of the nurses, his neck collared by a thick bandage. "Hey fellas! Really good too see you!" he beamed.

They all said their hellos and stood around a little self conscious until the nurse that Donald had been speaking to said, "Come on now grab a chair each and make yourselves comfortable."

"Feel a bit of a pratt actually Donald," said Rob with mock concern, "couldn't get you any grapes or flowers, they blew the shop up as we got there." They all laughed and then Tam stuck his hand inside his camouflaged smock, had a furtive glance around and handed Donald a half bottle.

"Only the best for a Scotsman Sor, somethin' ta keep ye warm at night."

Donald looked genuinely pleased and as he stuck it under his pillow said. "Thanks, thanks very much Sergeant McGregor, I really appreciate it." Donald's handsome face lost its smile to reinforce his sincerity.

"Och it's nothin…How's ye neck anyways?" enquired Tam. Donald touched his neck as if he'd just remembered.

"Oh! Just a scratch really, I'll be back in no time…"

"It almost severed the artery right through," interjected the nurse as she returned, "and he'll not be going anywhere for *some* time." she stated firmly but with a smile.

Donald looked a little sheepish and said quietly, "But it *is* nothing and I feel like a bloody fraud when you see guys like Sergeant Longthorne and some of these." He gestured to the other patients lying there.

"How is he? Vince I mean." Rob asked.

Donald took a deep breath, "It's hard to say, I think he is awake, he's at the end of the ward in that bed that's curtained off."

"Okay Donald if you don't mind….And seeing that you are so fit I'll mosey on down and see him." said Rob. They all turned to walk down the ward but Donald signalled for Wee Tam to stay.

As the other two walked off his face went very serious and once again he spoke very quietly to his little mentor. "I made a bloody arse of it didn't I?….Going to the wrong bloody house for God's sake."

"It wasna your fault Sor, that pillock Garland sent you to the wrong house. He said to you, count eleven houses up and it was seven, you did as you were told." said McGregor calmly.

"But you didn't want me on the arrest team in the first place. You knew I wouldn't come up to scratch.." answered Donald getting more animated by the second.

Tam's face twisted to a scowl and he took a pace toward Donald, his finger pointing to him from the waist. He spoke quietly but with conviction.

"Hey! Now just you hang on a wee minute. I didn't want to take you on a team in the first place because that meant that you'd have to lead it and you were not quite ready. You saw and heard all the shit that went on, even experienced guys got it bad. It was far better that

you were with the OC and his Rover Group. You would
have seen what was going on everywhere in the area and
yes, you would have had your share of action with them
and there will be plenty more of this type of thing...
I'll guarantee ye, that one day you will command your
own Company as a Major in this very town.... Nothing
changes.....You were unlucky that's all, shit happens all
the time. The only criticism I have is that as soon as you
were attacked you should have let loose and zapped a
couple of the bastards, you were within your rights....
But that's just inexperience...That's all"

"I know," said Donald dolefully, "I know that this
sounds stupid Sergeant Mcgregor but I tried to reason
with them. They saw me when I emerged from that alleyway and they came for me as soon as they saw that I
was alone.... I said to them...Oh! What does it matter
now what I said.....The hatred that was in their eyes will
stay with me for ever. They wanted me dead and by the
time I realised it, it was too late, I was down. Thank God
Corporal Garland and you arrived..." Donald swallowed
hard a couple of times.

Wee Tam shook his head and clapped Donald on
the shoulder. "Aye, but you're here to tell the tale, and
do you know what? There's going to be a lot of people
in this unit who'd give up a month's pay for a battle scar
like what you're gonna have. And listen, shall I tell ye a
wee secret? The first riot I was in, *I*, froze and that's no
shit. It's ..It's like a baptism y'understand? Ye need ta go
through it just once, so that ye know how ta handle it
next time. You know, just like them injections ye get at
the MI room before ye go abroad. It's like a weak ver-

sion of the disease so that your body can handle the real thing when it comes along. Well that's' what you've bin through and here you are, chattin' up all the lovely nurses and no doubt thinkin' evil things!"

Despite himself Donald laughed heartily, it was the tonic he needed and Wee Tam's little allusions always amused him.

Frank and Rob Thomas pulled the curtains aside and entered. Vince lay on the bed his eyes closed, a box like contraption covered from his legs to his chest with bed linen covering it. It had been a week since the shooting and their first opportunity to visit him.

Rob looked at Frank and made a sign for them to leave but Vince's eyes flicked open and he manage a weak, "Alright?"

"How is it brother?" asked Frank, smiling as he shook his limp hand.

"Aw man you know." slurred Vince, "I'm pumped full o' drugs and I canna get out of bed even for a shit… How's the blokes?"

"They're fine Vince." cut in Rob Thomas. Vince screwed up his eyes and turned his head slightly, aware for the first time, that someone else was in his space.

"Hello boss, didn't see you, thanks for coming."

"Sorry we couldn't get here sooner, but you know what the bus service is like, what's the prognosis mate?"

"I dunno, me wife and mother are here stayin' at the hospital. I think they know but they won't tell us… What a fuckin' mess eh? Heard you tried to get the bastards, thanks boss.."

Any further conversation was broken up by the ward sister, a pretty green eyed woman. She spoke firmly in a lovely Southern Irish brogue. "Come on now gentlemen, curtains up mean no visitors. Sorry Vincent but they'll have to say their cheerios."

"Ok Vince we'll see you again. Wee Tam is here too, bye." said Frank cheerily.

"Yeh! See you." said Rob and met up with Wee Tam and Donald again.

The sister followed them and said by way of an apology. "Vincent has had a hard time today. His family visited him for the first time just this morning, they were .. Shall we say, quite emotional and at this stage that's just what he doesn't need, so I would prefer it if he rested now."

"Sure we understand Sister." said Rob, "What's the prognosis? Can you tell me?"

"That's for the specialist to say of course and there are more tests to run.."

"But?" persisted Rob.

"But, he is not responding at the moment as well as he should, his legs that is."

"Oh Jesus!" groaned Rob. Frank and Tam exchanged glances, grim looks on their faces.

"Let's get the fuck out of here!" said Rob and without waiting strode off and out of the ward.

Podge Hopkins strode into the kitchen at Battalion Headquarters, he had just returned from an interview with the Commanding Officer who had shaken his hand and thanked him for his vigilance and steadfast behaviour in the face of the enemy. "It was naffin' Sir, anybody would have acted the same." he had said.

Word had got round and all of the cooks were in the kitchen, even those off duty, plus some of the Headquarters staff. He paused wondering what they were all doing there. Spontaneous clapping was followed by a cheer. Somehow, thought Podge as he stood there soaking up the adulation, cooking and dishing up slop to the ungrateful masses just won't seem the same any more.

Lieutenant Tony Orchard stopped by his Pig that was parked at Battalion Headquarters. He was bewildered, he had to stop and ponder a moment and go over in his mind exactly what the Commanding Officer had just said to him.

Earlier that day the Major, Alan Briggs had called him in his office. Alan had been uncharacteristically brusk and businesslike. "The CO wants to see you Tony, be down there for eleven thirty sharp!" Fear and uncertainty had gripped his guts. He churned over everything especially his actions during the Internment phase, his breakdown in the house when he had frozen instead of making a decision allowing a Private soldier to take command, he had shuddered.

He could not remember his trip to Battalion Headquarters. He had sat in the back of the Pig staring ahead thinking of the humiliation that waited for him. They would all know by the time he got back to the school thanks to the bush telegraph. Britton would be there sneering and all the men smirking and laughing behind his back, well damn all of them.

He waited in the Adjutant's office which was next to the CO's. Coffee had been served up but the Adjutant was non committal, he was busy answering the phone which seemed to ring every few seconds denying any real conversation. He saw the fat cook, Hopkins go in and come out all smiles, followed by others including Lance Corporal Norris.

Some soldiers were in front of the CO on disciplinary charges, the RSM barking and screaming at them in the corridor outside, then yelling out the time at a pace impossible to keep as the soldiers were marched in "Left right left right!"

Then after half an hour it went quiet. Tony had sat there hoping that he had been forgotten about, even the adjutant had stopped glancing in his direction.

Then the CO's door had opened and out strode Quentin Harper, he spied Tony and a huge smile lit up his face. "Ah! Tony, come in! Please sit down." He had gestured him to a large leather Chesterfield then parked himself on a stool opposite him. Tony sat rigid on the edge of the chair.

"Well young man, why do you think you are here?!" beamed Harper.

"Colonel I..." Tony just shook his head unable to get out the words.

"Well, I'll put you out of your misery," The CO's mood turned serious, "Tony being an Officer is all about leadership and setting an example and for those few minutes last week I saw those two qualities in you. You kept a cool head whilst helping an injured member of your patrol and organising those two other relatively inexperienced soldiers while under tremendous pressure from the mob. I have no doubt at all in my mind that even if I had not turned up, you would have turned that situation around and made it good. This is your first taste of action and you came through it very well indeed, keep it up, you have a great career ahead of you."

"Are you comin' Sir?" It was the Pig driver. Tony snapped out of his trance and nodded. He leapt into the back of the Pig in a single bound.

Big Norrie, Ronnie Gittins, Taff Reece and a few other members of the platoon sat around in the dining room having a brew ready to go on patrol. Norrie had just finished telling them for the third time how the CO had lavished praise on him for the capture of the Londonderry IRA man, much to the disgust of Ronnie Gittins.

Digger Davis approached them, his nose was red and swollen and he had two large black eyes but the stone that had hit him had done no worse than that. He had been detained overnight in hospital and released next day to be put on light duties for a week. He had volunteered for sedentary duties like radio watch in the Ops room or the Intelligence cell instead of being trounced for duties in the cookhouse peeling spuds.

Digger strode up to them, he looked a little agitated and glanced over his shoulder a couple of times before he spoke. "You bastards are never going to believe this and I wouldn't either, but I heard the OC talkin' myself, they're gonna give that wanker Orchard a gong."

"What the hell are you talking about man?" enquired Reece. A few others on the periphery of the group closed in to hear the reply.

"They're gonna pin a medal on Orchard. I heard Briggs myself talking to the CO, he didn't see me and his office door was open.." stated Digger his mouth hanging open in surprise.

Ronnie Gittins the self appointed barrack room lawyer took over.

"OK fine, we believe you Digger but let's just think for a minute. If you give someone a gong then there must be a citation to go with it, you know some written words, wot tells everyone why he's getting' it....So can anyone think as to why he's getting it?"

"Maybees you heard wrong Digger." ventured a voice.

"Yeh!" continued Ronnie, "What exactly did you hear?"

"Well, Like I said," replied Digger getting a little agitated, " I was next to the OC's office and I heard him talking to the CO.."

"How do you know it was the CO?" interjected Ronnie.

Digger, now really irritated raised his voice and said heatedly, "'Cos he called him friggin' Colonel, who do you think he'd be talkin' to? A Chinese friggin' take away!?"

"OK old mate, keep your shirt on, just trying to establish what was said." Answered Ronnie calmly.

"Well, like I was sayin', he was talking to the CO and I heard him mention Tony Orchard and what a *splendid chap* he was, so I go to the Ops room and picks up the extension and listens. The CO said that he was putting his name up for an award for his actions and example of leadership and all that shit.."

"Didn't the CO carry you and him out when you got injured?" shot Ronnie his eyes glittering with fervour.

"Yeh, apparently he came along just after I went down.."

"Then that's it! It's gotta be!" cut in Ronnie "He's come round the corner just as Orchard 's done something really neat like beating back the crowd or sammink."

"But the man's a friggin coward for chrissake!" roared Digger, "You've heard me tell you how he froze in that house and all the rest of it and now he's getting a medal!"

By now a sizeable crowd had gathered around Digger and a hum of disgruntled conversation filled the air.

Norrie sought out Frank, he found him talking to Wee Tam in one of the corridors. "Is it true? About Lieutenant Orchard I mean.. ..Getting a gong?" Norrie then proceeded to tell Frank what he'd heard, careful not to expose Digger.

Both Frank and Tam looked at each other then burst out laughing. "Norrie!" laughed Frank, "Someone's winding you up mate!" But even as he said it a part him knew that it was true.

Frank festered, it was not in his character to do so but he did. He had found out an hour before, that most of what Norrie had told him was true. He had phoned a contact in headquarters who had seen a draught of a citation for Orchard. He had no hate for Orchard but then he had no love for him either, he thought privately that at best he was an arrogant snob and at the worst a coward.

He had seen for himself and had heard the stories. He knew that for the benefit and well being of the platoon he had to forge a good working relationship with him but the news about the award had strained that to breaking point.

He thought of Vince lying in bed useless and all the other guys who had given a maximum effort even though sometimes scared shitless and what did they get? Then there was Orchard a walking contradiction of an officer and leader, now strutting around the base with a large smug look on his face. Frank swung his legs off his bunk, he knew that if he continued festering sooner or later he would erupt, he had to keep busy.

Nick Summers also pondered on the information that Alan had passed to him in confidence about Tony. His first reaction was to be pleased for him, after all he may have been going through a phase or something, being new and all that. Then he thought about the story he had heard on the grapevine about how he had cracked up leaving Digger to take charge. Rumours they may be but he had a feeling that they weren't that far away from the truth.

Tony Orchard walked into the front Sangar where the gate sentry was sitting reading a magazine. He was duty Officer and part of his job was to inspect the sangars at least once per day, he stood arms akimbo glaring at the sentry who had stood up and hastily ditched the reading material.

"You're bloody well on a charge, just who the hell do you think you are? Reading on duty! Now get this place sorted out! I'll be back in half an hour!" Orchard strode off toward one of the other Sangars. "There's going to be some bloody changes around here!" He murmured to himself.

14

Three weeks had past since Internment. Things had slowly returned to "normal". Shootings and bombing incidents dropped to more or less what they were before but confrontations and the riots that ensued, remained higher.

The workload of the soldiers also remained high. Patrols, guard, standby. Patrols, guard, standby. Over and over, day after day, week after week. This was only broken up by being pulled out to do searches or throw in cordons for searches.

A great change had taken place with Tony Orchard. He was no longer introvert and moody, his confidence had grown and he seemed to take a greater interest in the day to day running of the platoon. Any influence that Frank had over him because of his greater experience had gone. Orchard questioned and mostly argued about everything that Frank implemented or suggested.

Frank found himself losing patience with him and tended to avoid confrontations by keeping clear of him.

The lads in the platoon sensed the atmosphere. They had mistrusted Orchard at first but since his actions on Internment they disliked him, that dislike turned to loathing when they heard that he was to be rewarded for his cowardice.

Alan Briggs despite being a competent, well liked OC did not pick up on this under current of bad feeling. Nick failed to bring it to his attention because he in turn, did not realise just how high feelings were running.

They had one month to go before the end of the tour. A little excitement was beginning to ripple through the ranks. There was talk of five weeks leave and a trip to Malaya later on in the year. Strange faces started to appear from the pre- advance party of the Unit taking over from them.

Frank came in off patrol, he unloaded his rifle in the sandbagged area and emerged to find Lieutenant Orchard waiting for him. He used no words of greeting but just gave a nod and said, "Come on! The OC has a job for us and wants to speak to both of us at once."

Alan Briggs was in the Ops room talking to another officer in the uniform of the Princes Own. Frank and Tony walked in on them and Alan broke off and introduced the man as Major David Howells.

Alan then spoke to Tony. "Tony, I'm lending you and most of the platoon to David. He is based in South Armagh and has kindly allowed us to go on his turf. The experience will be invaluable, soldiering where we should be soldiering, in the open countryside." They all smiled at that. "Well, I'm sure you will enjoy it, David here will give you a briefing now in my office, if all goes according to plan you should be leaving the day after tomorrow."

Major Howells sat on Alan's desk. A large map of South Armagh had been hastily pinned to one wall. Frank and Tony were the only others present. Major

Howells lit up and spoke. "Your OC was being very kind when he spoke, the truth is I'm over stretched at the moment and finding it very difficult to cover my area of operation. I reckon that it needs another Company at least to share the responsibility, however, until the powers that be come round to my way of thinking I've got to beg, borrow and steal manpower from everywhere" He turned to the map and using a ruler to point, continued his talk.

"This," he said showing a large area outlined in purple, "is my area of responsibility. It contains over fifteen road crossings into the South known as unapproved roads, plus two main roads and a railway, these have got to be monitored all the time. Then of course, there is the border itself and all the responsibility in patrolling that." He turned to them, his eyes though bright and intelligent were tired and dark bags showed under them.

"Most of the roads in the area have to be cleared constantly to allow our traffic and patrols to use them, that means clearing culverts.."

"Culverts?" Interrupted Tony.

"Yes, you know pipes under the road, some are no bigger than ordinary drain pipes, others you can walk through two abreast, they have a habit of putting a few beer kegs in them from time to time filled with home made explosive and taking out our vehicles or patrols when they cross over them."

"I see!" said Tony. "And presumably they just sit on the high ground overlooking...."

"Exactly! And just press the tit at the appropriate moment. I have three dead already and we're just a month into the tour." stated David grimly. "You are not being invited down to a picnic, its tough work and it's dangerous, you will have to adjust quickly, very quickly indeed."

Frank looked over Belfast from the Black Mountain, shafts of sunlight lit up areas and buildings, it looked like any other city at work, smoke rising, the glitter of car windscreens, the huge Harland and Wolfe crane operating. He tried to pick out the Company area but it was lost in a fold in the ground.

Norrie crept over to where Frank lay and immediately lit up. After a couple of drags he spoke, "The Boss is kicking up, he's looking at the bleeding map again and reckons we're in the wrong place...Wants to see you."

Frank sighed and pulled away from his cover and walked along a dry ditch to where Lieutenant Orchard sat with Pinky Watson his signaller. A map was lying fully open on the bank of the ditch. Orchard was alternately looking at it and then to the field in front of him, a grim look on his face.

He ignored Frank for a minute or so then turned and without looking directly at him said, "We're in the wrong place, we should be fifty metres that way." he waived his hand further down the ditch. "Prepare to move everyone.."

"Sir!" Frank cut in, "It doesn't really matter a toss whether we are fifty or one hundred and fifty metres out, when the choppers come they'll be guided into this field anyway.."

"Look Sergeant Britton!" said Orchard sharply, "We agreed a bloody grid reference with the RAF and that grid reference is over there! On the edge of that line of bushes and we are *here*, and why do you presume that the helicopters will land in this field?"

"Because that's where Gittins will be, he will guide them in." Frank said, trying hard to keep the irritation out of his voice.

"Gittins for God's sake! He's a private soldier, what does he know about guiding in helicopters?" said Orchard, his voice incredulous.

"Sir!" said Frank with a blank expression on his face, "He's done the Heli Handling course, in fact he got top marks on it, he's more than capable, not that the pilots will take much notice of him…"

"Well I don't like it, not one bit, they're due here in ten minutes, we're in the wrong spot and everything is pinned on the abilities of a private soldier." Orchard savagely chopped at his map to get it back to pocket size. "Well? Get the men moving Sergeant Britton."

"Sir!" Frank growled, his voice getting a little louder, "At the moment the men are in all round defence, in a few minutes when we hear the choppers I will have to get them into stick order ready to mount the choppers while still maintaining as much as an all round defence as possible. Its tricky but we rehearsed it as best we could in the base, if I go chopping and changing now it will upset everything.."

"Just do it!" snapped Orchard, "And don't presume to give me a lesson on tactics.." Orchard stopped short, he realised that he was losing his cool. Pinky Watson the signaller pretended to be busying himself with something but Orchard knew that he was hanging on to every word, ready to inform his mates at the first opportunity.

Orchard considered insisting that Frank carry out his bidding but they were literally flying into unknown territory and he was very anxious indeed that everything went well when they were down there, an upset now he though may not bode well for the coming week.

"Very well, we'll do it your way this time..." The rhythmic thud of a helicopter cut him short, as Frank stood up he could see Ronnie Gittins already running into the centre of the field waving a coloured panel.

The grey Wessex helicopter circled once and then dropped quickly onto the field, the door opened and the Loadmaster signalled for the first group to clamber aboard, as he did so another Chopper landed a little distance away and the procedure was repeated. They took off almost as soon as the last man was aboard. One more trip would be made to move the rest of the platoon.

The base at Drumboyle a few years earlier had been a rural police station. A large brick building resembling a manor house with barred windows on the ground floor and a large court yard bordered with chain link fencing on the edge of a small village from where it took its name.

Looking down at it from the circling chopper Frank saw a slightly different picture. He noted the Manor house building and a court yard choked with Porta-cabins. The field next to the station was now tarmac and used as a vehicle park and chopper pad. The whole area was inevitably boxed in with silver corrugated iron, a sangar at each corner.

As soon as they landed they were ushered into a Portacabin which was rigged out as a briefing room with rows of chairs and a large map taking up the whole of the end wall. They left their bulging Bergin rucksacks outside, filed in and sat down. They were told by a young Lieutenant of the Princes Own, Alex Winter that they would be given a briefing as soon as the choppers returned with the rest.

Alex was their Ops officer, a young golden haired youth that spoke with a lisp. They didn't have long to wait and soon the briefing room was packed with the platoon. Major Howells welcomed them to the location then handed them back to the Alex Winter whose manner of talking reminded a few of them of the typical officer portrayed in black and white films of World War Two.

"Wight chaps, jolly pleased to have you all aboard, things are quite hectic and I'm afwaid that you are to be deployed right now on a road clearance task that should take you the rest of the day. It's a comparatively safe section so that you can shake out and use it to cut your teeth on but please, that doesn't mean that you can be complacent and I'm sure you won't be. Use it to iron out your problems because I've got a real humdinger for you tomorrow!" His cheery face lit up at that and they all laughed a little. "But the good news is that when you get back this evening the chef's will force feed you on T Bone steaks!"

His manner relaxed them and helped them to assimilate the briefing that he now went into, in detail.

They were to clear a four mile section of road from the base to a small village then return on foot across country. There were seven culverts and two bridges to be cleared. The good news was that the road was not overlooked by high ground and it was bordered by high hedges that made it almost impossible for an observer to see any traffic on it. Nevertheless the Ops officer ended the briefing on a solemn note.

"Well, that's it chaps it's now up to you and the professionalism that you are renowned for but let me tell you this, there is a great tendency to relax in this beautiful countryside. It's the lack of people that does that. In the city you are constantly on the edge not knowing who is friend or foe but here, here you have a sunny day with green fields, birds are singing and the few people that you do come across are generally pleasant. I'm sorry to do this but I will now show you a stark reminder of what soldiering can be like in South Armagh."

He took two steps to a wall that had part of it covered by a sheet, he removed the sheet to expose a black and white photograph blown up to about two feet square.

At first, it was hard to make out what was portrayed but then a horrible recognition took place. It showed a human torso blackened and ravaged lying on a white slab, placed near the appropriate places were the remnants of two legs and an arm.

The Ops officer's voice cut in speaking quietly, for one could hear a pin drop. "This poor lad went to examine a milk churn that looked like it had fallen off a lorry, there was even spilt milk surrounding it. They didn't find the head and an arm....Okay, *he* is dead but what can *we* learn from it? Treat everything with suspicion, don't go rushing in, call for the proper agencies like bomb disposal to examine anything that you deem suspicious. The bad guys have got time on their side, we have professionalism and caution."

Frank and Tony Orchard remained on the road with the dog handler. With them were Pinky Watson the signaller and a half dozen men who were to clear the hedges on either side of the road and the culverts when they came to them. Corporal Taff Reece was on the left flank about a hundred metres from the road and Norrie was on the right flank. Their job was to flush or "bump" any potential spots that a bomb could be triggered from. In between the two flanks and the road were three soldiers whose job it was to try and discover any wires that lead from the potential firing points to a culvert or hedge row.

The whole thing was controlled from the centre by radio based on the road, to either halt, speed up or slow down the flanks.

At first, caution ruled and they took a relatively long time to reach the first culvert. Orchard was continually on the radio to the flanks trying to get them to send their exact locations and getting frustrated and angry when they took their time in doing it.

When they got within sight of the culvert or to be exact, where they knew the culvert to be which was generally under a dip in the road, the handler sent in the sniffer dog to check if he could smell explosives. If this was negative then a couple of the road party would deploy to either side of the road and physically check the culvert was clear or otherwise. This was considered to be the dangerous part of a dangerous job, so the soldiers were swapped around as often as could be.

When the first culvert loomed, Orchard started flapping about a look of worry and uncertainty showed through his blackened face. This spread through to the two teams that were to do the clearing. They looked at each other hesitating, so Frank jumped up and took the initiative. He signalled to the team nearest him led by Ronnie Gittins, "Come on follow me!" he said. Orchard turned, his mouth open as if in shock.

"What....What the hell are you doing?!" he spluttered angrily to Frank. "I didn't give an order....We've got to contact the flanks first.. ..They're not responding, there may be a problem."

"It's okay Sir," reassured Frank, "if they had found anything we would have heard by now besides we'll go well out into the field and work our way slowly in. This culvert is a biggy and we should be able to see through it some way out."

"How on earth do you know that this is a large one?" demanded Orchard. "We were given no briefing about that."

"I asked the dog handler." retorted Frank a little too quickly and loudly, "He's cleared this route a dozen times or more." Orchard looked around to see who had overheard the conversation, as usual Pinky Watson was at hand with the radio, busying himself with something.

Orchard calmed himself then said in an authoritative manner. "Okay let's move it! We've wasted enough time!"

Frank moved off with the other two members of the team across the field in a diagonal line to the small stream that ran from the culvert. It was lined with willow trees and the odd Hawthorn. The only way to approach the culvert properly was to get in the middle of the stream, this they did and found themselves knee deep in cool, crystal clear water, lapping and gurgling over stones.

The trees cut off the sun and it was gloomy and cool under the canopy. It was a place where in better times you would soak your feet after a walk in the hills and perhaps enjoy a cool beer before continuing.

The words of the young Ops officer echoed in Frank's mind. *There's a great tendency to relax in this beautiful countryside...*Then an image of a blasted torso flashed in front of his eyes.

He turned and smiled to the other three, "Okay lads I'll lead, stay in the rear and keep your eyes open for wires or anything suspicious." He led off slowly, rounded a gentle curve and saw the wide mouth of the culvert about thirty feet away. Moving to the left slightly he positioned himself so that he could see straight through it, he saw through to the other side and made out the silhouette of a man at the other end, then heard a voice echoing through the tunnel.

"Okay Sarge! It's clear!"

Frank got back on the road and saw the leader of the other search team, the one who had shouted through the culvert, "You were too quick! Did you approach slowly from about fifty metres out like you were briefed?"

The young lad Thompson, looked a little sheepish and cast his eye toward Lieutenant Orchard who cut in loudly, "I ordered Thompson to go straight to the mouth of the culvert, it saves time, at this rate we won't be finished until tomorrow.."

Frank straightened up and faced Orchard, his jaw was set hard and his eyes were narrowed. "Look here Sir!" He said with anger at the edge of his voice, "If there had been a device in there and someone had been watching they would have pressed the tit as soon as the clearance team got down there! You heard the briefing, we can't rush into these things, it's fucking suicide if we do!"

"And let me remind you Sergeant!" Raged Orchard, a snarl contorting his face "This road is safe, it is *not* overlooked and we have to finish this task before dark, so don't try to make a big deal out of this! Besides, you had no business leaving your position on the road to do the task of a private soldier."

"Sir! *I am* the platoon Sergeant around here and what you did set a wrong and dangerous example! .."

"That's enough Sergeant Britton, your cheap popularity stunts in front of the men make me want to puke, now get this show moving .. And now!" He turned and strode up the road. Frank stared after him for a few seconds aware that his heart was hammering.

The rest of the culverts and bridges were cleared one by one. The men got more confident and competent and by the last one they had become slick and efficient. Orchard kept away as far as possible from Frank for the rest of the operation.

The Ops officer Lieutenant Winter had been right about most things and certainly about the T Bone steaks. The platoon sat in the small dining room polishing them off with piles of egg, chips and bread and butter. All the walking and tension had given each man a huge appetite, each man that is except Tony Orchard.

He sat at the table with the Alex Winter the young Ops officer. Always on edge when eating with the men, Tony was glad of his company. He sat and picked at his food and now and then glanced over to where Frank was eating flanked as usual Orchard thought, by his cronies, Norris, Reece, Gittins and the like. Now and then they would burst into laughter, no doubt directed at him.

Ronnie Gittins was in the middle of a story about an incident that had happened that day. As usual it was a skit at his good friend and sparring partner Norrie, "Anyway," he said to his audience, "Norrie come down from the flank to swap over with me on culvert clearance. So, what's the score then Ronnie? he says, so I says naffink to it Norrie. When you come to a culvert you go forward with the sniffer dog to check it out, the only fing is you've got to go on all fours with the dog, so's you don't upset him. Bollocks! Says Norrie. It's true I said, just look at old Tommo Thompson there with the knees of his trousers all worn out, that's through crawlin' with the dog. What Norrie doesn't know is that Tommo had torn them falling down the bank. So Norrie rears up don't he. No bastards gonna get me crawlin' on me 'ands and knees for fuckin' nowt!" said Ronnie in an exaggerated mimic of Norrie's Nottingham accent.

"You lyin' bastard!" roared Norrie in mock fury.

The table erupted in laughter and even some of the Princes Own lads on the next table joined in the mirth.

The lispy Lieutenant spoke in his exuberant manner and broke Tony away from his thoughts. "Well, congwatulations Tony, by all accounts you and your men did very well today but sleep well tonight as there is a big clearance to be done tomorrow and right on the border too!"

15

The bunks in the Police station itself and in the surrounding Portacabins were cramped even under normal circumstances, now that Tony Orchard's platoon had arrived, it was nigh impossible. Beds had been slotted in for them but it meant crawling over sleeping men to get to them or being crawled over just as you were nodding off, so most of the platoon including Frank, opted to sleep in the vehicle park in sleeping bags. The evening was warm and balmy and most of them were so knackered they would have slept anywhere.

Taff Reece had bashered next to Frank. Frank lay half in his sleeping bag propped up against the wheel of a trailer finishing a mug of tea. He could feel a wave of fatigue trying to envelope him. There was an early start in the morning and it looked like it was going to be a long old day.

Taff spoke in a soft voice. "I heard Orchard was kicking up again today, the twat."

Frank had given up trying to do his loyalty bit for Orchard with his closer friends, to the blokes yes, he had to keep up the sham but on these type of operations when you are just in your self contained group it was hard not to open up.

"Does a day go by when he doesn't?" Answered Frank.

"He's a fuckin' knob!" continued Taff, "He's got a great bunch of blokes who would get him through any situation.. And what does he do? He blows it completely, treats us like shit…It's really beyond me."

"It's working for him though," replied Frank, "the CO and the Major think he's the bee's knees and the worse thing is, he knows it. At this moment that man can do no wrong, he could probably walk around South Armagh in a fluorescent yellow jacket singing the full repetoir of Orange songs and nothing would happen to him."

"Problem is though Frank," said Taff gravely, "all those stood around him would get the chop."

"Don't you think I realise that?" said Frank.

It was first light, the base was a hive of activity, most soldiers queued up for a full "dead pig breakfast" as it was generally known. Bacon, eggs, sausages and fried bread. It seemed like they had hardly slept and drowsiness showed up in tight white faces. A now familiar cheery voice boomed out, "Bwiefing room in ten minutes everybody."

"Bollocks!" shouted an anonymous voice from the eaters.

Major David Howells was first to address the assembled group. There were RUC men in their black uniforms, two sniffer dog teams, Engineers and of course men from the Princes Own and Tony Orchard's platoon. The briefing room was full to bursting and some had to stand outside. Howells called everyone to order introduced himself then gave an outline of the operation.

"Gentlemen, we are to clear the stretch of road between the Derg and Sheelin Rock." He paused as a ripple of low conversation broke out amongst the assembly. He expected it, that particular stretch of road had claimed seven lives over recent years of both RUC and Army. It ran parallel to the border with the South and was overlooked by high ground that was mainly on the other side of the border, making an ideal set up for any road bomber.

It was cut by many culverts and bridges and its low stone walls and thick roadside vegetation made it extremely dangerous to clear.

The Major cleared his voice loudly and the room went quiet once more. "As you can see we have pulled in as many resources as possible for this task. We have two dog teams, Royal Engineers..." David was cut short when a voice with a Belfast accent cut in from the back of the room where a knot of RUC men stood.

"Why exactly Major, are we clearing the road?" It came from a middle aged constable. A military man would not have dared to interrupt a briefing with such a question, maybe it could have been asked more subtly at some stage but the RUC were not bound by such intricacies and were inclined to take a more direct approach.

The Major stopped talking and peered at the man, he recognised him and gave a slight smile before answering.

"Well, essentially we are clearing it because my Commanding Officer told me to clear it and I wish *you* had been at *that* briefing." Laughter broke the little tension that had grown.

"But," continued the Major, "I suspect that the order came from HQ Northern Ireland in the first place, probably due to some intelligence report or other.."

"But nobody uses the road except for a few local farmers." Persisted the voice, "*We,* never use it, *you,* never use it...But we continually clear the bloody thing. The only reason the IRA mine it, is because we go on it to clear it! And why is it that we are never made privy to these intelligence reports that dictate what we do? Surely to God if we are going into something where lives are at stake, we should know at least why." The Constable finished looking a little uneasy, the room was deathly quiet except for the rustle of fabric as people turned to eyeball the questioner.

"Well of course Jamie I cannot begin to answer those questions and it's neither the time nor the place to do so. If you permit me I will carry on, there is a long day ahead of us."

The long day started with them shaking out just outside of the small hamlet known as the Derg, a crossroads with two houses and a crumbling barn.

A Platoon from the Princes Own took the left flank of the road, the one that ran up the high ground to the border and Lieutenant Orchard's Platoon took the other flank. The Engineers, RUC and dog teams were based on the road with the OC, David Howells and Tony Orchard. Frank elected to go in the centre of his flank for better control, Orchard didn't argue, he thought that the further they were apart the better.

Slowly, the caterpillar crawled along the road, the sniffer dogs sent well in advance. They expertly worked their way through the hedgerows, tails wagging, responding to the whistles and shouts of their handlers.

Pinky Watson the signaller was close to Orchard, he noted that he hung back as far as possible from the front of the column, that was alright by him but he hoped the other units hadn't noticed.

The uniforms of the men on the flank got torn in many places as they negotiated hedgerow after hedgerow, not only trying to find a way through but also searching for wires which was their primary task. The men on the extremes of the flank heaved and sweated as they forged ahead to clear the high ground well ahead of the road party.

Now and then a halt was called to allow culverts or other obstacles to be cleared. On and on it went mile after mile, until just after one o' clock when the OC ordered everyone to stop where they were and take a half hour break.

Most just flopped and Frank spent another five minutes of precious rest time getting the men to take up some kind of defensive position.

He then dropped beside Taff Reece and Norrie in a shady ditch and took a long pull from his water bottle.

"Jesus Frank!" sighed Taff, "This is bloody hard work, gimme the city any day of the week."

"Come off it Taff," threw in Norrie, "an old sheep shagger like you should be used to chasing around the hills."

"Cheeky bugger, I only once tried to shag a sheep but I found that your father had beaten me to it so I gave up."

Frank was studying the map, he folded it away and said, "We're approximately just over the halfway mark now."

Taff came closer to Frank and whispered, "I wonder how shit head's doing down there?" He pointed down to the distant road.

Tony Orchard felt good. He was not in Command, so he had no burden of responsibility apart from making sure that his lads on the right flank were keeping to the tempo, which mainly due to Frank they were.

He noted the cool ease in which the OC directed the Operation, he was right behind the dog handlers but kept his signaller well back with the rest of the group. He let the men get on with the job they were trained for, neither hurrying them nor giving out continuous cheap praise. He dropped back now and again to his signaller and talked to his flank men on the radio to ensure that everything was going well with them.

Tony felt a surge of frustration well up in him for a few moments, if only, he thought, my platoon were as slick and professional as these, my job would be so much easier.

The OC stopped the Operation for a half hour break because he knew from experience that everyone especially those on the flanks would be tired and losing concentration. They were more than half way and three more hours would see it through, if all went well.

He walked back to where Tony and Pinky Watson were sitting on the road their feet in the ditch much the same as everyone else. He squatted by Tony.

"Learning anything Tony?" he said with a grin, "Piece of cake really, although one shouldn't really be blaze¢ about such things. You must be bored back here, so I'll tell you what, when we start again in twenty minutes, you'll have the reins for a bit okay? I'm going to nip up to the flanks and see how they're getting on. Before Tony could react David slapped him on the back and moved off toward some other members of the road party.

This sudden awesome responsibility nearly made Tony puke. His guts began to twist and he badly wanted to go and answer the call of nature.

"Does that mean I go with him and you have his signaller Sir?" asked Pinky warily.

"Just bloody wait Watson can't you!?" Shot Tony his voice full of irritation.

"Well I just thought," persisted Pinky, "if you're in charge like, you'll need to be in contact with everyone and my radio's no good for that."

"I know that Watson! For God's sake stop prattling on like some old woman!"

Pinky decided to push him just one more time, he took a breath and said to no-one in particular. "Well, we've got away with it for over four hours now if something's going to happen it's bound to happen on this half."

Tony Orchard swivelled round to tear into Pinky but he had already got up and was walking toward the OC. Tony fought hard to punch back down the anger and fear that had risen up.

"Okay Tony, she's all yours!" shouted David Howells and promptly burrowed through the hedge and disappeared. Pinky gave Tony a big cheesy grin and followed him.

The Dog handlers were crashed out in the ditch. Two yellow Labradors sat on the road panting, their faces took on an enquiring serious look when Tony approached. Tony stopped, looked at two men sprawled on either the side of the road and said brusquely "Right chaps! Let's get a move on then!" The older one that seemed to be the senior of the dog handlers half rose up and squinted at Tony.

"Where's the OC?" he enquired. Tony looked at the man with disgust, he wore a uniform but that's as far as looking like a soldier went, he thought. He took in the man's crumpled and dirty combat jacket, the woollen hat instead of a beret and the non issue high boots that looked like they'd never been cleaned. To top it all, the man hadn't shaved for at least two days.

Trying in vain to keep nastiness out of his voice Tony answered, "Look, the OC is not here and I'm now in charge, it's time to go so let's move it!"

The senior man looked across at his mate who had also risen, he was younger but of a similar scruffy appearance, he spoke to him in a strong Birmingham accent.

"How's your Gringo?"

The younger one patted his dog and replied loudly in a thick Devon accent. "Ee still ain't rested yet Corporal Bassett." The senior man Bassett, turned back to Tony and said in what Tony detected as a surly manner.

"Can't move yet boss, the dogs ain't properly rested like."

"Well, they look perfectly rested to me dammit!" shouted a perplexed Tony.

"Ah! Well they would wouldn't they?" said Bassett calmly, "To an untrained eye like yours that is but they's special dogs ye know, they have special food and special trainin' and they needs the rest."

"Aye that's right Corporal Bassett, they needs the rest." echoed the younger handler.

"And if they don't get the proper rest," continued Bassett "they make mistakes ye know, they miss things like."

"Yeh, they miss things like explosives, don't they Corporal?" said Basset's mate in a half soaked manner.

Tony looked at them for a couple of seconds, he was lost for words, he turned and walked back to the signaller as he did Bassett winked at his mate who grinned.

Tony took the handset off the signaller who asked, "Problem Sir?" Tony shot a glance at the signaller.

"Yes, the damn dogs need more rest. I will let the OC know that there's going to be a delay.." He was interrupted by Bassett whistling and shouting to his dog, he turned and saw that both of them had started to walk on, sending the dogs ahead of them. Tony looked flustered, his mouth hung open.

"You'd better tell everyone that we're off Sir, or else we'll leave them behind." Advised the signaller.

"No! you do it! That's what you're paid for man." snarled Tony.

An hour went by, the road party advanced snail like, yard by yard up the road. Tony stayed well back from the dog teams. The countryside started to open up, there were less bushes and trees and the ground on the Border side of the road rose steeply. The signaller shouted to him and walked up, "It's Sergeant Britton Sir, he has asked us to stop and let them catch up they're having a hard time going through some thick stuff."

"Very well, call a halt," ordered Tony. Damn Britton he thought, trust him to whinge and stop everything, he hoped at least that the OC would re- appear and take charge once more.

Bassett wandered back to Tony, he was rolling a cigarette, when he had stuck the straw thin smoke into his mouth and lit it, he spoke. "It's just as well we stopped, I was going to call a halt anyway."

"Oh! You were, were you?" asked Tony sarcastically.

"Yep!" replied Bassett nonchalantly.

"Don't tell me that the poor little things are tired again."

"No, as it happens, *they* are not tired but I am and my oppo is, so we're going to have a sit down and a smoke for ten minutes."

Basset started to walk back then turned and said, "This next stretch, I want it done extra slowly to let the flank men have plenty of time to clear the ground. We're overlooked from the border from now on and seeing as we can't exactly go over the border and clear any would be firing points and seeing that the bleedin' Garda and Irish Army won't clear it for us we need to search extra careful like. Oh! And yeh, you'll see a change in the colour of the tarmac round the next bend, there's a culvert there, last year they blew a Landrover up and killed three." He turned and walked on.

"Problem Tony?" It was the OC and Pinky. They had returned from the flank and had come up behind him.

"Problem's? No, no, none at all Sir. I decided to call a halt because the flanks are having a hard time and I want the dog handlers rested before this next stretch. According to the map we are going to be overlooked from here on in and the high ground is actually over the border so I was about to tell the flanks to really take their time and carry out an even more thorough search."

"Hmm, well spotted Tony, I was just about to tell you the same thing." said David a smile of approval on his face. Pinky looked at the other signaller who raised his eyes to heaven.

The day ended late with no incident. Every culvert, bridge and every inch of bush, wall and hedgerow on that road had been examined and cleared. They all got back to the Drumboyle Police Station at nine thirty pm to a huge meal of steak, eggs and chips.

This time Frank and a few others found themselves sharing a table with a couple of RUC men, one of which was the man Jamie who had spoken out at the briefing that morning.

He was still venting his feeling as he tore into the meal. "You see, that took what?…Sixty men, nine hours to clear, that's something like five hundred and forty man hours and what for? They could be out tonight laying more bombs in those culverts, the only time a cleared road is safe is if you were to follow the clearance team up in your car. I mean technically speaking that road should be cleared every day if it's to be declared safe at all but no bugger uses it, so why risk our lives clearing it?"

Tony sat with the OC and the Ops officer. He was feeling pleased with himself. David had praised him at the finish of the Op. He spied the two Dog Handlers, thankfully they were just about as far away from him as they could get in the relatively small dining area. "Those dog handlers David," he ventured to the OC, "they seem to know their stuff."

The OC finished chewing a piece of meat and said, "Yes, especially old Brummy Bassett. I believe he is former SAS, got booted out over something or other and opted to go as a dog handler. He's an odd bugger but the best, the very best, we're lucky to have him. The Engineers are always trying to pinch him and take him to the City but he won't have any of it, he's worth listening to if ever he bothers to talk to you."

He continued eating in silence for a while and then spoke again. "Tony, tomorrow afternoon we're going to get a VIP visitor." he looked around and continued, "This is not for publication. It's the General Officer Commanding Northern Ireland, keep it under your hat. Only Alex and I know at this stage and that's the way I want to keep it, right to the last minute. Security apart, I don't want cooks preparing something special and the Sergeant Major getting everything spic and span. I want to show him the base and the soldiers as they really are.. Worn out!" He said the last few words with a wry grin.

"You and your lads are on an Op tomorrow, Alex will fill you in on the details later but it's not too far from here and if you can possibly make it in for say around four thirty, I would like to introduce you to the GOC. It's not absolutely essential, so don't break a leg to get back but seeing a different cap badge here helping us out may beg a question from the General"

Tony agreed immediately and was elated to think that he would be able to meet the General.

As David was leaving the table he said casually, "Oh! I forgot, had a word with your OC Alan Briggs a half hour ago, he sends his best and says that they are just about coping without you!" They laughed. "I told him how well you were doing." he winked and walked away.

Alex, Tony and Frank sat in the Briefing room, there was no-one else present. "There's no need," began Alex, "for me to brief all the platoon, your lads have adjusted quickly and compared with what you've done over the last couple of days, this is small potatoes."

He swung around to the map and pointed to a section near the border. "This area is one of the few pieces of ground that overlooks the border from our side. I want you to patrol that area. Do you see these three roads leading to the South? They are unapproved roads and are used by all sorts of people from Farmer Giles to smugglers and of course now and again the baddies use them. Your mission tomorrow Tony is to stake out these roads and check out the traffic using them. If you find smugglers you can call the RUC. Try to get a feel for the frequency of use for each of the roads, in vehicles per half hour or something.."

"Can they not block these roads off permanently?" enquired Tony.

"Oh! Yes," replied Alex, "they frequently put barriers in but because they are not guarded they are pulled down again. Anyway, if you split your forces you can cut the three roads at the same time or cut two roads and have a sweeping patrol out, it's up to you, you know best…Any questions?"

Both Tony and Frank shook their heads and Alex left. Tony folded his map and made to go, Frank spoke, "Well, how are we going to play it?"

"Play it? What do *you* suggest?" Tony replied without looking at him.

"Well, I think it would be pointless to sit on all three roads all day because everyone who needs to know, *will* know within half an hour that we are there and go somewhere else. I think we should cut a road for half hour only, patrol some more then cut another for half hour and so on."

"No! I don't think so. We may well miss things doing it that way. The platoon will split in two, each will have its own road and area to look after. Some can cut the road, some can rest and some can patrol the area.." said Tony flatly and firmly.

"That's okay but it makes it too unwieldy with all these little patrols moving around..."

"I believe that I just made the plan for tomorrow Sergeant Britton....Goodnight. I will see you at seven sharp ready to move." He left the Briefing room. Frank stood there listening to his footsteps disappearing into the main building, his fists knotted.

Frank and his patrol walked warily through a wooded area. The men were spread out and silent, each man cradling his SLR with backsight flicked up and a round up the spout ready to go. They wore their camouflaged smocks, olive green trousers boots and puttees.

Their belt order consisted of two ammo pouches containing four full magazines for the rifle. Three water bottles and a couple of pouches containing first aid kit and emergency rations for twenty four hours.

The Gunner with the General Purpose Machine Gun (GPMG) universally known as the "Jimpy" carried a small belt of ten rounds on the gun and two pouches full of belted ammunition. His number two carried a Smallpack with more belts, they had quickly learned that carrying them on their body criss crossed like some Mexican bandit didn't work, they caught up on everything, were uncomfortable and could be seen miles away by reflecting the sun.

Frank signalled a halt and his men immediately went to ground facing alternate ways. He signalled for

Norrie to close on him, when Norrie squatted down Frank spoke in a low voice that Norrie could just hear. "I think that the road should be just a couple of fields away now. When we move off I want you to take the Gunner and his number two up to the high ground and dominate the area around us on the road but be careful there may be some other patrols from the platoon in the area." Norrie grunted and moved off.

Frank stood up, automatically everyone followed suit. He moved off out of the wood and made his way down a small tree line that formed the perimeter of a field, he paused and looked back to see if he could see Norrie, he couldn't so he carried on slowly in the direction of the road.

At last, after the second field he cut the road. He signalled a pre arranged manoeuvre and immediately two men came up to him and together they broke through the hedge and went onto the tarmac. Simultaneously two teams of three did the same. One, fifty or so yards to the left and the other the same to the right, these would act as cut offs if an incident occurred in the centre with a vehicle.

They didn't have to wait too long. A battered old Bedford Dormobile came along, they could hear it coming a minute away, barking and coughing its way slowly down the windy road. The cut off sprang out and waived it down, there was a painful metallic screech as worn out brake pads were forced onto hard steel disks which made hardly any change in the speed at all until the man behind the wheel frantically changed down. There was a horrible grinding in the gear box but finally it came to rest by Frank's group.

A squat, swarthy man in his fifty somethings got out, he was scruffy and dirty, a flat cap was pulled well down over his forehead. His brogue was so thick and spoken so quickly that neither Frank or Tommo understood what he was saying, so they got him to open the back doors of the van. Inside it was piled high with pink animal carcasses.

"Pork" said Frank.

Frank insisted that the load was taken off so that a search for something more sinister could take place. The man thought that Frank was confiscating his load and pleaded with him to stop, he even pulled a huge roll of ten and twenty pound notes out of his pocket and offered him a handful of the bills.

When the search was over and they started to load the pork back on, a big smile lit up the man's face and he slapped Frank on the back. Frank could just make out, "You're a lovely fella." As he drove off.

Tony Orchard checked his watch, it was just past noon, he calculated that he would have to start making his way back at about two thirty to get back in time to meet the General. He had chosen the road nearest to Drumboyle for himself. He was bored, he had decided to "sit" on the road all day with Corporal Reece and the rest of his men patrolling the immediate area. There had been no traffic down the road now for the past two hours.

Pinky Watson listened in on the radio to Frank's team. He knew by their messages that they had kept on the move between the two roads allocated to them, just putting in a road block every now and then.

Pinky had got his fill of Orchard. He was by far the worst Platoon Commander he thought, that he'd ever had in his five years in the Regiment. No sense of humour unless of course a person of senior rank cracked a joke, he flapped over the smallest thing and quickly blamed others, but he got away with it every time, it was almost as if someone unseen was looking after him.

Pinky enjoyed baiting him, it was a form of tension release, besides he knew that if he kept it up Orchard would have him replaced as his signaller and that would suit him just fine.

"Sergeant Britton has just stopped and searched his sixth car Sir."

Orchard frowned and opened his mouth to reply but then changed his mind.

After some minutes Tony Orchard stood up and said to Pinky, "I don't like this place, we'll move off up the road. Get Reece on the radio and tell him that my group are moving east on the road!"

"I thought we weren't s'posed to use roads to travel on Sir." stated Pinky.

"I'll tell you what you're supposed to do and what you're not supposed to do Watson, now get that message out at once, at once! Do you hear!"

"Hey Frank! You won't believe this, I've just heard Pinky on the radio to Taff Reece, telling him that they're moving along the road." Norrie said with an exaggerated look of surprise on his face.

"He's probably just moving a short distance." Frank said with some irritation, "Let's worry about ourselves shall we?"

"Oops! Sorry Sergeant Britton, only keeping you informed boss." said Norrie feigning hurt.

Taff Reece was moving along some fields parallel to the road on which Tony Orchard and his group were now using. He was ahead of them by some three hundred yards. He was not happy that Orchard was using the road at all, especially this near to the border.

Suddenly he froze, fumbled for a second with the zip of his smock and pulled out a pair of issue binoculars, he knelt and looked intently at something shiny on the road.

Through the binoculars he saw a car that looked like it was half in the ditch, he could only see part of it. He immediately got on the radio to Orchard and told him to stop. Frank, who had overheard the message told Taff to go a hundred yards ahead of the vehicle and block the road.Frank moved quickly and met up with Orchard who was pacing up and down looking agitated. "Sir I will take most of your men and start to cordon this off, you will need to call out agencies to deal with this.."

"Is that absolutely necessary? It's probably some drunk from last night who swerved into the ditch and then staggered home, if we call out the agencies we could be here all night."

"Maybe you're right sir, but what if you are not and it's a "Come On" ? We can't just leave it and pretend it's not there.." Frank let his words hang and Orchard, his face grim went to the radio and started the ball rolling.

Pinky had removed his radio and walked over to Frank, "You know what the problem is don't you?" he said with a big grin on his face.

"What?" asked a puzzled Frank.

"The GOC is due in the location this afternoon and our man was hoping to meet him, don't look like that will happen now." he chuckled

"How come you know so much?" said Frank.

Pinky tapped his nose, "Signals Mafia, we know everything that's going on."

After an hour during which Frank had put in a cordon and set up an Assembly Point for the agencies to arrive at, a loan Wessex helicopter circled and then dropped onto a nearby field for a few seconds then lifted off again and disappeared.

Brummy Bassett and two soldiers from the Princes Own as an escort came sauntering across the field with his yellow Lab toward the Assembly point where Frank was. He got on the road and started rolling a cigarette, he snapped his zippo lighter open and lit up.

He turned to Frank, "Have you had a close look at it?"

"Yeh, I got to within about twenty five yards, it's a grey Cortina half in the ditch, both doors are closed and there's no sign of anything else."

"Have you checked for wires leading to it?"

"Yes, and we've checked all the dominating ground."

"Good, I'm not being funny like but Bomb Disposal will need all that info when they get here and if it ain't done they don't half get upset. I've seen 'em clear off till the next day, leaving the cordon in all bloody night 'cos it aint been sorted out like." said Brummy.

"I appreciate that Brum. What's the score now?" ventured Frank.

"Well, if you'm sure its not wired I'll take me dog in to see if he indicates so that Disposal will know the full score when they get here, by the way where's that pratt officer of yours?"

Frank bristled slightly, he had his own differences with Orchard but even so someone from the outside had no right to speak like that about him, however, he didn't want to upset any apple carts in a situation like this. "He's at the other side of the car blocking the road."

"Good," said Brum with a wink, "just keep him off my back, he turns the dog funny like." Despite his feelings Frank laughed as Brummie urged his dog toward the car.

Tony Orchard looked at his watch, it was gone four and Bomb Disposal had only just arrived. He felt miserable, his chance to meet the General face to face had gone. He now realised that he should have joined Frank at the Assembly Point, took command and directed operations from there but it was too late now, he just sat in the ditch and festered.

The Major from bomb disposal turned up in his armoured Pig. He strode toward Frank but spotted Brummie. He smiled and spoke warmly, "Hi Brummie,

I know! I owe you a bottle of whisky, I haven't forgotten you bastard!" he turned to Frank still smiling, "This git bet me last time we met, that the stiff lying at the side of the road was a tailor's dummy. Nobody could make it out for sure through the bino's, but what we didn't know is that this bloody cheat had accidentally walked passed the bloody thing having lost his bearings when he got out the Chopper!"

They all laughed and when it subsided the Major went serious. "Sorry Sergeant, I'm Roger Miller and you?"

"Britton sir."

"Okay gents, what have we got here?" he said staring at the ground in concentration. Frank led in with the story from when it was spotted until the Dog Handler had turned up. When he finished Miller turned and asked, "Brummy?"

"Well boss, I took the dog in he went all round it and he didn't indicate anything at all. About ten yards this side of the car is a pile of day old spew, the remnants of a fish supper. My bet is a drunk crashed it into a ditch then legged it home, the plates will probably tell us it's a local."

"Yes, you're right in that respect. It belongs to a guy about three miles down the road but the RUC say there's nobody home so I'm going to have to clear it." As he spoke his assistant came up to them with a pump action shotgun. Miller spoke again, "Load it with two solid shot and one SSG, Ill try to get in through the rear window, what will be facing me Brum?"

"The boot."

"Good then the rear window *it is*. Prepare me a charge." he said, then with Brummy he went casually forward until he rounded the gentle curve and saw the rear of the car about thirty yards away.

He pumped the mechanism of the gun back and forth to load it, he looked at Brummy, "Ill bet you that bottle I owe you, that I smash the back window and open the boot at the same time."

"No bet! At this distance I could do it with a pea shooter." declared Brummie.

"Spoilsport." said Miller. He knelt and fired three shots in as many seconds, the window smashed but the boot stayed closed. "See, you could have had another bottle Brum my old son." Just then there was a metallic yawn and the boot opened slowly. Brummie looked smug and they both laughed.

Roger Miller walked forward to the car with the charge, behind him his assistant payed out the wire from a drum. He had a cursory look in the boot and through the windows, dropped the charge in and came back. "Warn everyone we'll be blowing in twenty seconds." he said looking at his watch.

Just then another of his team came up and said, "They've just located the owner Boss, he's on his way with the RUC."

"Hit it!" shouted Miller to his assistant. There was a dull "Wump" as the small explosive blew.

"What did you say?" he enquired.

The explosive had blown open all the doors and knocked out the windows. Miller took one last look at it and declared it safe. He shook Brummy's and Frank's hand and departed in his fleet of Pigs. "Now, *that's* a brave man, Frank." stated Brummy.

Frank turned and clapped Brummy on the shoulder, "Coming from you, that's praise indeed."

16

"What did I tell you?! ranted Orchard, "Some bloody drunken Irish bum gets his car in a ditch and we over react and get delayed for hours! I'm telling you, had we ignored it the owner would have driven it away by the time we had got back to base, but no! We had to do it your way didn't we?" Orchard was raving at Frank in the relative privacy of the briefing room.

"I just don't believe you sir!" snapped back Frank with undisguised disgust. "If you adopt that attitude, you're going to come unstuck sooner or later, you just can't take the risk!.. "

"You made us look bloody fools, we could have called in that registration number and went and got that guy ourselves." snarled Orchard.

"Its fucking SOPs Sir! Standard Operating Procedures, that's what we carried out! I mean, what is *really* the matter?" said Frank viciously, he was coming to the end of his tether. "We missed meeting the General did we? Wow! Holy shit! *I* won't be able to sleep tonight will you!?"

"I've had it with you Britton, when we get back I.." Orchard stopped in his tracks as the door opened and David Howells came in, he was beaming.

"Ah! Here you are! Tony, Sergeant Britton. Well done, very well done today! Your timing couldn't have been better. The General arrived early and I'd just finished telling him how over worked we were down here when your report about the car came in. It all dovetailed in nicely, nearly came out to you with him but he had to move on. Well, I said everything I wanted to say to him and I think I hit home. I'm pleased, I will probably be demoted and end up as an assistant dog handler to Brummy tomorrow, but right now I'm pleased! Very well done!"

Tony grinned at David, he instinctively knew that David liked him. Frank excused himself. When he had gone David said quietly to Tony. "Come on, I'll stand you a drink."

They both walked into the main building of the Police Station where David and Alex each had a room. There was a tiny canteen that Tony was unaware of, it was for police use only and off limits to the troops but David had an open invitation and at times took advantage of it.

They walked in and found two of the RUC officers relaxing in armchairs watching a portable TV. One of them got up. "Good evening Major! Was the General pleased today?"

"Yes Roy I think he was and I'll have a large Bushmills if I may and Tony?" Enquired David.

"Oh! Err.. A large Bushmills for me too please." he said without really knowing what he was ordering. Tony was not a drinker but he did not want to spoil the OC's good mood. The OC gestured to the two RUC and they nodded and accepted a drink.

They stood together and David offered: "Good health gentlemen!" He took a good swig and the rest followed suit. The whisky scalded its way down Tony's gullet and he gave an involuntary shudder but no-one seemed to notice.

Roy the RUC man then said, "Well, come on lads bottoms up! The next one's on me. I'm a Grandad for the first time today!"

"Congratulations Roy," laughed the Major. "I've got that pleasure to come."

"What are we celebrating like?" asked a broad Birmingham accent. They turned as Brummy still in his combat jacket and dirty boots swaggered in. He'd had a shave but had left long sideboards. He had a lopsided smile on his face.

Tony stared, he wondered what the reaction would be to this scruffy misfit barging his way into the company.

The OC was the first to speak. "Ah! Brummy you're just in time, Roy's a Grandpa and the Bush's are on him!"

"What about ye Brum?" smiled Roy.

Brum smiled back then let his eyes rest on Tony for a couple of seconds before turning and speaking to the OC. He spoke in a relaxed manner as if they were old friends, his arms folded across his chest. Tony bristled, it was beyond his comprehension. This damn scruffy misfit just inviting himself in the company like that! His chain of thought was broken by another large glass of whisky being pushed onto him.

"To Roy being a Grandad and may he be one many times over!" toasted a jubilant David, they all drained their glasses except for Tony who gingerly sipped at his glass.

Suddenly he was aware that Brummie was staring intently at him before saying, "Now come on Lieutenant Orchard Sir! It's a toast and celebration! Bottoms up!"

"Oh! Quite." said Tony and swallowed it all at once, again he shuddered and this time some of the liquid was forced up into the back of his nose, he started retching and coughing much to the delight of the small audience.

"Sorry, went down the wrong way." he managed to rasp out, which made them laugh even heartier.

"Bloody hell Frank!" said Norrie in genuine amazement, "Never thought I'd see the day when you smoked!"

Frank held the glowing butt up as if to inspect it then dropped it and crushed it out. He gave a sort of half embarrassed look and turned to go but Norrie pulled his arm. "What's up mate?" he asked, a serious look on his face.

"Nothing.. nothing at all." murmured Frank without looking at him. He broke his hold by walking off toward the vehicle park.

Norrie watched him go, Taff Reece came to his side and enquired, "What's up with him then?"

"Dunno," replied Norrie, "but you can bet it's that wanker Orchard. I tell you Taff, for two pins I'd punch that bastard's lights out, he's bought us nowt but trouble since he's bin here."

Frank sat in the shadows of the vehicle park, he watched and listened to the hum of conversations coming from the several different groups that had gathered for a chat before turning in for the night.

He felt alone and vulnerable which was alien to him. He was beginning to lose confidence in himself. Every time he had made a decision or took a course of action it had come into conflict with Orchard. Well maybe just maybe he thought, the man might be right. Take the car today for instance he thought, the old sweats from the Princes Own who had been here a couple of months would probably have left it for twenty four hours and then dealt with it if necessary.

He thought about all the conflicts and arguments that had taken place over the last two months between them. He hadn't smoked for ten years and these first few cigarettes were keeping his mind extra alert. His thoughts kept coming back to the same conclusion, that he was letting his personal feelings for Orchard cloud his judgement.

"You know the trouble with yow? Mister Orchard, *Old Boy.*" slurred Brummie, "Yow are one of these arrogant prats that need to stand on people to reach whatever you're reaching for. You're a stuck up bastard, the reason I'm 'ere is because I laid a bastard like you out once and maybe if I did it again they'd get me outa this shithole, Mister fuckin' Orchard old boy." They were still in the Police Mess, music was playing and a couple of more RUC officers and Alex the Ops officer had joined them.

Tony had been singled out by Brummie who now had him cornered. The whisky had gripped Tony and he felt disorientated but at the same time he felt good.

All he was aware of was this scruffy peasant in front of him who thought he could break all the rules and get away with it. "Now you listen here Bassett," he spat, "You don't speak to me like that for a start! Just who the hell do you think you are? Speaking to people like that. I'll have you on a charge tomorrow for gross insubordination and threatening behaviour"

"Hah!" exclaimed Brummie a sarcastic smirk on his face. "That's the way all you wankers act ain't it? Can't stand on your own two feet, got to hide behind army rules and regulations. How *do you* fuckers survive? I mean, do you fancy coming outside like and settling it? " He looked Tony up and down made a dismissive gesture with his hands and walked away.

Tony's temper got the better of him and he tried to close with Brummie who was now talking to an RUC man but the OC grabbed him, "Tony meet Inspector Ryan. Barry this is Tony Orchid…Sorry, Orchard, damn this fire water!" he babbled

"Good to meet you Son." said Ryan as a tray of Bushmills was bought to the group. Ryan grabbed two and gave one to Tony, "Here's knowing you son." he said and tipped the glass back, Tony followedsuit. The liquid flowed down his throat as easily as warm milk.

Tony was aware that someone was trying to wake him up but he incorporated the sound of the voice into a dream he was having. He was wading through an evil smelling swamp trying to find a bank to crawl up to dry land. The voice kept saying loudly "Come on! Wake up!"

he opened his mouth to tell them to shut up but as he did so a slimy green frog jumped into it.

Tony sat bolt upright and vomited over himself. He was still in his uniform boots and all. After another heave he became aware that Pinky Watson was at the end of his bed saying. "Come on Sir! The Chopper will be here in five minutes!"

Tony struggled hard to clear his thumping head, he had a raging thirst and his guts felt terrible.

"Just get out! Get out!" he yelled then flopped back on the bed. He tried hard to piece together the remains of the night, he remembered arguing with Bassett and trying to make conversation with the Inspector and the OC then sitting in an armchair unable to move and someone trying to pass another whisky on to him. That last thought made him retch a couple of times but had the effect of getting him off his bed and stumbling to the toilet.

He looked down at himself, he was covered in revolting slime. He unclipped the shower nozzle and sprayed himself down while gulping water straight from it.

"I called him again but he fucked me off Sarge!" said Pinky "He's ill, looks like food poisoning or something."

"I'll bet it was those greasy fackin' chops we 'ad last night." Threw in Ronnie Gittins, "Turned my guts an' all."

"Pissed, more like." added Norrie.

"Okay, If he doesn't make it there's no problem, just a little adjustment but the plan is still the same.

They were at the side of the Chopper Pad waiting to be lifted out. There was to be a search carried out by the Princes Own on a deserted farm complex. Tony's platoon were to put in the outer cordon to control anyone entering or leaving the scene of the search, a simple enough job that was designed to give the lads a little break after their last few hectic days.

The Choppers would drop them a mile or so from the target, they would advance to within a couple of hundred yards of it, split into two groups and encircle the farm from opposite directions.

The lads were crouched by their heavy Bergin Rucksacks in stick order ready to mount the choppers when they appeared. Suddenly heads turned as the Lieutenant walked toward the Pad. His face was white and ghastly and his step uneven.

Frank walked to him and said quietly, "Leave this one out sir, we can manage okay."

"I'll be okay Sergeant Britton just don't make a drama out of this.. Okay?"

Frank studied him for a second then motioned him to his stick where he flopped down.

They were dropped off in the middle of a large green pasture, three choppers landing simultaneously. Ducking low, the sticks ran to the cover of the nearest hedgerow.

The drone of the Choppers faded, Frank checked his compass heading and then signalled the Platoon to move off. Lieutenant Orchard stayed near the rear of the two columns and said nothing.

After a half hour Frank called a halt, he could see the farm complex in the distance, now they had to split, he would move around to the left with his group and the Lieutenant to the right with his.

He called the Lieutenant forward and he arrived some minutes later still looking pale and ill. Frank decided to make no comment and simply said, "This is it sir, move off to the right and I'll see you the other side." Orchard nodded and Frank led his column off.

Orchard turned to Pinky and said, "Pass the word back, we stay put for ten minutes." He reached for his water bottle and took a long swig. Cold sweat oozed out of every pore in his body, he lay his thumping head on his rifle and closed his eyes.

Frank worked his way around the farm which was about three hundred yards away, when they crossed a track leading to it he dropped off two men to control it, likewise with the metalled road that led to the farm itself. When he reached what he judged to be half way around he stopped and kept watch for the Lieutenant coming in.

Taff Reece made his way to where Lieutenant Orchard lay. He shook his shoulder and said, "Sir, we been here now for twenty five minutes do you think we should move?"

Orchard lifted his head, a trail of spittle connected his face to the butt of his rifle like a silver cord. He looked around him then wiped his face, he tried hard to gather his thoughts, "Where's Sergeant Britton?" he demanded.

"He's long gone Sir, he's probably in position by now." stated Reece matter of factly.

"Okay Corporal get back to your position, we'll be moving off shortly.. By the way which way did Britton go?" he asked.

"He went to the left Sir." said Reece and gave Pinky a meaningful glance.

Lieutenant Orchard led his men around the farm but became a little disorientated in some thick young birches, Taff made his way up to him, "Sir! We've cut in too close to the farm, we need to push out a bit more." he said forcefully.

Orchard snarled back, "I bloody well know that Corporal, now do me a great favour and stay with the rear section where you're supposed to be!" Taff nodded and made his way back.

Tony took another swig from his water bottle and emptied it trying to slake his raging thirst and clear the clag out of his mouth. That was his second and last bottle. He ploughed on until he came out of the birch grove. About twenty five yards away there was a small brick building with a sloping tiled roof, the door was hanging open by one hinge, outside was a stone trough with a water tap.

Orchard called a halt, he hadn't expected to see any building on his way around, his immediate thought was that it would make a good temporary HQ for the cordon, especially if that water tap worked.

Taff Reece went as near to the front as he dared, he did not want to incur the wrath of the Lieutenant any more that morning. He saw the building and said to Tommo, "Oh no! He's cut in that much that he's hit the outskirts of the farm complex! At this rate we'll get mixed up with the search teams when they come in."

"You'd better tell him Taff," said Tommo.

"Not fucking likely baby! Get my bloody 'ead bitten off again, he's got the pips on his shoulder let him work it out!"

The more Tony thought about the idea the more he liked it. "Okay Watson, we'll move to that building and set up in there, Reece can take the rest of them and meet up with Britton, come on!"

Tommo surveyed the scene his jaw started to drop, he turned and shouted urgently, "Hey Taff! Have you seen this? They're moving toward that outhouse! It hasn't been cleared for God's sake!"

Taff returned to Tommo and stared in stark disbelief of what he saw, "Oh! Fuckin' Jeez!" he exclaimed and started to run toward them.

Orchard got to the outskirts of the building first and went straight to the water tap while Pinky went past him to the building. Orchard tried the tap, it squeaked as he turned it but no water came out, he groaned as he did so he heard shouting from across the field and saw Corporal Reece running toward them waiving and yelling at the top of his voice, then he heard Pinky shout excitedly, "Sir, there's a rifle in here on the table!"

The crack of the explosion jolted Frank, it seem to come from the left of the farm, he had heard some yelling before but couldn't decipher it. The immediate silence after the explosion was followed by blood curdling screams. Without a word he sprang up and ran at high speed toward the noise.

Through two fields he ran, he could now see the black smoke rising above the trees. The screaming had been replaced with agonising shouts. He ran into the scene, a small brick building with no roof and one side blown away, some timbers were still smouldering in it. Taff Reece and Tommo were huddled over something just outside of the building.

Taff saw Frank coming and stood up, his mouth was open and his eyes staring, "Frank man! Frank man!" he yelled, "They've got 'im, they've got 'im! The bastards have got him! That bastard Orchard walked right up to the building! The crazy bastard!"

Frank pushed passed him and saw the blackened body lying there still propped up by the radio on his back, an arm plus half the shoulder was missing and one side of the head too had vanished leaving a grey ooze.

"Pinky,! Pinky!" screamed Tommo.

Frank looked around, he grabbed Taff and shook him, "Where is he?" he shouted, Taff looked at him trying to come round and answer, "Where the fuck is he? Where's Orchard?!"

Taff gestured toward the smoking building but Frank shook his head and shouted, "No, he won't be in there, not him but I'll find him!"

He didn't have far to look, under a tree some yards away sat Orchard. He sat with his back against the trunk his knees drawn up to his chin and his arms clasped firmly around them.

"Get up! Fucking get up you bastard!" He ran toward Orchard and lashed his foot out at his shins. Orchard rolled and cowered away but Frank grabbed him and dragged him toward the remains of Pinky. When he realised what Frank was doing he screamed and tried to break himself loose.

Frank kicked the legs from under him and dragged him the last few yards until Orchard's face was inches from the smouldering torso. "You'll no doubt walk away from this you scum!" raged Frank, "But you'll never walk away from the sight and smell of this moment." With that he leapt onto Orchard and started to throttle him with one hand and batter his head like a hammer with the other.

17

Alan Briggs sat in his office looking at the parade ground beneath his window. There were a group of soldiers in line listening to some words of wisdom from the RSM who stood stiffly to attention in front of them, his Pace Stick under his arm and exactly parallel to the ground.

In the outer office he could hear the Company Clerk bashing away on the typewriter, a chair scraped in the office next door and Reg Wallace came in, a sheaf of papers in his hand,

"Can't get over it Sir! First day back off leave and no absentees, unbelievable!"

"Come in Sergeant Major and please shut the door." said Alan who immediately started fishing in the draw for his pipe but eventually found it next to the telephone, he gave it a few dry sucks and motioned the CSM to a chair. Reg knew this routine well, there was something serious he wanted to say.

"Sarn't Major, I spoke with the CO yesterday, he had a small welcome back to work meeting in the mess with the company commanders." Alan paused and looked once more out of his window, the RSM was now barking orders and the squad in front of him carried out rifle drill with sharp crisp movements.

"Britton will not face a Court Martial it seems. The Department of Army Legal Services seem to think that

Lieutenant Orchard's evidence alone will not be sufficient. He was in shock for a far greater period than anyone thought and his memory about the incident is somewhat flaky. We *do* know that Britton probably lost complete control of himself and attacked him but we have no witnesses to that. He turned a tragedy into an embarrassing shambles." Alan spoke quietly with no vindictiveness.

Reg remained silent, he had heard on the grapevine about the growing conflict between the two men that had come to a head in that field a couple of hundred miles away beside the remains of Watson. When the search force had eventually got there they had found Corporal Reece in charge, Orchard was sitting under a tree silent and Britton in the bombed out building guarded by Lance Corporal Norris, who at first would let no-one near him.

When Orchard eventually talked Frank was put under bunk arrest. No-one came forward to say that they had witnessed any assault on Orchard, even under the Gestapo like interrogation of Staff Sergeant Stokes SIB.

The fact that Orchard had been in close proximity of the blast had earned him a great deal of sympathy, his lack of command and control after the event was understood.

The death of Pinky Watson shrouded everything. No-one quite knew what had happened. Tony Orchard stated that he could remember seeing the outhouse and realising he was too close to the farm moved away and that Pinky somehow had drifted toward the house and had seen a weapon on a table inside, unable to stop him in time, Pinky had entered and triggered a booby trap.

Only part of the bomb had gone off, which was the initiating charge consisting of a couple of pounds of plastic high explosive designed to set off a couple of hundred pounds of home made low explosive. It had failed to do so, if it had detonated the blast would have taken casualties over a wide area, as it was the relatively small charge was enough to get Pinky.

Corporal Reece and Tommo did not give evidence saying that they saw Orchard leading Pinky to the house, had they done so they reasoned, they would have to say that they saw Frank attack the Lieutenant. They had discussed it and decided that getting Frank off the hook was more important than trying to nail Orchard whom they thought would surely walk away from any charge. After all he was an officer and he was going to get a gong wasn't he?

"Am I right in thinking sir, that Britton was to be kept on leave until this is sorted out?" enquired Reg.

"Yes, that was the general idea, it's all such a bloody wicked shame." said a subdued Alan staring through his desk.

"A rising star like Britton who surely would have been RSM one day, high grades on all his courses and then.." Alan threw up his arms, "And God knows how young Orchard is going to come out of all this. The CO has extended his leave for a few weeks to ensure that he fully recovers. I visited him on leave, he still had one of those surgical collars on and his voice was shaky but what a fighter, he was all smiles and begged me to see the CO and ask if he could return off leave with everyone else." Alan shook his head. "And let's not forget Watson's poor parents, their only son chopped down like that. You know I couldn't look them in the eyes Sarn't Major."

There was perhaps ten seconds of silence, the shouts from the RSM on the square got louder as he marched his squad under Alan's window.

"Sir?" ventured Reg. "About Sergeant Britton, if he's not being Court Martialled, what is going to happen to him? I mean they can't keep him on leave indefinitely can they?"

"That's what I was coming to."

"Sorry Sir, I didn't.."

"No! No! Sarn't Major my fault I was drifting off the subject as usual," smiled Alan who sat up in his chair. "Britton comes to the end of six years service soon, if he was to transfer out to some other Regiment or indeed leave the Army it would solve a problem. You see the Old Man wanted to post him to our other Battalion but they won't have him, the CO is an old protege of Tony's father and feels that it would be both unfair to Britton and himself. Our CO is determined not to have him back either and there lies the problem, a simple posting to the TA or some other organisation would result in the same problem popping up a couple of years later and they.. That is the Regimental Colonel wants it solving now."

"I see." said Reg who was still confused.

"CSM, I hold no bad feelings toward Britton and that's the truth. Seeing people you are responsible for blown to bits has strange effects on people. I'll pull no punches, go and see him, tell him that if he wants to avoid a Court Martial he needs to terminate his service with the Army now!"

"But I thought he wasn't being Court Martialled anyway!" stated a puzzled Reg.

"He doesn't need to know that CSM! Look, what's the alternative? The old man will sack the bugger! I know Britton well enough to know that, that will finish him, the pain and humiliation…. But if he terminates of his own free will, he will retain his dignity, his red book will be signed 'Exemplary' .. "

"I'll see what I can do sir." said Reg grimly.

One month later on a Friday afternoon in the deserted camp lines when everyone had long since disappeared on a Long Weekend the Commanding Officer with the aid of just the Adjutant and RSM held two interviews.

At ten thirty exactly the RSM ushered Frank passed the Adjutant into the CO's office. He wore his best uniform with medals and boots bulled until they looked like black glass. The Commanding Officer wore a tweed suit complete with a flat cap that lay on his desk, an English Pointer lay in the corner panting.

Frank came to attention, the RSM announced him and stood in the back ground. Harper stared at the desk for a few seconds and then up at Frank.

"It gives me no pleasure to accept the termination of your contract. May you prosper in your next employment. Thank you for your past good service..... RSM!"

The RSM marched Frank out. In the corridor he offered his hand, "Good luck Frank." He said quietly.

"Luck? What's that? There's a coffin in the military cemetery half full of sand bags to keep what's left of Pinky company and the tosser that allowed it to happen is about to be rewarded for it."

Frank broke his stare and looked down. "Sorry, you're a decent man. Thanks and goodbye." He said and walked off. The RSM watched him receding quickly down the corridor and saw him fling something at the wall, he walked over and picked up a row of gleaming medals.

At twelve thirty exactly, a smiling Adjutant ushered Tony Orchard into the CO's office. He had on his "City" pinstriped suit, a crepe bandage around his neck. Harper let out a delighted "Tony!" And came from around his desk to shake his hand. "Sit down my boy, can you talk?"

"Just a little at a time Sir." he croaked, a big smile on his face.

"Well I'll cut to the quick Tony, I've just had notification, you are to receive the award of "Mentioned in Despatches" You will have an oak leaf to wear on your medal ribbon!"

There was a 'Pop' behind them and the Adjutant came in with a bottle of Dom Perignon. "The Brigadier will be down in a minute, so let's steal a march on him and I've a feeling that there are a few more bottles on ice in his mess!"

They all clinked glasses, "The Regiment!" They chorused.

KARUDA

1

The Dakota started losing height slowly, gently leaning to port. Paul Van Der Borg sat back against the fuselage sandwiched between two young men. One of them a lad of around twenty with hair shaved down to the skull had talked incessantly since the beginning of the journey a couple of hours before. He had tried to engage Paul in conversation and when he got no response talked across him to a similarly aged youth the other side who just gave a series of grunts as a reply every now and then.

Paul's eyes were shut but his brain was active. He had blanked out the drone from Shaven head and his thoughts drifted back over the events of the last couple of days. An observer would have noted that every so often a subtle expression slowly taking over his normally expressionless features, a slight snarl, the jaw jutting and hardening followed by the small glimmer of a smile. He thought about his arrival in Rhodesia and the rendezvous at the Hotel in Salisbury.

Paul pushed his way to the bar of the hotel. It was packed with men and women in various forms of camouflaged uniforms. It was loud and sweaty, a great deal of laughter came from the different groups that made up the crowd. "Beer!" he shouted to the black barman and a few seconds later a large frosty glass of golden liquid was pushed in front of him, he threw a note on the bar and waved the change away. He took a huge swig and waited a few seconds before slowly wiping the froth from his lips.

Paul made his way back through the crowd and into a large sitting room with smaller groups and couples also in uniform talking in a relatively quiet manner. Jordie had said that he would meet him at the hotel at eight pm, so he would work his way around the several bars in the hotel until he found him.

Jordie Jonsen lit up another cigarette, he was nervous and felt like knocking back his drink and leaving. He should never have agreed to meet him in the first place. What was Paul Maas doing here in Rhodesia? And how did he get to know that he was now serving with their army? Just phoning him at the camp like that and asking for him by his *new* name, speaking to him as if he was an old friend he had last spoken to the day before. Jordie had been on duty and couldn't spare any time with him so they'd agreed to meet that night at the Hotel. *My name is now Van Der Borgh. Keep quiet about seeing me.* Paul had said as he put down the phone.

He had last seen Paul when they were in the South African Army together, they had become close, too close. Jordie closed his eyes and blanked it out. He looked at his watch again it was three minutes past eight, if he didn't show up by five past he would go.

He looked up at the doorway and felt a grip of fear and uncertainty in his gut. There stood Paul. He looked different, had put on a few pounds without looking overweight, his moustache had gone and his head was cleanly shaved and tanned. He had on neatly pressed green jungle fatigues with high boots and stood in that way of his, legs apart, head slightly lowered, cold and menacing.

Their eyes met and Jordie put on a smile, "Hey man! Damn good to see you, sorry I couldn't talk to you for longer today but you know how it is!" He pinched the material of his uniform, "Fucking armies they're the same all over!" He laughed without conviction. "And talking of armies, the last I heard was that you were in the Brit Army." They shook hands warmly. He looked questioningly at Paul as he ushered him back to his seat.

Paul checked the surrounding area, apart from a couple that were wrapped up with each other there was no-one within earshot of normal talk. "Keep it down my friend," said Paul evenly with a smile on his face. "you could say I am here incognito eh!" He tapped his nose and laughed out loud. Jordie joined in and when the laughter died away sat nervously waiting.

Paul took a swig and finished his beer, a passing waiter stopped by the table, Paul looked at Jordie, "A drink?"

"No man, look I've gotta be out of here…"

"Duty perhaps." offered Paul with a smile and a hint of sarcasm, he turned to the waiter, "Just one beer."

"That's some uniform, what are you in?" Enquired Paul.

"RLI…Rhodesian Light Infantry, it's full of foreigners, Brits mostly…" he tapered off and waited for Paul to get to his point.

"We go back a space eh? Me and you," Sighed Paul, "Remember that time in Jo'burg, hey? By God we were lucky to get out of that one….You were a damn good back up Jordie and that's no bullshit man, I still owe you a big one for that."

"Yeh Paul they were the days, yeh! We were damn lucky," Jordie said enthusiastically, he wondered if Paul was still carrying the knife. "But things are different now, I got out of all that shit and started again here… Hey! And married with kids!" Jordie immediately regretted releasing that information.

"And a Sergeant to boot, I see." Beamed Paul nodding toward the chevrons on his arm.

"Yeh, they pin them on any bastard these days… As you can see!" He laughed. Paul didn't, he just stared at Jordie. He opened his mouth to speak but the waiter came up and placed a beer in front of him. Jordie dug in one of his pockets and gave a note to the waiter.

When he had gone Paul spoke low to Jordie.

"Jordie…This is not my town, it's good in one way because people don't know me but the fact is you are the only guy I can trust here. Yeh, I know there are others but they are shit. I need your help to get established here. I managed to get in the country alright but my passport is shaky, it won't stand up to too much inspection…."

"But if you got through Passport Control here surely to God Paul….."

"I didn't come through any Passport control anywhere Jordie." Paul took a sip of beer and sat back in his seat as if breaking the conversation off. Jordie's stomach started doing cartwheels. He now wished he had ordered a large scotch.

"I need to be legit in this country." Paul continued, "A passport for a start, preferably Brit and then an *in,* into the Army, it's the only thing I know. Don't worry I won't crowd you I'll go into the RAR or something else. You can fix things, you work in headquarters in charge of administration don't you? This is just an administrative problem, simple to a guy like you."

Jordie found himself nodding in agreement. He knew from old that when Paul was in a corner he was deadly, an argument at this stage would be useless and dangerous, he would just have to play for time.

"Jordie I have enough funds for about three weeks, a month at a stretch, how long do you need to fix things?"

"It's not as simple as you've made it sound Paul but it can be done. I have access to passports at the Depot, that's a start. I might have to get in touch with one of the old firm down South to fine tune one for you and it *will* cost. Give me ten days for a start. I should be well on the way to sorting it by then. Oh! And I'll need a photo."

"Married eh?" smiled Paul as he removed a small square snapshot of himself from his wallet and flicked it across the table.

The sudden change of tack startled Jordie. "Yeh! What about that eh?" He said woodenly.

"She's a pretty girl"

"She's gorgeous mate.... Look, about the Passport Paul...."

"You live on Fifth and Jacaranda, a lovely district. You've made it Jordie, well done."

Before Jordie could reply there was a commotion at the entrance to the lounge some of the rowdier crowd from the bar came in laughing and shouting. A big man in the group with a flattened nose and half an ear missing looked over at Paul and Jordie, a smile split his face and he came over to Jordie. "Hey Colin you old drop out, Missus let you off the leash?" he turned to Paul and Jordie spoke up quickly and awkwardly.

"Hey Tom meet er...Paul he's a buddy passing through, just bumped into him, he's a ..Just passing through like I said." Paul stood up and nodded to Tom.

"Great!" said Tom, "Come on, bring your beer." Before he could say anything Paul found himself being pushed to the small bar followed by Jordie and the rest of the crowd.

"Beers all round!" shouted Tom to the Asian barman.

"Sorry Sir, waiter service only in this lounge, sorry but if you sit down......"

"Set those fucking beers up on the bar now you fucking tar brush or I'll rip your fucking throat out!" roared Tom much to the delight of his comrades. Paul turned to Jordie and using the noise as cover said, "I am at the Oasis Hotel room 113 keep me informed on your progress. Just leave a note at the desk for Kruyer, I am relying on you Jordie, or should I call you Colin now?"

Tom clamped a mit around Paul's shoulder and said, "Are you joining us? The outfit I mean."

Paul reluctantly answered, "No man, I'm moving on..."

"Are you part of that lot going to Karuda?" He asked

"Karuda? What's going on there?" asked Paul.

"Oh! It's in shit street since the Brits pulled out a few years ago. The rebels were just about to oust old M'Punga when he started hiring mercenaries. There's a bunch of 'em in the bar next door flying out there tomorrow morning. Sorry looking bunch, no offence but I thought you might be one of them, you are a Brit aren't you?"

"Er, yeh that's right." He was glad that Tom thought so, he had disciplined himself to talk with a British accent since arriving. He looked around for Jordie but he had gone.

Jordie stopped in the shadows some way from the hotel he was not sure whether Paul would come out looking for him. He lit up and took a deep drag. He thought that he had seen the last of Paul a few years ago when he absconded from the Army in South Africa after knifing a fellow soldier to death. Paul had been a suspect for weeks but ran only just before they came for him. With Paul out of the way the others had set on him, beat him, humiliated him, until he too ran. He closed his eyes to blank it out.

Now the cycle would start again, no matter what he did for Paul he would always be there, a menace, a threat. He thought of his wife and children. Paul had made it known to him that he knew of his address and the way he had spoken of his wife and had said, "She's Pretty" as a statement and not a question meant that he'd been close. The bastard, it won't happen again. Jordie gritted his teeth and strode off.

Van Der Borg eased his way into the company of the would be mercenaries, mostly young lads but some older who looked like they'd had military experience. He had scanned each one of them from a distance to ensure that there was no one that he knew. They were drunk and their high spirits would soon turn to loutish behaviour he thought. He had seen a man in his thirties sitting at the edge of the group smoking a pipe, he looked mature and sensible unlike most of the rest. Paul sidled up to him.

After a few moments Paul ventured, "Are you all going to Karuda tomorrow?"

The man looked around in surprise and saw Paul's smiling face, he removed the pipe and cleared his throat.

"Yes, as a matter of fact we fly out tomorrow, who are.."

"Sorry man, shit, my name is Paul, I was interested in joining you guys."

"Good to meet you, I'm Seb, are you from England?"

The two talked for about half an hour and Paul had gently pumped him for all the information he could get. After standing him a few beers and spirit chasers he found out that Seb had been in an Engineer unit in the British Army for around ten years. He had caught his wife one night with his best mate and had gone off the rails going absent from his unit for months. When he had come to his senses and tried to put things right they had thrown him in Colchester Military prison for four months.

When he had got out he had no wife no home or job and after some time had been "recruited" by some ex army man he had bumped into to join the Karuda National Army as an adviser. After a couple of weeks he had found himself being flown to Rhodesia. They had been waiting for three days in this hotel for the flight to Karuda and now it was to be in the morning from an old military strip an hour north of the City. They had to be outside the hotel at six sharp ready to go.

Paul suspected that as well as his other problems he was probably an alcoholic, still he seemed honest and sincere enough, if a little morose. Seb had been appointed "senior" of the group and was made responsible to get them from A to B. The aircraft, he told Paul, was full, there was no room for anyone else.

Paul stored the information. If anything went wrong in the plan with Jordie, Karuda could be an alternative, it was about two hours flight away. The only problem was Seb did not know of any contacts in Salisbury for the recruiting agency. His instructions came by phone through the hotel from a guy calling himself "The Major," who did not leave any contact numbers. So if things turned sour for him he had no contacts at all to get out to Karuda.

He made Seb promise to write to him via the hotel within the next week or two to pass on any information regarding recruitment for the KNA. Paul was not hopeful that Seb would remember in the morning, still, was all he could do for now.

They were interrupted by some aggressive shouting, one of Seb's crew, a youth with a Scottish accent was arguing with a couple of Rhodesians in uniform. He was backed up by a lad with a skin head haircut who held a bar stool like a club. A bottle was smashed against the bar by one of the soldiers who then stood there threatening them with the jagged green shards.

"Time to go Seb, see you…And don't forget to keep in touch, eh?" He got up and walked out as the bar stool was thrown.

Jordie lay awake his wife Serena gently snoring beside him. He thought about her and the two little ones. How well he was thought of now, his good lifestyle and social connections. Serena's father was a Judge with wealth and influence who doted on his only child. When he finished with the army at the end of the year he would be set up for life.

The knot of fear and apprehension grew in Jordie's stomach. What if they found out about his former life? Not only the crimes but what he had become, the things Paul had made him do. Tears welled up and trickled down his cheeks and the knot tightened in his stomach until he could bear it no longer. He slipped the sheet back and padded downstairs to the telephone, he lifted it and dialled a number, a voice answered "Police."

Jordie spoke like a machine.

"I wish to report that a man is staying in this country without a valid passport and is wanted for at least two murders in South Africa. He is stopping at the Oasis Hotel and is armed and desperate." Jordie continued to talk to the officer for another two minutes giving as much detail as possible. He refused to give his name and replaced the phone in the cradle. The knot in his stomach was still there. He reached into a draw and took out a Star 9mm semi automatic pistol , he slid out the magazine, checked it and gently clicked it back into place, he carried it upstairs and placed it under his pillow.

Paul made his way back to his hotel, he had drank more than he intended but he could afford to lie in for a change, there was not much he could do now except wait.

Paul could not sleep, he lay there staring at the ceiling and all he could see was Jordie Jonsen, or as he called himself now, Colin Johnson. He congratulated himself again for keeping tabs on him, it was not all that hard he knew lots of people on the African Continent who were glad to pass on gossip and information.

Things had not gone well in the meeting with Jordie. Yes, he had smiled and promised a lot but not with the fire and conviction of the old days. Jordie had moved on and was settled. He had seen the nervousness in him. Now all I pose is a threat to all that, concluded Paul. He swung his legs out of the bed, drank some water and checked his watch, it was just after 4 am. He heard a noise in the corridor outside, swiftly ran and pressed his ear against the door. He could hear some muffled voices and the jangling of keys it seemed like next door.

He immediately got dressed and was just putting on his boots when all hell broke loose, voices were yelling and a woman was screaming. He slid up the window, he was on the first floor and knew it was a small drop to the patio below but he saw several uniformed police pacing around and looking up.

The noise and commotion had now spilled into the corridor. Paul chanced a look and saw several Police officers trying to frog march a naked, middle aged white man down the corridor. He was kicking and screaming at the top of his voice. A young black women also naked, cowered in the doorway sobbing and trying to cover herself.

Other residents had crowded outside of their rooms to get a good look. Paul walked back in his room grabbed his bag, slid into the corridor and walked in the opposite direction to the fire escape.

Walking quickly through back streets Paul, in the same breath both cursed Jordie and congratulated himself for giving the wrong room number to him. A bribe to the guy in reception when he had checked in made sure that to all intents and purposes he lived in the room next door. "Wife trouble," he had explained with a wink while shoving a pile of bills to the grinning clerk.

The next phase would be tricky he thought as he looked up at the Hotel where he had been drinking with the boys bound for Karuda. He entered the lobby it was 4.45am the sleepy night clerk, an Asian in his sixties looked enquiringly at Paul.

"There are guys here who are on a flight to Karuda this morning. I am here to ensure that they are on that flight." stated Paul with authority in his voice. He continued, "Please give me a list of their room numbers." He held his hand out expectantly.

"No problem Sir, I was supposed to call them all in ten minutes anyway." He tore a sheet of paper off and handed it to Paul who nodded and moved to the stairwell. Making it look like after thought he turned and said to the clerk, "You had trouble last night, a fight, which one of them was it?" The clerk hesitated, Paul returned to the desk a cold look of mounting fury on his face

The man became alarmed.

"It was the big one, he had a fight with someone in the army."

"Room number."

"My God, room number." repeated the clerk and went into a flap, he looked at the register and said. "Room 222, Mr Gowler, Henry Gowler."

"Give me a pass key, come on man snap it up!" said Paul loudly, exploiting his advantage.

The clerk handed over the key and Paul set off pleased that his fishing had paid off. He opened room 222 and was hit with a stench of stale booze and body odour. Lying on the bed fully clothed was a lad in his mid twenties, a pile of vomit trailed from his mouth to the sink which was half full of the stuff.

Paul walked over and shook him, much to his surprise the man woke immediately and sat bolt up right, his eyes wide with apprehension. "Whatsamatta? Hey who are you?" demanded a Glaswegian accent.

"Listen to me man, and listen good, are you Gowler, Henry Gowler?"

"Yeh! Who the fuck are you?"

"Never mind me for the moment, that guy you cracked last night is dead and as we speak the cops are on the way to arrest you. Get your kit now and leave by a fire escape...."

What de ye mean killed him? All I did was stick the head on him for fucks sake!"

"Fine, you want fifteen years in the slammer? Stay! I am *The Major,* and I need you in Karuda, stay low and meet me at this address tonight at 10pm." Paul scribbled an address in his note book and gave him the torn out page. "Let yourself in the back door. It's your only chance to get out of this......Well?" Gowler stood silent for a few seconds staring at Paul then grabbed his bag and threw some gear into it.

He ran for the door and turned. "This address!...10 PM?"

"Yes, let yourself in the back door and say The Major sent you....Got that?"

2

The Dak was now losing height rapidly. Shaven head and most of the rest had their faces pressed against the portholes like kids on there first school bus outing. He returned to his seat and noticed that Paul had "woken up". "There's your first view of Karuda mate." he said with an assumed authority, trying to impress. Despite himself Paul leaned and looked through the porthole window. He saw scrub land criss crossed with tracks that emphasised the rich red earth and now a concrete strip with a couple of square buildings at its centre. As it circled more he saw in the distance the outskirts of a town.

Wally Crabbe sat in the drivers seat of the battered Landrover and watched the Dak slowly circle the airfield. Just his luck he thought, Friday pay day and he had been dicked to pick up another bunch of dross and take them to the Camp. He could have been with his mates now in downtown Laka with Lula on his arm and a few beers but that bastard Mason had ordered him at lunch time to pick them up.

One of the blacks could just as easily have done it like on other occasions but no, that bastard Mason had got it in for him. For Christ's sake, as he never tired of telling people, Mason and him had joined the Brit Army together. They were buddies and then they'd come here and Mason had made it to Regimental Sergeant Major of the Training Depot while he was kept down to being a dogs body, Lance Corporal driver.

They had said that every white joining the KNA would be at least a Sergeant. That was eighteen months ago when he and Mason had landed on this very strip and Mason had shook his hand and said, "Its both of us Wally, not me and you but both of us mate, we've got to look out for each other." Now Mason was at the top of the heap and didn't give a shit about what he'd said.

Crabbe shouted across to the black driver of the green Three Ton Bedford truck. "Hey Syrus! How many we got comin'?"

"Dunno, Din ask Lance Corporal, Sir." Came the indifferent but somehow mocking reply.

"You useless black bastard!" shouted Crabbe irritably, knowing that he should have collected the information from the Orderly Room himself before he left for the strip.

The Dak taxied to within about fifty metres of the two vehicles and switched off its engines. A rickety mobile ladder was pushed up to the fuselage by a couple of workers. After a few minutes the mob led by Seb started to descend. Crabbe stood on the bonnet of the landrover his arms akimbo and balled at the group "Over here now you fuckin' lot .. And at the double!" The group immediately broke into a sprint except for Paul who sauntered across to the vehicles.

Crabbe, eyed him but said nothing. "Who's in charge?" he snarled jumping down to the ground. The group immediately cleared a respectful distance from him. Seb, looking the worse from drink spoke up and identified himself. "Are they all here?" Crabbe demanded.

"No, one person absconded but I have a replacement. Are you the Major?" asked Seb.

A howl of laughter came from Syrus, the black truck driver, who said while chortling, "The Major? No Sir! This the *General!* General Wally Crabbe is at your service!" he laughed again.

"Shut it! You nigger bastard or so help me!" Crabbe reached behind into the Rover and picked up an AK 47 Assault Rifle. He held it at the ready for a few seconds and then turned his fury on the assembly. "Get in the truck! At the fucking double!"

Once again they all moved quickly except Paul who stared at Wally for a few seconds and then walked slowly to the truck. Wally watched him and a twitch started over his left eye.

The training depot was five miles from Laka. A faded sign at the entrance showed the crest of the KNA. A shield and two crossed spears with a gold crown set on top. A scroll at the top of the main gate said: "Camp Lagonda." Wally Crabbe drove at speed through the gates and screeched to a halt on the main square which was black tarmac surrounded by palms. The Three Tonner was a few minutes behind. Syrus knew that Wally was in a rush so he just eased back on the pedal and took his time.

Wally was suitably irritated when it pulled up and screamed for everyone to get in a straight line in front of him. He took the precaution of getting rid of Syrus before he addressed them. With a sneer in his voice he told them that they would be bedded down in the gymnasium that night and that they were confined to camp, there was no food but a canteen was open for their use, reveille would be at six thirty and then he added with a leer, "The fun would begin."

The Gym at one time must have been a credit to Camp Lagonda but was now a dilapidated building with a scarred and dirty parquet floor and various broken apparatus dotted around it. They had each been given a straw filled blue mattress, a sheet plus a spoon and a brown tin mug.

Paul bunked down in a corner next to Seb laying out his mattress and using his rucksack as a pillow. He removed his boots and stretched out, hands behind his head.

The Shaven head who implored everyone to call him "Tex" was mouthing off to them about what he had done and what he had not done. He attracted a small group who looked no more than teenagers to whom he regaled fantastic stories of daring, loud enough for everyone in the room to hear. This did not bother Paul in fact he welcomed it. He had met his type before, insecure empty vessels as soft as egg yoke and desperately trying to build a hard shell.

Guys like him would automatically become a target for the regime here and therefore take pressure off himself. Then, just as Paul was starting to drift off Tex did a very stupid thing, he interpreted Paul's silence as a weakness. He was also upset that no matter what he said, it got no reaction from Paul at all.

A few of the lads had bought back beer from the canteen and had offered a couple to Tex while listening to his stories, after he had downed a few he directed his attention to Paul who seemed to be dozing on his mattress.

Tex shouted across to him, "Hey! You wanna beer? Hey baldy, yeh, I'm talkin, to you, you dumb shit." The small group around him laughed and Tex threw an empty beer can at Paul, it hit him on the chest.

Paul opened his eyes, sighed and sat up. He stretched then started putting on his boots. When he had tied the laces he stood up and walked toward Tex. "Yes, I"ll have that beer." He said with a slight smile on his face. Tex smiled back and picked up a can, as he handed it across Paul swung a long arching right hand, the fist caught Tex on the bridge of the nose which burst like an over ripe tomato. He collapsed without a sound the can of beer rolling across the floor until it hit the wall.

"Well," said Paul to the stunned group, "where's my beer?" Everyone moved at once and Paul found himself with the choice of about six.

Jordie stayed up when Serena went to bed. She knew there was something wrong but he had uncharacteristically bitten off her head when she had asked, a row had erupted and only moved on to a stony silence when one of the children came into the room crying.

Jordie was worried, a check with his mate in the police revealed that they had arrested the wrong man at the Hotel. There had been a mix up with room numbers and by the time it was sorted, this Maas come Van Der Borg character had gone and there was no trace of him.

He knew that Van Der Borg would come for him sooner or later. His inward eye saw him at work with his knife slashing a guy to ribbons in a bar toilet and on another occasion setting fire to a car with his victim lashed to the steering wheel. He still could hear the agonising screams and Paul's laughter. He reached down the side of the cushion and felt the Automatic.

The clock struck ten, he'd decided that he would try to sleep on the settee that night. He heard a noise in the room and stiffened. He had set a loose tripwire on the garden path attached to the handle of a cup with a saucer balanced on it inside the room. It was the saucer falling that he had heard.

Steeling himself he thumbed off the safety and inched toward the kitchen door. Through its opaque glass he could see a figure and saw the door handle slowly going down. The gun bucked up sharply as it discharged with an almighty boom, a small hole appeared in the glass and the figure disappeared.

Galvanised by the noise he ripped open the door and rushed out, the gun straight out in front of him. Five yards away, lying face up in the fish pond, a neat red hole at the base of his neck was the body of Henry Gowler, the address Paul had given him still clutched tightly in his hand.

3

At precisely 6.30 am the door to the Gym burst open and four soldiers rushed in wielding three foot long batons, "UP! UP! UP! They screamed as they kicked at the prone forms on the mattresses. Paul rolled off his bed and made quickly for the exit, he was dressed and ready, he'd had a feeling that the first morning would be all about surprise and instilling respect, that lovely comfortable word for fear. He had readied himself. Nevertheless, as he darted passed one of the soldiers he received a blow across his back that smarted like hell.

Outside they were herded into three ranks on the main square with more screams of abuse and threats. They looked like a bunch of refugees, bewildered, some still half dressed . "SHUT UP, AND KEEP STILL!" Balled one of the soldiers that seemed in charge. He was dressed like the others, camo trousers, boots and green T shirt. He was tall and powerfully built as if he worked out regularly with weights, his sinewed arms covered in tattoos. "I am Staff Sergeant Reeves, when I tell you to do something you DO IT! And when you do it, you do it at the double and before you do, you shout, YES STAFF! Is that clear!?......Well IS IT!?

The ragged bunch in front of him echoed back, "Yes Staff!"

"Right, that aircraft that you dross came in on is still sitting on the strip five miles that way!" He raised an arm and pointed back over their heads. His eyes were wild and staring and now and then flecks of froth tore off his mouth and jetted out in front of him. He continued yelling at the top of his voice even though the furthest man in the squad was only yards from him.

"We're now going for a little trot around the camp to see what you're made of! Those of you pansies who can't hack it just continue running on through the gate to the Dak, which I think by looking at you, will be all of you. Now turn to your left. Your left you dozey bastards! Follow me. Left, right, left, right!"

Reeves set out at a cracking pace in front of the squad his henchmen at the sides shouting and screaming an almost unintelligible, non stop stream of abuse, while laying into them with their sticks. Van Der Borg breathed deeply to enrich his lungs, over the last weeks he had got running fit in preparation for joining the Rhodesian Army. He found himself next to Tex who had a large cross shaped plaster over his nose and two black, puffy eyes.

On and on the pace went, left, right, left, right, people started dropping back, the threats and encouragement went on, even louder now. Paul sank his head down and sucked in huge lungs full of air, he kept his eyes pinned to the calves of the man in front of him whose legs were going like pistons in time with the rhythmic chant of left, right from Reeves.

They came to the perimeter fence and followed it along, Tex was having problems with his breathing and every now and then coughed up and spat out a bloodied goo, but still he kept going. Something was wrong with the guy in front of Paul. He started going out of step and wavering, now he lost speed and without hesitation Paul stepped around him and found himself at the front with Reeves just ahead of him. He had stopped chanting now but the pace continued unabated. They ran past the main gate if there was a time to quit this was it, but not for Paul where would he go?

He sensed that Tex who was still next to him was going for the gate, he started to lose speed but Paul grabbed him in the small of his back and propelled him on. Between gasps he said, "Don't quit now, keep fucking moving, it can't last for ever, come on!"

Tex bucked up and started putting more effort into it. On and on they went for fifteen minutes or more, once again they passed the main gate and Reeves glanced around to see who was left and once again he increased the pace slightly.

When Reeves looked back over his shoulder Paul could see that his face too was red and sweating profusely, it can't be long now he hoped rather than reasoned. As if he had heard his thoughts Reeves increased the pace even more and started to pull away from them. Paul opened his stride and started to leave Tex behind. One of Reeves' henchman was at his side but apart from the odd expletive to no one in particular remained silent and fighting for breath like the rest of them.

Paul could see nothing apart from Reeves' sweat stained, green T shirt a few paces in front of him, he heard nothing except for his own extremely laboured breathing. They passed the main gate a third time as they did he was dimly aware of Reeves turning around again to check. This time Paul tried a tactic, he increased his pace to his absolute limit and gained on Reeves, now he was at his side. Reeves unused to being challenged shot him a glance and increased his pace to keep the lead. Paul could hear his laboured breathing and stayed level with him. He knew that he himself, couldn't keep it up for more than a few seconds longer, then suddenly Reeves broke and slowed dramatically. Immediately Paul slowed until he was once again at his rear thankful that his tactic had worked.

He now kept well to the rear of Reeves, the pace had dropped but it wouldn't be wise to push him, this was his town, he could skin Van Der Borg ten different ways and he knew it.

Paul doggedly followed Reeves until he found himself on the tarmac of the main square where the rest were waiting in a straggly heap, some were doubled over and one guy was puking into the base of one of the palms.

He stood with them hands on hips unable to breath in enough air, sweat blinded him and his legs felt shaky. He lifted his wet shirt and wiped away as much of the stinging sweat as possible aware of someone else running in, it was Tex, he had made it round three times as well. It looked like that they were the only two to do it with Reeves. The plaster hung off Tex's face and fresh blood poured from his nose, he was all in but made it to Paul's side and just managed to keep standing.

"Get 'em showered and back on parade in fifteen minutes ready for processing!" roared Reeves who had seemed to have recovered completely.

Paul was still hot and sweating after the "shower". He pulled on his last remaining clean, green fatigue shirt. The rest had decided to languish as much as possible under the trickle of cool brackish water coming from broken shower heads in the ceiling of the ablutions.

He ensured that nobody was around then quickly rifled through the personal belongings of the squad. Moving from one pile of kit to the other he removed passports and any money. When he'd got three passports he stopped and went to a disused office, once in there he climbed on top of the desk and pushed the passports and money into the space between the wall and the roof. He was hoping that it was a double wall with a space in between, it was and he heard the flutter as the pile dropped down.

He marched quickly outside and stood at ease on the spot where they had paraded earlier. Reeves was there with his three henchmen he looked at Paul but said nothing. He checked his watch then sent his dogs off to round up the sheep. Reeves sauntered over to Paul. "So you think you can take me big man?" He was eye level with Paul and just a couple of inches away.

"NO STAFF!" Came Paul's immediate and loud reply. He had to get this man's respect not his hatred.

Reeves sneered. "Good because I thrive on breaking those who think they can." Any further talk was cut off by Reeves' staff shouting and balling at the rest of the squad who were still trying to dress as they doubled over to them. They fell in next to Paul still covered in sweat and breathing hard.

Once again Reeves flanked by his staff spoke to them. The maniacal type shouting was gone and replaced by a raised monologue that he snarled out. "Only four of you dross went through the gate but there's still plenty of time. If you think that was hard you've got a lot of surprises coming."

He let his words sink in and then continued. "This morning you will be processed by the clerk in the Orderly Room, once you have signed the dotted line you are under contract for two years from which there's no going back."

Again he let the squad absorb his words while he looked at each one of the twelve left. He continued, "You will each receive a uniform issue which you will wear at all times from then on. You will be given a barrack block to live in which is your responsibility to keep secure and clean. Until further notice you will be confined to this camp, you will not attempt to mix with or talk to anyone outside of your squad, me and my staff, is that clear!?"

"YES STAFF!"

"Good, now get back to your accommodation and fetch your passports, get back here in two minutes.

They all doubled to the Gym and started rummaging through their kit, it didn't take long for the first cry to go up, "Bollocks! Some bastard has had my money and Passport away!"

"Mine too!" shouted Paul angrily.

They lined up in the Orderly room waiting to see the clerk, he was a scrawny white man past middle age who looked totally bored. Red veins in his eyes showed that he had been on the bottle the night before and many before that. He looked up at Reeves questioningly. "What am I supposed to do? If they haven't got passports we can't prove identity, we can't prove identity they are on the next plane outa here." He stated simply to Reeves who let out a sigh.

"Look I've sent some guys down to the airstrip to search the four that dropped out, at least one of them is a thieving bastard, we'll get the passports back." He checked his watch and continued, "Look at least you can start the process, to save time. It is Saturday man for Christ's sake." The scrawny clerk gave a gallic gesture and called the first man forward.

As he stood in line Paul could feel Reeves' eyes on him. He avoided eye contact and just remained in the queue silent and staring ahead. Reeves approached him and once again stood with his face aggressively close. "Fancy a guy like you getting robbed, thought you were an old soldier, you have been in before haven't you?"

"No Staff!"

"Liar! But don't worry I *will* find out about you...." Reeves was cut short by the Clerk calling Paul forward. Paul was alarmed by the interest shown in him by Reeves it was the exact opposite of what he wanted. He now realised he had been wrong to stand out on that run around camp.

"Name?" shouted the clerk to Paul.

"Van Der........." Paul stopped himself in time, Reeves had thrown him off balance for a second and he had almost blurted out his real name instead of his planned one.

"Vander? Is that V.A. N. D. E. R. ?" said the irritated clerk.

Paul nodded and so with his new name he continued through the process.

Just as the last man was being dealt with one of Reeves' henchman the one he called Smiley came in shaking his head. "They were on the plane and starting to taxi, we got 'em off and strip searched the lot of them......Nothing!"

"Didn't you search the Dak? They must have stashed it when they saw you" Demanded Reeves.

"Tried to but the crew started kicking up big time, my bet is they've got stuff stashed there themselves....."

"So the thieving bastards got away with it."

"Not quite we gave each and every one of them a good kicking in turn, the crew had to carry one of them on the aircraft." said Smiley with a big smug grin on his face.

"Well?" demanded Reeves from the scrawny Clerk. Scrawny looked at his watch then at the small pile of paper that had not been processed because of the lack of proper identification. He sighed and reached for the stamp and ink pad. "As far as I'm concerned," he said to Reeves, "you have told me that *you*, have seen the Passports, am I right?" Reeves nodded and the Clerk started to stamp the paperwork.

Reeves smiled, although he would himself do his damndest to whittle this lot down he would do it his way and not the way of some broken down pen pusher. Yes he was happy but not as happy as Paul "Vander" now felt deep inside.

4

It was Sunday evening the squad sat in small groups in the canteen. The floor was a large square of concrete, the roof a high construction of atap leaves. It was open on three sides and the fourth was the bar. A black man in his sixties was on duty selling bottles of Lion beer and a small assortment of spirits as well as the inevitable Coca Cola. The cold drinks had gone and it was either warm beer or no beer, most chose the warm beer.

It had been a hectic weekend and they had finished just a couple of hours before. Reeves and his staff had run them into the ground again, this time Paul was wise enough to stay with the main squad. They had received some "History" from a bored white officer who looked and acted like a school master.

They learned that Karuda obtained independence from Britain in 1961 and M'Punga had been its first and only President. He also claimed Royal lineage and on official occasions answered to 'His Majesty'. Although he didn't call himself King, he was grooming his son Tasi to eventually become the first King of Karuda.

At first the Country had thrived, exports of minerals from copper to diamonds and gold. The Capital City was Laka. Karuda was a relatively small country with The Congo, Zambia and Rhodesia on its borders. A senior officer on M'Punga's staff had been accused of treason but escaped before trial some years before.

He had set up just over the border in the Congo and over the years had built up a large rebel force which had begun to challenge the KNA in earnest. The influx of a mercenary, mainly British force had checked this and a period of calm now existed. The Officer, Paul noted did not criticise the government or give any negative information.

Now they sat relaxing, a little self conscious of their brand new camouflaged uniforms that seem to drape on them like the cardboard boxes they came in.

Paul sat at a table with Seb, Tex and a few other young lads. Tex had now attached himself to Paul, gone was the bragging and loud mouth. He had asked Paul earlier why he had hit him, Paul had replied, "You needed a lesson and you got one."

"But you helped me on the run, if you hadn't I would have been on that plane with the others."

"I don't hold any hate for you Tex but someone sooner or later would have done it and they might not have been as *gentle* as me…. And you showed guts on the run, you were in a worse state than any of us and yet you completed it." Paul had held out his hand, Tex had hesitated slightly then shook it warmly.

Seb downed the glass of clear spirits and waved his glass at the barman, he turned to Paul and said, "So we meet the RSM tomorrow morning, they say he's a real bastard, makes Reeves look gentle."

"Ha!" said Paul. "RSMs are supposed to be bastards, that's nothing new."

"What's RSM?" said Tex, he like most of the others had no military background.

"Regimental Sergeant Major," stated Seb. "the embodiment of any military unit, usually a man to avoid like a plague!"

A disturbance at the bar made Paul turn, he saw the driver that had picked them up from the airport in a heated discussion with the barman. Paul got up and sauntered across. He heard Wally say to the barman in a low growl. "Now listen you black bastard, I settled my book last week."

The barman produced a large dark red book from under the counter and flicked through the pages, he underlined an entry with his finger.

"Look here Corporal Wally, no red line through means you not pay. Sorry but RSM Mason, he say all wog shop bills to be settled on pay day or no more credit.

"RSM fucking Mason says." mocked Wally who then became aware of Paul at his side.

"Do you want a beer Wally?" asked Paul casually throwing some notes on the bar.

"Who the fuck are *you*, to call *me* Wally? You fucking dross! I could have you thrown in the jail for just looking at me."

"And where do you think that will get you in the long run? I will be around for sometime yet Wally." said Paul gently as he offered him a bottle.

Wally stared at Paul for a few seconds, he had already heard on the camp grapevine about his fight with Tex. He shrugged his shoulders and took the beer, after a swig he turned to the barman and snarled, "Piss warm again, you useless bastard!"

It was closing time and the barman started to lock the stock away in a backroom. Chairs scraped as one by one, or in groups people started to drift off. Paul had been sitting with Wally for more than two hours now listening to him venting his spleen against everything and everybody that had to do with Karuda.

Gentle questioning by Paul and a steady stream of bottles kept Wally on the right track and build up a picture of Karuda that was slightly different from the lecture earlier that day.

It seemed that M'Punga the President of Karuda had gone the way of the despot, all his good intentions had vanished in his quest to amass a personal fortune and remain in power whatever the cost. He had executed or locked up his opposition and now it was rumoured he was relying on hard drugs to keep him going. The national infrastructure was beginning to break down and only the army and police were in receipt of regular pay as well of course as M'Punga and his gang.

However, about two years earlier an army officer on trial for treason had escaped and had amassed within a few short months a few hundred followers. They lived and trained over the border in the neighbouring Congo. The KNA had proved to be useless against the guerrilla tactics employed by the rebels and were steadily losing morale and the will to fight.

In desperation President M'Punga had turned to his country's old Masters the British and asked for help.

With their Army stretched in Northern Ireland and other world commitments they had turned M'Punga down but had also turned a blind eye to him recruiting British Nationals to fight for him.

Wally, Mason, Reeves, the Colonel and the Major and a few more had been the first to arrive and immediately took positions of power. The Colonel was a former Lieutenant kicked out for fraud. The Major, a former Corporal from the Intelligence Corps who had the right accent. The RSM, Wally spat out, was a former private soldier who like himself had gone on the run from his unit rather than face disciplinary charges.

Their aim concluded Wally was to recruit and train as many ex Brit or commonwealth army as possible to firstly supervise and then control the demoralised KNA and at the same time amass personal fortunes. At an appropriate time they would flee the country as wealthy men, "They think that it's all a big secret, ha! But Wally Crabbe knows!"

At first, Wally continued, they had took the rebels by surprise and had hammered them back over the border but slowly the rebels came back and many thought they were about to launch an offensive to regain the initiative

"You should 'ear them sometimes," slurred the drink soaked Wally, "Talking about how they are defeating the rebels but they're living in a fucking dream. They can't recruit enough people any more and the ones they do get is dross, fucking no hopers, who've done nothing except watch John Wayne movies. Do you know..." Wally stopped and checked around him to make sure no one was in ear shot, then pulled in close to Paul. "Do you know what? They fuck off in the bush on so called "*Operations*". They attack and loot the mines, they rob banks and businesses and blame the rebels, then shoot up some innocent fucking civvies, villagers and the like, dress 'em up in guerrilla uniforms and parade 'em through the streets piled up on the back of a truck and do you know what else? All of us are supposed to be paid in US Dollars but *Colonel* Hennings and that bunch hang on to them and pay us in Karudan Dollars that are worth jack shit outside of this country, but it won't last it can't. Somebody had a pop at M'Punga last week, just missed him by all accounts, the yellow bastard won't come out of his palace now."

The two got up and left the canteen and as they split outside Wally turned and said to Paul, "Watch yourself big man. Reeves has got his eye on you already." He tapped his nose and tottered off burping.

Paul set off towards his block, he saw a movement in the trees ahead and a smiling figure loomed out carrying a truncheon, smacking it impatiently into the palm of his hand, it was Smiley. Paul checked his pace and automatically felt for his knife, he inwardly cursed, he had purposely not worn it thinking that he would be safe from serious attack inside the camp.

He heard quick footsteps behind him, turned and saw the two other staff members closing in on him, they too were carrying truncheons. They stopped just short of Paul who backed against a tree. "So you big tough bastards need sticks," shouted Paul with disgust in his voice, "Gentlemen up to this point you all had my ut-most respect." He sneered and spat on the ground.

Smiley who seemed to be the leader flung his trun-cheon to the ground. "I don't need shit to take you, you fucking dross. Hard man eh? Well, we'll see." He took a boxing stance and advanced on Paul. The other two also dropped their truncheons and waited expectantly.

Smiley feinted a jab with his left, then swung a huge right that would have felled an ox if it had connected but it was telegraphed and a mite too slow. Paul blocked it and drove his head into Smiley's face, it caught him on the eyebrow, he staggered back stunned.

Paul's instinct was to follow up and finish him with his boots but Smiley's mates had other ideas. They closed in and started punching him. Despite his situation Paul laughed aloud, "Ha! You fucking amateurs, first you get talked into losing your weapons and then you use your puny fists instead of your feet." He slammed a right into the stronger one of the two and narrowly missed his groin with a follow up kick.

The weaker one backed away. Smiley his eye already swollen to the size of a chicken egg again advanced on Paul. Paul leapt back and picked up a truncheon, for a second everything stopped. Smiley lived up to his nick name by still having a big smile on his swollen face, the strong one and the weak one now circled. "Tosh," or-dered Smiley, "when I say, go for his legs, Roy, when I say, rush him!"

Smiley's grin turned evil. "Now!" He screamed and charged in.

Paul, without taking his eyes off Smiley who was the biggest threat swung the truncheon and caught Tosh in the face, the stick snapped in two. Paul dropped to his knees and Smiley piled over the top of him and on to his back. Paul stood up and Roy back tracked a few paces a look of fear and uncertainty on his face.

Smiley jumped up before Paul could give him the coupe de gras with his boots. Paul saw something glinting in his hand, it was long bladed combat knife.

"Okay! Break it up!" It was the unmistakable sound of Reeves' voice booming from the shadows, "Vander get to your bunk before I throw you into jail."

"Yes, STAFF!" boomed back Paul dropping the broken truncheon and coming to attention. He gave a last sneering look at Smiley then dashed away.

Reeves emerged from where he had been observing. He watched Vander trotting away then turned on his staff, "I said that I wanted *him*, roughed up! Look at the fucking state of you lot, I should've done it myself."

"Be my guest." said Smiley.

Paul's squad and another half dozen or so squads at differing stages of training were all stood rigid to attention on the square. It was eight o' clock and they were on the Monday morning "Muster". The sun was hot enough even at that time of day to send streams of sweat from armpits to waist. Reeves was in front of them, he also stood to attention waiting.

Soon the object of his wait came clip clopping down the road toward the square. An averaged sized man in an immaculate white tropical uniform carrying a sword marched on to the square. He stopped, Reeves marched up to him and exchanged words. Paul couldn't help but think that he had seen better drill come from week one recruits in his old Unit. It just proved to him what a Mickey Mouse outfit this really was.

Even though he was sore and bruised, he was glad the fight had happened. He had no doubt that Reeves had set it up. He reasoned that they would have more respect for him now and perhaps take the heat off, he hoped that he was right.

After the talk with Wally he had almost decided to quit and take his chances elsewhere but something was telling him over and over that if he worked hard at it, things would come good. It seemed on first impressions that the Camp regime was nothing but a bunch of loud mouthed egotists living as Wally had put it, in a dream. He was better than any of them he thought, give me time and I will have all of them in my palm.

"For the benefit of those who don't know it," shouted the white uniformed sword carrier. "I am Regimental Sergeant Major Mason late of the British Special Forces Division. I am your God now and don't you fuckin' well forget it!" His voice was thin and lacked natural authority. He too turned and waited for an arrival.

Two figures in similar white tropical uniforms casually strolled toward the RSM, the taller one who Paul took to be the Colonel made no pretence at any drill. He simply walked up to the RSM and gave a half hearted wave that was supposed to be a salute. The shorter one who was the Major stood with his hands on his hip gripping a black swagger stick which at one end was rounded into a tennis ball sized black orb.

The RSM screamed at the parade, "The Commanding Officer will inspect the new draft, the rest carry on!"

Down the line they came, the Colonel, the Major, the RSM and at the tail Reeves. Colonel Hennings stopped at each individual and asked questions. He was tall and thin, an aristocratic, arrogant look on his white boyish features. Major Pern followed close behind, smaller and darker, a good looking face but there was something about the thin lips that gave a warning.

"And you, what's your name?" The Colonel had stopped in front of Paul and looked down on him, his lips turned down in a disinterested scowl.

"Vander Sir! Recruit Vander!" answered Paul crisply while staring through the Colonel's Adams Apple.

"Have you seen service?"

"A little Sir, I was with the Legion for a short time." He had decided to admit to some former service, it was obvious to Reeves that he had been trained so he would give a little to allay suspicion. He had heard enough stories about the Legion from comrades over the years to bluff anything but a close examination.

"Did you desert? The penalty for desertion here is being shot. Do you know that Monsieur Legionnaire?" A little chuckle arose from the Major and RSM.

"Non, Mon Colonel, I did not desert."

"And less of that fucking froggie talk here Vandal or whatever your name is….Its SIR! Do you understand!?" Interjected the RSM fiercely. But Paul had achieved his aim to avert more questioning and the team moved on through the ranks. Reeves stopped for a moment and leered at Paul.

5

The weeks passed. They were drilled on the square and given weapon training. They were taught how to attack using fire and manoeuvre and how to handle explosives. The instruction Paul thought was generally sub standard, bullying and threats filled in for real knowledge and the ability to get it across. More than once Paul had taken over a lesson because his knowledge was better and now the instructors especially Smiley gave him more to do while they watched or slid off to do other things.

The pressure they had received at the beginning had slackened off. As he had predicted Smiley and the others had a healthy respect for him but Reeves was still a menace especially to Paul, to whom he seemed to hold a special hate. He didn't waste any opportunity to try and bring him down or humiliate him in front of the others.

Paul took it all in his stride and never reacted even when Reeves in desperation had ordered him to lick his boots, Paul had dropped to his knees instantly in front of the squad and had done just that, it was an embarrassed Reeves who had backed off hurling abuse at him.

Guerrilla attacks were on the increase, bridges blown, and key installations like electricity generating Plants attacked. It seemed or at least they were told that the army's counter insurgency tactics were working, after all they had paraded another fifteen dead guerrillas on the back of a truck the other day in Laka.

Paul was the natural leader of the squad, Seb and Tex his close allies. He had no problems from any of the others. Their numbers dwindled to eight over the weeks. The lads who had no experience at all benefited greatly from the instruction and guidance that Paul and Seb gave them after hours and slowly they became a close nit little group.

Gradually Paul became known to the other soldiers on the Camp most of them also recruits. They came to him for help and advice. He also enhanced his reputation further when he laid out a bullying NCO from another squad in the canteen one evening. The NCO had been too ashamed to take disciplinary action.

They had been confined to the camp and the canteen for five weeks now and this coming Friday they would be allowed into Laka for the night. They were all excited at the thought and even Paul looked forward to getting out of the Camp.

He had generally been happy. There was nothing they could throw at him that he could not cope with, even Reeves. The NCOs had respect for him. His old feelings had not risen up in him for months, he reckoned that he must have been too busy and he had layed off the drink which had helped.

They had been told that in a matter of weeks they would be going to either 1 or 2 Commando of the KNA as instructors and platoon leaders, then into the bush on Operations. Above all this filled most with anticipation or trepidation or both. But at this moment the prospect of a night on the town overrode everything.

"I'm gonna get me one of those little black fillies and shag myself stupid as soon as I hit town." declared Tex lying on his bunk and staring at the ceiling, he grabbed his crotch and gave a long "OOOH!" They all chuckled.

"Yeh! Me too." shouted another.

"Oh! Yeh and that'll be your first, cherry boy." shouted yet another

"This time tomorrow night, I'll be up to my ears in beautiful sweaty minge, roll on, just roll on." sighed Tex

Seb joined in but on a more sombre note. "You're going to have to get past Reeves first Tex boy, he's on duty and he'll be inspecting everyone who goes through that gate. It won't be the first time he's thrown someone in the jail for not being up to scratch, and for some reason he has a special dislike of us lot."

Paul lay on his bed eyes shut but listening to everything. If it was true what Seb said, he would be going no further than the jail tomorrow evening. The prospect did not worry him, they couldn't keep him down forever.

From further talks with his now "Old buddy" Wally Crabbe, he had found out what made Reeves tick. He had been a fitness instructor with the Royal Marines training recruits for three years and was married to a beautiful girl Lillian, whom he adored.

One day one of his recruits went missing and when he got home his beautiful Lillian was missing as well. The note had just said "Sorry". It transpired that all the recruits had known what had been going on for weeks.

Unable to stand the humiliation he had broken and ran. He had tried for the Rhodesian Army but the fact that he was a deserter stopped them accepting him and he had ended up in Karuda. A tin god, bitter and resentful.

They all sat on the side of their beds polishing boots and picking loose cotton off their sharply pressed uniforms. The great day had arrived, they were off on the truck to Laka for the night. The truck left at seven it was now a quarter to. Each inspected one another as thoroughly as any inspection they had received on the Parade Square.

Paul suited a uniform well, his figure had trimmed over the weeks of training and abstinence. They all left the barrack block in jubilant mood. Paul stayed at the back of the group with Tex and Seb. As they neared the Guardroom by the gate the tall athletic figure of Staff Sergeant Reeves came out and stood in the middle of the road facing them a sneer on his face. He looked at his watch, there was still a few minutes to go, beyond him they could see a Bedford truck, their carriage awaited.

"Line up here!" shouted Reeves. They formed a single line with Paul at the end. One by one he looked each of them up and down and said, "On the truck!"

He came to Paul who was now alone at attention staring straight ahead. He looked him up and down then walked around him.

"And where do you think you're going tonight Vander?" asked Reeves in a conversational manner." Paul stared straight ahead but said nothing.

"I asked you a question Vander, do you want to end up in the jail for dumb insolence?" asked Reeves a little more louder and aggressive.

Paul then bewildered Reeves by smiling at first then breaking into a chuckle.

"Are you fucking mad Vander?" asked an astonished Reeves. He looked Paul directly in the eyes. Paul stopped laughing and focused back into Reeves'. Their eyes locked and Paul held his stare, ten seconds, fifteen, it was coming almost up to the minute when the driver of the truck punched the hooter and shouted.

"Hey staff, are we going? Boy General Wally Crabbe say I got to be back to pick up supplies."

It was enough for Reeves to break off and tell him to get on the truck. When the tailboard went up and the truck was about to move Reeves came up to the back and shouted in. "I'm on town patrol tonight, I just hope and pray that one of you fuckers fucks up.!" He stared at Paul and held it until the truck disappeared.

Randy's Bar was heaving with men in uniform and scantily dressed women. It was the only bar in Laka that had been put "Out of Bounds", so naturally everyone made for it. They had the cheapest beer and a seemingly never ending stock of women of all ages and shapes. The noise and music was deafening. It only got worse when someone escorted a girl up the open staircase to one of the many rooms on the first floor and got jeered and cheered by the crowd. The long bar that seemed to have a sweating barman stationed every yard along it worked continuously to supply the thirsty soldiers who were three deep.

Paul, Seb, Tex and a few others had found a space at the end of the bar. The atmosphere and noise was too much for Paul but in spite of his inner feelings he felt happy. Like the rest of them he had downed bottle after bottle of the ice cold beer. A girl of about eighteen and a couple of similarly aged companions came over to them smiling, they put their arms around the men and started fondling them. Paul immediately stuck his hand in the pocket with his money in and kept it there.

Tex lasted about ten seconds then led one of the girls up the stairs, a great cheer broke out from the crowd. Paul downed another beer and nodded to one of his group to get him another. The girl that had attached herself to him now had her hand in his flies her other around his back. Paul started to get aroused, the others were in a similar position. The music, the crowd noise, the heat, the booze, the perfume and the women all started to have a hypnotic effect. "Come with me honey-bee, I give you good time, come on, ten dollar only, you fuck, fuck for short time, or as long as you like come on honeybee...."

Paul propelled the girl to the door of the nearby toilets, she resisted slightly but he pushed her into one of the cubicles and lifted up her short dress. It was all over in about twenty seconds, a short, savage brutal act. The girl that was much experienced even at her young age cursed him, "You dirty, white trash bastard, why couldn't you be nice to Lucy 'sted of treatin' me like dat. I want twenty dollar from you!"

Paul peeled off two tens and flung them at her, "If I get a dose off you, you bitch, I'll slice your fucking liver out!" With that she ran out and Paul went over to one of the sinks and looked around the toilet area. It was a filthy hole, a man was on his knees with his head in the urinal retching and spewing, the whole floor was an inch deep in urine and vomit. He flopped his penis in the sink and swilled water over it.

Paul joined the rest of them, Tex was not back yet. Seb was still getting the treatment off one of the girls who was telling him how much she loved him and wanted him. Paul was suddenly aware that someone was staring at him, he looked and saw a fat, balding white man in his fifties looking in his direction. With him was a giant black man about six foot four and twenty stone, he too was looking at Paul.

Together, with fatty leading they came up to Paul. In a slightly foreign accent fatty spoke to Paul. He was unkempt and greasy, his lank, thinning hair plastered to his head with sweat and grime. "You tore up one o' my best girls, she won't be able to work for a week. I lose money, you pay me."

Paul gave a look of innocence and a shrug , "Okay, how much? I don't want trouble." As he spoke, he moved a little towards the huge ox at fatty's side.

Fatty smiled and the oxen relaxed a little. "Oh! We say sixty dollar?" He turned to his escort and smiled, " Me and Vincent don't want trouble either."

Paul crouched a little and spoke to a person at the side of Vincent. "Hey can you help? I haven't got sixty dollars." Vincent turned his head slightly to see who

Paul was talking to, before the move was completed Paul sprang like a piece of coiled steel and head butted him on the corner of his forehead just above the eye. The huge man staggered back but didn't drop. Paul followed up kicking hard at the man's shins and slamming a hard left and right into the face, still he tottered backwards but didn't go down, finally he let fly a huge kick into the man's groin, who then staggered and dropped.

A barman with a broken bottle jumped over the bar and lunged at Paul, he side stepped but nevertheless the razor sharp ragged edge sliced through his shirt and flesh underneath. Paul backhanded the man who lost his balance and stumbled to the ground, he immediately delivered three ferocious kicks to the head and body.

The area of the fight had cleared, the only sounds were of women screaming at the tops of their voices. Fatty was cowering on his knees by the bar his face deathly white. Three men suddenly appeared with baseball bats but didn't move in, that was there first and last mistake. From nowhere Paul had the ten inch knife in his hand and grabbed a stool with the other. He flung the stool and followed up immediately slashing the knife in a great arc, one of the men buckled, screaming and holding his arm, blood spurting through his fingers. Then Tex came behind the other two and layed one out with a bottle, the other dropped his bat and ran. Now no one came forward.

Paul put away the knife and walked up to fatty who tried to scramble away on all fours, he stopped when he hit an overturned table and started gibbering in a foreign language, his hands working as if to push Paul away.

"You wanted sixty Dollars?"

" No! No! Sixty Dollars."

"Well I think ten dollars is a fair price I *was* a little rough on her." He peeled off a note and threw it to the ground next to fatty, as he walked away he stopped and turned, "You tell your big friend Vincent that if he tries to get even I'll kill him then I'll come for you." He walked out followed by Tex, everyone made room for him and was silent.

RSM Mason sat behind his desk in civilian clothes. He was angry, this was the first ever Saturday that he could remember being in camp. Staff Reeves stood in front of him. Mason looked up and said, "I don't understand it, I just don't understand it, if you are so sure it was Vander why doesn't any bleeder come forward and say so? This man hospitalises three men and God knows what else, he leaves a pool of blood the size of Lake Palla and no one has seen anything…..What about the girls?"

"They're tight lipped, somebody has told them to keep it shut."

"Only the owner could do that, whatsisname that fat Belgian bastard, Kokkos, Karlos?"

"Karbol," Corrected Reeves, "he wouldn't talk to the police if he saw someone murder his mother. He was the same last year when that crazy Aussie shot the bar up and killed one of the whores."

"And the other soldiers? It must have been packed." asked Mason getting more irritated by the second.

"By the time we got there the place was absolutely empty apart from some medics trying to lift a giant
black onto a stretcher...There's also a guy in hospital
with his arm near cut off. I heard some talk saying that
Vander did it.

"Talk?" who talked? One minute you say that no
one talked and next you say some one did talk, what's it
to be Staff!?"

"It was just something I heard from a group of soldiers as we toured the bars afterwards, I can't pin point
the guy."

"Well until you can Staff don't waste my time!" Mason made for the door, "As a precaution throw Vander in
the slammer and get him in front of me Monday morning, and it would help if you found a witness." Mason
held the door while Reeves walked out.

Paul lay on his bed, his stomach smarted and any
attempt to get up creased him in pain. They had got
back around two in the morning, the booze and adrenaline had kept the pain at bay until then. Paul had started to stitch the wound in his gut himself but Seb who at
one stage had been a medic took over. Paul told them
all to clear out of the room, they would come to arrest
him soon, he said and probably anyone else they found
with him.

At four thirty a.m. Reeves with two of the guard
came bursting in and tossed Paul out of his bed, the
stitches broke and fresh blood had pumped through his
T shirt. They had searched and searched until Reeves
demanded to know the whereabouts of the knife. Paul

had said nothing. To his surprise they left him and he lay back down and drifted into sleep.

A man who Paul had seen before as a clerk in the Headquarters came in the barrack room, he spotted Paul and came quickly over. "Paul you've gotta get out of here! They're comin' to arrest you. I just heard Mason talkin' to Reeves, they've got no witnesses but they're going to bang you up anyway!"

Paul didn't move but said woodenly. "Witnesses to what?"

"Come off it, everyone knows you sliced them geezers up and fucking right too. They've done enough of us over in the past, but no bastards talkin'!.. Look I've got to go, if they catch me here they'll know I've been..."

"Yeh, go, and thanks."

Ten minutes later Reeves entered the barrack room it was empty apart from Paul Lying on his bed. The wound was gaping, blood and gore oozed through his T shirt. Paul drifted in and out of consciousness.

"Get up Vander, I've got you a new bed space." said Reeves kicking the bed.

"I said Get Up! You useless piece of shit. Hard man eh? Good for beating drunks up and knifing defenceless half wits. I've met your type before Vander. You bluffed your way here, you had no passport and probably stole the others to give you credibility. I'll tell you what you fucking scum bag, I'll move heaven and earth, I'll use every trick and all of my power and influence to get you on the Dak back to Salisbury and do you know what? There's gonna be a reception committee waiting for you, my guess is you've fucked up there as well. What-

ever the outcome, you won't get back here. Now get off
that bed."

Paul heard all of Reeves' little speech. It was a pity
he thought, he had liked Reeves at the beginning, he
had seemed a good, hard man who's mission it was to
turn them into soldiers but he had a bitterness and hatred that clouded his judgement and made him a dangerous bully and adversary. It was a *great* pity he thought,
but now he was a threat and had virtually signed his own
death warrant.

With some effort Paul swung his legs out of the
bed and on to floor. With one hand supporting his belly,
he walked hunched over to the exit clenching his teeth
and breathing hard.

"MOVE IT! screamed Reeves and kicked him in
the behind.

Outside Reeves made him stand to attention and
then marched him around the square twice before going to the guardroom, each time he had faltered Reeves
had been on him, kicking and raving.

Paul made it to the guardroom, he stood there
while Reeves told the guard commander to lock him up.
Reeves left and Paul collapsed. The guard commander
looked in disgust at Reeves walking off. He picked up
a phone and spoke to the switch board, "Get an ambulance!"

"Have you gone completely mad Staff!?" shouted
the Colonel in genuine disbelief. Colonel Hennings,
Reeves, RSM Mason and Major Pern were all assembled
in the CO's office. All except Reeves were in civilian

clothes. The RSM was almost boiling over with fury, this was the second time he had been called in that day. He had been in a drinking session with some friends when he had got the CO's summons.

"Well Staff!?" Joined in Mason his eyes set hard.

"*You*, told me to jail him RSM!" said Reeves in astonishment. He was afraid because in his reckoning, he was cornered by three rats, three self centred, self seeking dangerous rats, who would think nothing of throwing him to the wolves to save themselves.

"I fucking well told you to arrest him! You, at no stage told me he was seriously ill, only a fucking idiot would try to march a man with stomach wounds and that's what you are Reeves, a fucking idiot!" Spat out Mason his voice contorted with rage.

The Colonel spoke again, he was nervous, he was not built to take pressure. He continuously paced his slim frame around the office scratching his elbow. He spoke in a pathetic sounding falsetto.

"Vander is white Godammit! That means potential trouble! Nobody gives a damn if a few of the natives are wasted but look what happened last year when that recruit died, we had his MP kicking up a bloody great fuss. If this one dies, it could blow the whole operation open. Bloody newspapers and intervention from the foreign office again. On the one hand we are trying to get more people to join us and then things like this happen…It's all too awful to contemplate."

Major Pern had been sitting down listening to the three of them. He was disgusted with the lack of guts and guidance displayed by the Colonel. He tapped his black ebony stick impatiently in his hand, "Does anyone know how bad this Vander really is?"

Mason turned and spoke "I called the MO ten minutes ago, he said that his wounds were deep, had penetrated the bowel and that the marching he was forced to do and the other physical assaults he received have turned a controllable situation into a dangerous one. He can't be moved." He had spoken in a heated voice, all the time staring at Reeves.

"If this turns sour, if he...Dies," The CO's voice thinned away.

Reeves blew his top. "He's not going to die for Chrissake! He's not the type, the man's a fucking pyscho! He damn near wasted three guys last night over nothing! He's gradually taking over this camp, people follow him like some demi god. There was at least sixty witnesses last night and no one will even admit that they've seen him....He's dangerous David...."

"Don't you call the Commanding Officer by his first name!" raged Mason.

"Oh for Chris'sake come off it Mason! Remember sitting on that Dak all of us? Less than two years ago? You, or any of you, didn't know shit from what was happening. It was my suggestions and my know how that set this whole thing up and what a mug I was, content to do the thing I know best, training recruits while you lot grabbed the top positions. And look at you! You actually believe in yourselves! You! A spotty faced Lieutenant thrown out for siphoning money from the Regimental account now a Colonel strutting around like Lord shit. And you two fucking drop outs, Special Forces my arse! Well I've had it up to here! And if I have to go to M'Punga myself and tell him what's going on and what you are planning I will. Oh! Yes, I know about all the cash and diamonds and God knows what else you've all got stashed away. When its starts getting rough you're all going to leg it........"

"That's enough Reeves." said Mason weakly. The counterattack had shaken him.

"If M'Punga knew what you were planning he'd have you all taken out and shot." continued Reeves. Pern casually reached inside his jacket, took out a small Mauser Automatic and levelled it at Reeves who stared in disbelief. Mason and Hennings got out of the line of fire quickly.

"M'Punga is not going to find out anything from you or anybody. RSM, the Staff Sergeant is showing signs of insanity, he has already subjected a recruit to treatment that is threatening his life and he is still show-ing dangerous and aggressive behaviour. Call out the guard, have him arrested and locked up."

"Oh! For Gods sake Julian is there a need for this?" whined the Colonel.

"What do want David? Do you want this frustrated, illiterate muscle bender to spoil everything? Make the call RSM."

"Fuck you!" shouted Reeves, he tipped a desk over and dived through the doorway. Pern took a quick shot but it was wide.

Paul sat up in bed, he was in the Camp Hospital, a square room containing four beds, the other three empty. One side contained a treatment room and office with an internal window that looked into the ward. The lights didn't work in the ward and it was illuminated only by the office light.

Paul watched the black medical officer put down the phone and come through to see him. He had a big smile on his face showing a gleaming wall of white teeth. "That was the RSM I told him exactly what you said, that you were dangerously ill because of the marching and beating...If they come here you gotta look the part though!"

"Yeh, don't worry Doc, have you got a smoke?" Paul had quit years ago but at that moment had an urgent craving for one. He looked down at the bandages around his midriff, they felt firm and painkillers had got rid of the throb. The wounds were little more than superficial, a large sliver of glass had been left embedded and that had caused a lot of the trouble, the MO had removed it and carried out some good needlework.

"So Mister Paul you owe me some money." beamed the Doctor.

"Yeh, I can give you fifty now and fifty on pay day, okay?"

"You said a hundred right now!"

"Okay, so phone the RSM back and tell him you made a wrong diagnosis!" Both men laughed out loud.

Paul had reasoned that the only way that he could get some respite and send the head shed into a flap would be to convince everyone that he was very ill. He had genuinely collapsed in the guardroom and had cooked up the plan after listening to the Doctor ranting about the Camp Regime while he stitched his wound.

A recruit had died on a run. He had collapsed and they had just left him on the side of the road for three hours. By the time the Doc had got to him he was dead. They had done their utmost to shift the blame on to him but had failed. It had been easy to get the Doc to go along with his plan.

The Doc had just left leaving a medic on duty when the door opened and the same clerk that had warned Paul earlier came in the ward. Paul had time to lay back and look half comatose.

"Paul, Paul, listen!" said the clerk, gently tapping him on the arm. "I saw the CO, Reeves, Mason and Pern going into the CO's office for a meeting, so I goes in the office next door, the walls are thin.." The clerk related the meeting to Paul leaving out nothing. When he had finished he sat back and waited.

"Thank you my friend." whispered Paul, gripping the clerks arm. "Keep me informed."

"It's a pleasure." said the clerk looking a little embarrassed. "I'd do anything for you Paul." He got up and half ran out of the ward.

Paul re-assessed the situation in the light of what the clerk had told him. Reeves on the run, where would he go and what would he do? Perhaps they would all come to their senses when things had calmed down and unite again but Paul doubted it.

He had sensed rather than seen, the underlying tensions between all of them. Neither of them trusted each other. They were in it to get what they could out of it, whether it be financial reward, or the slaking of some thirst for power. It was bound to have blown at sometime and he Paul Van Der Borg had been the catalyst. At this thought Paul allowed himself a smile.

"Congratulations Vander.. If that is your name." said a voice that was quiet and conversational. Paul who had been drifting in his thoughts felt a jab of fear as he opened his eyes and saw Reeves sitting by his bed relaxed just as if he was visiting an old friend. "You are here what?.. Six weeks and you have the whole lot of us disappearing up our own arseholes. I knew from the first time I clapped eyes on you, that you was a problem, what are you after Paul Vander?"

Paul noticed that the duty medic had resumed his sleep in the office, he had studied Reeves while he talked and reckoned that he had flipped. Month upon month in this pressure cooker situation, trying to channel and vent his frustrations into his training regimen and then turned on and nearly killed by the very men he had guided and supported.

"Help me." said Paul gently.

"What?" answered Reeves, raising his head, "What did you say?"

"Help me." repeated Paul.

Reeves gave a low chuckle and shook his head. "Me help *you?*"

"Yes," said Paul sitting himself up in the bed. "help me get rid of those bastards."

"You are off your rocker Vander." sneered Reeves as he started to get up. He was sounding like his old self again. He leaned forward to get out of the chair, as quick as a snake strike Paul grabbed him by his shirt and dragged him toward him the point of the knife in the corner of his eye. Reeves lost his balance, he stumbled to his knees on the floor and Paul's iron grip held him in close.

"You wanted my knife Reeves? Well now you have it, one flick of my wrist and you are dead and who would blame me? Poor old Vander lying on his sick bed and nasty Staff Sergeant Reeves who put him there in the first place comes to finish him off."

Paul venomously spat the words out and increased his grip, the point of the knife just breaking the skin at the point where the nose met the eye socket. He continued savagely. "You fucking sorry moron, why *shouldn't* I finish you right now eh?! Your lovely Lillian wouldn't miss you would she? She's probably still getting banged ten times a night by half of your recruits in Plymouth. What makes you such a fucking sorry loser Reeves?"

Reeves heaved and started sobbing, large tears rolled down his cheeks.

"Go a fucking head Vander....Do it!" He blubbed

"Listen to me Reeves, I said help me and I meant it! You....and I together we can clear this scum out!" Suddenly there was a noise, the door opened and Mason followed by Hennings and Pern entered the office, startling the duty medic awake.

Paul whispered to Reeves urgently. "Get over into the corner and under the bed, get a grip man and go now!" He released Reeves who didn't hesitate to do as he was told. Paul just had time to put away the knife and ease down the bed. He forced dribble out of the side of his mouth and made his breathing laboured as the door to the ward opened. Mason fiddled with the light switch but gave up in disgust when nothing happened.

The trio approached the bed and Hennings spoke in a thin weak voice. "Vander….Vander are you awake?" Paul groaned a barely audible yes and nodded his head slightly.

"Good…Er, are you feeling better?" Again a groan.

An irritated Pern broke in. "Listen Vander, Reeves is under arrest and will stand trial for what he did. Attempted murder carries twenty years out here, he won't survive for two of them. So get well and you'll see him go down, things don't take too long around here…Right?!"

He looked at Hennings as if to bring it all to a conclusion. Hennings leaned forward and patted Paul's shoulder. "Good man." he said and led them out of the hospital.

Some two minutes later, when all was quiet again except for the gentle snoring of the medic, Reeves left his hiding place and approached Paul's bed. "What have you got in mind?" he said woodenly.

"That depends on you and what you can tell me." said Paul evenly.

"Oh! I can tell you a lot my friend." sighed Reeves.

Paul took his arm from underneath the sheet and Reeves automatically sprang back. Paul offered his hand. Reeves stepped forward and shook it.

6

Colonel Hennings was nervous an armed guard outside of his office testified to that. Reeves had been on the loose now for a second day. Pern and Mason were also rattled and took similar precautions. They had mounted a block on the Road to Laka in case Reeves had tried to make it to M'Punga and carry out his threat. The phone rang, "Colonel Hennings."

It was the Doctor. "Colonel, my patient has taken a turn for the worse and we must take the risk and move him to the Peoples Hospital in Laka, if we don't he may slip."

"Very well, do what you must…and keep me informed."

"We need a pass, the road block may turn us back."

"Yes! Yes! Send your man around and I'll sort it."

Hennings put down the phone and cradled his head in his hands.

Paul and Reeves sat in the office of the Camp Hospital talking. Paul in an arrangement with the MO had got rid of the Duty Medic and ordered the ambulance, they had locked the door so no one could surprise them. Reeves sat uneasily, forever flexing his muscles and cracking his knuckles, a worried grimace replaced the usual look of confidence.

Paul on the other hand sat back smoking, an air of confidence and excitement about him. He knew he was on the verge of something big, he knew there were many traps and pitfalls to overcome but living on the edge was like a drug to him.

"The ambulance will pick us up from here and take us to Laka, once there it's up to you to get me to see M' Punga." stated Paul.

"Ordinarily that wouldn't be a problem, up until last week I went to the Palace a couple of times a week to train his son on weights but after the assassination attempt he's become a virtual recluse, plus we don't know what Hennings has poisoned his mind with, so as soon as I come out in the open I could be arrested." whined Reeves.

Paul countered, "My little spies tell me that Hennings and the other two are playing this close to their chests in the hope of catching you soon. I have put word out that you have been seen living rough in the jungle area north of the camp. I believe they are about to mount a huge search operation there, there's a price on your head too, five hundred dollars was mentioned."

"Five hundred fucking dollars." sneered Reeves. Paul pushed the phone across the desk to Reeves.

"Phone him!"

"Phone who?" puzzled Reeves.

"The President's son, phone him and tell him you are coming in to do whatever you do, you've done it before. Tell him you have an instructor in unarmed combat with you, he has got an interest in that sort of thing you said. At least it will get us into the Palace."

"Yeh but.."

"But nothing, he can only say no." insisted Paul.

"And what if I do get you to see M'Punga? What then? We'd tell him all we know about this supposed fortune and the plan to flee the country with it but we've got no proof, just our word, no loot to show him, just me on the run and you, an unknown rookie. Hennings and Pern are so well in they would turn the story around and have us both shot! No, you may have got it right up to now but that's ludicrous." said Reeves in a sullen dejected manner. Paul came to a rapid conclusion that Reeves was right.

"Come on Reeves think! There must be something we can use to convince M'Punga. Where do you think they would stash all the loot?" Things had come on so well for Paul he refused to believe it must all come to a sudden halt now. If it was the end of the road for this particular plan he would have to kill Reeves immediately and bide his time until another opportunity arose. It amused him slightly that unwittingly Reeves was thinking for his life.

Reeves got up and started pacing, his situation and being confined to the hospital was telling on him, Paul guessed that it wouldn't be too long before he cracked. Suddenly Reeves' eyes widened and he smashed a fist into the palm of his hand. His voice was loud and he spluttered as his brain worked ten times faster than his mouth. "That must be it! That slimy bastard Pern, that jumped up fucking corporal, he was Intelligence Corps in the UK. Ha! Ha!" Laughed Reeves.He sat down a cruel grin on his face, he looked at a puzzled Paul. "Mr smart arse Pern at one of the first meetings we ever had to discuss our long term aims took minutes, you know what I mean? Who said what etc."

Paul nodded his interest growing.

"He tried to impress every bastard with his knowl-edge of *proper procedure*." Mimicked Reeves, using Pern's pseudo upper crust accent. "Later on, Hennings stopped any records being taken in case they fell into the wrong hands and ordered Pern to destroy those already taken!"

"So you were in on these meetings?" said Paul his face a mask of concentration.

"In the beginning yeh, but when things took off and they started actually getting the loot rolling in, they cut the likes of me out of it."

"And so did he destroy the minutes of those early meetings?"

"No, he fucking didn't!" shouted Reeves his eyes wide, little flecks of foam darted from his mouth as he spoke.

"How do you know for sure? Did you see them re-cently?"

"As recently as two weeks ago." said Reeves his voice subsiding to a more normal pitch and volume, "He keeps them in a big safe in his bunk room, he also keeps the keys to the Armoury and Ammunition store in there and I had to get them off him. Usually he brings them to his office on a daily basis but on this occasion he had forgotten and I went to his bunk with him and I saw them in the safe!"

Paul, still apparently unmoved, jabbed at Reeves, "How did you know it was them? Did you see them? Did you read them? All of it?"

Reeves' face fell, "No of course I didn't read them! What the pissing hell did you expect me to do say? *Excuse me Major Pern Sir, can I read those stupid bastard minutes you took, you know, the ones that could get us all fucking shot.*"

Paul ignored the outburst, "Then how do you know they were the minutes?" he asked simply.

Reeves ran his fingers through imaginary long hair. He took his time answering and when he did his voice was back to normal. "He wrote them meticulously in longhand in a large red book with a stiff cover. A ledger type book and yes, I know there are many such books but this one I recognised. It had the word "CONFERENCE" printed on the cover but the F had been filled in to look like a P. It's a stupid little thing but I noticed it and there it was, still in his safe.

"Does he keep the key to the safe on his person?"

"I dunno, must do."

Paul studied the floor in deep concentration for a minute then snapped out of it and picked up the phone. "It's Paul, come and see me." He replaced the phone and spoke to Reeves. "Go back to your hidey hole I'm expecting a visitor.

Paul unlocked the door and let the clerk in, he was a little surprised to see Paul on his feet but said nothing. After sitting down Paul asked for an update on events.

"They've mobilised all the camp and are just starting to move off and search the overgrown area of the Camp for Reeves. The order is to shoot on sight, they say he's deranged and has a weapon, the RSM is conducting it personally. Hennings has a headache and retired for the day."

"And Pern."

"Major Pern is making ready to go on a short break, he has a shamba somewhere in the Bush."

"I mean right now, where is he?"

"He's not left camp yet and he's not at his office he must be at his bunk…Is everything alright Paul? I…We are so worried for you, Reeves may come here.."

"No, don't worry my friend. I am safe enough, go back to your duties and keep me informed. One other thing, get Seb and Tex to come here immediately."

The clerk nodded and turned to go, he looked at Paul and said, "My name is Gary." He looked embarrassed as he shot for the door.

"That little pansy is queer for you." said Reeves with contempt as he re-entered the office. Paul ignored the remark and started to think aloud.

"The ambulance should be ready soon, once it is here put bandages on your face and get on the stretcher, my men will then bring it around to Pern's bunk.."

"What the hell are you after Vander?" said Reeves, his eyes were hooded and he looked dangerous, "I mean, really after? I mean, you're not just going to go up to M'Punga and say, *'Scuse me sir, I have unearthed a plan to rob you and your country blind sir, look what a good boy I am sir.'* mimicked Reeves in a school boy voice.

Paul thought for a few seconds then decided to include Reeves in his plan, it was a risk he knew, the guy was unstable but as long as he was on the run he was controllable.

"Look Reeves," said Paul approaching and standing close to him, "this country is wide open. I sensed it the minute I got out of that Dak, so did Hennings and the rest of them and in a way they are doing alright. No doubt they have a fortune salted away ready for the quick flight out of here one day. But we," Paul was careful to gesture to Reeves when he said spoke, "*we* will replace them. We *will* resurrect the army and defeat the rebels and once this is accomplished, we from a position of power will dictate the next moves! The possibilities are endless" Paul finished by breaking off his stare at Reeves and returning to the desk.

Reeves could not make up his mind whether Vander was madman or genius. He flashed over the couple of months he had known him. He had tried to crack him but despite his best efforts he had failed and now here he was, his life virtually in Vander's hands. Vander, he realised was a natural leader with a magnetic personality that compelled the men to do their utmost for him but most of all Vander, he thought, was a cold, calculating predator. Essentially a planner but nevertheless an opportunist who could think on his feet. He was definitely ruthless, had probably killed and had probably more than once planned to kill him. The last thought made him surface.

"I'm with *you* Paul, watch that bastard Pern! He's more dangerous than all the rest of them put together."

7

After a few minutes Tex and Seb turned up at the hospital, they looked in alarm when they saw Reeves. "Look, don't worry Reeves is with us now. We are on the verge of something very big. I have no time to explain in detail but I will tell you now, that if we are successful you will be extremely well rewarded but if we fail, we will have to fight for our lives!"

He looked at both of them in turn. "It's up to you, you can walk out now and it will mean nothing to me but if you are *in,* you are totally committed." Seb went to say something but checked himself. Tex looked at Reeves and said a little nervously.

"I don't get it Paul, why is this bastard all of a sudden our friend?"

At that, Reeves clenched his fists and started to close with Tex. "You jumped up little bastard..." he hissed.

Paul stood between them and said with authority. "Okay, get it out of your systems if you must! But if we are going to pull this off we've got to stand together, we've got to plan together and if necessary, fight and die together......Together! Well?"

Tex sighed and said, "Count me in."

"Seb?"

"Aye, in for a penny in for a pound."

"Reeves?"

"Yeh, yeh! Count me in…And God help us."

The ambulance arrived. Paul obtained the pass for the road block then dismissed the driver, "Give me half hour then turn up at Pern's bunkhouse."

Paul carrying a rucksack approached Pern's bunk-house. It was a complete Nissen hut secluded in the trees divided up into a bungalow type house. There was a Landrover parked outside but no sentry. He decided on a direct approach in case he was being watched from a window. For effect he held his stomach and leaned slightly forward as if in pain. Paul got on the path and walked stiffly toward the door. He tapped the door briskly and stood back. He heard Pern's posh voice ask, "Who is it!?"

It's Vander Sir!" The door opened a few inches and Pern looked out and beyond Vander.

"What is it man? I thought that you were on your bloody death bed!"

"I need to speak to you sir, it's about Reeves. It's something you ought to know."

"Very well come in." Pern opened the door, he was naked apart from a yellow towel around his waist which made his tanned body look even darker. He was hold-ing the Mauser which he now let drop to his side. Paul found himself in a study type room, a table strewn with paper, a filing cabinet and writing bureau. Pern turned and looked at Paul expectantly.

Paul went to speak but fastened his eyes on the Mauser, his mouth hung open. Pern looked puzzled for a second and then said in an irritated voice, "Oh! For

God's sake," and put the gun on the writing bureau. As soon as he began to turn back Paul moved in and sunk a powerful blow into the bottom of his rib cage, Pern jack knifed and fell to the floor groaning.

Paul let him recover for a few moments careful to step behind him and get the pistol, the hammer was back and there was a round up the spout. Pern was definitely taking no chances.

When he judged him to be okay he snarled viciously at Pern and kicked him in the back. "Up! Up! To the safe now! Move it!" Pern knelt then still breathing heavy rose to his feet his towel slipped to the floor and he walked unsteadily to a room. It was his bedroom, a single bunk lay on one side of the room and on the other, a large green safe.

"The keys to the safe!"

"If you want money Vander, you have got the wrong safe." said Pern contemptuously.

"Open the safe Pern!"

"You'll fucking well hang for this Vander! I have the army and the complete police force of this country at my disposal. Now put that bloody gun down and let's talk! It's not too late, I could use a man like you..."

Paul moved toward Pern who fell backwards onto the bed. The knife now replaced the gun and he held it at Pern's throat.

"I am no stranger to death," said Paul in a conversational tone. "I know many paths that lead to it. I have no need to kill you but if I don't have that key you will choke on your own blood! Now what's it to be?"

Pern lost the colour in his face. "In my trousers." he croaked.

"Lie on your stomach!" Ordered Paul who went to the wardrobe and pulled out a couple of wire hangers. He slid the loop of one up to Pern's elbows and twisted it until it pinned his arms together like a trussed chicken. In a similar manner, he bound his feet. He found a bunch of keys and surmised that it must be the huge brass one. It was, and he swung open the door of the safe.

At the bottom he saw the red book with the F turned into a P. He took it out and flicked the pages stopping here and there to study some of the content in detail. After some minutes Pern who could not see what Vander was up to spoke. "Vander, look the CO will pay you anything you want, ten thousand US, twenty even" Pern was no fool, he knew that Paul was desperate and possibly a lunatic to boot. Death, he felt, was just around the corner. He would say and do anything to alter that.

Paul carefully put the book in his rucksack and un-twisted the wire on Pern. To avert his suspicious mind and keep him on the wrong track Paul snapped, "You bastard there is no money in there! Get dressed quickly! Your uniform. Hurry man!" Paul shut the safe.

Pern talked as he put on his uniform trying to es-tablish a rapport with Paul.

"Ye know, me and you would work well together. Hennings, well Hennings has always been weak, just be-cause he had been to Sandhurst he got the CO's job, unlike sloggers like you and me who've had to work for every penny we've ever had. That bastard gets it on a bloody plate. I need a man Vander...I mean a real man like you who could put things right. With my inside knowledge...."

"Tell me about M'Punga." said Paul quietly.

"M'Punga?" quizzed Pern in a puzzled voice, not sure now of Paul's motives. "I..I don't quite understand."

"What makes him tick?" said Paul tapping his head with the Mauser. "Don't be afraid to talk, I want to know."

"Well M'Punga is slippery fish, Hennings could answer this question better, he sees him on a weekly basis."

"No! You answer me! You slime ball." shouted Paul viciously.

"Oh! God, M'Punga, where does one start?" spluttered Pern nervously. "He's a vicious thug who killed, lied, bribed and bullied his way to the top..."

"Apart from scum like you, who keeps him there?"

"There is his Services Chief of Staff, Juba, he keeps the Army and Airforce Generals in line and loyal. Ha! Airforce, three bloody Dakotas and two Hunter Jets." He blabbered nervously. " He's also a great influence on M'Punga and keeps him supplied with everything from Scotch Whisky to a never ending supply of young women and drugs. We, that is Hennings despite his best efforts has to deal with Juba rather than M'Punga."

"Where exactly is all the loot stashed?"

"So that's it." said Pern matter of factly, "Well, there's enough for everyone you know. We can cut you in, your share to date would be about sixty thousand.... Pounds Sterling that is but that is nothing it could treble or more in the next year. Come in with us Vander!"

"Where exactly is the loot stashed?" repeated Paul.

Pern looked crestfallen, he had always imagined that it would be the weak Hennings if anyone who blabbed. "I honestly don't know, Hennings is the only one who does."

Paul saw through him immediately. Hennings might be the CO but Pern was definitely the brains and drive in the outfit. Pern had finished dressing.

"Very well," said Paul, "I have no further use for you. Hennings will tell me all I need to know. Bye." He levelled the gun at Pern's chest. Pern backed away his hand in front of him.

"No! Wait Vander! There is a room below the armoury, it's all in there! Don't kill me man! There's no need, I can still be of use."

"Okay Pern, I will tell you this. We are going to make a trip to see M'Punga today, you co-operate and you will live, if you don't you will die."

"I'll not rot in one of M'Punga's prisons if that's what you have in mind because if it is, I would sooner..." whined Pern on the edge of hysteria.

"You will live and I will get you out of the country...."

"How the hell can you guarantee that?" yelled an exasperated Pern, "*You*, don't know M'Punga, he's so bloody ruthless.."

"Well what's it to be Pern? You either trust me or I end it here! What's it to be?"

Pern sagged, "I have Hobson's choice old boy and that's no choice at all. I will do all I can to help...Let me start by saying that if you are going to meet M'Punga you need to look the part. It's no good going there dressed like that, he doesn't talk to anyone below the rank of Colonel and you need a chest full of medals, a DCM or at least an MC." Pern turned and went to an oak cabinet.

"Watch it!" shouted Paul bringing the gun up. Pern took no notice and began throwing small flat cardboard boxes onto his bed.

"Medals and insignia old boy, a hobby of mine. Okay lets make you a full colonel in my old Corps with an MC, shall we say earned in Aden, plus a General Service Medal with bars for the Radfan, South Arabia and of course Northern Ireland. An OBE of course and let's see what else we have."

Seb and Tex waited outside of Pern's Bunkhouse for Paul to emerge. Reeves had unsettled them by saying that if Paul fucked up they would all be shot. Seb, not knowing what was going on in detail had started to have doubts but Tex remained strong.

Presently Paul came out with Pern. They stared at Paul in his green uniform that had been festooned with golden rank insignia, medals and a maroon cravat, to finish off with he wore a hat that looked like it had been stolen from a South American General. Pern looked with surprise at Reeves.

After a slightly self conscious look Paul barked out his orders. "Reeves, make that call now to the Prince. Use Pern's phone. You tell him I'm a special forces colonel on a visit and that I'm an unarmed combat instructor...You know the usual woffle. We need to gain entry to the palace this afternoon or tonight at the very least.

You two up front, Seb drive. I will be in the back with Pern and Reeves." After two minutes Reeves emerged from the building an uncharacteristic smile on his face.

"He bought it, we can go straight there. You'd better be good *Colonel* Vander. Prince Tasi may be an oily, fat, spoilt bastard but he'll see through you in a second if you're not."

The ambulance bumped down the road from Lagonda, Reeves leered at Pern and then started chuckling. "You had your shot at me *Corporal* Pern but you missed!" he reached over, slapped Pern hard in the face, grabbed his hair and rocked his head savagely up and down

"Enough!" interjected Paul.

Reeves switched his savage gaze from Pern to Paul. "If this bastard is going to die, I want to be the one to do it!" He forced out through clenched teeth.

"Right now we need him." said Paul evenly. Reeves sat back but kept his savage gaze on Pern. Paul again wandered if he was wise taking Pern with him, he may have underestimated Pern's influence with M'Punga. The Minute book may not be enough and he hadn't checked to see if the loot was below the armoury as Pern had said. Pern could argue that the book was a forgery and if there was no loot…. Paul closed the thought off. He hoped that he could trick Pern somehow into tripping himself up or betraying his feelings in front of M'Punga.

"Road block ahead!" warned Tex through the hatch. Reeves immediately lay down on the stretcher and placed the mask of bandages on his face. Paul held the Mauser under Pern's ear. The ambulance braked to a halt and they heard some talk. After a few seconds there was a shout and some scraping of wood on tarmac and they were back on their way.

Reeves pulled the bandages off his face, sat up and said in an agitated fashion, "Paul as soon as you get to the Palace this shit Pern will have you arrested. He is well known to them, he's had two years to worm his way in, kill the bastard now! I'll do it! Don't trust the bastard man!" Pern looked truly shaken, he looked from Reeves to Paul and tried to formulate some words but failed.

"I have a deal with Pern," said Paul evenly, "if he co-operates he lives, if not..."

"Okay this is the plan." said Paul with calm authority. He had stopped the ambulance just outside of the City limits and grouped them around the bonnet less Pern "Me and Reeves go in, once there, I try to find an opportunity to see M'Punga. You Seb and Tex wait with Pern at the hospital. Tie Pern up and don't let him talk to anyone. I will get a message to you via the hospital to bring Pern in, if you don't get a message today or hear that anything has happened to us, kill Pern and look to yourselves. All the loot you want is below the Armoury in Camp Lagonda.. Good luck." Paul handed Pern's Mauser to Tex and pulled him to one side out of earshot. "Have you got a problem about using it? On Pern I mean."

"No."

"Good, don't untie him until you get the message from me and don't trust him an inch!"

Reeves and Paul walked toward the Taxi rank having just left the ambulance.

"This looks good, a colonel arriving at the palace by a taxi." muttered Reeves.

"How we arrive is the least of our problems Reeves. I would be more concerned with how we left."

The taxi meandered through Laka's baking streets that were teeming with people. Every type of fruit was being sold and beggars seeing white men in the taxi hammered on the windows with their fists and gestured for anything they could get.

Presently they left the thronging streets and drove through leafy residential areas. They came upon a tree lined road newly surfaced with tarmac. At irregular intervals army jeeps with machine guns mounted were parked. Soldiers lounged around in the shade. The avenue ran to a huge set of wooden doors set in a fifteen foot high stone wall. "M'Punga's den, the Palace." whispered Reeves.

The sentries used to seeing Reeves let them through. "The next set of guards are the bastards." said a nervous Reeves. The taxi on Reeves' order stopped in a court yard just inside the gate. "This is it, shit or bust!" he said grimly. Both men got out and Paul followed Reeves to a metal door. Reeves pressed a bell and they waited.

After a minute or so a small metal slot at head height in the door opened and then closed. A bolt was drawn and after some seconds a voice shouted "Enter one at a time!" Reeves went in and the door closed. Paul could hear nothing. After a minute the bolt slid again and the voice commanded, "Enter!"

Paul found himself in a large ante room, it was brightly lit with no furniture apart from a small table. Reeves was not there. Two very tall black soldiers in camo trousers and green T shirts looked at him with contempt. "Empty your pockets!" Paul did so, some dollar bills and some change. "Identity!" Paul went to his map pocket and pulled out his ID card issued at Camp Lagonda to PRIVATE Vander, in it was thirty US Dollars. They searched Paul's small rucksack and thumbed through the book , it meant nothing to them. "Turn around!" he was frisked. "What is the purpose of your visit?"

"I am here at the request of Prince Tasi to instruct him...You can check."

"I have checked, were it not true, you would be dead!"

Paul was ushered through the door and saw Reeves, he was talking to a black officer who eyed Paul with some hostility.

He followed the Officer and Reeves through some passage ways, at each turn there was an armed soldier. They stopped at a door, the officer knocked and went in. He came out almost immediately and waived them in. As Paul passed he stopped him and hissed quickly, "Do not look the President in the eye for more than two seconds, and address him as His Royal Highness and bow your head!" So M'Punga *was* there! Paul felt a rush of excitement.

Paul entered a large square room with a beautiful
Persian carpet but no other furniture. At one end was a
huge ornate fireplace and around this stood a group of
people. They were in uniform apart from two men, one
was a tall fat youth with large jowls, bulging stomach,
the other small and intense looking. Both were in track
suits.

The officer that had accompanied them halted
with Paul and Reeves a respectful distance from the
group and waited. The fat youth who Paul guessed was
Prince Tasi, looked at them with interest, the others totally ignored them. After some minutes the group broke
into a peal of laughter and a small man in an army uniform turned around and looked toward his officer.

Paul saw that he was around five foot two with a
slim frame, his face though Negroid showed some Asian
influence in the domed forehead and slightly thinner
nose. His eyes were narrow slits of mistrust and hatred.
This, thought Paul, must be M'Punga.

The Officer bowed, Paul and Reeves followed suit.
"Your Royal Highness,"

The officer began in a voice that sounded as if it
had said it a thousand times before. "Your Royal Highness it gives me pleasure to present to you Staff Sergeant
Reeves who has come to instruct His Highness, The
Prince Tasi and Colonel Vander, late of the British Special Air Service and Intelligence Corps and visiting our
army in the role of advisor, he too comes to...."

"Yes, yes, you are dismissed." chirped the little
man. The officer bowed again and left walking backwards to the door. The little man whom Paul was now in

no doubt was M'Punga came toward them. Paul could feel his eyes on him. "Colonel," Came the high pitched voice from M'Punga, "tell me, why wasn't I informed of your presence in my country?"

"Your Royal Highness I only made my presence known today, I have come to you on a mission of great importance.."

"Oh! Did you? I thought you came to instruct my son or is that your *mission of great importance* !" He chuckled and the group at the fireplace roared with laughter.

"He is an unarmed combat instructor Papa, keep your distance!" It was the boyish voice of Prince Tasi. M'Punga turned and laughed, this time the group at the fireplace howled, bent double and slapped their legs.

"Very well Tasi," said M'punga slyly, "You had better test him out, see if all your expensive training has paid off…eh?!"

Tasi stopped smiling but then turned to the smaller track suited man at his side.

"Jokko." was all he said and the small intense man started to walk warily toward Paul. M'Punga moved back to the group.

"It's all on you sunshine." hissed Reeves, "Lose this and we're all fucking dead!"

Paul studied the man whom he took to be Tasi's bodyguard. He was not the usual run of the mill giant that normally took these parts. He was relatively small with a large completely flattened nose. His almond shaped eyes had a burning intensity about them. He had no bulging muscles and didn't adopt a fighting stance. This, to Paul meant that he was very dangerous indeed.

Paul took off his medals, put them in his hat and hand-ed them to Reeves who backed away.

Jokko stopped a few paces away from Paul who had not moved. The group were silent and expectant. Jokko made a movement with his arms and started to move around to Paul's flank forcing him to turn. Suddenly Jokko leapt in the air, just as Paul put his arms up in a defensive cross a foot came bursting through just catch-ing him on the chin, a light flashed in Paul's brain and he found himself falling backwards. Instantly another bang on the side of his head, he felt the floor rise up and hit his back.

He instinctively rolled and rolled then leapt to his feet, his head clearing by the second as adrenaline ham-mered through his system.

Jokko was now crouching, Paul had his back to the wall so he couldn't be outflanked. "Finish him Jokko! Kill the trash!" Yelled Tasi. Jokko waited, he wanted Paul to move into him. Paul could feel the blood pour-ing from his nose and mouth. He dabbed the back of his hand in the blood and looked at it, he then acted as if he had gone crazy. Yelling, he took two quick steps toward Jokko but then stopped abruptly. Jokko fell for it and again lashed out with his scissors kick, another inch and he would have connected but he didn't and Paul moved in sweeping Jokko's legs even further up in the air. Jokko landed badly but recovered quicker than a cat and tried to scramble out of distance but Paul followed as quick and managed to get a hefty boot into the side of his ribs as he got up.

Jokko grunted then instantly swung around and lashed out again with his foot. This caught Paul behind the knee and he went down on his back, he instantly rolled over on to his chest with his hands splayed as if doing press ups. He was facing Jokko whom he saw step in for the Coup De Grace. As fast as his adrenaline soaked muscles would allow, he swung his legs around like a crocodile's tail one hundred and eighty degrees while twisting onto his back he felt his legs connect with Jokko's sweeping him off his feet, again Jokko landed badly and sprang back up but this time not as fast as before.

Paul was on him and grabbed his track suit in a judo fashion, he danced a little with Jokko, then swung and slammed him onto the floor, he heard his breath exhale sharply and knew he had him. He rolled him over on his front, hammer locked his arm within a centimetre of breaking it and with his knee planted firmly in Jokko's back cupped a hand under his chin. A wrench back and his spine would snap at the neck. In gladiatorial fashion he looked at the group of onlookers.

"Finish the trash!" Yelled Tasi in a temper laden voice.

Paul pretended he didn't hear, stood up and bowed toward M'Punga, who started to clap as he said, "He needn't kill him, he has never been defeated in front of me before, the shame will do that!" he laughed, the chorus laughed and clapped louder.

Paul turned and went to Jokko who was now rising, he held out his hand to help him up but it was shrugged off. M'Punga came up to Paul and said quietly. "And now Colonel, your mission of great importance?" Paul saw the narrow bloodshot eyes burning into him, before he could answer M'Punga cut back in, "But of course, you must wash up first, I will see you in half an hour."

Pern tried to wrestle himself into an upright position on the stretcher in the back of the ambulance when he failed he looked across at Seb who was guarding him. "Hey! Look old man can I have a drink? Er.. Water I mean, I'm as dry as a bone." Seb pulled back the blanket and inspected the ropes that bound him, satisfied he replaced the blanket and reached for a water bottle.

"Aye, take a swig o' this and make it a good one. I'm not getting up and down for the likes of you every five minutes." Seb propped him up and tipped the bottle, Pern greedily slugged back the water.

"Thanks old man, that's better. Don't suppose you could stretch to a smoke?"

"Aw for fucks sakes man!" gasped Seb, he fished around in his pocket, lit two cigarettes and placed one in Pern's mouth. Between puffs Pern started a casual conversation, he had tried with Tex when he was on guard but received a back hander for his efforts.

Seb he thought, was a little different though. He sensed a weakness and uncertainty in him, he also detected a slight smell of alcohol on his breath. He was agitated and becoming afraid. It seemed that they were guarding him in stags of half hour on and half hour off, he didn't have much time until Tex's return .

"Seb, I don't want to alarm you old man but this *is* all going to end up in tears you know."

"Aye and who's tears Mister, Major, bloody Pern, Sir. Yours or mine?" shot back an agitated Seb.

"Quite!" answered Pern gently. "M'Punga is no fool you know. I once saw him investigate a minor theft at the palace, some bloody trinket or other had gone missing. Using sheer logic and deduction he traced the theft to his Chef and do you know what he made him do?"

"No Major bloody Pern! I don't bloody know what he made him do!"

"He gave him a choice, either he would shoot him on the spot or he could cut his own hand off with a meat cleaver and live...Imagine that eh? His favourite Cordon Bleue Chef too and just over a trinket worth tuppence, that's what we're dealing with here you know."

In spite of his feelings, Seb enquired, "What happened?".

"Oh! M'Punga has it mounted now, the hand that is, as an ashtray I believe. Looks like a large spider on its back apparently.. Ghastly. And that was all over a bloody useless piece of glass. You know, Vander won't stand a chance he's probably under arrest right now. M'Punga and me we trust each other, he knows I'd never betray him. It's still not too late Seb. I can still get us out of this, maybe not Vander or Reeves they're in too deep, but you and maybe Tex, I could swing it. My influence is great at the palace."

Paul sloshed water over his head for the sixth time, his shirt was torn and heavily blood stained, his head hammered like the worst hangover anyone had. The stitches had burst and he felt blood trickling from his old stomach wounds. Reeves and he were alone in an ornate toilet. Paul carefully dried his swollen face.

"You cut that fine." stated Reeves.

"Cut it fine? If he had worn anything other than those canvas training pumps he would have finished me with that first kick. Shit, that man can fight! That kick I gave him in the side, busted three or four ribs for sure, did you see the blood he coughed up, all frothy? That's blood from a punctured lung, he is as hard as they come, and then some!"

"So you're saying you're harder, is that it?"

"No! I'm saying I'm lucky, dead lucky!"

"Let's hope it holds." said Reeves.

Just then the door opened and a flunky carrying an armful of green fatigue shirts came in. "Please try these for size Colonel, his Royal Highness will see you in ten minutes."

Paul was ushered by the Officer into a different room, it was more businesslike with a filing cabinet a desk and a battery of phones. Reeves was told to wait outside.

Soon a large fat Officer of middle age came in. Paul had seen him in the fight room. "How do you feel Colonel Vander?"

"To tell the truth Sir, not too well, that Jokko hits hard." said Paul in a subdued voice. The Officer laughed and then went serious.

I am Field Marshall Juba of the Karuda Defence Force. His Highness has instructed me to interview you…. Something about a matter of great importance I think you said Colonel?"

"I need to speak to M'Punga personally Sir.."

"How dare you call our Royal Highness that! I could have you taken out and beaten to death for that Colonel!" Screamed Juba, struggling to get his huge, fat frame out of the seat. Suddenly he stopped his diatribe and came to attention. Paul knew that M'Punga had entered the room.

"What could he be beaten to death for Juba?" said the high thin voice.

Before he could answer Paul broke in. "It was my fault your Royal Highness, I am a field soldier and unused to the ways of court. I heartily apologise for my lack of manners and will ensure that in future I will proceed with more care.

"Hmm, I very much doubt it. Tell me, why did you not kill Jokko when my son ordered it?"

"At the time Sir, I was unsure of exactly who your son was, having not been introduced beforehand, however Sir, had *you* ordered it then it would have been done without hesitation." Stated Paul loudly and confidently, he was still rigid to attention with M'Punga behind him.

"Very well Colonel, relax." said M'Punga casually. He came around to the front of Paul and sat at on the desk. Only then Paul became aware of the three bodyguards that had entered silently with M'Punga, they stood just behind him. Juba remained standing behind the Desk.

"State your reasons for seeing me." said M'Punga casually. Paul took a deep breath and began to speak.

Reeves paced up and down like an expectant father. Paul had been with M'Punga an hour now, this in itself he thought was a good sign. The door opened and a bodyguard beckoned him in. He saw M'Punga now sitting at the desk with Paul the other side, a tray of what smelled like coffee between them. The bodyguards were relaxed and even Juba was slouched. M'Punga looked up at Reeves and smiled, "Thank you Staff Sergeant Reeves. Colonel Vander here was telling me how you were instrumental in the exposeȼ of this whole affair, you should have come straight to me though." he wagged his finger in mock rebuke.

"Sorry Sir, I didn't think.."

"Ah! But you *did* think and you will be rewarded for it ." He waved him away and a bodyguard opened the door.

"Look Seb, before they come and arrest you cut me free and get me to a phone! It's your only chance man!" Pern said in an excited whisper.

Seb got up and tried to move in the hot confined space in the back of the ambulance but banged his head. He reached into his equipment, pulled out a water bottle and took three deep gulps. He retched a couple of times but kept the liquor down.

"What about Paul and Tex? Fuck that bastard Reeves but what about *them*?" He snivelled.

"Seb, I will do my best for them but they're probably dead as we speak! Cut me free man! Save yourself. Seb reached to his equipment and pulled out a knife.

"If you're kiddin' me, I'll kill you meself." He blubbed as he sawed through the ropes.

The back door of the ambulance was wrenched open by Tex, "What the? What the hell are you doing? You drink soaked, crazy bastard!"

"It's the only chance we got Tex, Paul is dead, they're comin' to arrest us man!" Tex looked at Pern he was sitting up, hands free but feet still bound, he looked pale and frightened, he had been seconds from getting free.

"Dead is he? Well that must have been a ghost I was just speakin' to on the phone then." said Tex and punched Pern as hard as he could in the face.

M'Punga watched Reeves leave the office. "You tell me that these people had cheated me, giving false body counts, plundered my mines and businesses, diverted cash used for paying my soldiers to acquire a fortune, while all the time the enemies of my country are building up to strike? And you yourself want very little? This I find hard to believe."

Paul seized his chance, his face changed to a mask of staring fanaticism . "All I want Sir is a chance to build up your Army into a great force! That is what I do well. That is what I was put on this earth for, to lead men into battle. To fight and struggle for a belief, to watch my enemies die before me. I can do it, with Field Marshal Juba's help, I can do it! All I want is my soldier's pay and one year to complete my strategy.."

"And what is your strategy?"

"We have at the moment something like two hundred and fifty white soldiers here mostly former army from Britain. Good soldiers who are wasted by being split up and sent in penny packets to serve in the Commandos as advisors or platoon leaders, some even as drivers. With your permission, through the Field Marshal, I will retrain these people and form The Royal Karudan Combat Commando that will crush all opposition in the land. We won't pussy foot around and shake sticks, we will pursue these pigs to the very borders of our land and then pursue them in their so called havens across the border, there will be no let up and no mercy!"

Paul could see a fire light up in M'Punga's eyes. "Let me demonstrate Sir, how lax your army has become under the leadership of Hennings and Pern. Your own palace guard frisked me, they stole thirty US Dollars from me but missed this!" With a deft motion he reached to the back of his neck and pulled out the knife, he flicked it and it thudded into the table, he stepped away from it before the bodyguards could react.

M'Punga's eyes widened, he turned. "Juba?"

Juba too had been stirred by Paul's speech and shocked at seeing the knife, he new M'Punga well enough to know that he had found this British Special Forces Colonel to his liking. M'Punga had fared well under the British and still had a lot of liking and respect for them. If he went against him he might lose favour himself, however, if he backed him now it would keep his options open. "Well, your Royal Highness," spoke Juba in his deep rich voice, "the Colonel thinks the same way as me, must be our Sandhurst training!" he laughed.

"I'm more than willing to take him on as an advisor on my staff for what did he say? One year?"

The ambulance stopped outside of the palace. Tex was glad to get out of the cab. Seb had thrown up several times on the journey from the hospital. Between heaves he had cried and sobbed, even a couple of back handers had proven ineffective against his breakdown. Tex couldn't put him in the back with Pern and he couldn't trust him to drive, so he'd had to endure the sobs and the acrid stench of vomit laced with stale booze.

Tex stopped outside of the Palace main gate and opened the back of the ambulance then acting on Paul's phoned orders, cut Pern free. Pern was shocked but when he recognised his surroundings he couldn't believe his luck. He clambered out and rubbed some life into his numb limbs. He straightened his uniform as the ambulance drove off. Still slightly bewildered, his face caked in dry blood he walked to the guardroom. The guard commander leapt to attention when he recognised Pern."Sergeant, get that ambulance stopped and arrest the two occupants. Watch it they're armed!"

The guard commander ran out and went through the motions to do as he was told but he had already been for warned by Juba not to take any real action.

M'Punga, Juba and Paul now sat in M'Punga's Presidential Office. It was a huge room with thirty foot high ceilings and walls covered in oak panels ornately carved. A fitted carpet with the design of the Karuda flag covered the entire floor and Corinthian columns rose to the ceiling. The whole thing a monument to bad taste.

On a raised marble platform at the end of the room was M'punga's desk, the top of which had the dimensions of a full sized snooker table. The three of them sat at one end of the desk in enormous padded leather chairs. Juba put down the phone and said. "Your Royal highness, he is on his way up." They waited in silence. The tall oaken doors swung open and the escort officer stood and waited, Juba made a signal and he spoke.

"Your Royal Highness it gives me pleasure in presenting Major Pern OBE DCM MC who craves an urgent and personal meeting with Your Royal Highness." M'punga nodded and Juba gestured, almost immediately Pern came strutting toward them. He had cleaned up the best he could but still looked pale and unnerved. He stopped and quickly bowed. "Your Royal Highness I have an urgent matter to report, there is a person in the palace grounds who is going to attempt to take your life. I was a captive of them until I just broke free! I have had two of them arrested the third needs finding as a matter of urgency. I suggest..."

"Is this the person you are talking about Major?" said M'Punga quietly.

Paul rose from the chair and faced Pern who spluttered and went for a gun that wasn't there. "Yes! Watch it Your Majesty, he's dangerous.."

"Mmm, lets see who's dangerous and who's not shall we? Approach!" Ordered M'Punga. Pern came face to face with Paul.

"Sir, this man is armed with a knife and has sworn to kill you. This morning he tried to coerce me into his plan and when I refused he kidnapped and tortured me to get my co-operation. When I still refused he ordered his two henchmen to take me in the Bush and kill me but thank God I escaped. Call your bodyguard Sir, I warn you!"

"This *would be* assassin Major, tells a somewhat different story. He says that you, other white officers and indeed maybe some of my own officers had meetings and conspired to rob me and then flee the country. This would be assassin tells me that operations against the rebels are non existent and that all the time they get stronger while you get richer by robbing me and blaming the rebels."

"Meetings Sir!? Operations!? I know nothing of these things! I am purely administration, a ruddy pen pusher Sir!"

"Ah! Yes, and talking of pushing pens perhaps you will recognise this?" M'Punga lifted the red Minutes book off his desk, opened it and flicked through the pages, he stopped and read from it. "Thursday the 18th, now let me see...ah! RSM Mason suggests that the cash should be shifted out of the country immediately in case the rebels attack and makes things difficult, however, Major Pern does not agree, he seems to think that arrangements to keep it safe in another country are incomplete.. and so on and so forth." M'Punga's voice trailed off and he handed the book to Pern with a smile on his face.

Pern stared in disbelief his jaw worked but no sound come out. Suddenly it all fell into place. Vander was not the get rich quick thug he had thought. He was bold, clever, devious......His thoughts were interrupted by the three bodyguards running into the room. Juba barked "Arrest this man, search him thoroughly and keep him under close observation!" Pern was dragged away, shouting and begging almost incoherently.

"Your first mission Colonel is to round up and arrest the other conspirators. My Palace Guard are at your disposal....And then there is the loot Colonel. I will inspect it *all*, here tomorrow." said M'Punga, who then left the room.

The next few days saw Hennings arrested plus Mason and a few other officers and men. Paul, with Juba and a couple of his staff present personally supervised the opening of the vault beneath the armoury, where plundered diamonds, gold, silver and US Dollars lay neatly boxed or crated ready for a quick move if necessary. This is what in M'Punga's eyes had made Paul's story about resurrecting the army and defeating the rebels a credible one.

What ordinary man could ignore a fortune there for the taking and instead set himself an enormous task? To him, like many before him, Paul Van Der Borgh remained an enigma. Madman or genius? Or that deadly mixture of both?

8

Brigadier Paul Vander newly appointed Commander of the Palace Guard and Director of the Laki Garrison removed his name card off the seat, sat down and carefully flattened out any potential wrinkles in his crisp white tropical uniform. He was one of the last to take his seat before Juba and M'punga arrived. The officers in his Command filled the remaining three tiers of seats.

The photographer, a thin birdlike white man in his sixties continually stuck his head under the black canopy that covered his camera, emerging to shout instructions to the periphery of the group. He was sweating profusely in the late morning sun and continuously wiped his brow, he made no attempt to remove his thick, worn hacking jacket and spotted bow tie.

The photograph had been Paul's idea to celebrate his new appointment. M'punga had readily agreed, it had never been done before. Thirteen months had now passed since Paul's fateful first visit to the Palace, already it seemed like a lifetime away.

Paul had been given a free hand by Juba who had expected him at any time to fail but he hadn't. He formed the new Commando which at Juba's insistence had been named Royal International Special Commando. A potent mixture of former professional soldiers

He had dug out former experts in intelligence and surveillance to build up an intelligence gathering unit whose patrols relayed vital information on rebel movements and activities. A job made easy because the rebels had become lax in the absence of any real harassment

Small but numerous, well equipped Strike Forces using newly acquired helicopters that the Loot helped to buy, acted upon the information and ambushed or raided the rebels at every opportunity. The rusting Hunter Jets were resurrected and used to put in air strikes on known positions. The small artillery Regiment was retrained, expanded and used to support operations. Finally, totally demoralised the rebels withdrew to their safe havens in the Congo to lick their wounds and regroup.

This is what Paul was waiting for. His surveillance teams had pinpointed these camps and acting upon information from spies who had infiltrated the rebels, he put in a co-ordinated strike when these camps were full. The rebels who thought that the KNA would never cross the border were mostly taken by surprise.

After a large battle that lasted for two days the Royal Special International Commando, backed up by Commandos from the KNA finally overcome the last and largest of these camps. The Rebel leader was found badly wounded. They kept him alive long enough for Juba to arrive and hack him to death.

The government of Congo only became aware what was going on when it was long over. Noises were made but it was all too late. It had taken eleven months and twelve days before Paul could report that the war was over.

Paul, during the whole period of operations had been in the field. His headquarters could be packed on the back of two trucks and could set up within an hour of arriving anywhere. He lived rough in the bush and the rain forests with the rest of them. He even took part now and again in ambushes and raids much to the worry of Juba. Paul was wise enough to ensure that Juba got a huge part of the praise and credit at all times.

The photographer shouted and gestured to someone on Paul's left at the edge of the group, "Oh! Shut the fuck up you old women!" came the reply, the group sniggered, pleased at being entertained during the boring wait. Paul smiled too. It was Tex, now known as Major Terrence Potter of The Palace guard. His faithful ally and loyal comrade.

As keen as he was Tex had proved an awful soldier, unable to understand even simple tactics or basic fire and manoeuvre and least of all take orders off anyone, so Paul had kept him as a personal bodyguard where he could keep an eye on him, much the same as it was now.

It was a pity about Seb, if he had kept his nerve, he too, mused Paul would have been looked after, but drink had destroyed his confidence and judgement. He had sobbed huge crocodile tears when Paul and Tex bade him farewell from the airstrip a few days after the incident at the Palace. Paul had placed a huge wedge of US Dollars in his hand as severance pay. "I really blew it didn't I? Sorry" Were the last words they heard him say.

Hennings, Mason, Pern and a few other more petty conspirators had been put on trial. It was an huge open affair that some correspondents called a "Show Trial." The world's press attended for the nine days it took. Colonel Vander was neither seen or mentioned. They were all found guilty. The Karudan nationals involved were sentenced to death which was carried out by firing squad almost immediately.

The rest were also sentenced to death but after a few seconds which was enough time for Hennings to break down sobbing, the Judge commuted it to an indefinite gaol sentence which made Pern choke.

After six months in Laka Military Correction Centre they were marched from the Prison to the Airstrip barefoot and in chains. The last thing they saw and heard on Karudan soil was *Sergeant Major* Wally Crabbe hurling abuse at them and making obscene gestures as they hobbled aboard the Dakota.

Reeves although mentioned in the infamous Minutes book as a conspirator did not stand trial. Paul had dissuaded any such action, however, M'Punga despite his initial praise did not trust him and refused to ratify any appointment that gave him power. He returned to Camp Lagonda training recruits.

Dispirited, Reeves turned to drink for solace. Two months after the Palace incident he was found in his bunk at Lagonda dead on his bed. Pern's Mauser was still gripped in his hand and his brains were over the pillow. A scribbled note on his bedside table simply said, "Fuck all of you."

A movement to his front brought Paul out of his thoughts, it was M'Punga, Tasi and Juba looking resplendent in their uniforms and feathered cocked hats. They casually sauntered past the photographer who gave a nervous exaggerated bow and came to the group, who all rose and stood stiffly to attention. He smiled up at them and said "Gentlemen." As soon as he turned he sat down and everyone followed suit. Juba sat between Paul and M'Punga.

"All look this way and smile!" Shouted the effeminate voice of the photographer.

Paul Beamed. .

THE OPERATION

1

Frank saw the three youths come into the lobby of the Night Club, they were very drunk and they were very loud. The girl in the kiosk shot a glance at Frank who shook his head to signal that they were going to be denied entry.

The biggerof the three was fumbling for some money from a huge wad of assorted notes while shouting something at his friends. Frank went up to him and smiled, "Sorry, I can't let any of you in tonight."

The big youth swung around tried to focus on Frank then slurred in his loud voice, "Whatsa matter? I got money.. Look! Probably more than you'll earn in a month....Here!" He tried to stuff a note into Frank's top pocket but his hand was brushed away and once again Frank told them that they would not be allowed entry.

Tanya the girl in the kiosk reluctantly trod on the silent alarm, a red bulb would now be flickering behind the bar. A few seconds lapsed then the large swing doors to the bar area swung open letting out for a moment the deafening thump of disco music. Brad North the head Bouncer appeared, he was around five feet six tall but massively built with broad shoulders, no neck and a livid scar on his forehead that distorted his eyebrow, all this and his stone grey eyes told anyone at a glance, what they were up against if they tried it on.

He went straight for the big man and punched him as hard as he could in the guts, as he buckled he kicked and pushed him toward the exit, the other two looked bewildered and one even raised his hands in capitulation to Frank who also began to herd them out. As they got to the outside step Frank could see Brad scooping up five and ten pound notes that were scattered around, the big fellow was puking against the wall.

Once back inside Brad straightened his bow tie, brushed imaginary dirt off his worn evening jacket and laughed, "You're too soft with 'em Frank! The only thing drunks understand is this!" He held up his big meaty fist and winked at Tanya who gave a weak smile back.

Brad reeked of booze despite his warnings to Frank and the others to lay off it during working hours. He flexed his broad shoulders and marched back into the bar area. Tanya lit up a cigarette and glanced at her watch, "Another bloody hour." She moaned. She was in her mid thirties and very thin. She must have been a looker at one time thought Frank but two failed marriages and three packs a day had taken their toll.

Frank moved nearer the kiosk and Tanya looked at him and smiled, "This game's not for you Frank." she said gently, "Brad enjoys it, he couldn't live without it but he'll get his one day. He's roughed up too many from round here....... Just doing it for pin money love?"

"Yeh! More or less." said Frank returning her smile, "Just filling in time before I get a real job."

In fact, it was the only steady income he had at the moment. Frank had taken leaving the Army hard.

When he had walked out of the CO's office he still had two months to serve but nowhere to serve it, the humiliation of rejection shattered him.

His marriage to Ann had shown some cracks over the last couple of years especially when the frequency of tours in Northern Ireland seemed to speed up.

When he was returned early from the tour she had not been at home in their Quarter in Aldershot but at her mother's place in Swindon. She had taken her time coming back blaming her Mother's poor health for the delay.

Ann had been shocked to hear what he'd been through and at first felt sorry for the way he had been treated but then the grape vine had started at the wives club and Ann had heard a version of how Frank was drunk and attacked the officer for no good reason. The final blow came when she heard that Frank was to face a Court Martial and maybe kicked out of the Army.

They had rowed bitterly one night and Frank had been so over wrought that he had grabbed her, eyes staring and teeth clenched, he had let her go almost immediately shocked at what he'd done but it was too late. Ann had rushed to the bedroom and slammed the door, all Frank could hear was her deep sobs as he too buckled and broke down.

When he got back the next day from the building site where he had got temporary work she had gone. A note just said that she had to; *Sort things out* and for him not to follow her. A check of the house revealed that she had taken most of her clothes and personal things. The next few days were a blur to Frank, he didn't go to work and instead went on the drink.

By now all his mates from the Regiment were returning from the tour and he spent his afternoons drinking with them. When they returned home he either went with them to continue the session or found a pub that had a 'lock in' for the afternoon and then started on the evening session.

Norrie was unmarried and had gone home to Nottingham, likewise Ronnie Gittins to London. Wee Tam also lived nearby in quarters with his equally small wife Mo and their two young children. He made it an open house for Frank but he declined through embarrassment and the fact that he didn't want to cramp their family life.

After waking up one morning at the foot of his stairs covered in vomit and no idea how he got there he started to straighten himself out and laid off the drink. His knew his army money would soon dry up and he needed to sort himself out.

He caught the train to Swindon to be met with a closed and locked door at his Mother in Law's house. After some time she came out on the step and in steely fashion told Frank that her daughter wanted nothing more to do with him. He had barged past, neither Ann nor her clothes were there, just the old chap who sat in the chair sucking his pipe too embarrassed to say anything except for muttering "Sorry Frank" a couple of times.

He guessed that she would be at one of her sister's houses in the area but he reasoned that if she had really wanted him, she would have waited at her Mother's for him, had a good row then made up and gone home with him. Taking it a stage further had only strengthened his belief that she really didn't want him.

He had lost his job on the building site but a chance conversation with an old army buddy who had been out some time had put him on to the job as a Bouncer in the Guildford night-club.

He did three evenings a week, the money was good but as he expected the hours were lousy. Brad, he thought was a sadistic bully who took great delight in his work especially when it came to beating up young drunks. Brad also had a fiddle going on the entrance fee, this involved Tanya who through fear complied, also at this moment in time her and Brad were an item and living together.

They both heard the car skid to a halt and all the doors slamming, followed closely by another car. Five men in their twenties, swarthy looking and in rough clothes came bursting in swinging pick handles. Leading them was the large youth who they had thrown out a half hour before. "That's one of the bastards!" he screamed, "And there's another little fat bastard in there!"

Frank knew there was no room for negotiations here, he guessed instantly that they were a bunch of lads from the fairground just outside of town and were out for big trouble.

They closed on Frank, he parried a blow from a pick handle and threw a hard right which slammed into a face. A crack on the side of his head sent sparks flashing in his brain and he started to lose it. As he went down he could hear the sound of the kiosk smashing. He was fortunate in a way that so many were trying to get to him as he lay there in a ball, they all got in each others way and made much of the attack ineffective.

Suddenly it broke up and the sound of a police siren outside gave the reason why. Uniformed officers piled in and started grabbing everyone in sight. Frank was yanked to his feet by an officer who immediately kneed him in the stomach and helped by another threw him into the meat wagon outside. Just as it was about to pull away the door opened and Brad stood there with a policeman, "That's 'im." He shouted and Frank was pulled out.

The foyer was a mass of broken glass where the kiosk had been. Tanya sat nervously puffing on a cigarette having her arm dressed by one of the bar staff, she looked across at Frank with a hint of a smile. Frank was in tatters, his jacket had been ripped off his back and the front of his shirt torn out, blood trickled from a couple of head wounds.

In contrast Brad was still comparatively immaculate standing in the middle of the foyer talking and gesticulating to a tall police inspector who was almost bent double trying to speak face to face with him.

Frank went over to Tanya, "Gizza fag love." he said, she offered him the packet.

"I Didn't know you smoked."

"I don't." He smiled and lit up.

"Get out while you can Frank," she urged, "If them coppers hadn't turned up they would have killed you, and as for lover boy there he took one look and went back inside."

The barman who had put a bandage on her arm patted Tanya and went back into the bar area. Tanya motioned with her hand for Frank to come closer, as he did she slid him a bundle of notes.

Frank looked at her sharply, "I can't have that!" He said in an astonished whisper.

"Go on!" she urged, "Take it! Everyone will think the Gypos took it and lover boy would only have it anyway. You took the beating for him so take it!" Without further argument he stuffed the roll into his trouser pocket and stood up.

"Hey Frank!" shouted Brad in amazement, "The cops here say that we rolled that punk we threw out of here!"

The tall inspector came closer to Frank. "It's lucky for you laddie that somebody tipped us off that they was coming back here mob handed. Seems he wasn't all that bothered about getting punched and kicked for *nothing*," he said sarcastically, "but someone also relieved him of fifty or so quid while doing so."

"Well they knocked the Kiosk off!" countered Brad aggressively.

"So you admit you have it." stated the Inspector quickly.

"No! Have I bollocks!" shouted an indignant Brad and proceeded to pull the linings out of his pockets.

"And you?" said the inspector turning his watery, tired eyes on Frank. A policeman at his side held up a rag that was once Frank's jacket and shook his head.

Frank still a little dazed from his beating shook his head and backed away, the police officer dropped the jacket and said "Come on, hands up!" The shake down revealed the roll of notes.

Brad shouted, "You thievin' bastard!" And went to close with Frank but was pulled back by the Constable. "It's bastards like you that give night clubs a bad name." he ranted.

"I gave it to him!" screamed Tanya, "I fuckin' gave it to him for safe keeping, it's the takings from tonight!"

Brad looked angrily at her but said nothing, "Go ahead!" she said sobbing, "Check it out! It will all tally up."

"I don't know what's going on here! But it stinks!" Snarled the Inspector, "You can tell your boss from me, he's going to have his work cut out renewing his licence!" With that the inspector and the uniforms that were left walked out crunching over the shattered glass.

Brad flared, "I don't know what you two have got going but you're outa here!" He motioned aggressively for Frank to go then turned on Tanya, "And you, you bitch!" He trailed off lost for words in his rage, Frank thought about saying something but changed his mind, he was bruised and sore from his beating and Brad was all keyed up ready to let fly, he turned and walked out.

2

Peter Gant stepped carefully down the stairs leading from the aircraft to the concrete runway. He saw the huge red sign, *Salisbury Airport* and scanned the observation balcony with his one good eye but could see no familiar faces.

He reached the ground and aided by a walking stick limped toward the airport building.

"And how long do you intend to stay Mister Gant?" Asked the Immigration Officer in his thick Rhodesian accent.

"Oh! I haven't really thought about that I'm afraid." said Peter in his soft boyish voice. The Officer took in the patch over his eye and the out of shape nose that didn't fit on his otherwise fresh soft face. The sturdy walking stick was now hooked over his arm. "You see Sir," he continued politely, "I will be flying out to Karuda eventually.. I have relatives there.. I'm on rest and recuperation after this lot." He gave a big smile as he pointed to his defunct eye.

The officer smiled and gave him back his passport, "You're lucky, things are pretty stable there these days, my brother was there for a while flying Gunships for them in their little war.. You be careful. Eh?"

Just as he was about to go, two men dressed in suits approached him. One of them flashed a card to the immigration officer who promptly lost interest and turned to his next customer.

They steered him to a small office by customs and after taking his passport off him bade him sit down. The man who had shown his ID was slim and around six feet tall, in his forties, with fair to auburn hair and eyebrows and cobalt blue eyes.

"I'm Hanlon." He stated. The other with a stern face set like stone just nodded.

Hanlon continued, "Why are you visiting Karuda.. er Mister Gant?"

"Forgive me but I don't really see what this has got to do with anyone. I don't even know who you are."

"Let's just say we represent the government of Rhodesia I think that's all you need to know apart from the fact that one phone call could have you on the next flight out of here, not the next *available* flight Mister Gant but *the next* flight. So why are you going to Karuda?"

"I have a relative there."

"Brit.. ex Pat?"

"Yes."

"Name?"

"Richards."

"First name.?"

"Alec.. Alex!"

Hanlon nodded to Stone Face who went out of the room. "You don't seem sure, is it Alec or Alex?" bullied Hanlon. Peter steadied himself. Paul had warned him in one of his coded letters that Rhodesian Immigration or Military Intelligence may make life difficult for him.

He had supplied Peter with a Bona Fide name and Address to use and told him to use his injuries as an excuse for coming out to rest. The next question was so direct it jolted him.

"Do you know Paul Van Der Borgh?"

"Paul Van who.. Sorry?"

"Don't fuck me about man or else I will get flat with you." sneered Hanlon, "Now, do you know him?"

"I have never heard of him." stated Peter firmly, although he had a premonition that he was just about to get flung out of the Country. The door open behind him and Stone Face returned, he nodded to Hanlon. The mood changed dramatically.

"Very well Mister Gant, it would not be my choice of a holiday destination. When are you passing through this way again?"

"I.. I'm not too sure, my injuries you see.."

"Are you stopping in Laka, the capital?"

"Yes.. I suppose I am, Alex lives there."

"There is a man there Mister Gant." Hanlon stood up and stared at the desk top for a moment before he went on. "I will put all my cards on the table Mister Gant, there is a man there who we are very interested in. We believe he is Paul Maas alias Paul Van Der Borgh, who is now using the assumed name of Vander, he is highly placed in the hierarchy of the government and Army there. We need as much information as possible about this man, especially his movements, also a photograph if possible. Now I know that the chances of you coming into contact with him are negligible but the Ex Pat community there is small and Laka is small, Goddammit the whole country is small, so there is a chance that you may come in contact with him."

Hanlon held out his hand and Stone Face passed across a large brown envelope. He pulled out a blow up of a shot of Paul and handed it to Peter. It was large and grainy showing Paul in a foreign military uniform smiling broadly. "That's all we've got I'm afraid, have a good look and I'll have it back."

"Why all the interest in him?" asked Peter.

Hanlon glanced at Stone Face and said, "Let us just say that he is of interest to us at the moment and we pay well for information. *Any,* information that you can gather would be welcome Mister Gant. Here is my card with a telephone number, it is a travel agency here in Salisbury. Ask for me, Daryl but if you phone from Karuda the line may be tapped. I am sorry to have delayed you, if anyone is waiting tell them it was Immigration…. Goodbye." He handed Peter back his passport and watched him limp out of the room.

When the door had closed Stone Face spoke first, "We are indeed grabbing at straws Colonel."

"Yes," replied Hanlon. "maybe, but at the moment we must take what we can get. Karuda is as tight as a drum, there is no information coming out at all. I'll say one thing for our friend Borgh, he knows how to run an army, that border is sealed tight and when they get their International Airport built, we shall lose a lot of control over them."

3

The phone rang and woke Frank from a stupor. His good intentions of laying off the drink for a while and finding a decent job had been put on hold. He had been on a lunchtime session with Wee Tam and some others and had learned that Vince Longthorne had lost the use of his legs permanently. He was still in Ulster but was being shipped home soon to a specialist Hospital.

Frank with an effort rose from the chair, he was still bruised from his beating at the club but his face was almost back to normal, he answered the demanding ring.

"Hello Frank old boy, how's tricks?" asked the smooth well spoken voice. Frank recognised the silvery tones but could not place a face for them and said so.

"It's Nick, Nick Summers, look I can't stay on the phone long, can I meet up with you tomorrow, say lunchtime at the Trafalgar?"

"Yes, no problem Sir, " said Frank automatically using the respectful address, "is anything the matter?"

"No, on the contrary, but I need to see just *you*, for now."

"Better not meet at the Traf. then, say the Red Lion at One."

"Okay, the Red Lion at one." Echoed Nick and put the phone down.

Frank walked down the hill out of Aldershot, there was a chill wind and dead leaves lay around in profusion. He passed Manor Park and came to the Red Lion. He checked the bar on the left, it contained a couple of old men playing dominoes. In the right hand bar he saw Nick sitting at a copper covered round table, a half glass of beer in front of him. He was reading a newspaper and was unaware of Frank's presence until he sat down. They exchanged greetings and Nick got in a pint for Frank and renewed his half.

They started with some small talk in which Frank learned that Nick too, was finished with the army and was on "gardening" leave. He omitted to mention his imminent marriage break up.

Frank skirted around the events of his departure from the Regiment. He knew that Nick would be aware of them and if he wanted to know more he would ask. After a pause in which empty glasses were replenished Nick lit a large cigar and got down to business.

"Frank first things first, from now on let's be on a first name basis okay? Good, now through a contact I met up with a very odd fellow some days ago. He's offering work and is willing to pay big money. He wants former soldiers only, a small group to carry out a task. I know nothing more apart from the fact that it's abroad and it contains an element of risk." He sat back and let the words sink in.

"That's it?

"Yes, until he thinks I am taking him seriously that's all we have."

"Are you? Taking him seriously I mean?"

Nick didn't answer for a while, he took a large drag from the cigar and blew it out slowly while studying the table top, finally he looked at Frank. "The man is offering ridiculous money Frank, I must admit I'm tempted."

"How much?" Asked Frank.

"Look I'm not being evasive but I don't want to lead you up the garden path. I need to sound this guy out more.. Are you interested?"

"At the moment yes, in fact the sooner the better for me."

"Okay Frank, I will be in touch, and Mums the word eh? Come on, I'll give you a lift to the Traf." The two men shook hands and left the pub.

The train pulled into Waterloo, Frank and Nick alighted and joined the throng to exit the platform. It had been three months since they had last met. Nick had called him the day before and reminded him about the conversation.

Frank had almost forgotten about it. He had a job with a small security firm in Camberley but was still restless. Nick had told him that their 'would be' employer had asked him to a meeting at a pub near Pimlico. He had cleared it for Frank to come along.

They grabbed a taxi and a few minutes later turned up at the Fox and Hounds pub.

Julian Pern had a last look in the mirror before leaving for his appointment. He had never quite regained the good looks he had before entering Laka prison. The eyes were duller and premature crows feet had embedded themselves in the corners. His hair was still dark and thick with a few silver lines now showing above his ears. There was some jagged scar tissue around his mouth that was partly hidden by a thick moustache curling round into a short goatee beard.

When sentenced, he had immediately contemplated suicide. He knew Laka Military Prison only too well. On many occasions he had taken great delight in visiting the grey decrepit building and observing what went on in the filthy, rat infested highly overcrowded conditions, watching the beatings and the torture that was routine in this stinking hell and more than often taking part.

His prisoner 'welcoming committee' had set about him trying to cut his lips off with a blunt knife, they had almost succeeded before they were dragged off by a guard.

He and three others were the only white men in the gaol and the authorities were a little uncertain how to treat them at first, that was the reason Pern had been saved.

The vicious assault had been a kind of blessing in disguise because they were transferred out of the main body of the prison to an annex that had been a chapel in the colonial days. Pern had spent a month in the Prison sick bay. Life, apart from the odd 'visits' he got, was comparatively good there and had helped him get over his initial shock and thoughts of ending his life.

Also a rumour had started that they would all be set free soon and booted out of the country, this kept a glimmer of hope alive for them and was a topic of conversation as they huddled around a guttering candle, whispering into the night.

Then one day, after six months, something unheard of in Laka prison life happened. A doctor examined them and prescribed drugs for treating their various ailments, they were given meat and vegetables to eat and allowed exercise in the sunshine. A limited Press was allowed access and they answered questions about their treatment, they were told what to say and of course they said it.

Five days later they were given a blue boiler suit each and after being chained together were marched at night and bare foot to the airfield near Lagonda Camp and flown out of the country.

For months back in England Julian Pern could not be in the same room as a black man and if he saw one in the street he had to fight down the urge to kill him. His mother had finally got him on therapy and his condition had improved.

He had lost touch with the others until one day Hennings had called on him. Hennings although weak and wet had come through his ordeal virtually unscathed apart from the weight loss and humiliation.

He had come straight to the point with Pern, he said that he was suffering from terminal cancer and had but a month or so left to live. He had always lived alone and now he had to die alone and he didn't want that. Julian had sensed that there was more to this, he knew that Hennings came from a wealthy family, so it might just be in his interest to look after his old 'chum' in his hour of need.

He moved Hennings into the accommodation he shared with his mother. The large flat in Pimlico had been ample. Julian's mother had been a wartime nurse and had coddled Hennings to his last day.

Shortly after Hennings had moved in, he had told Julian of a large horde of gold bullion, diamonds, other precious stones and American dollars that he had stashed in Karuda. Pern had been astonished and at first disbelieved the story. How could this seemingly weak, indecisive man have had the guts and know how to pull of a stunt like that, with no-one knowing or finding out?

Hennings had seen the disbelief on Pern's face and smiled, it had been all so easy. Did he remember the rebel convoy that they had captured and bought back to the camp? It had been ransacked by the troops.. yes? All apart from the trailer that fifteen or so bodies had been dumped in, ready to be paraded through the streets the following week.

Left over the weekend, the stench had got so bad that on Sunday morning he had gone to investigate where it had come from and found the trailer full of corpses dumped in the forested area not far from his house.

He had summoned the guard to get rid of the trailer but they couldn't shift it because of a punctured tyre, so he made them unload the bodies onto another trailer.

When the last body had been lifted he had seen three Tea chests. He got rid of the guard and had prized the lid off one of them and found the sealed bundles of high denomination US Dollars. He had struggled to remove and conceal the tea chests, then summoned the guard again and told them to get rid of the trailer. There was at least ten gold ingots and enough precious stones to fill two sandbags as well as hundreds of thousands of US Dollars.

He personally saw to it as a precaution, that within a month all the members of the guard had been transferred out of Camp Lagonda.

He had painstakingly buried the loot under the rockery in his garden and 'sat' on it, not knowing quite what to do with it. After being freed he had nurtured hopes of recovering it one day but now that day would not come.

In his Will, he left Julian's mother two thousand pounds and his own mother's diamond brooch. To Julian he left his house in Kent and sixty eight thousand pounds with a sentence that his family solicitor read out: *Hoping that it will be used to fund an enterprise of sorts.*

Julian had contemplated just taking the money and forgetting the horde. Maybe, he had reasoned, it had been found by now. But sleepless night had followed sleepless night as he tossed and turned trying to estimate the wealth that was lying just below the ground. The thought of returning to Karuda had terrified him at first, the image of Vander sneering and laughing at him made his guts twist and cramp but as the weeks rolled on he began to plan in his mind how he could get his hands on this wealth.

First, he would need a small team, special forces if possible, trained to live and fight in hostile conditions.

Basically honest men who would deliver without taking advantage, was there such men? He would have to find out. A guarded conversation with one of his few remaining military contacts led him to a fledgling security firm run by a former Captain. He, personally had not shown any interest but said he would ask around.

Some time later Nick Summers had phoned him. Julian found out that he was a decent officer with integrity, who was leaving the service for personal and domestic reasons, he if anybody could put together such a team.

"Julian!" His thoughts were shattered by his mother's shrill, strong voice. "Julian! Will you be long on this business meeting? I am going to your Aunt Mildred's and I want Sasha to have her walk at five."

"No mother, I should be back." He replied without taking his eyes off his reflection. She came into the hallway and strode up to him.

"God! Just look at you, why on earth don't you get yourself a decent suit? Really that tailor of yours, your father wouldn't have had a handkerchief made there. Now I'm off!" She stopped and turned, her shrill tones became soft and a look of concern came over her face. "Take care." And she was gone.

Julian walked to the rendezvous. Initially he would have to disguise his name. The events that had happened to him in Karuda and his homecoming had not escaped the press. The photos portrayed in all the daily nationals, were poor and the only close up of him showed a hollow cheeked, bearded, ill man.

Nick stood up and smiled as Julian approached, Julian smiled and held out his hand, he then turned to Frank who was also now on his feet.

"Julian, this is Frank." said Nick warmly, both men shook hands and they all sat down.

After drinks were ordered and the small talk dried up Pern looked at Nick and said, "Well, did you think it over?" His eyebrows were arched in apprehension.

Nick leaned forward a little and said, "We need to know more.."

"Of course you need to know more, a lot more. The object of this meeting was for me to find out whether you had thought the general idea was feasible or not." Pern spoke quickly with a degree of irritation in his voice.

Nick hardened his voice but without raising it said firmly, "And I told you, that I needed more information. What drops you gave me were not enough. Me and Frank are partners in this now. I realise that you cannot trust us completely until we have made a firm commitment, but we won't commit until you give what you can to us!"

Pern started to blink and twitch. As a child he'd had a stammer which he overcame well before his teens but in times of stress the symptoms reappeared, since Laka Prison they came more often. He took a deep breath and let it out slowly while staring at the desk top, then spoke in normal tones.

"M'my dear Nick we seem to be at an im...Impasse."

"Well," said Nick with a sigh, "you either trust us now or the deals off. If you give us the details and we don't like it, we will turn it down and keep schtum about

it and you have our word on that.. Frank?" Frank nodded.

Pern looked at his watch, "Come on!" he said,
"Back to my place, it's not far."

They reached Pern's flat after about ten minutes
walk. They had both noted how Pern had a slight limp
and needed to stop every so often as if to let pain ebb
away. Pern had remained silent during the journey.

Frank and Nick were surprised at the size and el-
egance of the flat. Many original works of art adorned
the walls and the furniture and fittings all had taste.
The kitchen in which they sat was a complete contrast.
All the surfaces were stainless steel as well as most of
the utensils that hung in their correct places. The whole
room was like an operating theatre and totally devoid of
any character.

Pern poured coffee from the steel percolator and
sat down. "For a start my name is Pern." He paused to
see if it had any effect, it didn't. "You may have read in
the papers a year or so ago about…. About Karuda."

"That's right!" said Frank, "Julian Pern, impris-
oned in Karuda then set free!"

"Okay, are we now all in the picture as to my identity?" again the irritation in his voice. He continued,
"There is a fortune waiting in Karuda for anyone with
the guts to go and get it. I can only estimate the wealth
from the description that I've had but it is very substantial. I am willing to pay the leader of a successful operation…. Twenty per cent of the total cash value."

"What's the fortune in?" asked Nick, "Is it cash or gold.. what?"

"Mostly cash, some gold and precious stones, the cash is US Dollars." said Pern.

"How do we get in and out?" queried the ever practical Frank.

"Getting in and out should present no problem, I have put a lot of thought into it and am finalising the plans..."

"Is there anyone else beside you in on this?" shot Frank.

"No! Just me.."

"How good are the Karudan Army?" Frank again.

"They are, they *were*, quite good," barked Pern, he was getting irritated again, he liked to be in the driving seat, the nerve started to twitch around his eye. "But if you ch...Chaps do your job professionally y..you should be in and out before they realise you're even in the country!" He ended up by taking a huge breath in and holding it for a few seconds.

Nick spoke, "Things *do,* go wrong Julian, *you* ought to know that. We need as much information...Recent information on the Karudan Army as you can get, with unit locations and strengths.. Have you anyone still inside Karuda who can help?"

"No! No! Impossible! We're on our own.. Now look, as important as this is, I have other things to do.."

"You still didn't answer my question, persisted Frank, " How do we get in and out?"

"That is a detail that I will not c..commit on until I know that you are both in!" glared Pern, "Now what's it to be?"

Nick looked at Frank then said to Pern "Give us a minute would you old boy, matters to discuss." Pern nodded and left the kitchen. "Well Frank?"

"I need time Nick, I can't think while I'm on his patch." Frank gestured at his surrounds.

"Yeh! I agree," said Nick, "but this guy is getting impatient.. Leave it to me." He got up and went through the door, he found Julian staring through the window at the street below.

"Julian we need a little more time.."

"I see! How much?" Came the terse reply from Pern who still had not turned around.

"Say three days maximum."

"Very well, three days to the hour maximum, you have my number, please see yourselves out."

4

The Limo sped towards Camp Royal, two outriders on huge silver and white Honda motorbikes were thirty yards in front and a Saladin armoured car followed thirty yards behind.

Brigadier Paul Vander sat alone in the back of the Limo. He was in full regalia. Once clear of the Palace he removed his gold braided hat and tossed it on the seat. He had a bitter taste in his mouth. He had just attended a ceremony for Field Marshal Juba.

It was disgusting he thought, the bloated elephant could not have himself promoted any higher than Field Marshal so he invented yet another decoration to add to his chest full of medals. One day he would invent a rank higher than Field Marshal and then have himself promoted.

Juba, he recollected, had a huge toothpaste grin as a smiling President M'Punga had pinned on the cross after delivering a rousing citation. What was the medal? The Karuda Freedom Cross? The Cross of Karuda? No, that was it, The Royal Cross for the Liberation of Karuda, what fucking crap! Paul's face screwed up into snarl and he spat on the glass screen behind the drivers head.

The outriders slowed as the gates to Camp Royal swung open. The Limo pulled up at the red and white barrier just inside. A black soldier in a white helmet bearing the royal coat of arms looked into the back of the Limo. Paul opened the back window and showed his ID card, the soldier straightened and saluted as the barrier rose and the Limo purred away.

Paul had insisted that everyone, including the President and Juba must show proof of identity before gaining access. It was part of his never ending struggle to enforce discipline into his troops. His palace guard were housed in Camp Royal and were good, the rest of the army were slacking. At the end of the war with the rebels the army was disciplined and motivated but that was a long time ago now it seemed and they had become sloppy.

The budget had been slashed after the war and now there was not enough money to train them hard or for them to fire their weapons regularly. To top it all, Juba had them doing stupid projects like clearing huge spaces in the jungle only for it to be neglected so it overgrew again with secondary foliage making it less accessible than it was before or digging roads that led nowhere. This had started to demoralise the troops.

Because in effect, Paul's Battalion was the Praetorian Guard for M'Punga his budget was left virtually intact. The Palace Guard was one area in the army that Juba did not have direct control over. Paul had argued vehemently in the early days that he could only serve one master and that master was M'Punga. This of course had appealed to the President and Paul got his way.

Paul knew that Juba mistrusted him, he had never quite accepted Paul's claim that all he wanted was to be a soldier and be allowed to get on with it, he thought that Paul was far more ambitious than that but at this moment in time could find no proof.

Juba was right of course, he himself had started off as a Private soldier in the British run Karuda African Rifles after trekking seventy miles bare foot to join them, so he new all about ambition and ambitious people.

On the surface they were smiling friends but Paul knew that Juba had spies in his camp and Juba suspected the same of Paul.

He knew that if Juba could be removed from the scene, that he, in all probability would become Number three in the country and if both the President were removed plus the spoilt brat Tasi? Now there was a thought! Paul allowed himself a little smile as he walked from his car up the steps of his Villa situated in a quiet corner of the camp.

He was met in the hallway by his head servant, a six foot four inch Somali called Kinga who took his hat and cane. In a deep rich voice he said, "Sir, there was a message from a Mister Paul Gant, he says that he arrived in the country this morning and that he is in residence in the villa you provided but could not gain access to the camp and could you please contact him, sir."

Paul nodded, "Anything more to report? Good, then get Major Potter over here, lay out my fatigues, leave some supper then retire. I won't need you till morning." Kinga bowed and left. Paul walked to the drinks cabinet and poured himself a large Johnny Walker Black label and gulped it back.

His main room smelled of the bush, the floor was covered in animal skin rugs mostly Kudu. There were huge easy chairs made of elephant hide and draped in zebra and giraffe skins, the obligatory lion skin complete with snarling head lay in front of the huge stone fireplace above which, guns and muskets from a bygone age hung, giving off an oily gleam.

Paul entered his bedroom and stripped off his uniform, he detested wearing it, the brocade and gaily coloured lanyards meant nothing to him. The only medals on it were his General Service Medal from the British Army with bars for South Arabia and Northern Ireland and the Karuda Defence Medal that all participants in the war received. He also wore the Grande Cross of Karuda that M'Punga insisted he wore because it was a personal gift from him. The fact that he held no store in wearing rows of medals had always baffled M'Punga and Juba.

After a shower he put on his jungle fatigues, the green, brown and yellow splinter camouflage pattern were faded through over washing, the material was soft and made Paul feel a lot easier. He couldn't remember the last time he wore civilian clothes. Opening a small cabinet by his bed he took out a belt and holster and buckled it on. In the holster was the Browning High Power 9mm automatic pistol courtesy of Captain Hugh Perry, Int Officer of the Princes Own Yeomanry. He slid the knife into its hard leather scabbard and clipped it on the back of his belt in such a fashion that it lay parallel to the belt and snug in the small of his back. This was his normal relaxed dress.

As he descended the staircase he heard a Landrover pull up, Kinga moved swiftly to the door and let in

Major Potter. Paul beamed, "Tex," he shouted and then to Kinga, "You may leave now."

"Paul," Smiled Tex.

Paul ushered Tex into a hide covered easy chair and poured him a whisky. Paul then padded around his villa to make sure that Kinga and the other house boys had left. He returned and poured himself another stiff shot then proceeded to unload his tensions and venom on Tex by recounting the day at the Palace.

Tex listened intently to his friend and mentor. Although he knew that Paul genuinely liked him and they had been through a lot together in the last two years he still had a deep rooted fear of him. He knew what he could be capable of when the mood took him.

When he was loud and aggressive and releasing his tensions like he was at the moment, it was not so bad, but when he was in his silent, black moods of depression he was dangerous. Since the end of the war these moods came more frequently.

Tex also strongly suspected that he was a killer, not the type of killer that a war produces but a stone killer. His mind flashed upon an incident in the war when they had captured some rebels. Paul had become very interested in two of them and took them away for 'special' interrogation. He had returned the next day saying that the prisoners had killed the escort and escaped when he had left them for a few minutes.

Nobody had thought any more about the incident, after all people were getting killed every day. Then, quite by accident a day later, in a remote disused copper mine, a patrol came across the scene of a slaughter. Tex had been there when the reports came in and decided to look for himself.

The scene was horrific; two of the bodies had been horribly mutilated. They were naked and bound, their scattered uniforms identified them as rebel forces and he deduced that they were the 'escaped' prisoners. But the most unnerving thing was that when they found the two escorts it was discovered that they had been executed with one shot in the head each. They had been dumped down a shaft and were found when Tex had ordered a search of the area. He had never broached the subject with Paul.

Paul stopped his ranting and refilled their glasses. He now looked more relaxed and his tones returned to normal. Tex knew that he would be through it in a few minutes and then he would get down to the real reason he had called him. He often had talks with Paul like this; he was the only real person that Paul could relate to. Tex suspected that he was bisexual if the rumours around the camp were anything to go by but drew comfort from the fact that he had never made any advances on him in that way.

"Do you know what the problem is Tex? I mean do you know what the *real* problem is? We haven't got a war any more. When we did have one that bloated pig Juba kept out of the way and that simpering faggot Tasi dived for cover if anyone as much as farted. The only guy that showed any guts was M'Punga himself and now look what's happening to him, he's out of his skull with drugs and booze most of the time and every day Juba gets more powerful. M'Punga listens to him more and more, you know what I suspect will happen one day?"

Paul's face went deadly serious and he paused, staring Tex full in the face. "I will be summoned to the palace on some pretext and once there, arrested and executed within minutes." He tossed the rest of the whisky back and made a grimace.

Tex sat forward in his chair, he was alarmed. He knew that Paul had an uncannily accurate sixth sense about impending danger. "Jesus Paul, what makes you say that?" He blurted, fully realising that if Paul went, he would surely follow.

"Juba cannot and will not accept me; he regards me as a rival. The war gave me a lot of credibility, he realises that M'Punga accepts me and even likes me and I control a battalion of crack troops who he knows are loyal to me. He suspects or rather he knows that I'm after his job. He has spies in *my* camp and even in my house trying to find the least excuse to remove me from the scene...I tell you Tex, I feel the walls closing in on me." He paced the room smashing a fist into his palm over and over.

"Well?" shouted an excited Tex jumping out of his chair, "Strike first! Have the bastard over! Fucking wallop him before he wallops you!"

Paul gave a mocking laugh. "Things are not so easy my friend. M'Punga regards Juba as a brother. They go back a long way, their families are intermarried, there's a strong tribal bond, and to kill him would mean big trouble..."

"Well get some other bastard to kill him!" shouted Tex.

"And if they fucked up what then? Juba would immediately suspect me...No! If it's to be done, I do it personally.

"You said that M'Punga is now hooked on shit.. yeh?!" said Tex, his voice reverting to normal. "I reckon he's on hard drugs, who supplies it? I mean there's hardly any in the country except for the Pot that's grown locally and that *is* shit, I know 'cos I've tried it. You get to M'Punga's supplier and you get M'Punga.. I mean if you control his drugs, you can turn him on and off like a tap, that way, maybe, you can get to Juba."

Paul stopped in his tracks; this was an angle that he hadn't thought of. He abhorred drugs. Tex, he knew had a liking for soft drugs, he had grown up in that culture and therefore had more of an understanding of such matters.

"Thank you for that my friend, you must go now it's late." He said clasping Tex's hand. "We will talk more on this." Tex turned and walked toward the door but stopped when he heard Paul sigh.

"Shit! I knew there was something else Tex. I have a distant cousin over here visiting me. He is in Juba's old house, his name is Peter Gant. Go to him tomorrow morning and tell him.. Tell him I'm indisposed. Look after him for a day or two, any problem?"

"No, none at all Paul." Tex nodded and left.

5

Kinga paused to look around, making sure that he had not been followed. Darkness had fallen and there was no-one else on the red dirt road. If he carried on walking for ten minutes he would arrive at the outskirts of Laka, but he turned off the road and through the bush. Presently he came to a perimeter fence and followed it round until he came to a guard hut by a gate.

He heard the strains of some western music coming from a transistor radio inside the hut, a rifle was propped up against a sandbagged wall but he saw no sentry. He noiselessly ducked under the barrier and walked quickly up the drive.

Juba's Indian servant gave a disdainful up and down look to Kinga and led him to a door, "Knock and wait." He said before flouncing off.

"Enter!" Roared Juba and Kinga bent low to enter the room. Juba was pulling up his trousers; there were two young women in the room, one completely naked and sobbing on the floor. Red wheals covered her light brown flesh. The other had on an army uniform, the jacket of which was open and Kinga caught a flash of huge pendulous breasts, she carried a long whip. "Out!" yelled Juba and the two women brushed past Kinga, the naked one who was also bleeding from the nose grabbing at some clothes on the floor.

Kinga could smell the dope and realised that Juba was high on drugs. He now sat behind his desk with just his trousers on, his huge belly forcing the desk away. He gestured Kinga closer then said, "Well?"

Kinga drew in his breath and started to speak in his quiet, precise manner. "Nothing unusual has happened this week, after he return from duties he relax with a drink in the house, on one occasion he went out unescorted in his jeep for two hours, I know not where. Tonight the Major Potter visit him and he ordered the house cleared.."

"What was his mood?"

"He seem normal."

"What is normal, you fucking monkey eater?!" Yelled Juba standing and smashing his huge fist on the desk. Kinga paused, he showed no sign of fear but carried on in the same quiet manner.

"He never smiles; his thoughts are behind his eyes."

Juba took a large service .45 revolver from his desk drawer and placed it in front of him. He looked from it to Kinga and spoke slowly and menacingly.

"Something tells me in here," Juba tapped the side of his skull, "that you are not trying hard enough to do my bidding. For six months now all you have ever given me is drivel." Juba slowly picked up the gun, aimed it at Kinga's chest and thumbed back the hammer. "Perhaps this is a good time to have you replaced.. No?"

"He trusts no-one master, the only one he talks to is the white Major and they are always alone." said a completely unruffled Kinga.

"Okay, go! And I warn you monkey eater, my patience is wearing out!"

Peter Gant looked at his broken face in the mirror and let out a cry of frustration. He had been bottled up in the villa now for two days, he had tried in vain to contact Paul but to no avail. He now began to think that it was a big mistake coming out to see him. After all who would want a one eyed one testicled freak like me? He thought bitterly.

The beating that he received courtesy of the kangaroo Court in Belfast had put him in intensive care for a fortnight and a further two months in hospital. He never rejoined his unit and was given a medical discharge. The ringleaders of the attack received a year in Colchester Military Prison and discharged from the army.

After a year of hearing nothing at all from Paul an odd incident took place that ended the mystery as to Paul's whereabouts. He was at an Out Patients clinic in Woolwich Hospital, he had trouble with his eye, the boot that had smashed the eye had also shattered the socket and it needed lots of extra treatment.

A man had approached him and engaged him in conversation, he too was receiving treatment. Peter had noticed the livid scar tissue around his mouth and wondered whether it was anything to do with that.

The man who said his name was Gerald had chatted amiably with Peter while they waited for their appointments. Later, he took Peter for a meal and then drinks at his flat in Pimlico where he seduced him. Peter had stopped for three days and nights before Gerald said that his mother was returning and wouldn't understand.

During the course of their relationship he discovered that Gerald had been a Major in the SAS and had dealings in Karuda with his Rhodesian counterparts. He had mentioned Paul's name one day in conversation, saying that he had come across him once in Rhodesia.

Peter had gushed excitedly; although Gerald had called him Paul Vander he knew instinctively that it was Paul. Gerald had generously supplied a contact address but told Peter never to mention him to Paul as it might compromise his former secret work in the area, even now that he was retired. When Peter told him that he would, if possible, visit Paul, Gerald gave him a small list of places to visit and made him promise to call him when he was there.

At first Peter received no replies to his letters, and then curiously a hand delivered letter from Paul was dropped on his mat. The letter was printed and anonymous but made clever references so that Peter knew without doubt it was from Paul. It told him to stop all communication with him until further notice and that when he was ready, he would send for him. The letter also contained the key to a simple code so that future letters could contain more information. Nine months had past, then the letter with a summons and now here he was.

A Landrover skidding to a halt on the gravel in the driveway snapped Peter from his thoughts. There was a loud sharp rap on the door. Peter quickly fixed the brown leather patch over his dead eye and pulled open the door. He saw a man of slim build and average height in a khaki military uniform complete with a holstered pistol and swagger stick. The smiling face spoke in a London accent. "Peter Gant? Major Terrence Potter at your disposal, seeing as you're white and a friend of Paul you may call me Tex!" He gave a mock salute with his swagger stick and walked past Peter into the large hall.

"This used to be old Juba's place until there weren't enough rooms to put all his whores in.. Oops! Shouldn't have said that, me and my mouth."

Peter took an instant dislike to this swaggering loudmouth but at the same time was glad to see someone whom he could talk to. "How is Paul?" He asked

"Paul? Oh! Paul is as well as can be expected as they say." Tex strode into the large dining room, "I tell you mate, we've had some good do's in this place. I'll say one thing for old Juba he knew how to throw a party..... That was during the war of course, things are a little different now.."

"When shall I see him?" Asked Peter quietly.

Tex stared him in the face for a couple of seconds, despite the eye patch and slightly deformed nose he could sense rather than see the effeminacy in Peter. At once he knew what type of relationship he had with Paul. His gut knotted slightly and surprisingly for him, he felt a stab of jealousy. He quickly buried it and said, "Paul is rather indisposed at the moment..... Matters of state I'm afraid. Have you known him long?" Shot Tex.

Paul had warned Peter to keep quiet about any past life, he was to say that they were distant cousins who met up now and again.

"Well yes, we're cousins you see...I had some free time and thought.."

"Come on!" interrupted Tex rudely, "Get into the Rover and I'll show you the sights of lovely Laka.

Paul stood up from bending over the map table. His head of training, Major Bindi threw some paperwork in his brief case and looked expectantly at Paul.

Paul turned and poured some coffee from a flask and said. "Okay Victor, you now have my training directive for the next three months, should there be any problem in implementing it I want to know immediately.. Yes?!"

"Yes of course Sir!" Snapped Brindi who saluted crisply and walked out of the office. He looked at his watch, it was way past lunch time. He and Bindi had been in conference for three hours. He pressed a button on his desk, the door opened and his adjutant entered. "I'm finished for the day, tomorrow I'm taking a rest." He walked out of his headquarter building and down an avenue of Jakaranda trees. His driver slowly bought the Limo level with him but he waived him away, today he would walk back to his villa.

Kinga met him as he walked in. Paul walked into his hide scented living room and Kinga followed. He sat on an armchair and began to remove his boots, normally Kinga or one of the other house boys would have done this for him but they had long ago learned that

Brigadier Paul had no time for such personal attention, however he did nod in the direction of the drinks cabinet and moments later Kinga had poured him a tumbler of Black Label.

"Did you make your report last night?" asked Paul casually.

"Yes Master."

"And?"

"The Field Martial grows impatient, he threatens to replace me."

Paul knew exactly what 'replace' meant. "How do you feel about that?" asked Paul as he slid his remaining boot off.

"I think I can last a little longer, but it grows difficult Sir, he cannot believe that you are not plotting against him and urges me to do more."

"What do you know about Juba's drug habit?"

"He smokes Dagga most of the time Sir."

"Is this locally grown stuff?"

"Sir?"

"Is the Dagga from the villages?"

"I think so Sir, it is quite common."

"What about harder drugs.. cocaine, heroin, that kind of thing?"

"I know nothing about these things Sir."

"Okay Kinga, it is your mission to find out where M'Punga gets these drugs from, someone in Juba's circle will be supplying him. Use your contacts and find out, I will pay extremely well for good information.. You may go."

Tex pulled up outside of a huge, grey stone building topped in coiled razor wire, "And this is the infamous Laka Military Prison, we can go in if you like. Those prisoners get up to all sorts in there, bottled up like sardines five to a one man cell, would hate to think what they got up to, all those sweaty, steaming, writhing bodies." He said, while looking at Peter with a sickly grin on his face.

Peter got very uncomfortable, he had been with this obnoxious, megalomaniac for most of the morning, listening to his endless innuendoes and thinly disguised insults and how close he and Paul were. Tex, he thought, typified all the others who had tormented him in his life. "Get me back would you please." said Peter.

"Hah! Heat getting to ya is it? Yeh! It takes time to get used to it. Take me and Paul, we fought the war together in this heat. All them insects and snakes in the jungle. You know we lived in a swamp for six days me and Paul, waiting to attack this enemy camp.."

"Look...Tex! Just get me back, my head is killing me!"

"Yeh! I meant to ask, what happened to your eye and your leg? Didja get hit by a bus or sammink?" Laughed Tex.

Peter could contain himself no longer. "If you must know, I was kicked and beaten, almost to death by a bunch of loud mouthed swaggering bullies.. And yes they wore uniforms too!"

"Oh! *Sorree* sweetheart! Keep your knickers on!" Countered Tex. The twenty minutes it took to get back to the Villa was driven in silence. Once there Peter got out and without a word, hobbled inside. When he heard the Landrover pull away he dropped onto a couch and burst into tears.

After a half hour Peter got up and showered then padded to the well stocked drinks cabinet. He was mostly teetotal apart from an occasional wine but nevertheless, selected a bottle, poured himself a half tumbler of golden liquid and gulped it back. He gagged but held it down, then had another and another. Before he passed out he had formulated a simple plan, in the morning he would rise early, pack his bag, get a taxi to the airport and start for home.

How long had someone been hammering on the door? His brain refused to open his eyes, scared at what they might see. Something was wrong, he didn't know where he was. "Jesus!" shouted Peter and opened his eyes. He was on a rug in a large room but where? His mouth was bitter with bile, his hand went into a pile of cold sticky goo, it was vomit, his head pounded and he was on the verge of throwing up, he felt wet and cold around his waist.

Through the pain, his good eye picked up a movement at his side and a familiar voice said, "Congratulations Peter. I believe that you have evacuated from every orifice in your body, take a shower, I will call back in an hour." And with that Paul walked off and slammed the door.

Peter retched and staggered to the toilet.

Precisely one hour later Peter heard a vehicle crunching on the gravel drive. He had showered and put on some decent clothes but his head still hammered and he felt nauseous. Grabbing his stick he hobbled to the door and opened it. A black soldier in a smart uniform smiled at Peter, "The Brigadier sends his compliments and asks if you will join him for lunch at the Officer's Club." He turned and gestured to the gleaming black Limo.

Paul stood in the bar of the Officer's Club with a group of black officers, most of them were his Company Commanders. Even though his Battalion's main duty was to provide security for the President, he trained them as an Infantry unit ready to deploy into the field and fight at a moments notice if necessary.

The Majors, hung on to Paul's every word. They feared him but most of all respected him as a leader. All of them had fought alongside him in their war against the rebels.

Paul rarely talked to them in a familiar manner about personal things or sociable subjects, it was always about training or his observations on differing matters to do with the unit or the Army in general.

He never criticised anyone in authority to them by word or gesture, even though he felt certain that they were all loyal to him, he knew that Juba was powerful and held them all in the palm of his hand, one flex and they were crushed.

Tex wandered over and joined them. He never felt at ease in the club, he had a feeling that they all secretly laughed or sneered at him behind his back, except for Paul of course. He could never quite understand why Paul had befriended *him*, he had never had any real friends even at school. It wasn't as if he were the only other white face in the camp because there were others.

He knew he had let Paul down during the war. If it hadn't been for his personal intervention he wouldn't have made it but Paul had taken him under his wing and gave him status although he never had any real power behind his rank. His title of Brigadier's Personal Assistant meant absolutely nothing. He had his own office and was always on call if Paul wanted him, but that was it. Through boredom he poked his nose into other people's affairs in the camp which made him even more unpopular. What was more, everyone knew that he reported everything back to Paul.

When Tex joined the group the Majors made their excuses and drifted to one side leaving him with Paul. "I thought your cousin was supposed to be here," ventured Tex. Paul looked at his watch but said nothing. Tex continued, "He's a little touchy your cousin...Was he always like that or was it the accident?"

Paul looked curious, "Accident?"

"Yeh, didn't you know? Some geezers kicked his head in, he's blind in one eye poor sod, crippled too by the looks of him." Before Paul could react, he caught some movement at the entrance. Standing next to a tall servant was a small forlorn figure, a patch over his pale face, leaning heavily on a walking stick, it took a couple of seconds for Paul to realise that it was Peter. The servant caught sight of Paul and pointed him out to Peter who gave an embarrassed smile.

Paul strode toward him hand outstretched, they shook hands a little stiffly. Paul was grinning and said, "Well Peter you look a lot better than you were an hour ago, ha! You have met Major Potter, he tells me you were a little unwell yesterday. I hope you have an appetite, I fear the chef has laid on a feast!"

Peter listened to the ebullient Paul, full of smiles and laughter that he knew was barely skin deep, he was covering his embarrassment. Physically, Paul seemed taller, maybe because he was slimmer than he remembered. His fully shaven head was as nut brown as his tanned weathered face, suddenly he was aware that Paul had stopped talking and he was expected to say something in return.

He smiled and made his replies saying how good it was to see him again etc. etc. But inside he was dead. The times he had gone over this moment in his head were innumerable, they saw each other and hugged and hugged, saying how much they had missed each other, then Paul would lead him to a secluded cottage and say *That's it Peter that's ours, for ever together.*

Peter found himself being ushered along between Paul and Tex through some curtains to a seating area. Along one wall was a huge buffet, lines of silver dishes complete with silver lids and behind each one a smiling chef in perfectly starched whites. Paul led them down the glittering line where they were served from fresh salads, roast pig, sides of beef and whole smoked chickens.

Once sat down, Paul carried on a conversation with Tex and one of the Majors, the content of which, was complete double Dutch to Peter who just sat picking at the meat on his plate. Then once again Paul swung his attention to Peter.

"I trust you find the Villa to your liking Peter, we had it specially renovated for VIP visitors."

"I feel honoured." replied Peter with an edge to his voice, "A VIP villa, a luxurious Limousine and escorted by a tank, it's all so…*Wonderful.*" Those around him fell silent.

Paul looked up sharply then managed a smile and said, "The armoured car was necessary. There are still isolated groups of former rebels, they would think nothing of cutting your face off, that is after they had…But who wants to know all about that?" He looked around and laughed, immediately a half dozen others joined in and broke the little bit of tension that had built up. Tex sneered at Peter.

A small eruption of noise reached their ears as the door to the Dining room swung open and Prince Tasi entered with Juba and a few other gold braided officers. Immediately the officers in the room fell silent and stood up.

Paul was the last to do so, even though Juba outranked him and was the head of the Army this was Paul's club and etiquette demanded that he be invited in by Paul. He walked over and gave a bow to Tasi, he smiled at Juba and stretched out his hand, Juba took it and smiled back, "My dear friend," oozed Juba, "we were passing and His Highness expressed a wish to stop and say hello."

"Of course," replied Paul, "I will have a table set.. "

"No!" Interjected Prince Tasi, "You carry on, we will go to the bar, you may join us when you've finished." He turned and walked off with Juba. Paul returned to the table careful not to let any type of message exude from his features.

He carried on with some small talk for a couple of minutes then said to Peter as he rose from the table, "Come! You can meet The Prince Tasi."

Peter got up knocking his stick to the floor, he bent stiffly to pick it up, then limped after Paul who waited for him by the entrance. Looking Peter full in the face he said slowly and firmly, "Peter, these people are extremely powerful. Phrases and even a single word, no matter how well meant, can often be taken wrongly, please be careful...eh?" Paul gave a smile and said "Come!"

They entered the bar. Juba stood there telling one of his stories. He was, as usual in full dress uniform. Tasi was in the uniform of a Marshal of the Royal Karuda Airforce today, the amount of medal ribbons worn by him and Juba were dazzling. Paul had not seen Tasi for some time, he looked as if he was putting on weight. His nineteen year old face was bloating over his collar, he was not at all like his father M'Punga who was small and wiry. Paul thought that he must take after his mother who, he believed, was Juba's half sister.

Paul and Peter stood a respectful distance from the group. Paul knew that Juba and Tasi were aware of his presence, but ignoring him for a while was just part of the never ending unnecessary game that told people exactly where they were in the pecking order. Peter began to say something but Paul motioned him to be quiet, when you waited, you waited in silence.

A figure stood by the entrance of the door, hands folded in front of him. It was Tasi's personal bodyguard Jokko, silent, brooding and watchful. Paul acknowledged him with a nod but Jokko just held Paul's gaze for a few seconds with his deep moody eyes and looked away. Paul assumed that he had never forgiven him for beating him in that contest in front of M'Punga and Tasi.

"Ah! Brigadier Paul there you are!" exclaimed Juba jovially, beckoning both of them to the group. "I was just telling his highness how you have transformed this place into a really good club!" Juba's face turned to Peter and Paul introduced him to them. Juba shook Peter's hand but when he offered it to Tasi the Prince just turned away and whispered something in Karudan to one of his Aides who laughed aloud.

A waiter came up with a tray of drinks but Tasi waived them away. Juba read the signs and said almost apologetically, "Well gentlemen, we must leave, the Prince has had a hard day." With that Tasi and his entourage swept out of the bar and the building leaving Peter and Paul alone.

"Paul, would you please get me home, I'm extremely tired." said Peter softly while looking at the floor.

"Yes of course, I will take you.."

"No! There's really no need, I can get a taxi if necessary.."

"Nonsense! I will summon the car." said Paul loudly as he walked off.

The Limousine with its usual escort sped along the road toward Peter's Villa.

They both sat in silence in the back for a minute until Paul spoke, he sounded false and forced much like when a man argues with his wife to the point where she breaks down in tears and he is forced to say something conciliatory even though he knows it will be rejected.

"We have a full day tomorrow Peter, just you and me, we will see the sights.."

"Paul," interjected Peter sharply, " just get me home, I want to be on the first flight out of here." .

"That's impossible, there are no flights out of here until next week.."

"Well then I'll drive or walk or bloody well swim if I have to, but I will get out of here somehow, tomorrow if not today!" shouted Peter in a rare fit of temper.

Paul ensured that the glass separating them from the driver was fully closed. A few seconds of charged silence followed then Paul spoke again in his quiet, slow and deliberate way.

"Peter, you must believe me when I say that I must watch every step that I take in this country. If for a moment my enemies saw that I was weak they would close in for the kill...Literally. If they thought that in any way there was some kind of...Attachment between us other than distant blood relatives it could spell disaster for both of us.."

"Then why for crying out loud did you ask me here in the first place?" croaked Peter his voice breaking with emotion.

Paul pondered, he indeed new that bringing Peter into the country may well be risky, but in the UK Peter had been a loose cannon, asking everyone for any news of him keeping the name of Van Der Borgh alive instead of letting it die. Then there were his letters which Paul must assume had been intercepted either in Rhodesia on the way through or in Karuda, he had to stop him.

Paul thought that by bringing him here he could assure him and take all the mystery out of the situation thus neutralising him, but it was all going wrong. He no longer desired Peter as he had done in the old days, it was nothing to do with his injuries, it was the just the way he was, a man incapable of any long lasting emotion or attachment.

"Well!" repeated Peter sobbing, "Why?…Why did you bring me here to be humiliated and laughed at? Ha! Ha! Peter the one eyed pufter, see how he hobbles along in the wake of Brigadier Paul.. "

"That's enough Peter!.. That's enough! You are tired and upset. I will pick you up at ten tomorrow morning.. Don't do anything stupid and lay off the booze. Tomorrow I will explain the situation to you fully and you will understand…. You'll see!" He patted Peter who had crumpled into a hyperventilating dribbling mess.

The Limo stopped outside the Villa and Paul motioned for the driver to stay where he was and went around to help Peter out but as he got around the car

Peter had limped quickly up the steps and disappeared through the door.

Once inside he made for the drinks cabinet and poured himself a large Brandy. This time, when he gulped it down he didn't retch. With the liquid giving him a lovely warm sensation in his stomach, he carefully made his way up the stairs to his bedroom and started to pack his case. He had stopped sobbing, his emotions had hardened a little and were replaced with purpose and hate.

6

The Taxi pulled up outside the Royal Hotel in Laka. A Doorman in full livery came down the steps and grabbed Peter's suitcase. Peter was slightly tipsy and went to walk normally without the use of his stick and tumbled to his knees. "My stick!" He slurred and it was placed in his hand.

The Hotel was but a faded reflection of its glory days when it used to accommodate the high echelon visitors to the country as well as high ranking officers from the British Army alongside wealthy mine and land owners. Then it had been the venue for grand parties, balls and the place had oozed with the wealth and opulence of the very best of Karudan white society.

Now as Peter limped across the large badly lit foyer to the check in desk he could smell the decay and dust. He booked a room and on finding out that there was no room service he asked the porter to get him a bottle of Brandy and bring it to the room.

After his second glass he picked up the phone and told the Hotel switchboard to put him through to a travel agents in Salisbury Rhodesia. After some minutes Peter's phone rang and the operator told him he was through.

"I will be arriving in Salisbury soon and would like to visit places of interest and wondered if you could help? There was a particularly helpful guy there last time his name was Daryl, could I speak to him personally, my name is Peter Gant." The woman on the other end of the phone said that he was out with a client but took the name of Peter's hotel and room number and said that he would call soon.

Peter then called "Gerald" at his flat in Pimlico. A woman, who he took to be his mother answered and in a shrill upper crust accent she said that there was no-one called Gerald there, then changed her mind. Peter could hear her calling "Julian". Gerald or Julian came to the phone, Peter did not take him to task over his name but simply blubbed, "Gerald it's so good to hear your voice!"

"Peter!" enthused Julian. They carried on with small talk for some minutes, then Julian remarked with a serious tone. "You're upset, do you want to talk about it?"

"Oh! It's nothing I won't get over, I just feel low at the moment."

"Did things not work out with.. With our mutual friend?"

"Something like that" replied Peter softly and took another swig of brandy. "I feel bloody awful Gerald, I wish I was back home.. I really I do, this dump depresses me. Oh God! I wish you had never told me about him.. I..."

Julian Pern could not believe his luck, not only had Gant made contact with Borgh but they had actually fallen out and Gant seemed bitter and miserable, should he put all his cards on the table with Gant and exploit the fact that he had eyes and ears right in the middle of enemy territory? He decided not to for the moment. "Listen Peter!" shouted Julian, "Snap out of it man, get a good night's sleep and I will call you in the morning.. Okay?.. Peter are you listening?"

Peter replied that he was and that he would await his call in the morning, they both said there goodbyes and Peter relaxed on the bed. He felt better now that he had unburdened himself a little.

The phone rang, he must have dozed he thought. He fumbled for it, cleared his voice and said "Hello."

"Salisbury on de phone sah!" Came the operator's voice.

"Mister Gant? Daryl here, I hope you are enjoying your holiday, Mister Gant."

"Daryl.. Yes I am, I.. I saw the sights you recommended, just like the photographs you showed me. Will probably go out and see them again tomorrow.."

"Good I'm glad you liked them, try and get fresh photographs if you can to update our posters and do keep in touch! Look I'm sorry but I have to go now, I will call you tomorrow there is lots more to see and do there…Goodbye for now Mister Gant."

The phone went dead, Peter lay on his bed and tried to analyse his reasons for talking to Daryl. He knew that he was some sort of spy and was using him to get information. If Paul had been there to meet him when he had arrived in Karuda he would have immediately reported his meeting in Rhodesia with Hanlon and Stone Face. Now, all he wanted to do, he concluded was to help and in some way hurt Paul and badly. With that thought he drifted into a drink induced torpor.

Paul's chauffeur stood trembling in front of the massive frame of Field Marshal of the Army, Montgomery Juba. They were in the large double garages attached to Juba's luxurious Villa on the outskirts of Laki.

Also present was Juba's own Chauffeur and his personal bodyguard. In the darker part of the garage and unseen by the victim stood Tasi and the ever present Jokko.

Juba flexed a baseball bat in his hand, he was not in a good mood and periodically swung it in front of the hapless man menacingly. At Juba's instigation his two henchmen tied the man's arms to a hook in the rafters so that he stood almost on tiptoes.

"For three months now," growled Juba through clenched teeth, "You have reported nothing! Absolutely nothing about that stinking white filth! Are you under some kind of spell that he has put on you?!"

"Please, please great father do not punish me," snivelled the petrified driver, "the white filth never says anything in front of me...!"

"Aaaah! Screamed Juba and swung the bat in a great arc toward the man who screamed and tried in vain to turn away from the blow. The blow however, did not come, Juba had faked it and pulled up short of hitting him. The man wailed.

Prince Tasi suppressed a giggle of amusement, he was enjoying the spectacle immensely and looked forward to carrying out something similar one day.

"What about this other one eyed filth that came to visit him? You drive them around, what were the words between them?" Ranted Juba.

"After the dinner at the club the visitor was upset and crying," said the chauffeur, pleased that he had something to report at last. "They were arguing and shouting in the back but I could not hear properly. The Brigadier was very upset after and called for the other white filth officer Potter when he got in...This much I know great father..."

Juba rested the bat on his victim's nose and said slowly. "I need more! Double.. Treble your efforts. I will expect more off you in three days..."

"But Uncle!" interrupted Tasi from the darkness, disappointed that the show was to conclude. "This cowering dog is a liar, he is indeed under the spell of the white pig. Finish him now and replace him with someone more reliable.. Go on! Beat him to death!"

Juba didn't hesitate, using his enormous weight and brute strength, he swung the bat time and time again until the rope snapped and he stood panting over the blood soaked corpse.

Tasi was breathless with excitement.

Peter Gant felt remarkably well, he inspected the brandy bottle and found that it was two thirds empty, he had no hangover and a cold shower had woken him completely.

He vaguely remembered the phone calls he made the previous evening but paid scant attention as to what was said and to whom. He would make a good effort today to leave the country by any means he could. In town there was one European travel agent, it would be a good place to start. A vision of Paul flashed on his inward eye and he felt the loathing that is born of rejection. He looked at his watch and saw that it was seven fifteen, at ten he knew that Paul would be arriving at the empty Villa to pick him up. He allowed himself a smile

He heard the door opening and swung round to see a man enter. He looked sixty something and dressed in an off white linen suit and straw hat, his rosy face sported a ragged, white goatee beard, his frame slight. He motioned to Peter to be quiet then whispered, "Are you alone?"

A shaken Peter nodded and the man continued, "We can't speak here, too dangerous, the cleaners are coming around. Go out of the hotel and turn right, cross over the road and keep going along The Royal Avenue, keep on the left hand side of the road.."

"Why on earth should I?!" exclaimed Peter, "And who are you? Are you mad?!"

"Daryl! Daryl sent me," said the man nervously with a refined English accent. "Didn't he say I was coming?" he looked around furtively and groaned, "God! I'm too old for this! Look chum, you can either take it or leave it. I'll give you fifteen minutes!" With that he walked out of the room after first looking both ways down the corridor.

Colonel Harry Macmillan retired, late of the King's Shropshire Light Infantry and Karuda Africa Rifles, again mopped his brow and looked back up the Royal Avenue to the Hotel. The waiter at the small pavement café loomed and Macmillan waived him away.

He looked at his watch and sighed inwardly, he would give that arrogant one eyed sod the remaining eight minutes of the fifteen and if he didn't show up, that was it, he was off.

Damn Hanlon calling him in the middle of the night like that, how long was it since he last heard from him? Was it one year or eighteen months ago just after the war finished here? I've retired for God's sake! Didn't the man appreciate how dangerous it was out here now?

It was fine when he had left the army in the fifties, he found it exhilarating to freelance for the security services of Rhodesia and South Africa while still being in the pay of MI6. He was fit and tough then but they never let go, it was always just another little job. The jobs nowadays had been small admittedly, check a hotel register here, find out what unit is where, get a photograph of this person or that.

It had all gradually faded away and stopped until the war against the rebels then they had re-activated him, pushing him to do more and more dangerous tasks. One of these tasks was to find out more about Vander the mysterious leader of the fight against the rebels. He was white and maybe of South African , English or even Dutch origin and that's all that was known.

He found this mission nigh impossible. Vander was never seen in public and was only photographed once on his appointment to the Palace Bodyguard. Getting a copy of that photograph had aged Harry ten years, he had been arrested for being in an off limits area. His bungalow was ransacked and he was questioned for hours. They didn't find the photograph, the transmitter or any other incriminating evidence. His doddering old fool act paid off and he was released with his feathers ruffled and no more.

All this exacerbated a heart problem and Harry announced his retirement from the "Game." Then last night out of the blue Daryl Hanlon had called.

He checked his watch again, six minutes to go. A Mercedes truck with the camouflage and markings of the Bureau of Internal Security came slowly rolling past, a soldier in reflective sunglasses leaned on the 12.7mm Machine gun mounted in the rear.

Macmillan averted his eyes and stared at the scruffy menu, a stab of fear twisted its way through his guts and he involuntary broke wind. He called the waiter back and ordered a large glass of the local raw cane spirit. He could have ordered gin or vodka or even whisky but it would have been dressed up cane spirit and more expensive.

He downed the slug in one and ordered another, he looked back up the avenue which was brilliantly lit in the golden morning rays and saw a figure limping across the street then down the pavement toward him.

"Damn the bastard!" He spat, downed his second drink and got up.

Peter had thought about the situation when the old man had disappeared. He had concentrated and dug up his conversation with Daryl the night before, something about pictures and posters. Christ, he thought, what the hell am I getting in to? But what was his alternative? He would at least see what was on offer.

He limped down the pavement, the low sun glaring in his eye. After some time he came to a junction on his left and paused before crossing it. "Gant! I say Gant! Over here man!" Peter looked down the small road and saw the old man waiving his straw hat at him, he stood next to a faded blue Morris Cowley car and beckoned urgently for Peter to get in.

As they drove along Macmillan kept his eye on the rear view mirror almost constantly, his head moving from mirror to windscreen in short nervous nods. He pulled up at a dilapidated, deserted petrol station careful to park at the rear out of sight

"You *are* Peter Gant?" he spoke quickly his eyes darting around their surroundings.

"Yes! And you?"

"Who I am is neither here nor there, have you got a camera?"

"No! I.... "

"Well take this," Macmillan pulled a small camera out of his rumpled jacket, "it's got twenty shots in it..."

"Look! For God's sake slow down man, what the hell is this all about?" shouted Peter.

Macmillan sighed, then laughed and shook his head. He remained silent for a few seconds while looking through the windscreen and breathing heavily, he then turned to Peter, "Okay.. Mister Gant, the camera is for you to get a photograph of Brigadier Paul Vander.. I take it that you know him?" Peter nodded, his mouth hanging open in confusion. "Good, you are also to get as much information as possible on Vander's movements over the next few weeks, day by day and better, hour by hour, this is vital information. When you get the information call Daryl and he will arrange to pick it up."

"No! No! I can't do that!" howled Peter, "I'm leaving today, I don't ever want to see that bastard again!"

Suddenly Macmillan turned on him, he gripped the lapel of Peter's jacket. His face was twisted, yet it seemed to lose years as his ice blue eyes flashed and shook off their dimness, he gritted his teeth and snarled, "Now listen here *chum*, I don't know who you think you are, or where you think you're at, but let me tell you this, you're up to your ruddy neck in it. There is no way you will leave this country until *we,* are ready.. Just try it *chum*. Rhodesia will refuse you entry and then what? Hack your way through the bloody Ulu until the rebels get you and tear your balls off?! No! You do as you're told and if you don't? Then the Bureau will be tipped off that you are a spy and believe me, they *will* find evidence to support that!" He let go of Peter's jacket and stared straight out of the windscreen again.

"If everything goes well," continued Macmillan in a normal voice, "and you get the information needed, Daryl will get you safely out and you will be rewarded, if you don't...I have already told you what will happen, this is not a game Mister Gant, please believe me.. I will drop you near your hotel."

Back at the Hotel Peter was too numb to cry, he lay on his bed looking up at the ceiling and trying to slow down the thoughts that raced through his head. He swigged a mouthful of brandy straight from the bottle and slowly let it trickle down his throat.

The shrill of the telephone snapped him out of his torpor, it was Gerald.

"Peter! How are you? I've been trying your room for the last hour." Oozed Pern.

"Not too well actually Gerald.. or is it Julian?" Peter didn't much more care who he upset now.

"That was necessary at the time old man. Look I *will* explain, could you do me a favour? Go to the European Travel agents off the Royal Avenue. Outside is a battery of telephone boxes one of which is international, give me a ring, reverse the charges if you like.. Peter are you there?"

"Yes, go to the phone box by the European travel agents, give you a call." repeated Peter sluggishly, "What will happen if I don't, will you tip them off as well?"

"Peter are you okay? Listen! Lay off the sauce for a few hours then call me okay?!"

Peter said that he would then rose and looked at his watch. Paul would be at the bungalow in an hour, he had time. He reached for the telephone to call a taxi but the bottle was in the way, he took another swig.

7

"Where is my regular driver?" enquired Paul abruptly. He stood on the steps of his villa talking to the new chauffeur of his Limousine who sat impassively behind the wheel.

"He got drunk last night Boss, got knocked down killed."

Paul inwardly flinched, he knew that his former chauffeur was one of Juba's plants, he also knew through Kinga that Juba was getting impatient with his informers and had probably made an example of him.

He sat in the back of the limo, the feeling that everything was closing in on him was getting stronger. In any other situation he would probably cut and run like he had done many times before but this was different. He had an overwhelming feeling that his destiny lay here in Karuda. In just over a year he had risen from a criminal on the run from three countries, to one of the most powerful men in Karuda.

There and then in the back of the car as it ran through the suburbs he decided to kill Juba, it was just the timing he had to get right.

Paul was surprised to see that Peter's mood had changed for the better, although he looked tired and drawn he had managed a smile and an apology for the his behaviour the day before. He blamed it on his old

wounds, when Paul had asked about them he said that
he had been beaten up by yobs and left it at that.

The convoy consisted of Paul's Limo, the armoured car and two Landrovers full of young, tough
looking soldiers from Paul's Battalion. It was necessary,
Paul said, because he wanted to show Peter the jungle
which increased the ever present security risk. As they
drove along and chatted, Peter gently probed Paul's
short term and long term plans.

Paul had replied that he would be busy for the coming weeks with no particular schedule apart from one
project that he would show Paul later. They had stopped
by a waterfall in the rain forest and Paul explained that
the area had been a temporary Headquarters of his during the campaign against the rebels. There they had a
cold lunch provided by a chef who had travelled with
them.

Peter studied Paul and could see how relaxed he
had become once he was in the field. He started to talk
of the old days and Peter found his heart warming to
him again. He knew that it was pointless to push their
relationship any further, that was stone dead. Peter remembered the camera but decided against using it yet,
the day was good, the best yet and he didn't want to
spoil it.

They left the jungle and Paul showed him the new
International "Airport." All Peter could see was a huge
area that had been cleared of forest and bulldozed flat.
Huge mounds of earth were everywhere but precious
few Plant vehicles or workers. Once this was complete,

said Paul, they would be independent of Rhodesia for air travel, it would be a new beginning, he said.

In the late afternoon they headed back to Laka, despite his former experiences Peter had enjoyed the day, he and Paul had been relaxed and even happy. The soldiers had kept a discreet distance which made it a lot easier. Paul had been in his element acting the part of the tour guide.

They turned off the main road and after some minutes Paul pointed to a strip of tarmac with a couple of Nissen huts at the side. Paul motioned the driver to slow and said to Peter, "That's it mon brave, that's where I first entered this country.. On an old Dakota .. It seems like a lifetime ago." They travelled a few miles more and pulled up at a large double gate, a soldier sprang to attention and opened the gate but Paul ignored him and got out of the car beckoning Paul to do the same.

"This was my training camp when I got here!" said Paul enthusiastically, "Camp Lagonda!" He walked through the gate oblivious of Peter limping to keep up with him. Inside was a hive of activity, the square was temporarily being used as a storage base for all kinds of building materials. A bulldozer and other Plant vehicles were parked in the corner.

"This is *my* project!" He exclaimed to Peter a large grin on his face, "Starting soon most of the existing buildings will be pulled down and replaced by modern barrack blocks for *my* Battalion. I will officially open it on March the eighteenth before the wet season begins and my soldiers will move in soon after that, come! I will show you where my villa will be built."

He enthusiastically marched ahead continually turning to talk to Paul, "We are to name it Camp Vander after yours truly, not my idea," added Paul quickly, "the President insisted."

They stopped at a large piece of ground that had been levelled. "This will be where my villa will be built completely to my specifications and the grounds land-scaped to remind me of my homeland…" With that he seemed to lose his ebullience and went silent. He turned and strode back to the Limo which had followed them up.

On the way back Peter asked if he could be dropped into town, Paul agreed and apologised that he couldn't join him, *Things to sort out,* he had said.

With some difficulty, Peter got through to Julian's flat and listened to the faint ringing tone at the other end. He was in a filthy call box outside of the European Travel agents that had closed for the night. The light was failing fast and he had only just made out the numbers. The street was beginning to fill up with an evening crowd and there was a none stop cacophony of hooting taxi horns as they spotted prospective clients on the broad pavements.

"Hello." It was Julian although through habit Peter called him Gerald

"Gerald .. It's Peter can you hear me okay?.. you are faint."

"Yes! Yes! Peter do you feel better?"

"Yes .. Sorry, I had a bad day yesterday…"

"Good, listen! Firstly are you alone and in that call box I told you about?"

"Yes of course."

"Peter you now know what my name is but don't use it over there.. Okay? That's important. Listen, I want you to do a favour for me.. It's nothing illegal, but it's best if you do it fairly casually without causing a stir if you get what I mean. I want you.. And please don't write anything down, I want you to go to a place just outside of the town called Camp Lagonda and let me know how it's looking. You know the sort of thing, is it deserted and if it isn't, who are the troops there.. It will be on the sign just outside the gate. Act like a dumb tourist and flash some money about, they'll let you get away with murder and probably show you around the place.."

"I went there today.... With Paul.."

"You did?! What luck! Did you go in ?"

"Yes, he gave me a guided tour as a matter of fact."

"Well? How did the place look?"

"It looked okay I suppose, they're going to rebuild it and rename it "

"What!?" Julian almost screamed, "What...What are they doing?"

"They're going to flatten some of the camp and make a new one." There was a silence from Julian but after Peter called his name several times he responded, his mood had changed.

"W..When is this to happen? When do they start?" He asked sharply.

"All that I know is that it will be soon. Look why is this so important?"

Julian ignored him and said tersely, "You must find out the date when they start! Do you understand me? Well do you?"

Peter was sick of being pushed around, treated and spoken to like he was dirt. Again he felt a surge of fury erupt in his chest and like people who rarely reacted in anger, once he let fly he had no control over it.

"Listen you fucking damn bastard!" he raged at the top of his voice, "I don't have to do fucking anything for you or anybody! Do *you* underfuckingstand me? And do you know what I'm going to do? I'm going to Paul and anyone else that will listen and tell them all about you...You Gerald fucking Julian Bastard!" With that, he slammed the phone down.

An eventful evening was in store for Paul. As usual his servant Kinga briefed him on the trivia of the day and followed him into the main room and poured him a Scotch. When Paul had taken a sip and removed his boots Kinga drew closer to Paul.

"Sir, I have news on what you asked."

Paul motioned to the door and Kinga said, "The house is empty, I told them all to go."

"Very well, go on." said Paul relaxing in a hide arm-chair.

"The drugs that you talked of, the ones that the President uses are supplied personally to him by Field Marshal Juba. The drugs come into Karuda from an-other country. This is controlled by Juba's sister Mara, who then gives them to Juba.."

"Mara?!" interjected Paul, "Is she the one that is a captain in the Bureau of Internal Security?" Kinga nodded. "How does Mara get the drugs in?" Asked Paul his brow wrinkled in concentration.

"This I could not find out Sir, nobody seemed to know." said Kinga in his quiet manner.

"Does anyone know that you are getting this information for *me*?.. This I must know Kinga."

"Your name was never mentioned, most of the people I talk to believe that I hate you because I spy for the Field Marshal."

Paul nodded in approval and asked, "Have you any thing more?"

"No Sir.. Not about that." said Kinga suddenly averting his eyes to the floor.

"What is it Kinga? Tell me." said Paul gently.

"Master, the people here are like old women, everyone is afraid. If they speak out the bureau visits them and they are never heard of again, so they talk to each other in the safety of their homes and among their tribesmen about many things and this is how I can get information by listening to them."

Paul nodded patiently and after a few seconds Kinga spoke again coming to his point.

"To get *this* information about de drug, I had to ask not one but many people. Juba has his spies everywhere and soon, someone will inform him that I have asked these questions." He stopped his head bowed.

Paul understood, he rose and said to Kinga, "I have no further use for you, you are discharged from your job as House Servant Number one as of this moment. Get your things now and report to me before you leave." Kinga bowed to Paul and left.

Five minutes later he reported back to Paul who said, "Leave the country tonight, you know how to do that safely?" Kinga nodded. "Here, take this." Paul handed him a large open envelope that had a thick wedge of US Dollars crammed in it.

"Good luck, you are a good man Kinga." said Paul. Kinga nodded to Paul and said, "Be careful Master and watch the Hyena." With that he turned and left.

Paul heard the door slam and flung his glass at the stone fireplace with all his might. "Damn!" He exclaimed and sat in the chair his head in his hands.

How long he sat like that he wasn't quite sure, he turned things over and over in his mind. Damn Juba, he thought, why was the bastard so paranoid, he had everything he wanted but trusted no-one. Sure he was after his job but if things were normal he would just have waited for him to retire or die. This is my country now, I want to go nowhere else in this world. I want to grow old here and die here and between times maybe take a wife and have three sons, he wouldn't beat them like he had been beaten.

A vision of his father, a giant Boer with a long red beard laying into him with a leather strop flashed on his inward eye. His mother screaming and trying to hang onto his beating arm being punched fully in the face and dropping to the ground.

His mind jumped forward a few years to when he found the knife in a disused mineshaft, he had been the only one of the gang who dared to climb down the crumbling half collapsed shaft and crawl through the underground passages, the crudely made kerosene fuelled brand guttering and threatening to go out.

He came across the knife standing up, stuck in something and it was a few moments before he realised it was jammed through the breastbone of a skeleton. Although not yet in his teens he had showed no fear, after all, it *was* dead. The knife fascinated him standing there still bright and powerful. He had prised it out gently and hid it from his friends.

His mother's screams had woken him again, his younger brother was already cowering in terror as he heard the cursing red beard, clump his drunken way up the stairs yelling and screaming what he was going to do to them.

It had all ended abruptly when Paul lunged and rammed the knife through his large gut, he had let the knife go and it was immediately swallowed whole, sucked into the gaping wound.

With the help of his mother, before first light, they had carried him on a pony to the shaft and flung him in but not before Paul had placed his hands inside the gore and tugged out the knife which was stuck somewhere in his father's back bone. He had stood staring at the black hole in the ground, grave to two people who had died by the knife.

A noise made him surface from his vivid memories, his face was tear stained and his eyes out of focus, mucous ran down his nose and bonded with silvery threads to the back of his hand when he wiped it.

The noise again, it was a tapping on his window. Paul became instantly alert, he knew no-one could see into the house. He drew his Browning pistol, the hammer was on half cock and he thumbed it back fully. Again the tapping, just audible, not insistent, just three well spaced taps.

Paul went to the front door and turned on the hall light as if he were going to exit there then moved quickly to the servants entrance at the side of the house, thumbing the safety off he opened the door and slid into the inky darkness. He looked in the direction where the window was being tapped but saw nothing, he crouched waiting for his eyes to adjust more.

"Mister Paul." It was no more than a whisper and it came from behind him, he swung around, finger on the trigger, his heart thumping but he saw nothing.

"Mister Paul, I am not armed and I mean no harm." said the voice in a low tone.

Paul was looking directly at source of the voice, it seemed to come from a point about five yards to the front of him, where there was a low brick barbecue stand.

"Who are you? Show yourself!" said Paul in a normal voice.

"I cannot speak my name but I will show myself, please lower your gun." Paul did so. "Look to your left, Mister Paul." Paul shot a glance to his left and a figure emerged from a recess in the wall of the house with his hands in the air. It was Jokko.

"Your accomplice, where is he?" enquired Paul sharply nodding toward the barbecue area.

"There is only me, Mister Paul." Jokko had advanced and stood about three yards from Paul his arms still raised. Jokko made an enquiring gesture and Paul nodded, Jokko dropped his arms and spoke softly.

"Mister Paul, I have only a short time before I am missed, so I won't talk in parables. I will warn you however, that we will never speak again. Juba will move against you soon and kill you, he will say that you were plotting to overthrow the President and will have witnesses and other *proof* to back his story up. You will not be given a chance to defend yourself it will be said that you resisted arrest or some such thing and you will be shot dead.

"When will this happen?" asked Paul evenly.

"Exactly when, is a time you will have to judge but I can tell you that two things will happen first. One, the Hyena will go missing and two, you will be separated from your Battalion, or it will be separated from you."

"The Hyena?" quizzed Paul, that was the second time he had heard the name that evening.

"Major Potter, he is known by that name. Juba knows that you confide in him and will try and break him first before he comes for you. His evidence would be important to his case, whether he does break him or whether he doesn't won't matter, he would die with you anyway. I do know that it will not happen for at least three weeks, Juba and my Prince are holding a celebration for the President's birthday and he wants nothing to spoil that."

"Why Jokko? Why do you tell me these things?"

Jokko grimaced for a smile. "My Prince Tasi was a good master. I looked after him since he was five, he was a good pupil. Then Juba took control and is shaping him into a hate filled twisted creature as devious and deadly as himself. Now he provides him with the filth that bends his mind. One day my Prince will be King of Karuda and Juba wants to hold the reins." Jokko's face contorted in a rare show of emotion.

"Who can I trust if I move against Juba?" asked Paul, realising that this was the reason that Jokko was telling him this.

"The President thinks you are a good man and he trusts your judgement, this infuriates Juba. There is one person who hates Juba but equally fears him. He is one of his Battalion Commanders, Chimba. Juba wiped out his family but doesn't realise that Chimba was a survivor, he waits for the day when he can settle matters."

"How can I trust *you* Jokko? Why should I believe that Juba wants me dead? After all, you want rid of Juba because of what he has done to your Prince. How do I know you have not made all this stuff about killing me up in the hope that I will do your dirty work for you, you have no reason to love me ."

"Mister Paul, some time ago you and I met in mortal combat. I am better than you but that day in the Palace you were fighting for your life. Everything that has shaped you and kept you alive during the years of brutal adversity that I know you must have suffered was also in that room. I had little chance and yet you let me live when you could have killed me. From that moment I was in your debt. After today, I consider that debt repaid…I have one request.. Spare my Prince, without Juba he can recover."

"Just one more thing, why did you say that you could not speak your name?"

"My name would mean nothing to you. The name that you know me by was given to me by my Prince when he was five, he named me after...After a brand of tea Mister Paul." Jokko allowed himself a smile then turned and disappeared in the darkness.

Julian's Mother couldn't recall Julian being so upset, even when he came back from imprisonment in Africa he wasn't as bad as this, pacing up and down in his room and raging aloud like that. She heard furniture being smashed then silence. She was about to enter his room but heard him sobbing and shouting something inaudible in his grief.

It had started after a phone call he had received earlier. Damn him, she thought, if he wants to act like a spoilt brat let him, I'm off. She straightened her hat and left the flat slamming the door as loud as she could.

Julian left his room and resisted the urge to have a drink, he had to maintain a clear line of thought. He felt weak and helpless. He could not think of a way out of the situation. Peter Gant had snapped, threatened to expose him and possibly blow the whole plan, it would certainly put Vander on his guard. All the planning and preparation he had put into it would be wasted now.

He had traced Van Der Borgh's history back to the Princes Own Yeomanry and through investigation had come across Gant. He had made their first meeting at the hospital look unplanned and natural. He had needed eyes and ears inside Karuda and couldn't believe his luck when Gant had been more than willing. And now? Nothing.

The phone rang and Julian stiffened, with his heart thumping he picked up the receiver, before he could answer a voice croaked, "Gerald?"

"It's Julian, not Gerald." he said in a cool distant manner.

"Julian! Julian, I'm sorry, look.... You don't know.. You don't *want* to know what I've been through, it just so happened that you got in the way.. Julian?"

"It's okay Peter, really it is, it *was* my fault. I get carried away at times.. Look old man, are you still in a position to talk to me?"

Peter replied that he was and Julian pumped him for information about Camp Lagonda and the airstrip and confirmed the fact that Vander would be there on March Eighteenth.

After going over it a few times, Peter asked him what it was all about, Julian was silent for a few seconds then spoke, the lies oiled and smooth.

"Peter I'm sorry, you've probably guessed by now that I work for a government organisation and I must tell you that what we have discussed is highly sensitive. I advise you for your own good to leave the country as soon as possible. Talk to no-one, just leave and I will meet with you on your return and explain the whole picture to you. I must go now, take care my friend." Julian heard Peter beginning to form another question but put the phone down, he immediately picked it up again, flicked a small book on the phone table open and dialled Nick's number.

8

Frank came back from the bar with two drinks, it was Saturday night and his night off. He hung on to the pint and handed the smaller glass to Tanya. She smiled and Frank sat down. She was craving for a cigarette but knew Frank disapproved so tried to push it to the back of her mind, not that Frank would ever say anything, she just thought that she should make an effort.

She and Frank had been together now for three days, she moved into Frank's small flat on the day that they had met up for the first time since the incident at the club when Frank got the push.

He had gone to Brad's house to see about the money he was owed but no-one answered, he then drove to the club. Brad was not there but Tanya was, she was with the owner collecting a few things. Frank learned that she had just been discharged from the hospital after Brad had given her a beating one night. He had also thrown all her belongings in the street and a neighbour had taken them to the club until she was well enough to recover them.

At Frank's insistence she moved in with him until she could fix herself up better.

At first, it was a little embarrassing and they were both a little self conscious. Frank had opened some wine and they had celebratory drink, exactly what they were celebrating they were not sure.

Tanya recounted how things had rapidly deterio-
rated after the incident at the club. Brad had accused
her of having an affair with Frank. He had brooded for
weeks on it, then after a particularly bad night at the
club, when Brad had been on the receiving end of a hiding for a change, he had turned on her. The police had
visited her in hospital but she didn't make a complaint
and they let the matter drop.

Either through sympathy, or just to comfort her he
didn't know but he wrapped his arms around her and
they made love, they had no real love for one another
but they were two lonely people who needed comfort
and reassurance.

They hit it off, she was easy going and undemand-
ing and he the same. Frank had got a temporary job
looking after a warehouse at night and part time barman in the Princess pub at lunchtimes. Tanya was to
start part time in the Laundrette under the flat.

They finished their drinks and started for home,
a figure walked toward them from the shadows. It was
Lenny Clark, one of the bouncers from the club, a tall,
quiet Scot.

"Frank, you didnae hear this from me you understand?" he said quietly with a serious look on his face,
"Brad is after you and Tanya, I mean big style. He thinks
that you and Tanya were doing the business behind his
back, especially now she's moved in with you. Watch him
Frank, you know what he's like."

Frank went to thank him but Lenny walked quickly
away. Tanya suppressed a sob, "It's all my fault Frank I'll
move out tomorrow.."

"You'll move nowhere, nothing is your fault." assured Frank gripping her arm and continuing to walk on. He had once considered taking some kind of action against Brad, not only for what he did to Tanya but for not paying him. He had decided that what happened to Tanya before they were an item was not an issue and therefore decided to take no action, as for the money, he had decided that he would give it one more try, but Lenny's warning had put a different slant on things.

There was a note shoved under the door, it was from Nick. *Call me first thing tomorrow,* it said.

Frank surmised that the note was something to do with Pern and the operation. He and Nick had accepted the job from Pern and he advised them to put a team of six together. This was not as easy as it sounded. All the good blokes were still serving and those that had recently left had moved away and were difficult to trace. Word had got round but so far only one man had approached them, he was an ex member living in the area, a known alcoholic and trouble maker, they had turned him down.

Nick was waiting at the end of the phone, it was eight in the morning and raining hard. He said for them to meet in a café in town.

Frank walked into the warm café that smelled of coffee and fried bacon. Nick was waiting at a table.

"The Operation has been called forward, he wants us to be ready as soon as possible, he wants us to fly out on Friday!" Nick stated with a touch of urgency in his voice.

"Fly? Fly where?" quizzed Frank sitting down opposite him.

"As yet I don't know, I was more worried about not having a team, we've got but a few days. I placed an advert in two national dailies last week. I've had two calls, one I eliminated straight away, the other one is coming down for an interview next week I'll have to bring it all forward."

"I'm working on the ex members of the Regiment," replied Frank, "I'll get a move on with that."

"Frank," said Nick a serious look on his face, "I said we would be there whatever we've got with us, are you still on for that?"

"I said that I was *in* Nick and I meant it."

"Both men stood up, shook hands and agreed to contact each other a couple of times a day with progress reports on recruitment.

Julian hardly slept since he had talked with Peter. When he had drifted, horrible distorted pictures had formed in his mind of the inmates of Laka prison chasing him He was naked and his feet were heavy, he could smell their breath on his shoulders as they hooted with laughter and pawed for him, he had woken up sweating, all the nerves ends around his scarred mouth tingling.

Then he dreamt of Paul Vander sitting on a Royal throne, Julian had levelled his gun at him and pulled the trigger but nothing had happened. Vander had given one of his sneers and had thrown his knife at Julian's groin, the shock had woken Julian completely and he had lain there sweating.

He suspected that he was losing his mind. He rejected everyone, even his mother repelled him most of the time. She and his father had shoved him in boarding schools since he was five, and most times on his holidays they themselves had been elsewhere on holiday, leaving him to relatives or a temporary Nanny.

He'd never had a real relationship with anyone, as soon as he got close he would be rejected. His one steady girlfriend was Stella, a horsey country girl from good family stock, even Julian's mother had warmed to her and encouraged the relationship. She and Julian had spent long hours together, he had felt comfortable in her company and had sensed that her parents had been fond of him too.

Then he was expelled from the Royal Military Academy at Sandhurst. What details did leak out were sordid and involved another young man. There was a whiff of scandal about the whole affair and Stella's parents had picked up on it. She no longer wanted to see him and a few weeks later got engaged to some Cavalry Officer whom she later married.

When he had failed Sandhurst his father virtually rejected him. What a blessing it was, Julian thought, when the old bastard died. They were living in Rhodesia at the time and Julian was out there visiting them *between jobs* he had said. His father went out to work in the morning and never came back, a stroke, while sitting at his desk.

His friends had diminished over the years. A spell in the Army had steered him in a straight line for a bit. Because of his educational qualifications they had accepted him in the Intelligence Corps and he had got promoted to Corporal very quickly but was disliked for being a loner as well as for his know all, arrogant attitude.

His OC's cheque book had gone missing and over a hundred pounds had disappeared from his account before he had realised it. Suspicion fell on Julian, a raid of his bunk turned up the missing cheque book and some of the money. He ran before he could be arrested and ended up back in Rhodesia.

It wasn't long before he had heard of the troubles in Karuda. His mother decided that they would go back to England. That was the last thing he had wanted and had approached the Karudan government with a view to recruiting a white mercenary Army.

Depression had always been waiting to surface from the black depths of his mind and since his imprisonment it had shrouded him more and more. He often mused that if things had been allowed to develop in Karuda he would have come through everything fine. He had never been so happy in his life as when he strutted around in his uniform, manipulating the puppet Hennings and accruing a fortune to boot, but that bastard Vander had ruined everything at a stroke. And the worst thing was he had never even seen it coming.

Julian came to the conclusion that even if he pulled off the operation and got his hands on all the riches it would not be enough. He had to strike back for his months of suffering and torture in Laka Prison. He had to strike back to regain his sanity, he had to kill Vander.

Frank and Norrie left the parked car and walked down the dark street. The drizzle formed a halo around the streetlight that was working. Frank looked at his watch it was one thirty am. They walked up the path of one of the council houses on the sprawling estate. Once round the back they stopped and listened for around ten minutes, then on a signal from Frank, Norrie produced a crow bar and gently started prising the back door off its hinges. It wasn't long before the door yielded, they waited for another few minutes then entered.

Brad North paid the taxi off and walked towards his house. He was in a fairly buoyant mood, not only had he made good headway with the new girl in the kiosk but he had managed to clip twenty quid off the night's take.

He entered the house, the hall light wasn't working but he saw that there was a light on in the kitchen from the gap under the door. Curious, he strode towards it and as he passed the front room door a figure dived at his legs and floored him. As soon as he hit the deck another figure pounced on him and forced a crow bar across his throat.

He struggled but was fighting a losing battle for breath, he heard the voice telling him that if he lay still he would let him breathe. He had no alternative, so he lay still and the strangulation lessened, however, when he got a few good breaths in he made an almighty effort to get up and almost made it but the crow bar was on his throat again, he felt something snap in his neck and his breath was cut completely. Again the voice was telling him to relax and it would be alright. This time he did and when he breathed again was not tempted to struggle.

The figure above him had on a black balaclava, he didn't recognise the voice but knew it was from somewhere up north. Another person sat on his legs and was tying them together.

"Listen you little fat bastard! I hear that you are going to do Frank Britton and his girl over! Is that right? Well is it?" snarled the voice, the crow bar started to put pressure on his throat again.

"No! No! That's not right!" he rasped. "Yeh, me and Frank fell out but it's nothing, nothing at all and as for Tanya…. Good luck to them."

"I don't fucking believe you, you shit! Do you know what Regiment Frank belongs to? Good, he's our mate and we don't want anything happening to him or his girl, tomorrow or the next day or ever.. Do you understand?!" raged the voice. "Cos if it does, we're coming for *you*, even if you were a thousand miles away when it happened and you'd better believe that pal 'cos for two pins I'd stripe you up now!" There was a few seconds silence broken only by the panting of both men, then the voice again.

"Okay fatty, we're leaving, now roll on your stomach, and remember this, we can always reach you." Brad received a kick in the ribs and felt the two men walking over him to the front door , seconds later it clicked shut. He pushed himself up by his arms but his legs were tied to the radiator, he slumped back down, he just felt relieved that they had gone and so tired, so very tired.

Frank and Norrie got to the car and as they were about to get in a torch flashed in their faces from the garden they had parked adjacent to. As they raised their arms in alarm an old sounding male voice shouted. "If you park 'ere again I'll inform the police, we've had enough of you drug pushers around 'ere! Now get!"

"Yeh! Fuck off and don't come back!" said another. Without bothering to argue Norrie started the car and sped away.

"Jesus! That was the most frightening part of the night!" Exclaimed Norrie.

"Thanks mate, that's one I owe you." laughed Frank, relieved that it was over. "I couldn't have gone away knowing that bastard might have got to Tanya."

"So you're really off on Friday? Fuckin' good luck to you mate." Norrie said warmly, "Have you got all your crew?"

"No, we're still short of the six we need but it will have to do."

"Still can't tell me what it's all about then eh? Me, your old mucker and all?" chided Norrie.

"If only it was as simple, my old mate, I really don't know what it's about myself yet."

On Wednesday night Frank and Nick entered the Heron pub and went into a side room that they had hired for the night. They were to meet the two men that had been recruited the day before.

One of the recruits was answering an advert that Nick had put in the paper and the other was a former soldier who was living in the area, neither Nick or Frank knew either of these two but both also knew that they would have to be pretty bad for them to be refused the job.

The first one was due at seven thirty, it was to be the guy who lived locally. He was five minutes early, Frank shook his hand and ushered him into the room. His name was Jim Walker, he was around five feet ten inches with a stocky frame and short, curly ginger hair.

He said that he had been in the Royal Electrical and Mechanical Engineers for six years and was a qualified vehicle mechanic. He had tried and failed selection for the SAS through injury, he lived in a flat in Farnborough and had no ties.

Nick explained that the Operation was abroad and hazardous and that he would have to be prepared to move out on the coming Friday. Jim enquired about pay and Nick told him that this would be settled on Friday when they were all to meet their employer and given a final brief. After more questions about his background they asked Jim to wait in the bar for them and he left.

"Well, what do you think?" asked Nick taking the first sip from his now flat pint.

"He seems okay, we just haven't got time to check anybody out. I say yes let's take him."

They were interrupted by a knock on the door, it opened and Jim stuck his head around it and said, "There's another bloke here to see you." Frank checked his watch he was half an hour early, he looked at Nick who nodded.

"Okay show him in."

The door opened fully and a black man of average height in a brown raincoat walked in, he looked at Frank and a big smile, accentuated by large, gleaming white teeth split his face.

Frank at once, both recognised the face but failed to place it or put a name to it. He automatically stood up and shook the proffered hand. The black man laughed and said, "You don't recognise me? Riff Riffington, late of The Princes' Own and you're Frank right?"

Then it came to Frank in an instant, they had both met in Belfast when Riff had visited the school with his OC about that psycho killer.

"Riff! Good to see you!"

"And you Frank, heard you had a spot of bother on the border, some lame joke of an officer dropped you in it."

"Yeh! Something like that," Frank felt a little awkward and gestured quickly to Nick, "Look, meet Nick Summers he's heading the Op."

Riff and Nick shook hands warmly. They ushered Riff to a seat and with a few questions ascertained that he had just completed nine years service and was enjoying a spot of leave at home in Birmingham.

Someone in his local pub had told him about the advert that Nick had placed in the newspaper, advertising: "Interesting work for former infantry soldiers."

"Look Riff," said Nick at length, "we're going to Karuda. We may, if it comes to the crunch, have to kill Karudans…"

Riff immediately knew what he was getting at and interjected by saying, "Hey! They're Kruds, I'm a Brummy."

They called Jim back in and told him that it was his last chance to back out, he didn't and Nick told everyone to be at Waterloo station on Friday at ten pm with passports.

"So that's it old boy," said Nick as he was driving Frank home. "we need at least thirty guys in my estimation and we are just four."

"Still, we'll be able to move quicker." Shot Frank. There was a seconds silence, then both men burst into laughter.

Frank started down the stairs of his flat to answer the hammering on his door. It was six in the morning on Friday, he could have lain in for another hour or so. When he was half way down in just his underpants he suddenly realised that it could be mates of Brad North's.

He hesitated at the door and shouted, "Who is it?"

"It's me Frank, Norrie, open up man!" came the urgent reply.

Frank did so and as soon as the door was open Norrie forced himself in to the narrow space at the foot of the stairs, he had a bulging sports bag in his hand. "Frank! Have you heard?"

"Heard what Norrie, what's this all about?"

"It's North! Brad North, he's dead! They found him yesterday in his house!" Norrie was speaking loud and excitedly. Frank calmed him and he continued in a more even tone. "It were on the local news but I didn't hear it, then someone said that North was found tied up and dead and police were looking for two men in their twenties seen in the area the night before."

"Stay calm Norrie they won't get as far as us." assured Frank.

"Don't fucking kid yourself mate, those vigilantes or whatever they were must have clocked the number of that banger I was driving. The cops were there in the Battalion car park where I left it, this morning first thing. I only found that out 'cos Taff Reece was guard Commander and told me straight away. Luckily it's not taxed or insured or registered to me in any way but it's only a matter of time, that damn crow bar is still in the boot and the balaclavas. For Chrissake! Listen Frank! I don't know where you are off to today and I don't much friggin' care but I'm coming with you!"

9

Paul entered the tented encampment of Number 2 Commando. Instead of the usual Limousine and escort, he was driving himself in one of his Landrovers. He wore jungle fatigues without insignia and a pair of large sunglasses in an effort to keep knowledge of his presence to a minimum. It was just after first light and the encampment was starting to stir, wood fires were being lit with huge kettles and pots suspended above them.

This was Colonel Chimba's Commando. They were on border duties for two months. Their job was to control a thirty mile stretch of border well known for guerrilla activity. Paul had met Chimba a couple of times before but only on formal occasions, he had seemed moody and quiet, yet his record was good. He was an above average officer who had excelled himself as a young subaltern during the war with the rebels.

Paul had done his homework and found out that Chimba had come from the South of the country, a place that had always been regarded as bush country, hardly developed or visited even when governed by the British. How and when his family had been wiped out Paul could not find out and chose not to dig too deep for fear of arousing suspicion. He knew that Chimba was married and had two children.

He was a good officer, well thought of by his men and from the south of the country, that was it, that was all Paul had to go on. If Jokko had misled him about Chimba's feelings for Juba, he was about to sign his own death warrant. With that thought in his mind Paul walked from his Landrover to a tent that had a small sign outside simply saying, "CO".

Paul hesitated at the flap then softly called Chimba's name. A brusk voice inside told him to enter. Paul did so and came across Chimba stripped to the waist swilling himself in a canvas bucket supported by a wooden frame. He didn't bother to turn and see who had entered but reached for a towel and rubbed himself down, he threw the towel down on his camp bed picked up a pair of thick rimmed spectacles, put them on and turned to look at Paul who had taken off his sunglasses

For a fleeting second either shock or fear flashed in his eyes, then he recovered, came to attention and said, "Sir! Welcome to my camp!"

Paul smiled and offered his hand, Chimba took it and smiled stiffly back. When Paul spoke to him, he made sure that he addressed him by his rank and surname, to do otherwise would have highly embarrassed Chimba and the meeting would flounder.

"Colonel Chimba, firstly I want you to be at ease. I am not here to carry out any surprise inspection. I am here to see you personally about a great matter that is troubling me. It is my hope that you can help me."

Chimba looked slightly confused, here the White Brigadier, he thought, a huge and powerful friend of Juba and the President who travels dressed as a private soldier to my camp miles into the bush and he asks *me* to help *him?*

"Please sit down Sir, I was just about to have tea served, will you join me? Or do you prefer coffee?" queried Chimba as he put on his shirt.

"Tea would be fine. Colonel I would prefer it if only you knew that I was here, your sentry just waived me through, I don't think he noticed."

"Of course." Replied Chimba and put his head through the flap and shouted something in Karudan, Paul could make out the words 'tea' and 'bring quick'.

"Is my tent good Brigadier or do you prefer we talk somewhere else? Perhaps we can walk to the observation post? It will be quiet for another hour or so."

Paul nodded, there was a sound outside the flap and Chimba took hold of a large aluminium pot of tea. He placed it on his small table and took two metal cups from his equipment, he blew on them and went to find a cloth but Paul took one of them and said with a smile, "Don't worry about a little dust Colonel, a little more of it after two hours on the road won't make any difference."

Chimba gave a little embarrassed laugh and poured the tea. "We are a little short on milk out here sir."

"Since when did a Karudan Commando need milk?" Laughed Paul, and was glad to see that Chimba also laughed.

They walked side by side up the small hillock to the observation point, bouncing small talk off one another. Finally halfway up, Paul knew that he either had to take the plunge or get in his vehicle, drive back and think of something else.

He stopped, removed his sun glasses and turned to face Chimba. "Colonel.." he paused for effect and then continued, "I don't know quite how to put my feelings into words, so please be patient." Chimba nodded.

"I am in an awkward position, a very awkward position. I came here to this country two years ago to fight a war, not for vast amounts of money like many of my own kind but because I have a soldier's heart and that heart lies here in the bush with the smell of wood fires and rifle oil. I have a will to seek out the enemy and destroy him just like you are doing now, just like we *both* did in the big war against the rebels." Paul paused and broke his eye contact with Chimba, he looked across the slopes in the distance for a few seconds before carrying on.

"Now, through no fault of my own I have an enemy who vows to kill me, not a rebel but a person in the army and government, a person who is jealous because President M'Punga supports and even likes me. This same person poisons the President's mind every day with lies and filth drugs so that his will weakens and becomes under the control of this talking snake. One day he will take over and will become President and then the earth will shake in Karuda."

Paul let his words sink in, then after a few seconds silence Chimba spoke, "Sir.. Who is this person?"

Paul turned back to Chimba and spoke the name. "Juba, Field Marshal Montgomery Juba, he is the Snake, he suspects that I know these things and has a plan to kill me soon, I have little time…"

"There are many ways to leave the country Brigadier…"

"I will not leave the country and the President to the Snake! I am stopping and fighting him. I did not come here my friend Chimba for an escape route, I came for your help in overthrowing Juba."

Chimba raised his hands, threw them down again and turned from Paul with an agitated look on his face. What they were talking about could get them both sentenced to immediate death. The only safe avenue for himself thought Chimba, would be to have the Brigadier arrested now and immediately report him to Juba.

Paul eased his hand behind his back while rubbing his ear with the other, he felt the handle of the knife and looked up and down the hill, it was as Chimba said it would be, quiet.

"Brigadier why!? Why did you come to me? What is to stop me arresting you right now?!" Spat Chimba, his eyes glaring behind his spectacles.

Paul looked down and saw that Chimba had a small pistol pointing at his stomach, he must have had it concealed in his pocket, thought a slightly alarmed Paul.

"Go ahead Colonel arrest me, after all it is your duty. I have asked you to help me kill Juba. Even if you let me go without pulling that trigger or arresting me, you are sending me to a certain death."

"You still have not answered my question Sir! Why me? Why did you come to me?" glared Chimba.

This is it, thought Paul, "Three days ago my security section intercepted a messenger." The lies rolled easily and convincingly off his tongue. "This messenger was going to report directly to Juba, one of these messages concerned you."

Chimba flinched and furrowed his brow, before he could speak Paul continued.

"It said that you were a threat to Juba because you knew that Juba was directly involved in the slaughter of your family.."

"Who wrote that message!" shouted Chimba.

"Captain Mara Imbekwe of the Bureau of Internal Security and Juba's sister, this much I know. Now listen to me Colonel, put the gun down and we can find a way out of this."

Two huge tears welled up in Chimba's eyes, his face screwed up and he turned and let out a sob, doubling up as if he had stomach cramps.

After some time he straightened up and blew his nose on a handkerchief, the pistol had disappeared.

"Well Brigadier it looks like we are on the same side, how much time do I have before they come for me?" asked Chimba in a forthright manner.

"The message…And the messenger for that matter, have disappeared and will never surface again.. "

"But what of that witch Mara? She knows.."

"I am taking steps this very day to neutralise that matter, the message about you was one of hundreds where she has similarly denounced someone, so I doubt that she will contact Juba direct about it for some days yet." Paul stepped forward to Chimba and placed both of his hands on his shoulders.

"At this moment my friend, we are two condemned people, we have no chance unless we strike first….. Together! Juba does not suspect we know anything…."

"But if I move my Commando against him it will mean another civil war! I cannot do that!" countered Chimba.

"You do not have to move against Juba, I alone will do that, but I need help...Are you with me? I need to know now!"

"Yes! Yes I am with you!" declared Chimba, both men clasped hands in a double handshake.

"Good!" smiled Paul, "Let us go back to your tent and talk some more."

Captain Mara Inbekwe started her working day much as any other apart from the fact that someone was lying in her large bed softly snoring. She showered and put on her robe. The presence in the bed irritated her, it had been a great night of passion but she was unused to having lovers during the week. Friday and Saturday were good but to get up for work with a veritable stranger still lying about was upsetting her routine and she was having none of that.

"Come on! Get up, time to go! Get your clothes on and leave.. Come on, up!"

The figure stirred, Mara peeled some notes off a bundle she pulled out of the draw and threw them on the bed, "Get some decent perfume and a pair of those long leather boots that you were whining about last night, come back on Friday evening! Now get out!" She ordered.

The young girl looked annoyed at being woken so early, she clutched the sheet to her breast and picked up the money with her free hand. She knew enough about

Mara not to complain or delay. She hastily dressed and with a forced smile left the flat.

Mara dressed in her black uniform of tight trousers and short sleeved shirt with silver rank insignia on the collar and the crest of the Bureau, the head of an eagle in silver on the right arm.

She looked at herself in the full length mirror, her rear she thought was getting a little too large but all in all, not a bad figure for a woman of thirty five.

Just before she left the house she strapped on a Colt .45 Automatic. It was far too big for her frame but she would have nothing else.

She left her house that was in an estate on the fringes of Laka reserved exclusively for highly placed persons in the forces or government and went to her black Mercedes saloon. She gunned it through the estate and up to the barrier which was lifted quickly by a policeman who gave her a salute as she passed.

Mara was in charge of administration at the Bureau headquarters. Her boss was a Colonel. Because she was Juba's sister many thought that she would have run the Bureau but Mara had far more insight and control over the organisation because she was at the centre of it. Nothing passed over anybody's desk without Mara knowing about it first. The Colonel was a figurehead who rubber stamped decisions suggested and formalised by Mara and her conspirators. It was perfect, if a problem arose that could not be surmounted or a mistake was made that could not be rectified, the Colonel took the flak.

She turned off the tarmac road onto a dirt track her usual shortcut. Presently she came to a bend in the track, as she slowed to negotiate it she saw an army truck in the ditch and a soldier lying on the ground, another soldier blocked her path with his hand raised to halt the car.

She wound down her widow and barked at the soldier, "Get out of my way!"

Suddenly she was aware of another formerly unseen soldier closing in from the side, as she turned she faced the barrel of a submachine gun, shocked she glanced forward and saw that two other soldiers were pointing guns straight at her.

"Get out of the car!" ordered the man at her window. She did as she was told and saw that the soldiers were not rebels as she had first thought but bore the insignia of Number 2 Commando.

"Do you realise who I am?" She hissed with unconcealed venom, "I am Captain Imbekwe of the Bureau of Internal Security, sister of Field M..."

She was cut off by the soldier backhanding her hard across the face. She crumpled onto the wing of the car and the soldier kicked her until she collapsed to the ground, he removed her Pistol and held her arm while his colleague stuck a hypodermic needle into it.

When she slumped they forced the limp body into a sack and threw it on the back of the vehicle in the ditch. When they had done this Paul came out of the trees.

"Good!" he said, "Now get the car into the ravine." They pushed the car off the road and through the foliage to a crack in the ground about twenty feet wide and the same deep, with a final heave they pushed it over the top and it smashed to a halt on the ravine bottom.

Paul entered the deserted barracks of Number 2 Commando. A small rear party manned it while the Commando was deployed for its two months on the border. He followed the Commando truck with Mara on board and stopped at a large building, one of the soldiers with a bunch of keys opened a metal side door and beckoned his two comrades.

They carried the sack with Mara in it like an old carpet to the door then down a long flight of concrete stairs to another door, behind it was a large room with a bare bedstead and a couple of chairs. One of the soldiers flicked a switch and a naked bulb gave off a weak, amber light.

Paul entered behind them. "Okay," he said looking around the room, "this is ideal. Bring her round and soften her up anyway you like but be careful, I need her to talk and later it's got to look like she died in that car. I will be back in one hour, have her ready!" He turned and left the room.

They snatched at the sack and pulled it off. Mara was groaning and starting to move, one of the soldiers produced a hypodermic with a shot to bring her round but the leader said to wait and removed her top, he stood back and looked at her semi nakedness, her two small pointed breasts standing erect. He looked at the others and they all burst into a nervous fit of laughter, then they started to tear off her trousers.

Paul showed his face in the office, he had time to go and change into his proper uniform, to all intents and purposes it was another routine day to his staff. Paul looked at his watch, he should be getting back to Mara soon, time was tight. He made his excuses and left.

He banged on the metal door and after a minute one of the soldiers opened it a crack to see who it was then admitted him. Paul descended the flight and entered the room. Mara was bound to a chair, she was fully clothed, her head hung down. Paul told the others to leave and wait for him outside.

At the sound of Paul's voice Mara lifted her head, her eyes were bloodshot and seemed slightly out of focus. Her face turned into a vicious smile, "So it's the white Pig! Where is your hyena, Pig? You know, when you die after watching all the rest of them die, I will take particular care that you don't go too quick."

"Yes Mara my dear," said Paul casually as he sat on a chair opposite her, "I hear that you are pretty good at things like that, especially with any young girls that come your way down in the cellars of Bureau Headquarters."

"Get on with it Pig!"

"I see my men didn't do a good enough job of softening you up.." Paul was cut off as she spat a large stream of bloody goo at him, it splattered in his face and he slowly wiped it off, first with his hand and then a handkerchief. He then reached behind him and pulled out the knife. He regarded it with a smile on his face for some seconds then spoke again.

"Mara, I want some information off you, give it to me and you will die quickly, but if not." He looked from the knife toward her his face set hard..

"Go to hell Pig!" she sneered.

"Very well," replied Paul, "you had your choice." He stood up and went to the door and shouted up the stairs. A few seconds later they heard the thud of boots as the soldiers returned.

"When I leave here," said Paul, "take this knife and slowly cut off an ear, then her nose and then an eyelid and then a finger in that order, if she tells you at any time that she will speak to me, you are to stop and call for me. I will be at the top of the stairs.. Any volunteers?" They all said yes quickly but the man in charge actually grabbed the knife off Paul. He turned and went to go up the stairs but Mara shouted,

"Stop! Ask me your questions!"

With disappointed faces the soldiers trudged back up the stairs.

"Now Mara, I hope that you are not wasting my time, if you are I will take a personal hand in the proceedings and there'll be no going back...Do you understand?"

Mara nodded then dropped her head.

"Do you supply Juba with drugs?" The reply was inaudible but she nodded her head up and down.

"How often?"

"Every three or so weeks." Came the soft reply.

"When is the next shipment due?"

"Soon."

"How soon?"

"Tomorrow."

"Are you sure?"

"Yes of course I'm damn sure, I organise it!" She flared.

"Mara, I am now going to ask you about that shipment down to the last detail." He paused then spoke again in a quieter tone but closer, so she could make out every word.

"Mara, there is a small village in the South called Kimbala. A very small village, five maybe six huts. In one of the huts lives a white haired old lady who looks after two boys one about twelve and the other..... About fourteen..."

"You leave them alone!" screamed Mara, "You just leave them alone! Do what you will with me but don't you touch them!"

"So when I ask you about those details, you are not going to lie to me are you Mara? Because you know that if you do, we are going to build a big bonfire in that village..."

"I will not lie to you," she sobbed.

They talked for half an hour, going over details three, sometimes four times until Paul was satisfied that he had enough to work with. He jotted nothing down but retained every detail in his mind. Finally there was nothing more to be said.

Paul placed an arm at the back of her head, he felt her tense then after a few seconds relax, he pushed her jaw with the heal of his other hand and stepped back.

Mara's head rolled to the side and hung down.

Paul checked that Mara's body that had been jammed back in the Mercedes behind the wheel properly and that her pistol had been returned to the holster, after sprinkling some of the shattered windscreen in her hair he switched the ignition on and rammed the stick into fourth gear, the arrangement he felt sure, would not look too suspicious at first and give him time.

Chimba had been most helpful with his inside knowledge of Juba and his immediate family including Mara. No doubt he would have made good use of that information himself when and if the opportunity had arose. Knowing about her two children by her own brother, had been the key to getting her true co-operation.

Paul eyed the three helpers and thanked them for their good work, "Be on time tomorrow, there's a full days work to be done but you will be well rewarded." They smiled and went there separate ways.

Paul regarded Tex as they sat on Paul's veranda sipping whisky and ice. Tex was recounting some trivial incidents that had happened during the week. Tex, Paul thought, was blissfully unaware of all the intrigue and skulduggery going on around him, apart of course from the snippets that Paul had fed to him.

Having Tex close to him these last two years was going to pay off. He genuinely liked Tex, who often spoke aloud Paul's very thoughts on certain matters. Tex needed Paul, without him he would be nothing especially in Karuda. He had accrued enough enemies over the last two years to guarantee an unpleasant end.

Paul had been amused to see the jealousy in him when Peter had arrived on the scene, the insecurity in his voice and the way he had subtly put Peter down at every opportunity.

Would he break when Juba's torturers got to work on him? He thought that it was likely he would. Tex's shell was hard but brittle and Paul suspected that the yoke was still soft. It never crossed Paul's mind to warn off his friend that one day soon he would be abducted, subjected to hell and then killed. If he did tell him, his reaction would warn Juba or his spies which might force Juba to act quicker than the three week space he had got.

Jokko had said to Paul that one of the things that would happen before Juba moved against him was Tex's disappearance. This would be a very valuable marker, if all his other plans against Juba failed then this would be the sign to get out and quick.

"Well Paul, what other plans you got for Peter?" Asked Tex, pulling Paul away from his train of thought.

"Er.. don't really know, by the way get through to Rhodesian Immigration, my adjutant is having a hard time getting him a flight out of the country, seems there's an admin foul up with visas or something and Rhodesia won't allow him back in to get a UK flight.."

"Bastards!" interrupted Tex, "The sooner we get our own airport the better!"

"Tex, the other thing I want you to do is report to me wherever I am, every day, once in the morning and once before say eight at night. Phone if you have to, I want you to do this for the next month or so until I am happy that things have settled down…. Okay?"

"Yeh! Sure Paul, is this.." Tex lowered his tone and looked around before continuing, "Is this about Juba and that feeling you've got?"

"No, not at all, that Juba thing was just a feeling and nothing else, it's passed now. No, this is something else not nearly as sinister." Laughed Paul, "I will let you know in good time, but in the mean time indulge me my friend and report to me twice a day as I asked."

Tex felt an alarm going off somewhere, for Paul to dismiss his earlier feelings about Juba was uncharacteristic. Paul, he knew, lived by his fears, feelings and gut instincts. According to him it had saved him many, many times. And now he was pushing them to one side. Now, thought Tex, I *have* a *feeling* about all this, maybe it's time *I* got out.

"Tex, tomorrow I will be gone all day from early, hold the fort, intercept every message that comes into the camp and hold them for my return. If you need a cover story say that I have gone into the bush for a walk-about."

Tex knew that would stand up as it was well known that Paul did this periodically, he ventured a question. "Where *are* you going Paul?" He immediately regretted asking it. Paul stood up and said brusquely, "Don't forget my friend, report twice a day, tomorrow may be an exception but after that…"

"Yes of course Paul, every day, twice a day."

The three Number 2 Commando soldiers that had helped Paul to abduct, torture and kill Mara Imbekwe were waiting for Paul at the appointed rendezvous in the bush, a crossroads with and old water tower as a marker looming above it.

It was still dark but there was a full moon which gave an eerie light over the landscape. The soldiers looked uncomfortable, night time was for them to sleep and for the demons to come out. They sat huddled in the front of their jeep, smoking and talking in subdued tones.

Paul's Landrover without lights closed on them and as he got out they too emerged shuffling and shivering slightly in the cool.

Without any greeting or preamble Paul barked, "Did you bring the rifles and plenty of ammunition?" One of the soldiers nodded and with the help of another bought three rifles out of the jeep for Paul's inspection. He shone a torch and grunted in approval at the bolt action, .303 calibre, Number 4 rifles, main personal weapon of the British Army for many years. Each Commando kept a dozen or so for sniper type activities when a steady bolt action rifle was needed.

"Did you zero them to yourselves?" The NCO among them spoke up and said that they had. Paul had asked Chimba for three of his best, most reliable soldiers, they had certainly come through so far.

"And the Gun?" Queried Paul. Again an item was produced for inspection, it was a slim wooden butted machine gun on a bipod. The Bren Gun was complete with a pack full of banana shaped magazines loaded with ammunition.

Finally Paul ascertained that they had water then spoke, "From here we leave the vehicles and go on foot, it is a long trek and will take a few of hours but it is necessary to approach silently. You are on operations as of this moment! Now put these on." He flung three shirts at them, they quickly stripped off their own and without question did as they were told.

When he saw that they were ready he put the pack of Bren mags on his back picked up the Gun and strode off into the darkness, he checked back once to ensure that he was being followed then set a firm purposeful step.

10

"Is that it?!" Asked an incredulous Harry Macmillan. Once again he and Peter sat in his old Morris Cowley car at the back of the disused petrol station. Harry still wore the crumpled linen suit and Panama hat, his eyes darted around nervously.

"No bloody photographs! Just one date, March the eighteenth at Camp Lagonda.. And that's a definite.. Yes? Vander *will* be there?!"

"Yes!" replied Peter irritably, "He said he would!"

"Well, I suppose that's better than nothing.. Just!" said Harry sarcastically, "But the order was for a photograph, you had a bloody camera! And I want that back incidentally young man! You'd better get that photograph and be damn quick about it." He prattled on getting more nervous and agitated by the second. "Daryl won't like it I'm telling you, he can be a tough turkey when he wants to be, I can tell you that! You let him down and…"

"Oh! For God's sake!" spat Peter.

"Ha! Ha!" laughed Harry aloud and excitedly, "You know what? I think a spell in Laka Prison would do you the world of good.."

"Oh! Yes? Would it?!" replied Peter with uncharacteristic venom in his voice. "Well, you'll know as well, because you'll be there with me! Just remember this, if I go down, you'll be right there with me, *old man!*"

"Damn you! You dirty little shit! Damn Daryl! Damn the damn lot of them!" Shouted Harry pounding the steering wheel with his bony fists. He stopped and rested his head on his arms that were now draped on the wheel. He breathed deeply a few times then sat upright and stared ahead, his nervousness seemed to have gone and his voice had almost gone back to normal. He spoke with authority and confidence as if he had reached a final decision about the way ahead.

"Be in your hotel room tonight, I will speak to Daryl on your behalf. Obviously you are not cut out for this sort of thing. I will get you out the country as soon as I can. I will see you tonight with the outcome of my talk with him, speak to no-one and wait in your room... Clear!?"

"Ye.. Yes, look thanks.. Thanks, thanks really." Peter sat back in the now moving car and almost cried with relief.

Paul looked out over the lake with his binoculars, it was deep blue almost black measuring about three hundred yards to the far shore, they were in an 'arm' of the main body of water which was unseen off to the left, thick vegetation lined the shores. On his side, the shore formed a little bay and jutting out was a wooden pier about fifty yards long.

At the shore end of the pier a Landrover was parked with three Bureau Policemen sitting in it, talking and laughing. Parked a little separately were two Mercedes trucks with 12.7 mm Machine guns known as Comma Sevens mounted on mono pods. All vehicles bore the silver eagle crest of the Bureau of Internal Security. Some of the police milled around these vehicles smoking and talking.

To no-one in particular Paul said quietly, "I make nine in all, two women and seven men, three with the Landrover and six with the trucks." He slowly lowered his binoculars and gently squeezed himself back into the small dip in the ground where his three soldiers lay sweating and exhausted.

It had taken three hours hard march to get to the lake. The going hadn't been too bad until they were within a couple of miles of the lake, then the terrain had changed from hard stony bush land and rocky canyons to thick secondary jungle that slowed them, yet made them exert their energies twice as much to get through. The road that led to the Pier was long and straight, any approach on foot or vehicle would have been spotted a long way off.

They had stayed parallel with the road and had steadily made their way to the lake and the dip in the ground which was about a hundred and fifty yards from the Pier.

Paul checked his watch, if Mara was right he thought, they had an hour before the plane arrived. Swallowing a mouthful of water from his bottle he looked at his three soldiers lying there covered in sweat with their eyes closed, they wore shirts with the camouflage and insignia of the Rebel Forces. He would give them another ten minutes rest and then deploy them.

Mara had said the shipments of drugs came in at regular intervals by light aircraft from The Congo.

Sometimes she accompanied the pick up, sometimes not. She would not be missed. The drugs would be taken back to Bureau headquarters then picked up by Juba, some would go to M'Punga, the rest sold on at enormous profit. Money in the form of US Dollars would change hands at the Pier.

He roused the three soldiers and they set about checking their weapons and adjusting ammo pouches. They weren't happy that they had single shot rifles when the 'enemy' had automatic weapons.

"Listen to me, and listen to me carefully." said Paul quietly but firmly. "When the shooting starts, you must know exactly what to do." Paul pointed to a long stick he had lain on the ground between them. "This represents the Pier." The soldiers looked at each other puzzled and Paul realised that it was a word that they would not have heard in their landlocked country.

"You know the wooden structure that points out into the water." They all nodded, "This," said Paul picking up a piece of stone, "is the Landrover." He placed it at the shore end of the Pier. "And these are the two trucks with the Comma Sevens," He placed two pieces of wood slightly separate. "If they at any time get the Comma Sevens trained on us we are finished.. Kaput! You understand me?!" They all nodded now fully awake.

"I, with the Bren Gun will keep them from using those machine guns on us. And you," he pointed to the NCO. "will stop the Landrover being driven off. You will use only carefully aimed shots, the Landrover must not be hit, it will be our escape vehicle and must be in working order. You two will pick off the remaining soldiers one at a time. Yes, I know they have automatic weapons but they are inaccurate and no good at this range, your weapons are perfect for that. Apart from the vehicles they have no cover, I will stop them getting to the jungle for that cover, you must remember three things. You only shoot when I give the order, you stop when I give the order, and the Landrover is not to be hit."

Paul then carefully placed them so that they had space between them yet he could maintain control, he then carefully cleared the vegetation to his front to give himself a clear field of fire.

Despite being on a high, the last couple of days started to creep up on Paul. His eyes gradually closed and his head sank until it rested on the wooden butt of the Gun. An insect crawled up the side of his nose and he lazily scooped it off. Some time later another buzzed around his ear but didn't land, it grew louder, suddenly Paul awoke with a start, it was the sound of an aircraft.

Peter Gant felt really good, this was the happiest he had felt since he had landed in this miserable country. Harry Macmillan's promise to get him out quick still resounded in his ears. He had been round the market stalls buying trinkets and some clothing in preparation for his return. In the hotel he went to the dining room and ordered a meal, the first proper thing he had eaten in days.

It was mid afternoon, Paul it seemed, had lost interest in him, that was fine by him. He returned to his room for a siesta, as he closed his eyes there was a knock at the door, he wanted to ignore it but habit took over and he limped to the door wrapped in a towel, he opened it and his heart sank, it was Tex.

"Hello! Hello! Not interrupting anything am I?" he said in a mock voice of concern as he strode into the room and looked around, he seemed disappointed that no-one else was there. "What did your boyfriend do.... Jump through the window?" he laughed. "Wow! That's some socket you got there!" He said gawping at the dead eye, "Makes ya feel fackin' sick don't it? No offence but I never seen one before."

Peter was now used to this goading routine from Tex, he disassociated himself from it and sat on the bed saying nothing just staring ahead. Finally Tex stopped and came to his point. "I've been talkin' to Rhodesian Immigration on the blower, seems that you fucked up somehow. They say that according to their records you ain't never been through Salisbury Airport, therefore you can't *return* there...Get it? If you weren't there in the first place, how can you return? Was it on your blind side when you went through or sammink?" Tex threw his head back and laughed. "Ha! Ha! I've heard of turning a blind eye before but this is ridiculous!"

When he saw that Peter didn't react he decided to turn nasty. "Listen you shit shover, if you don't get your act together, the Immigration this side are going to get funny, they're gonna start askin' questions and believe me, they won't fuck about, now show me your passport pretty boy!"

Peter rose from the bed and let the towel drop, Tex stared aghast then moved back a pace. "Is this what you want Tex?" Asked Peter a smile on his face, "I've heard of you macho queers before, all huff and puff, if you'll excuse that expression, but all they want is a bit of this." He turned and bent over slightly.

"You raving pervert! You dirty shit shoving bastard!" yelled Tex backing away to the door. "There's a law in this country about people like you! Ten years you'll get!"

Tex slammed the door and the room was quiet again. Peter sat back on the bed, laughed and reached for a bottle.

The light aircraft circled the arm of the lake a couple of times and jiggled its wings, a couple of the Police waved back. It lost height and straightened up on its approach, three of the Police broke away from the main bunch and walked slowly down the Pier, one of them carried a briefcase, he had no weapon noted Paul.

The floats on the plane skimmed across the lake and slowed almost to a halt, it turned and slowly made its way to the end of the Pier, once there the engine cut and a small hole appeared in the fuselage as a door was removed from inside, a rope was thrown and the craft was secured to a bollard.

Paul watched intently, he glanced to the trucks, no-one had manned the Comma Sevens, they were slack… Good! Three boxes were unloaded onto the Pier and a white man in shorts and singlet jumped from the plane, he checked the contents of the briefcase and turned back to the plane. This was it, decided Paul.

"Okay the four on the Pier first, open fire when I do!" shouted Paul as he took aim at the bunch by the trucks, he pulled the trigger and all hell let loose as the three other rifles fired together. Paul gave a two second burst at the group and cursed as he saw the strike was low, nevertheless one dropped but the others took cover behind the trucks. He looked across at the Pier, two bodies lay still and one was writhing and screaming.

"Where's the white man?" Yelled Paul, he got his answer when the prop of the plane turned and fired with a plume of smoke. "Hit the plane! Hit the Plane he screamed. There was a rapid Crack! Crack! Crack! over their heads as the ones by the trucks recovered and started to return fire. Paul glanced at his three soldiers, they lay in the bottom of the dip in the ground cowering.

Get up and return fire!" screamed Paul, a round smacked into the tree by his head showering him in stinging splinters of wood, he dropped down just in time to see one of the Bureau levelling a Comma Seven in their direction. He took careful aim and gave four short bursts of fire, the man behind the Comma Seven screamed as he was knocked clean off the back of the truck.

Paul then turned his attention back to the plane, it was trying to move forward but was still tethered to the Pier, as he swung the Bren around the white man appeared briefly by the door a knife flashed and the plane was free! Paul squeezed two bursts into the fuselage and the Gun stopped, he quickly changed mags as the plane started turning to get a straight run, he fired three bursts at the nose and the prop stopped, orange flames started to appear, licking out of the engine cowl.

Boom! Boom! One of the small trees around the dip disintegrated, Paul knew immediately what it was. He leapt away from the dip leaving the three soldiers cowering even lower, he chanced a look at the trucks and saw a figure on the Comma Seven, pumping burst after burst at the dip.

Paul stood and aimed the Bren from his shoulder, he put a long burst on the back of the truck, the Comma Seven stopped and the truck tilted as the tyres burst. He raced back to the dip, "Get up! Get up, come on! Or else we will die!" They got up and looked toward the vehicles. Two men crouched by the Landrover, "Get them with your rifles, don't hit the Vehicle!" ordered Paul. Two other men tried to break and make it to the cover of the jungle but Paul cut them down with a long burst.

It went silent apart from the odd pop and crackle from the slowly burning engine on the plane and some shouting from the vehicles. "Did you get them by the Landrover?" Demanded Paul.

The NCO spoke. "They are saying that they want to surrender Sir!"

"Okay tell them to come out in the open and drop their weapons." He ordered.

The NCO shouted in Karudan and almost immediately one of them stood up his hands raised another came by his side bent almost double holding his stomach.

"Okay finish them off!" ordered Paul, the NCO looked at him as if he didn't understand.

"I said finish them.. Now!" He screamed. There
was a volley of shots from the three of them and the two
men dropped noiselessly to the ground.

"I make that nine down, the one in the plane ten,
come on there's work to do yet!" barked Paul and led
them toward the three vehicles, a small explosion from
the aircraft made them flinch. They got within fifty
yards of the three vehicles when a figure that was lying on the back of one of the trucks jumped up and
grabbed the Comma Seven.

Paul aimed the Bren and pulled the trigger nothing happened, he flung it to one side as the first couple
of shells exploded just to their rear. Paul tore his pistol
out the holster, ran to his right then at an angle moved
toward the still firing Comma Seven. The firer, intent
on getting the other three didn't see him at first. Paul
then walked forward taking careful aim with his Browning, there were twelve rounds in the magazine and he
counted each one as he squeezed them off.

It took three rounds before he saw the strike, Four!
He saw it clang low off the protective shield. Five! It hit
high and left on the shield, the firers head was hardly
visible at this angle. Six! No strike, it was too high. Seven
eight nine, they all clanged off the shield at shoulder
height, suddenly the firer realised that he was being shot
at from his left and swung the Gun round to Paul and
exposing his head, this was it! Him or me! Ten eleven
twelve! The last two hit, the Gun stopped.

Paul knelt and changed mags, he then walked
warily up to the vehicles and checked out all the bodies,
two in the open, two by the trucks, two by the Landrov-

er, he walked down the Pier and saw the three bodies there, all dead. The boxes of drugs and the briefcase lay on the wooden boards, he checked the briefcase it was crammed full of money. There was a woomf! and the fuel tank on the plane caught sending columns of flame into the air, that accounted for the pilot.

Paul saw that his men had just emerged from the cover of the jungle and shouted for them to help. They loaded the boxes onto the Landrover. Despite his warnings the vehicle had been hit, but through the side and doors only. When all was loaded Paul thanked his three soldiers and told them he would pay them well.

Paul was all smiles and pulled a camera from his bag. He bade them to pose and hold their weapons aloft as if in victory, when they did so he drew his pistol and shot them dead.

11

Harry Macmillan parked a little way from the hotel. Carrying a small bag he walked round the back through the deserted area used for deliveries and rubbish removal. He stopped at a Fire Exit door at the top of some steps ankle deep in litter and dead leaves.

He looked around casually, then satisfied he wasn't being observed, inserted a thin steel spike through a tiny hole, when he felt it connect onto something solid he yanked down and pulled the door to him, carefully scraping debris away from the bottom of the door he pulled it open just enough to allow his slender frame to slide inside. He reset the metal Push Bar to re-lock the door then made his way silently up the stairs.

Harry took a careful look down the corridor in the direction of Peter's room, it was deserted. He saw the worn and holed maroon carpet beneath his feet and for a fleeting second he could hear the grand orchestras that used to play in the Ballroom, the popping of champagne corks, the laughter. He quickly pushed it away and made his way to Peter's door, he put the key in the lock and slid inside the room.

Peter was on the bed but awake, he look startled and blurted, "Jesus! Don't you ever knock?!"

"Sorry chum, old habits die hard." said Harry, a smile breaking out on his face. "Good news old man! I spoke to Daryl and it's okay. I convinced him that you were not up to it."

Peter leapt off the bed a look of astonishment and joy on his tired face.

"Thanks!" he blurted.

"Of course he was not pleased, not pleased at all but I took the brunt of his anger.."

"Sorry! I…"

"But that's of little consequence, the main thing is you are free to return through Rhodesia, my advice is that you go as soon as you can young man."

Peter nodded and went to say something but Harry took a bottle out of the bag he was carrying and offered it. Suddenly he looked worn and tired, his filmy blue eyes stared at the floor and he said quietly, "Look, I've been a bit hard on you these last few days.. I'm not used to it any more, I'm just too bloody old."

Peter took the bottle and clasped a hand on Harry's thin shoulders, "Come on sit down." He said gesturing him to a chair, "What say we crack the bottle and have a drink?" Harry nodded and gave a tight smile, he removed his grubby Panama hat and sat in a chair while Peter got another glass.

"Hope you like Brandy, er.. Peter isn't it?"

"Yes it is and yes I do like Brandy, though funnily enough if you had asked me two, or even one week ago you would have got a different answer." said Peter smiling, he was in a happy mood, just the thought of leaving the country elated him.

They clinked glasses and Harry proposed, "To your good health Sir!"

"And to yours *chum!*" Replied Peter using Harry's favourite form of address.

"Ah!" gasped Harry, "This is real fire water compared to the jungle juice I usually drink, where's the water.. In here?" Before Peter could react, Harry strode to the bathroom, with his back to Peter he deftly poured the drink down the sink and topped the empty glass up with water, holding the glass in a way so his fingers masked the contents he re-entered the room and sat down, he noticed that Peter had almost finished his.

"Who are you? I mean I don't even know your name." asked Peter as he sat on the edge of the bed.

"Who am I?" mused Harry, "Well my name is Harry and I know what I was, but right now I'm not sure.. Not sure who, or what I've become. Sorry for being so enigmatic chum, it's just that I have no-one any more. My wife...My wife, God bless her memory, has long gone. Do you know we used to come to this very hotel, my God the parties we used to have here! We, may have slept in this very room!" Harry sighed, then rebuked himself, "Oh! Shut up you boring old sod! Come on Peter, bottoms up! Let's have another!"

They drained their glasses and Peter re-filled them saying, "No Harry! Come on! What was it like in the old days?"

"The old days? Where, here in Karuda? Oh! They were absolute magic. We had a large house you know, in the same avenue as the Governor, some minor bloody official has it now, a right bloody shambles.." Harry looked at Peter, he saw that his eyes were blinking shut and he was gently swaying.

"Yes, the good old days, used to box for my Battalion you know, First String Welter most times. The only Officer that got in the ring.. And I saw them all off ye know, bloody strapping young Private Soldiers that would have given a month's pay to knock an Officer's block off and get away with it!"

Peter, his eyes shut, fell forward but was caught by a waiting Harry, he pushed him back on the bed and lifted his feet on. Peter stirred a little then gave away and softly snored.

Harry sat back down and continued talking. "And now what have I become? A weak, frightened old man who doesn't want to end his days in front of a firing squad...Or worse, rot in some stinking gaol, and you Peter my young friend would have put me there sooner or later.. It's so sad, so damn sad."

Harry rose and took a flat metal box from his inside pocket and lay it on the bed, using a length of thin rubber pipe he tied a tourniquet around Peter's leg. He pulled a syringe from the box, selected a vein in Peter's foot and emptied the contents into it. He sobbed.

Juba was worried, firstly his sister had disappeared and secondly the shipment of drugs had not arrived. He had ordered the Bureau to search the route his sister took to work but they had come up with nothing.

The shipment had been due at Bureau Headquarters at around four, it was now eight and there was no sign that it or the escort had arrived or indeed been seen anywhere. First he suspected that Mara had somehow double crossed him and taken the money and the drugs but he quickly dismissed this idea.

He then he feared that the chief of the escort had done the same, but he knew that the person in charge of the escort, a woman was very close to Mara and very loyal.

He paced his office in the palace deep in thought then punched a button on his desk, after a few moments an officer in full ceremonial dress entered and stood to attention, it was Juba's adjutant.

"Get hold of that Colonel at Bureau Headquarters and tell him to send a force of his men to Lake Palla at once to look for his missing men. This is to be a secret mission and he is to report only to me! I want him to go personally and be here at my desk for eight tomorrow morning to make that report!"

Juba then sat down and tried to busy himself but the two events were troubling him. M'Punga he knew, was running short of drugs, so too was Tasi, he had to maintain the supply. They both thought that the supply was never ending, they knew nothing of the fragile operation in force to keep that supply coming.

Juba knew that just lately he had become a little greedy keeping most of the drugs back to make money from the main pushers in the town. There was hardly enough to go around and everyone was clambering for them and paying stupid prices. Now M'Punga wanted more and more for himself and his women. He had tried to up the supply from the Belgian but in turn he had wanted to up the price to a ridiculous level, so he had kept importing the same amount but now it was not enough.

He saw some reports on his desk and glanced through them. They were the daily reports from his Battalion Commanders. His eye caught a report from Number 2 Commando on border duties, it said that rebel activities were on the increase and border incursions had taken place. It listed a number of areas where these had been, one of them he noted with alarm had been not far from Lake Palla.

A knock on his door snapped him out of his thoughts, "Enter!" He roared in bad temper, it was Desma his personal bodyguard.

"Master, I have bad news, your sister Mara has been found…She is dead Master."

"How did it happen?"

"In her car master, she had crashed."

Juba flopped his great frame back in his chair, his face wrinkled up, "Go!" he croaked and large tears started rolling down his big face.

"He's fackin' dead Paul!" blurted Tex in genuine bewilderment, striding into Paul's office. "Gant! They found him an hour ago on his bed!"

"In Juba's old house?"

"No he was still in that bleedin' hotel. I've been talkin' to the Chief of Police and it looks like he drank 'is self to death, there was bottles everywhere apparently!"

"Okay, calm down, are the police sure that no-one else was involved?"

"As far as I know, yeh."

"Get that half Asian detective, what's his name? Anyway get him! He's good, tell him from me, to go over that room and the body with a fine tooth comb and to report direct to me, he is to work independent of the police."

"That's a lot of trouble to go to for a useless pansy who drank 'iself to...."

"Just fucking do it!" Roared Paul at the top of his voice. This was the first time that Paul had talked to him in that manner and it was like a huge slap in the face to Tex. He stood there flabbergasted, his mouth open, then turned and quickly left.

Paul flung his pen at the wall and dropped his head on his chest "Jesus!" He sighed.

Harry Macmillan stood in his overgrown garden and looked at the bungalow he had lived in for the last ten years. It needed lots of repair and badly wanted a good lick of paint. The only rooms habitable now were his bedroom and living room, the rest were crammed full of old furniture and rubbish slowly rotting with dampness and neglect.

He had no friends as such to ask back, those he did spend a little time with now and again at the Ex Pat's club were to him, broken down old has beens who were drinking themselves to death while wallowing in the past. He was now virtually a recluse.

He forced his way through the vegetation until he saw on the ground, mostly buried by leaf debris, a wooden trap door. After clearing the top he pulled the door back and stared down into the blackness of the well.

Harry made his way back to the house, ripped the telephone out of the wall and threw it on the garden path. In the kitchen, he swung the ancient cast iron cooker to one side and with a great deal of wheezing and straining, lifted a radio from the cavity beneath it.

He stopped to get his breath back then lifted the set onto a work surface. He connected it up to the car battery he had placed in the sink and flicked the power switch down, a red light came on and the set emitted a humming noise. After connecting it to the aerial that was concealed in the roof. He pulled out a Morse key, checked his watch then started tapping out a message to Daryl.

He reported that Peter Gant had been found dead in his bed from acute alcohol poisoning and that he was signing off, after a few seconds he added "For good".

Staggering with the awkwardness of the radio he made it to the well and without hesitation dropped it down followed by the telephone. He carefully scooped the debris back over the lid and walked unsteadily back to the bungalow. "I'm too old for this." he groaned.

12

Tex looked at Tula preparing his dinner. She's beautiful, he thought. They had been together for three months now, a record for him. "Tulip." he called softly using his pet name for her, "How is your tummy?"

She turned, smiled and patted her slim waistline, "Little Tex is fine," she said and continued with her preparation.

Tex had lived with a string of women since he had been in the country, all had been prostitutes. They had come and gone. At first, flattered and honoured that a comparatively wealthy white man in such a high position was interested in them, then the realities of living with an immature, insecure, violent pervert drove home and off they went, usually taking everything they could carry.

They were easily replaced, he now owned half of Randy's night club and had interests in others so had the pick of the bunch. Then his "Tulip" had come along, she was different from the others. Apart from being beautiful and speaking good English she understood him, understood his need for constant reassurance and love. She could soothe him when he came home ranting and raving. He had once grabbed her and drew back to slap her and she had urged him to do it because she said, she deserved it. This had completely thrown Tex.

All of his life he had been on the receiving end
of violence, from his early days in Kilburn where he
and his sister were routinely beaten and kicked by their
mother's boyfriend as she wandered around indifferent
in a drunken or drug induced stupor. Then there were
the children's homes and the bullying and violence by
the staff and older boys.

By the time he had graduated to Borstal he had
become a survival machine. He trusted no-one and
thought that anyone showing emotion was weak and
there to be taken advantage of. Girls were sex objects
to be used and discarded at will, he never formed any
relationships of depth with anyone.

Then he had come to Karuda and met Paul. Paul
had given him the order and discipline he subconsciously craved, also he had offered him an unconditional
friendship and heaped reward on him.

Tula, no-one had ever effected him like she had
and when she had said she was pregnant, he had feelings he couldn't describe or understand.

And now? He thought, was all that finished? He
had been shouted and balled at many times in his life,
often followed up with violence. Although not quite getting fully used to it, it had meant nothing to him. But
that small outburst from Paul had shaken him to his
roots.

He had known deep down that something had not
quite been right with Paul for the past few weeks. He
recalled Paul's words about being arrested suddenly and
executed, his loathing for Juba and general unrest.

He looked across again at his Tulip gently arranging vegetables in a dish and humming to herself. Having never received or given love he could not even begin to understand the emotion that was welling up inside him, he turned away, tears springing from his eyes.

At precisely eight o' clock Juba's Adjutant ushered Colonel Janka head of the Bureau into the office. He was still dressed in Combat fatigues and his boots dusty.

Juba looked at him expectantly Janka started to apologise for his dress trying to explain that he had come straight from the Bush but Juba waved him on.

"Your report man!" he shouted.

"We reached the Lake and found that the convoy had been attacked by rebels, all were dead and the bodies of three rebel soldiers were also found...."

"Did you find the special shipment they were picking up?" interrupted Juba.

"There was nothing Sir. They left two trucks but stole the Landrover, there was a burnt out plane partly submerged a little way out in the lake.."

"Get some men to search it as a matter of urgency!"

"We did sir, we managed to pull it to the shore, apart from the body of a white man it was empty."

"Damn it to bloody hell!" raged Juba smashing his huge fists on the desk. "Get out! Get back to your bloody paperwork you bloody paper soldier!"

Just as the terrified Janka was about to shrink out of the door Juba stopped him and snarled menacingly. "You will personally ensure that my sister is buried with full military honours, it will be the finest funeral that this Continent has ever seen and Laka is to mourn her for one month, now get out!"

To his adjutant Juba barked, "I need to speak to the Commander on the Border…"

"Chimba Sir."

"Yes Chimba, get a radio link to this office now!"

Tula was aghast, "But life is good here Tex! We have a nice house and money, I cook you good food…"

"It's not that Tulip darling! If we don't get out now while the going is good it may all.. It *will* all finish!"

"What do you mean finish Tex?" Tula started sobbing, tears rolled down her cheeks and her beautiful almond eyes became bloodshot, "Why do we have to run like frightened chickens?"

"Oh! Come here love, don't cry, please don't cry." snivelled Tex holding her close and shutting his eyes against the tears.

"But why Tex? Tell me!"

"Trust me darlin', this…This whole thing is going to fall apart soon I feel it.."

"It's the white devil isn't it? Your big friend Paul, he has told you to go and you are running like a startled deer!"

"No it's not that! It's nothing to do…" Tex let go of Tula and stared at the floor.

"I thought as much," said Tula quietly, "the white devil means more to you than me or our baby." Tex tried to hold her and say something but she turned away and convulsed.

"Oh! Lord help us!" Sighed Tex and flopped in a chair.

Paul was ushered into President M'Punga's office, Juba was already there, he looked rumpled and tired. The shock of his sister's death still gripping him.

"Ah! Brigadier Paul," greeted M'Punga, "come sit! It seems we have a problem." He turned to Juba. "Field Marshal?"

"There has been several Border incursions by the rebels," said Juba looking directly at Paul, "It seems that they were not quite beaten after all Brigadier, however, let us proceed.."

Paul ignored the jibe aimed at him and the rest of Juba's monotone, he knew that he would be summoned sooner or later. The reports from Chimba were fictitious and part of a carefully laid plan to get Juba out of Laka and into the Bush. He also knew that Chimba had reported to Juba that he had found some sealed boxes on the stolen Landrover.

Juba was not primarily interested in the rebels that would be why Paul was summoned, he would be interested only in getting his hands on the drugs in the boxes.

When Juba finished Paul stood up and said to M'Punga, "Sir I need your permission to accompany the Field Marshal when he visits Number 2 Commando, and with your permission Excellency I will provide a squad of your own personal bodyguard to protect him!"

Juba was taken aback; he had no intentions of leaving the palace. He rose about to say something but M'Punga cut him off. "Yes, yes of course, your personal intervention Field Marshal will do good and you can give me an accurate assessment, but don't spend too long there Montgomery my friend, I need you back here!"

Juba forced a smile, "I will go tomorrow and return before nightfall, Excellency."

Outside the office he turned to Paul, "Why did you say I was going to visit Number 2 Commando?"

Paul feigned shock then acute embarrassment "I.. I thought that.. My God, I am sorry Sir! I would never have presumed to.. I feel a total fool.. Look Sir, *I* will go alone and give my report direct to you for the President..."

"Don't be a bigger bloody fool Brigadier. I was going there anyway, it's just that I don't like any one presuming my intentions." Juba was pleased that he had got Paul on a back foot, to see this perfect, white pig squirm was reward enough for the inconvenience of travelling to the border. Also he would personally supervise the recovery of the drugs.

"Make sure that your column meets me at the Palace gates tomorrow morning at seven sharp. I will have an attachment of The Bureau to do a proper job of looking after me." With a final scornful look he walked away. Paul watched the receding figure followed closely by a tail of aides and flunkies, his smile turned to a sneer.

Detective Inspector Kompe was waiting for Paul when he arrived back at the office. His straight hair and thin nose showed Asian ancestry, he pulled out a notebook and started to talk.

"I got there just before they removed the body, the room had not been cleared. His personal effects were mostly packed as if he was leaving shortly. There were several empty bottles of locally produced Brandy. Apparently the Bell Boy had been delivering a couple every day, However, there was one bottle that was imported French Brandy that I believe cannot be obtained in this country unless imported exclusively or he bought it in himself. The body was cold and had signs of rigour mortis, I would say he died last night or evening. The body was fully clothed minus shoes, he had vomited..."

"Your conclusion?"

"He either died of alcohol poisoning or choked on his vomit, there were no signs of suffocation or strangulation. Oh! He had only one visitor that afternoon, Major Potter, he may throw more light on it...And I found this on the floor Brigadier, it puzzles me." He pulled out small piece of coloured plastic and placed it on Paul's desk. It was Peter's false eye.

As Kompe left, Tex walked into Paul's office, he looked scruffy and drained as if suffering from a bad dose of flu. He had come to confront Paul and find out what was going on. Seeing his Tulip upset and crying had given him the resolution to come to grips with his situation, whatever that may be. Now that he was in Paul's presence he felt his resolve falling away.

Before he could speak Paul shot a question, "When did you last see Peter Gant?"

"Gant? Oh Lord! Must've been a couple of days ago..."

"You saw him yesterday afternoon, just before he died." said Paul evenly.

"What?! Oh yeh, forgot, had to see him about that Rhodie immigration problem.."

"What was he like?"

"Who Gant? He was okay…"

"Just okay?"

"Well yeh, you know.."

"Did you check his passport then?"

"N.. no! He wouldn't hand it over." Tex looked shifty and stared at the floor. A few seconds of silence followed with Paul staring intently at Tex, finally he spoke.

"Tex, something is troubling you about all this. I doubt if you can shock me so let's have it."

Tex grimaced, he could feel tears coming and didn't trust his voice to speak, he made a fending off gesture with his hands, recovered and spoke falteringly. "Paul, you know you get feelings about things? You know, you've often told me," Paul nodded slightly, "Well, fing is, I got 'em now, feelings that things are not right.. I.. I don't know what it is Paul."

Paul smiled, he stood up, went to a cabinet and pulled out a bottle of Black label. He put his hand on two glasses but changed his mind, taking a swig directly from the bottle he walked to Tex and offered it. When he too had taken a swig Paul spoke. "Tex, we've been through some times eh? Remember driving to the Palace in that ambulance? You, Seb, Reeves and Pern, not knowing what we were up against? Me and you were the only ones to come out of that, do you know why Tex?"

"Yeh! Because we didn't lose our bottle!" shot back Tex who had perked up some.

"Yes exactly, we held our nerve! And look where we are today. All I am saying Tex, is hold your nerve a little longer, take a few days off."

"Do you still want me to report in?"

"Yes."

"Paul, I'm sorry, I've had a bad day, I think I'm going down with sammink, I *will* have them days off."

They exchanged a few more words then Tex shuffled away.

Tula was waiting for him when he arrived home. The talk with Paul had made him feel better but he was still a little angry at himself for not being more forceful and demanding with Paul. He was glad to see her and she gave him one of those beautiful radiant smiles.

"Come Tex, sit down I have done your favourite meal!" With a flourish she lifted the lid of an oven dish.

"Blimey! Bangers and Mash! What a little darling you are!"

Tex relaxed with Tula on the large settee, the meal had been great and they now sipped large whiskies.

"Texy my love, tell me what is troubling you." said Tula stroking his hair gently.

"Nothing my Tulip, nothing, as long as I have you, nothing."

"You have been to see Paul yes?"

"Yeh!"

"And he made you feel better?"

"What makes you say that my love?"

"Well you don't talk of running away any more, so he must have made you feel better.. Yes?"

"Yeh, I suppose, look, change the subject eh love?" He slipped his hand in her blouse and fondled her breasts, "Come on love relax." he then slid his hand up her skirt, but she rolled off and he groaned.

"Tex honey, how can I relax, tell me what Paul said to you, it's important that I know what makes you feel better." Tex sighed and sat up.

"Paul's…Paul's Paul. I don't know what goes on in his skull any more than you do, you only know what he's thinkin', when he's doing it."

"Does he hate the Field Marshal Juba?" Tula asked casually at she lit two cigarettes and passed one across.

"Juba?" Why the hell did you…Tula, did someone tell you to ask that?"

"No!" Why should they!? It was a simple enough question…Come on Texy, let's go to bed." Tex stood up and held off her advance, he had known her only a short time, he thought, but long enough to know when she was being false.

"Whose been talking to you Tula.. I need to know."

"Tex! Come on Baby, you're too worried these days…" She took of her top and shook her breasts at him.

"Tula, I need to know and now!" shouted Tex.

Tula turned, slipped her top back on and walked out of the house, leaving Tex staring after her. He flung his whisky glass at the wall and followed her, as he stepped on the veranda he saw three policemen from the Bureau five yards away on the drive pointing their sub machine guns at him. To his side carrying a sawn off shotgun was Desma, Juba's personal Bodyguard, a huge grin on his face.

Juba waited in the garage for his "guest". He had decided to move against Paul as soon as he had the drugs under his control once more. Originally he wanted to wait until the president's Birthday celebrations were out of the way but he feared that the increased rebel activity would once again raise Paul's profile and make him more of a favourite with M'Punga and more difficult for him to strike.

Once the visit to the Border Battalion was over he would invite Paul back to the Palace so he could make a personal report to the President. He would travel with him and just the Bureau escort then make a detour to the garage. The thought of having Paul strung up in front of him was very satisfying indeed to Juba.

First things first, he would have the Hyena picked up, he was slightly disappointed that he had not got better information from Tula. He had set it all up of course. Tula had been Juba's mistress for a month she was a good find, intelligent, beautiful and a good actress to boot.

From her, Juba knew that Major Tex Potter hated him but he never spoke in detail of his meetings with the white Brigadier except to say that he too loathed Juba. Juba had got impatient and urged her to intensify her efforts.

When he decided to move against Paul earlier than planned he ordered her to do all she could on that last evening to extract information from Potter the Hyena before they arrested him. When Tula walked out of the house it was a sign that she had done her best and for the waiting squad to arrest him.

Prince Tasi turned up at Juba's garage, he was not expected by Juba but he had heard on the grapevine that he was going to interrogate that evening and didn't want to miss anything.

Paul walked out of his Communications centre next to his Headquarters, in disguised tones he had let Chimba know on the radio that all was going to plan and to be ready. He thought about Peter lying on a slab somewhere in Laka, he would get Tex to phone the British Consulate in the morning and arrange things.

Peter's body lay in a drawer in the state morgue on the outskirts of Laka. The Pathologist had not even given the body a cursory glance, he was far more worried about his other "patient": Captain Mara Imbekwe of the feared Bureau and Juba's sister.

His examination had revealed rope burns on her wrists and ankles, needle puncture marks and bruising all over her body but more important than that, she had been violently raped and tortured, finally, her spine snapped at the neck.

He was worried because he had delayed the examination. Juba had wanted to know immediately how she had died, he had panicked and reported on the phone that it was through multiple impact injuries caused by the car striking a solid object. He had not examined the body because he had been drunk at home most of the day.

Shaking, he picked up his phone and asked to speak to The Field Marshal, after a delay he was told that he was not available. He replaced the phone and covered the body with a sheet. He took his set of notes to the urinal and started to burn them.

Juba was not happy that Tasi had turned up, he would have to explain in detail why he was about to torture the Hyena, Potter. If Tasi even suspected, even if it was false, that there was a plot against his father he would have alerted M'Punga immediately and Juba would lose control of the situation.

Juba met Desma when the squad came back with Tex. Reluctantly he told him that there was a change of plan and to keep Tex in the cellar till later, he then instructed Desma to find a replacement from the Prison.

An hour later Juba handed a baseball bat to the breathless Prince Tasi and invited him to go to work on the helpless prisoner.

13

Paul rode in the back of an Armoured Personnel Carrier, he was a little concerned, Tex had not contacted him that morning and when he had telephoned his house there was no reply. He had no time to follow up because he had to meet up with Juba at the Palace and drive to the border.

Perhaps, he mused, Juba would arrest him at the Palace when he arrived, he doubted it, it was too near M'Punga, nevertheless he carried an Uzi sub machine gun and plenty of mags. He ordered his large escort to load their weapons and be ready for anything, if he was going to die, he would not go like a lamb.

Juba's escort of two landrovers packed with Bureau Police and a Mercedes truck complete with Comma Seven was waiting for him outside the Palace gates. The gates opened and Juba's gleaming black Limousine complete with bright pennants rolled smoothly out. Desma emerged and told Paul that the Field Marshal would travel in the middle of the convoy. Paul nodded and ordered his APC forward, in a pre-planned move his other two APCs broke off and tagged on to the end of the convoy behind the Bureau.

Tex was shocked and bewildered. After he had been arrested he thought that he was going for a one way ride, he had fully expected to be driven in the Bush and pumped full of lead. That was bad enough but when they bundled him gagged and blindfolded into a building he became petrified, it only meant one thing in this country, a long slow death.

He had been left alone now for hours. He wrestled against his bonds but they were tight and strong, the steel chair he was bound to was set firmly in the floor. If only he could get the hood off. He cursed himself over and over, he should have gone….. Got out of the country when he knew things were going wrong.

He'd had enough nous to secure himself a route out of the country and the means to travel it. Why? He screamed at himself, why didn't I have the balls to carry it out when every fibre in my being, told me to do so. He thought of Tula and groaned with pain, they must have forced her, threatened to kill her if she didn't co-operate, the baby! Oh! Jesus! God! get me out of this!

He guessed that it was about eight in the morning. A sound of footsteps broke his train of thought, he heard a key turning in a lock and a door grating open. He braced himself. There were at least two people, they were whispering and one suppressed a giggle.

Someone got hold of the hood and removed it, the room was gloomy, a pencil thin shaft of sunlight temporarily blinded him and he blinked furiously.

"Do you want a drink Texy baby?" spoke a familiar voice.

"Tula?! Tula!" Tex could now make her out, she stood in front of him legs apart and hands folded across her breasts. She was in the black uniform of the Bureau

Police and wore Sergeant's chevrons on her arm. "Tula?" he repeated weakly.

"Tula, Tula, Tula." she mimicked and the tall slim man at her side chuckled as he fondled her breasts and crotch. "That is not my name you dog!"

"Tula, don't talk like that please.." wailed Tex

"Oh?! And how should I talk Texy baby.. Is that better?" She walked forward and backhanded him hard across the face followed by another. Tex sobbed.

"My God! You are even more pathetic than I thought!" laughed Tula in mock astonishment, "The great Tex Potter, the worlds greatest lover.. Huh! How I used to squirm when you touched me!" she screamed, "Putting your rotten filth in me, night after night! My God, how I fucking hate you!" She pulled her pistol out and whipped him about the head several times before the other man spoke urgently to her and she stopped and stepped back panting.

Tex, only half conscious, his face running with blood raised his head and muttered. "Baby."

"Baby!" shrieked Tula, "If I had anything belonging to you in me I would take a knife, cut it out and throw it on the fire!"

She went to move in on him again but the other one stopped her and said urgently, "You just said you just wanted to talk to him! The Field Marshal will be angry!"

"Very well, get me out of here, and don't worry *Texy baby,* I will be there when you are screaming for death!" she spat at him and they left.

Despite everything, Tex's survival machine clicked into motion. Well, he thought, at least the hood is off, that's a start.

Paul looked through the back slit of the APC, he could see Juba's Limousine bouncing up and down as the roads lost their tarmac and gave way to pitted red soil.

"Road block ahead!" shouted the Driver. Paul felt a surge of electric tingle through his entire body. The APC lurched to a halt and Paul clambered out of the back and walked to the Officer on the road block, "Have you received orders from Colonel Chimba?"

"Yes Sir!" Came the crisp reply.

Paul walked down the convoy to the limousine, Juba lowered the window to hear what Paul had to say.

"Sir, there maybe some rebel activity to our front, there is only a little danger but I would be a lot happier if you travelled in the armoured car with me until we're through."

Juba didn't hesitate, with a worried look on his face he eased his bulk from the back seat and hurriedly walked to the APC, Desma his hulking bodyguard loped after him carrying Juba's bags.

Once they had sat down in the back and the heavy iron door had clanged shut Paul tapped the driver and the APC juddered forward then took off at speed. Paul looked through the back slit and saw that the following vehicles had been delayed as planned. The terrain became thick with vegetation and presently they came to a fork in the track, a soldier waived them to the left and when the rest of the convoy caught up a half minute later, he waved them to the right.

Paul kept up a non stop dialogue with Juba in an attempt to disrupt his thought process. He knew that Juba also survived on thoughts and gut instincts. The threat of danger had given him something to think about but in the relative safety of the APC Paul was afraid he might start getting suspicious.

Juba answered now and again with a grunt or a nod but Paul could see he was nervous. Desma just sat there, he was in civilian clothes and carried a sawn off shotgun on his lap plus other back up pistols on his person, he in contrast seemed relaxed and just rocked back and forth with the motion of the vehicle.

Suddenly the APC turned in a half circle and pulled up. "We're here!" declared Paul and opened the door, he leapt to the ground and as Desma bent double to get out Paul shot him twice in the head with his pistol.

"Come on! Get off!" said Paul irritably to the open mouthed Juba who puffed and struggled his bulk onto the ground in the clearing. Paul stripped him of his pistol and told him to kneel. Juba blubbered and dropped to his knees with difficulty.

The driver of the APC came around to see what all the shooting was, he had been briefed that he was taking them to a rendezvous. Paul levelled his pistol and shot him.

Juba wailed. "Mister Paul, whatever have I done to you to deserve this?! We have worked together so well, if the rebels are paying you I will double it and yes.. I will retire and you can have my job, I will go out of the country.. Immediately.."

Paul glared at Juba, "Did you kill Tex?"

"No! no, he is alive, they wanted him killed Mister Paul but I saved him!"

"Where is he?"

"He is in the cellar at my house. Let us go there Mister Paul and discuss matters in a civilised way. I have many riches..." His monologue was broken by a soldier in jungle fatigues coming into the clearing, he was prematurely balding and wore thick rimmed spectacles, it was Colonel Chimba, he looked from Juba to the dead driver.

"Was that necessary Brigadier? Is that what happened to my three soldiers at the lake?"

"It was necessary in order for this mission to be completely successful. Colonel, if anyone even suspected that Juba was killed by us it could still be extremely difficult...You had better get on with it, we still have a lot to do."

"I have changed my mind, I want this pig brought to trial for all that he has done wrong, not only to me but the Karudan people."

"Okay Colonel!" Paul spat at Chimba. "Take him back, tell his blood brother and good friend the President, that he is a criminal and should be bought to justice, or shall we take this a step further and arrest the President too and bring him to trial plus the heads of the Bureau and army who have tortured, maimed and killed to stay on top.."

"It's not right.. I can't do it..."

"What exactly did Juba do to your family Colonel? Come on, let it out. What was so bad that made you plan all these years to kill him?"

Chimba swung around to face Juba, he closed on him and in his fury yanked his bulk into a standing position. His eyes were wet and hate filled, he ranted in Karudan to Juba who shook with fear. Then Chimba turned to Paul and said in a detached voice, "He was a captain in charge of a squad whose job it was to seek out rebel sympathisers in remote villages and take appropriate action. I was a boy of six and watched as Captain Juba shot and killed my mother and father and my two younger sisters.. but only after he had.." Chimba broke down.

Paul became impatient, he rounded on Juba, "Name the people who are your spies in my camp, do this and you will go quick, lie to me and your family will burn, name them!" Without hesitation Juba began to reel off names.

Chimba recovered and when Juba had stopped talking he said to Paul, "I'm ready." Paul ordered Juba into the back of the APC and Chimba emptied the chamber of his small Pistol into him.

As they soaked the APC and bodies in petrol there was a sudden loud and prolonged burst of firing and explosions in the distance, "Goodbye Bureau escort." Paul murmured to himself.

Finally, Paul straightened up and threw the petrol can to one side. He had done many unpleasant things in his life, sometimes he had enjoyed it, mostly he had been totally indifferent and sometimes like at this moment he felt uneasy about it.

"Colonel Chimba, you are a good man and I will personally ensure that your family is well taken care of." Chimba turned from his task, his brow furrowed with confusion, he managed to sneer, "You are no better than him." Paul shot him dead.

As the APC and the bodies burned he removed his shirt and started burning parts of it with a brand, he rubbed thick oily black ash on his face and arms, he shouted aloud in pain as he held the flaming brand against his arm.

Using the tip of his knife, he gingerly gave himself superficial wounds to the face and arms and finally fired off a half dozen mags through his sub machine gun.

He waited for twenty minutes until he heard the sound of vehicle engines straining at full pelt along the jungle track, he tied some rope around his legs, then crawling as near as he dared to the flames still dancing from the burning APC, he lay down and waited.

Two Landrovers full of the Royal Personal Bodyguard pulled up at the entrance to the hospital and took up positions on the broad flight of stairs leading to it. Some entered the Hospital and checked out the route to the Wards.

Two minutes later the armoured Limousine of the President rolled up. M'Punga and the Prince Tasi were met and escorted into the building. Confusion rained about the shootings on the border and the President was taking no chances.

Paul heard all the noise and fuss approaching down the corridor and braced himself, he knew who it was and realised that this was going to be a vital meeting, it could swing either way. He tightened the fingers of his un-bandaged arm around the handle of his knife and waited.

M'Punga entered through the door of the Private room and saw a figure lying on the bed, bandages masked most of the face and left arm that was also supported. The figure was moaning softly rolling its head from side to side, oblivious of his presence.

M'Punga stared for a few seconds then nodded to an Aide who roughly tried to rouse Paul. Paul turned his head and with his uncovered eye saw the President, he struggled to sit upright but flopped back on the Pillows. The President came nearer and Paul could see that he had been crying heavily for his great friend Juba.

"How did he die?" he asked simply.

"I failed you sir!" gasped Paul, "Chimba led us into an ambush, somehow he split our convoy and then shot the Field Marshal..."

"Why?!" croaked M'Punga his voice breaking with emotion, "Why did he kill my friend?"

"While he held us captive Excellency, Chimba was shouting at the Field Marshal in his native tongue about a massacre many years ago in his village called Chibuki, and accused the Field Marshal of murdering his family..."

There was a wailing and screaming behind M'Punga and the Prince Tasi broke through and shouted, "Where is Chimba now, white pig?!"

"He is dead, as soon as he started to shoot at the Field Marshal I managed to get a gun and shoot him, but my legs were still tied and I fell back into the flames of the burning vehicle." Paul laid back breathing heavy as if exhausted, he closed his eyes and waited for the next question or tirade but nothing came. He heard some shuffling and then the door banged shut. When he opened his eyes again the room was empty.

Everything now, was a gamble thought Paul. He knew that M'Punga or Tasi in all probability would not go down to the border to investigate personally, they were too afraid of the "Rebel activity" down there which had taken lives. If the appointed investigator spoke to the troops involved in the massacre of the Bureau Police in the escort, he would find out that all orders had come from Chimba and nothing from Paul.

From the information that Paul had released about Chimba they would find out indeed that he survived the massacre of his family by Juba. It was all hanging by threads. All he had to rely on was M'Punga's insecurity about the rebel situation that he had got Chimba to build up in his reports, plus his faith in Paul as a military strategist and leader and any rapport that he had built up over the last year.

Paul had planned to stay in hospital for at least two days for effect but his usual iron self discipline snapped and he roused himself from the bed, things had not gone as he quite expected. If they were going to come for him, he would at least be on his feet and fighting. Careful to retain the bandages, he shuffled down the corridor and phoned his adjutant to bring his car around.

The adjutant was embarrassed, he relayed to Paul in subdued tones that he had just received instructions from the Palace not to obey any order given by him and furthermore, if he appeared in the camp he was to be arrested without hesitation.

Paul got back to his room, arrest must be imminent he thought, I must get out. He was about to put on his uniform when there was a commotion in the corridor and heavy boots came pounding toward his room. His pistol had been taken away when he was admitted to the hospital "unconscious" but they hadn't got his knife, he reached for it and held it beneath the sheets as he lay back on the bed.

The door burst open and four Bureau Policemen entered, the leader looked relieved to see Paul was still there. He spoke in official tones to Paul. "Brigadier Vander, it is my duty to tell you that you will remain in this room and you will not be allowed to leave it unless under escort." They all carried Uzi sub machine guns and looked young and tough. Paul lay back and closed his eyes.

Colonel Janka, head of the Bureau of Internal Security was a very happy man. In just days, two of the most feared and detested people in his life had been wiped out. Firstly he mused, that bitch Captain Mara Imbekwe had killed herself in a car wreck and then Juba got himself shot to bits by a crazy Colonel on the border.. What luck!

The vacuum gave him prominence, he had been summoned by the President himself who sought his advice. It was obvious that at this moment in time he didn't trust the Army.

Suspend all the Army Commanders, he had advised until things were more clear, and the President had agreed! Block all main routes to the Capital with the Bureau, call in the reserve Bureau and so on and so forth, and he had agreed to all of it!

He felt like celebrating but he had to remain calm and unruffled, these were still uncertain times. There was a knock on his door and the Woman Sergeant, Eva Saputo came in, she was very attractive and Janka knew that she had been a favourite of Juba for many months, hence her rapid rise in the Bureau. At the same time, so the rumour went, she was also mistress to Mara. She had been on special assignment for some time now, it seemed weeks since he had last seen her.

"Colonel," she began, "For over two months I have been on special duties for the Field Marshal." She stopped and stared down as if in sorrow, "Just before he was cut down by the cowards on the border, he ordered the arrest and death of the white Major Potter. I was assigned to spy on the Hyena for three months. He is now held by us but I have been prevented from carrying out the execution by the Lieutenant in charge of him. I want your permission to carry out the Field Marshal's order."

Janka's mind raced, he had heard nothing about this operation. It was probably another plot by Mara and her brother that he would have had to pick the pieces up for at a later date. "Why was he arrested?"

"He was plotting something, the white pig Vander was implicated. I think they plotted to kill the Field Marshal and eventually overthrow our beloved President."

"Have you proof of this?" asked a shocked Janka.

"They have been plotting for months! Juba knew this!" shouted Tula her eyes bulging with frustration.

"Don't presume to speak to me like that *Sergeant* Saputo!" Yelled Janka. "I am your Commanding officer and advisor to the President. I will not be shouted at!…. Now, where is your proof?"

Tula crumpled. Mara and Juba had always laughed and said that Janka was a weak idiot, but now the fact was driven home to her, that both Juba and Mara were just memories and reality sat in front of her, far from weak. "There is no proof Sir. I am so confused, all I was trying to do was carry out orders." She started to sob but Janka was having none of it.

"You! *Sergeant* Saputo, will bring the white Major to me here! Unharmed and in one piece! Do you understand that, *Sergeant?!*" he screamed with pent up fury. As an afterthought he rushed from behind the desk and with some difficulty, tore the chevrons off her sleeve. He grabbed her by the face and pushed her out of the door.

Tex knew that his gaoler was worried and nervous about something but could not find out the reason. His bonds had been eased and he had been given a drink, a little food and was allowed to relieve himself. He had heard Tula in the corridor outside arguing vehemently with the guard but she hadn't come in the room again.

The thought of Tula pained him less and less, she was just like all the others, he thought, and tried to bury any feelings he had for her. He was totally confused about his situation. I must have been here for twenty four hours now, he thought, and no-one has laid a hand on me apart from that bitch. Where was Paul? Why hadn't he done something? He started to fear the worst for him but pushed it away. His head ached like hell and the congealed blood on his head and face made him itch badly.

More talking in the corridor, it was that bitch again, this time the door was unlocked and she entered. This is it Tex, he muttered to himself, one way or the other, this is it.

He was untied and told to stand, he did so but collapsed, he had no feelings in his legs or arms. The gaoler helped him to his feet and snapped some cuffs on him.

"What's happening?" He asked

"Come with me!" said the gaoler, it was the first words that he had spoken to him.

"I said, what the fuck's 'appening!" shouted Tex collapsing defiantly back to the floor.

Tula spoke, "You will accompany me to the Colonel of the Bureau." she spoke firmly but the former viciousness and dominance had gone from her voice. Tex sensed something had gone wrong for her, making her nervous. He decided to push it just a little more.

"Well, no thank you, I don't feel like seeing him, I'm quite comfortable here." He crawled to the chair and draped his cuffed hands round the steel arm as if to anchor himself. The gaoler raised his stick but Tula stopped him and said something quickly to him in Karudan. She then squatted near to Tex.

"Tex," she said evenly, "These guys are not used to prisoners who talk back, I will not be able to help you for long, now get up please and follow me."

Wow! Thought Tex, she *is* worried. He staggered to his feet and was led out of the cell room to another with a dirty sink in the corner, the gaoler drew a pistol and Tula undid his cuffs.

"Wash!" Ordered Tula.

"No!"

"I said wash, damn you!" shouted Tula.

"And I said no!" stated Tex defiantly. She had stopped him getting walloped and now wanted him to soften the results of her beating, she *was* frightened.

The gaoler started shouting something, not at Tex but at Tula who looked sullen but said nothing until she turned to Paul and put the cuffs on again. "Very well, follow me" she said and walked out.

Tex sat next to Tula in the back of the bureau car, he decided to keep pushing and fishing.

"You know Tula, when Paul gets to hear about this.."

"He is in no position to do anything!"

"What's happened to him?" asked Tex a little too casually.

It was then that Tula realised that he didn't know anything that had happened in the last twenty four hours, she had to think fast. She knew that Vander was under guard at the hospital but was unsure about how long that would last. The President, she knew, liked Vander and this is what had started Juba's jealousy, hence the secret campaign against him. But now Juba was dead and the Pig was alive, if things turned around it could be very bad for her, she was running very short of friends.

"Look Tex you must believe me!" she whispered so the driver wouldn't hear. "It was me who persuaded Juba not to kill you, he knew I had really fallen for you that's why I had to put that act on in the gaol! Tex, it really hurt me to do and say those things but I was fighting for my life!.. And yours.. believe me!"

"Okay, so where's Paul?" he repeated, seemingly unmoved.

"He is under armed guard at the General Hospital.."

"Why the hospital?.. Come on dammit, what's been goin' on?"

"He was injured at the border, an Army colonel went berserk and .. and killed the Field Marshal.."

"Juba? Juba's dead?! How bad is Paul?" he asked excitedly.

"He's okay, he's wounded and burned…Keep your voice down!"

"Why is he under arrest?"

"The President ordered all Army Commanders to be suspended from duty in case of an uprising against him.."

"So with Juba out of the way who's No 2 to the President?"

"Janka."

"Janka?.. Who's he for Chrissake?"

"He is my boss and that's who we're going to see, Tex you must be careful.."

"Why did that Colonel kill Juba?" interrupted Tex totally unconcerned about her warnings.

"It was some blood vendetta, no-one really knows yet."

"And Paul was with them when it happened?"

"Yes, apparently so."

"What happened to the Colonel?"

"He was killed."

"Gimme a cigarette!"

Tex relaxed after puffing furiously for a few seconds. He slowed his thoughts down and tried to get some order and reason. It's my bet, he mused, that Paul killed Juba and made sure the Colonel got the blame, but it seemed that things had not gone quite to plan. M'Punga was suspicious and couldn't make up his mind if Paul was implicated, he concluded.

The car pulled into Bureau headquarters and Tex, still stiff was helped up the steps and along corridors full of staring, uniformed people. He was put in an office and his cuffs removed.

Janka had not been idle, he knew that Paul had been a favourite of the President and now he knew that Juba had a surveillance operation on him and Potter of which Saputo was part. Paul's story about Chimba's family being massacred was still being checked but was likely to be true.

As he saw it, he had a choice, either he could advise the President to finish off Vander and the other Army Commanders, or he could back Vander, have him released and thereby gain a powerful ally. He had never met Vander formally but had heard that he was a resourceful man with a strong spirit looking after him.

Janka was a realist, he knew that his own standing with the President could not last. He was essentially a bureaucrat, an office manager, not a political advisor or strategist. There were others though, he thought, who were far more capable of fitting the slot as number two to the President. Some, he knew, had a dislike of him and could make his life uncomfortable to say the very least if they came to a position of power. To have Vander in that position, a man who owed him a great favour, seemed the best option.

His thoughts were interrupted by a soft knock at the door, Eva Saputo entered looking sullen and contrite. "Major Potter, Sir. He is waiting to see you."

"Good Saputo, show him in."

Tex shuffled in, he made himself look more dazed and disorientated as if he had been drugged, Tula stood at his side.

Janka was shocked at the state of him, his head looked like it had been through a meat grinder. He was well aware of what his unit could get up to but he personally never had anything to do with that darker side of Bureau activities.

He gestured for Tula to sit him down.

"Major, who gave you those wounds?"

Tex closed his eyes in concentration, and Tula braced herself. "It was .. Desma." He croaked.

"Well, there's not much we can do about that, why were you arrested Major?"

"Juba, sorry, the Field Marshal, told me I was being arrested for plotting to kill Brigadier Vander, so's I could take 'is place like...But that was a load of old cobblers, I said that I would never be able to replace him.. I told him that. Look, just fetch Paul, he knows that I wouldn't do such a thing..."

"Saputo?" Queried the Colonel swinging his gaze to her.

She looked startled then said, "Yes, yes, the Field Marshal Juba was afraid that an attempt would be made on Brigadier Vander's life by this man..."

"And?"

"Well, I.. I told the Field Marshal that it was not true. I did not discover any evidence.."

"Look!" said Tex, "Get the Field Marshal here, or get me to see him, this whole thing can be straightened out, especially if Paul is here too, it's all a big foul up."

"You don't know about the Field Marshal?!" Janka looked from Tex to Tula who shook her head.

"But of course you wouldn't would you.. Why then Saputo, did you demand that this man be put to death if you had no evidence against him and knowing the Field Marshal was dead?"

Tula winced and Tex shot her a glance. "I thought.. I thought, well the thing is, I was not thinking clearly at the time..."

Tula was saved by Janka's phone ringing, he answered it, immediately straightened in the chair and said "Yes Excellency, I will come at once!"

Janka stood and shouted a name, the door opened and an officer entered.

"I am now going to the Palace, have my escort ready, ensure Major Potter has treatment for his injuries and freed. Arrest Saputo! She is to be kept incommunicado until I send for her.

"So there it is Excellency, the beloved Field Marshal arrested Potter because he thought there was a threat on Brigadier Vander's life. I know that despite a sometimes circulated rumour that all was not well between them, that they were on very good terms."

M'Punga nodded, his eyes were still bloodshot with grief and he seemed to have shrunk. He continually clasped and unclasped his hands and shivered now and again.

An Aide entered the room, when M'Punga acknowledged his presence, he spoke. "Excellency, it has been discovered that there *was* a massacre in the village where Chimba was born over twenty years ago," he hesitated before going on, "It is on record that the Field Marshal was carrying out duties in that area as a captain in the…"

"Yes! Very well." said M'Punga waving him away. "It looks like Chimba lured them all into a well prepared trap, there was not much anyone could have done."

Janka entered Paul's private room at the hospital, he dismissed the guard and was all smiles as he shook Paul's hand. "Brigadier, I hope that you are recovering well, can you walk?" Paul nodded, "Then come! Let us not keep the President waiting!"

The door was swung open for them, Paul and Janka walked into the President's private quarters at the Palace a hitherto forbidden area. The President stood there surrounded by four women and a dozen children from babes in arms to young teenagers.

The President smiled and walked toward Paul his arms outstretched. "I know you only have one good arm Paul, but you may embrace the President and then meet my family."

The Prince Tasi was inconsolable, he had wept and blubbed since he had heard of his uncle's death. He lay on the bed in his rooms at the Palace, dishevelled and miserable. He wanted a fix badly but there was none. Jokko stroked his hair and soothed him. "But Jokko, the white pig Brigadier had him killed I know it!" He wailed.

"No, no, my Prince, I have no love for that devil after he nearly killed me but I know that he loved the Field Marshal. I heard him say so myself many times, was it not he who killed Chimba trying to defend the Field Marshal?"

Tula was bought before Tex at Bureau Headquarters. After five days in the cells she was dirty and dishevelled, she could hardly stand and the light hurt her eyes.

"Well, well Tula, you do look a state," he leered, "Ye know what I am now? Haven't got me uniform knocked out yet, but I'm Colonel Potter, Commander of the Bureau of Internal Security. Seems to fit me don't it? Potter of the Bureau, bit like Fabian of the Yard, innit? But you wouldn't know about that would you?...Well, what *are* we going to do with you my Tulip?"

Tex started tutting and then continued, "You know, I might have really gone for your little story about stopping Juba from killing me and all that garbage, but Janka spoiled all that didn't he? Let the old pussy cat out of the baggy waggy didn't he. Oh! By the way he's a Brigadier now, got Paul's old job, he'd forgotten all about you in the cells. I'm just going to throw you back in there and let you rot, or should I let the other prisoners at you? Ha! You might enjoy that though!"

Tex stopped his little game, he stood up and went round the desk to her and clasped her shoulders, his voice started cracking, "I fucking loved you, you know? You meant more to me than any of them tarts and I mean all of 'em. When I thought...When I thought you was having my baby..." Tex let her go and doubled up with grief, he sobbed hard and couldn't get his breath.

Suddenly Tula put her arms round him, patted his head to her breast and rocked him. "Oh Tex! It can still happen my love, those days alone in that cell made me realise what a damn fool I'd been. If you could only know how I was bought up never knowing my father, manipulated by people I trusted, all I wanted was for someone to love me..."

"Did you mean it about the baby Tula? Can we still make it happen?"

"Of course my love, together we can make anything happen…. Just me and you."

Paul arranged the State Funeral of the Late Field Marshal Juba leaving nothing to chance. He went over every inch of the route with the people concerned. Soldiers of his old Bodyguard Commando were drilled until they were perfect. With difficulty, black horses were found to pull the hearse and stone masons were employed to make a monolith of a headstone out of black granite. Paul paced his home hour after hour practising the eulogy he would deliver.

The President was more of his old self especially after Paul had restarted the supply of drugs. He was still a Brigadier without portfolio until the day of the funeral. When the funeral itself was over, M'Punga summoned Paul into the throne room of the Palace. When he walked in, he was surprised to see it thronged with all the Senior Officers of the Army and Airforce. "Until my great friend was buried Paul, I could not bear to give you this." M'Punga handed him the Baton of Field Marshal and all the room cheered.

In the following week the border situation was "stabilised". Field Marshal Paul Vander took up offices in the Palace and was a constant companion to the President. Prince Tasi under gentle but consistent pressure from Jokko softened toward Paul but avoided him whenever possible. Colonel Terrence Potter warmed to his job as the head of the Bureau and he and Tula (as he still insisted in calling her) moved into sumptuous quarters on the private estate in Laka.

All of Juba's family, friends and co-conspirators paid homage to the new Field Marshal. Paul had a list in his head, thanks to Juba, of those that would be removed permanently in the fullness of time. Janka was the puppet head of his old Commando and slowly, very slowly, thought Paul, I will replace all the key positions in the Palace and the Military with my own trusted and loyal men.

On a warm, sunny, February morning, Paul, with the help of a few men from his staff loaded the casket containing his old friend Peter Gant onto a plane bound for Salisbury Rhodesia on its way back to England. Paul had a feeling that was close to regret but even that had dissipated before his car had left the airfield.

14

"I'm pissed off with this Frank!" hissed Jim Walker for about the fifth time that day, "We've done nothing except hang around airport lounges for the last three days, I tell you that Julian is off his friggin' rocker.."

"Yeh! Look Jim, I know, we're *all* pissed off." said Frank with a sigh, he rubbed his tired eyes and took a swig from the half empty bottle of coke. "Just bear with it eh?.."

"But Frank, you should say somethin'. "

"Okay, but let it drop for now Jim." replied Frank his voice betrayed a growing irritation. Jim gave a hands up gesture and slumped back in his seat.

They had been in the airport at Luanda, Angola for over eight hours now. Ten minutes after they had arrived there from Cape town Julian had disappeared after telling them to stay put until he returned.

Norrie lay on the floor in a sleeping bag snoring loudly and Nick had shuffled off to the toilets, Riff was sipping a coffee listening to the conversation but saying nothing, his eyes were bloodshot through lack of proper sleep.

Frank tried to fight down the feeling of insecurity that was starting to grow over him. It's just tiredness, he thought, a good nights sleep and I'll be okay. A lot had happened in the last three days and it was just a matter of adjusting.

They had all travelled together on the train to London to meet Julian and get their movement instructions, an initial payment and a detailed brief before they shook hands with him and departed but it wasn't to be like that.

They had met as arranged in one of the pubs just off Sloane Square. It was a rainy wind swept morning, the pub had just opened and was empty. Julian arrived a couple of minutes later, he said nothing but stared at Riff, a twitch beginning in his eye. He gestured to Nick and went back outside. When Nick joined him, he blurted out loudly, "Is this some kind of joke?! Bringing that black bastard!…"

"Hey! Just steady on!" launched Nick, "I chose him, he's a perfectly good soldier, besides, what's it to you? *We're* the ones taking the risk not you!"

Julian was a little taken aback by the intensity of Nick's reply. He drew himself up and went back inside followed by Nick. The little group looked at him, silent and brooding, they hadn't heard the conversation but knew what it was about. Riff looked up at Nick and was about to say something when Julian, staring at the centre of the table began to speak.

"Gentlemen, I am about to take you on an important mission, a mission that if succeeds will make each of us a wealthy man," he paused and looked around the table, careful to avoid Riff's eyes. "But I need an oath of loyalty off each of you…"

"Wait on!" It was Nick, his brow furrowed questioningly, "Do you mean that you are coming too?!"

"Yes, I will lead the operation.."

"Hey! Just hold on a minute matey," interrupted Nick nastily, "The idea was for me, with Frank to pick a team and lead it. There is no way that's not going to happen, come along if you wish, that's your prerogative, but there's a big difference in planning and advising to actually leading a hazardous Op. like this…"

"We don't know your ability Julian," threw in Frank, "You might have been an officer and that but we don't know what you're like…"

"And what's yer problem about having me along like?" added Riff, his normally happy face set hard.

The group fell silent and uneasy, Julian sat tapping his fingers on the table, he was breathing deeply.

Jim Walker broke the silence. "Oh! For fuck's sake let's knock this on the head straight away. We *vote* in our leader right?!.. Stick your hands up for Julian as our leader…No bastard. Right, stick 'em up for Nick!" Frank and Jim stuck up their hands, "Okay.. just two." stated Jim getting a little flustered, "Okay then let's see it for Frank." Riff and Norrie stuck their hands up.

"Okay it's a hung vote…" started Jim.

"No it's not!" said Julian raising his hand, "I vote for Frank too."

"And I second that!" Shouted Jim.

Frank looked surprised and a little embarrassed, he looked at Nick who smiled and made a Gallic gesture.

"Nick's our leader, it was he who put this together.." began Frank.

"But you've been voted in Frank," said Norrie, "You are now the man.. Is that correct boys?" He added looking around, they all nodded including Nick.

Frank took a loud intake of breath then clapped his hands at the expectant group, "Let's get a drink in first!" He said, then broke off to the bar, he had to give himself a space.

"I hope all your decisions are as good!" laughed Jim.

The group broke up to collect their glasses from the bar, Nick sidled up to Frank and gripped his wrist, "Get to it old son, I'm with you." He said softly.

They sat down again and fell silent. Frank cleared his throat and began in a firm voice, "All right, you've elected me the leader, I accept, so let's get some things out of the way. Firstly, you Julian, it's been said that it's your prerogative to come along…. Good, you will be in an advisory capacity en route but once on the operation itself you will be an equal member of the team. Now let's get things out in the open. Julian have you a problem with any member of this team? If so, spit it out here or forget it, what's it to be?"

Julian raised his eyes from the table to the ceiling and said.

"No problem."

"Good, then I suggest you let us know what is happening."

Nick came back from the toilets, the airport was beginning to wake up. His face looked drawn and white and his thick black hair was wet and plastered down, he eyed Frank and smiled, "Just had a scrape," he said rubbing his jaw, "Thought it would make me feel better.. It doesn't!" he laughed. "Those bloody bogs are God awful, I mean for an airport you'd think.. Oh! Forget it!"

Frank laughed along with him. His respect for Nick had grown enormously since that first day when the leadership vote had gone against him. He had not raised the matter or shown any type of emotion about it, he had just remained the same old laid back Nick, always there for help or advice.

"This had all better be bloody worth it! That's all I say." It was Jim Walker again. "I mean, he keeps on about us being wealthy men after all this but he's still told us Jack shit about any details...I mean, do you know any more than us Frank?"

Before Frank could reply he carried on his monologue. "I personally think he's off his rocker, do you see the way his eye twitches when he's under pressure and that colour he goes sometimes? And you can't get a word of decent conversation out of him.... I just hope he knows what he's doing that's all."

Jim dried up and picked up a well thumbed Sven Hassel novel. He had echoed all their thoughts. Julian had certainly not come across as a character to have confidence in but his hints at instant wealth kept them going, at least, that is what Frank kept telling himself. The truth, when he forced himself to confront it, was something else. After being rejected both by the Army and his wife, he felt he just had to get away and find himself a new life.

For the past few years the Regiment had been everything to him. All his friends were there. They thought the same thoughts, they talked the same way, drank in the same pubs, got cold and wet together, argued amongst themselves, lived, laughed, fought and sometimes died together. A large boisterous, good natured family of intelligent, hard men that possessed a unique espirit de corps.

And now he was out of it, rejected by the very people he had been loyal to, an unwanted son, rejected and kicked out. This was the escape, the illusion of being part of a team again amongst like minded people who understood one another. But as each day dragged by, more and more of that illusion was melting into reality.

He looked across at Nick and wondered why he was really here, he had not said much about his private life, ever. Frank knew that he was married to a very beautiful woman, he had met her once at a Company Smoker and was bowled over like most of the others with her charm and beauty. Surely he didn't need the money? Pondered Frank. He wasn't surprised that Nick had resigned, he had always seemed at odds with the hierarchy but to leave and then come on a job like this? He must be regretting it, he concluded.

Suddenly Julian was amongst them clutching a briefcase and looking very dapper in a pinstriped suit. A black porter came up panting behind him carrying two heavy suitcases.

He gestured the man to leave his cases. The team started to stir, Norrie sat up in his sleeping bag checking his watch and rubbing his eyes. Jim put down his book and looked at Julian expectantly, Frank and Nick rose, Riff sat, hands in his pockets, bored.

Julian looked around him and then turned to Frank, "Are we ready to move?" he said sharply.

"Yeh! We're ready to move Julian...Can you tell us where?" replied Frank a little testily.

"We need to get going..."

"No Julian! We're not a bunch of school kids on an outing.. We need to know!"

The others had now stood up and were looking at Julian, tired, hostile faces.

"Very well," he said in a resigned manner, "I've been negotiating with the aid of hard cash, a lift out of here. There are no scheduled flights to Rhodesia, so I've managed to charter an aircraft that will take us via Lusaka to Salisbury. Once we are safely inside Rhodesia I can give you all the information you require and more...But until then gentlemen, I will say no more about the operation. If questioned you are to say that you are employed by me. My father passed on to me various business concerns in Rhodesia, some of which are still running. Let us say that I am worried about various robberies and vandalism at some of the sites and am employing you as security consultants.... Say no more than that to anyone. Now we must get moving, the pilot is refuelling and is anxious to get moving as soon as that is completed."

Nick cramped and cold like the rest of them craved a smoke. The scruffy, surly South African pilot had told them it was forbidden but what the hell, what was he going to do, throw him off?

He clamped a cigarette between his lips and flicked his lighter. A movement across from him caught his eye, it was Norrie sitting up in his sleeping bag the hood of which was half over his head making him look like a hideous monk. He gestured for Nick to throw him one of his cigarettes.

Moments later the two men sat facing each other hunched, puffing away and now and again waving their hands to dissipate the smoke. Talking was out of the question. The roar of the engines on the Hastings made it impossible. The main cargo was made up by a number of boxes like Tea chests netted and secured to the floor. They rested where they could, either sleeping or drifting in and out of sleep.

Nick found a plastic coffee cup, dropped his cigarette end in the few drops of brown liquid at the bottom and watched it fizzle out. He gathered his sleeping bag around him in an effort to trap in the little bit of warmth that was left.

Nick regretted ever thinking about coming on the Operation. It wasn't a sudden realisation. He knew at the beginning of it all that he wasn't reasoning properly and that he would most certainly come to this conclusion.

Before he started the tour in Belfast he had tendered his resignation so that he would be released when the tour was over. Anne had been waiting for him and they had a glorious week in Anne's parents place in the South of France. Nick had sensed that all was not as it should be especially when he had talked of their future. She hadn't contributed but rather just smiled or agreed as he spoke. Nevertheless, they had a good break, then it was back to the grindstone for Anne, commuting to London most days and often staying overnight.

Nick tried a few of the contacts he had made before he joined up and some he'd made over the years when he had been serving but apart from some part time work delivering and collecting antique furniture there was no firm offers of work from any of them.

The first major row had broken out on a Saturday morning. Anne had said that she was working over Friday night. Nick was not unduly bothered, he knew that her work was very important especially at this moment in time when her boss was trying to land a large contract.

She turned up at around ten on Saturday morning. Nick had greeted her with a kiss and immediately smelled stale booze on her breath. She looked a little more ruffled than her usual immaculate self and when she said that she had a headache and was going to bed for an hour he knew that she had drunk more than a couple of G and Ts.

"Working late darling?" he ventured as she swallowed a couple of tablets.

"Mmm, not so much that, I think I'm going down with flu or something." she replied and then added, "Oh Nick, I left my briefcase in the car, be a love and get it for me. My address book is in it and I need to make a couple of calls before I lie down."

Nick complied, he went to the car parked on the drive, it had just started to rain. He crawled onto the back seat where she usually kept it but it was not there.

He flicked the boot catch and went around the back and lifted the lid, it was not there either but something caught his eye, it was the handles of a white plastic supermarket bag sticking out from underneath a spare blanket that was always kept in the boot.

He lifted it out and checked inside, he saw a dress that had been rolled neatly, he shook it out, it was small and chic, he had never seen it before, he put it to his nose and inhaled deeply, he also found a pair of tights with knickers tangled up in them and a pair of high heeled shoes.

He found the briefcase stuffed in the passenger seat leg well. Anne was coming out of the bathroom in her nightie, Nick handed her the briefcase.

"Thanks darling." she said smiling as she went into the bedroom.

"What did you do last night exactly?" he tried to sound casual but he could feel tension creeping into his voice.

"Oh! I, that is JK, me and the other girls worked on the project until around eleven thirty...Pm that is and then I crashed at the flat with Pam...Pretty boring stuff really."

"You didn't even have a drink then?" Anne stopped in her tracks, sensing that this was more than just casual interest.

"As a matter of fact Pam and I had a couple of G and Ts as a night cap...Is there a problem or something Nick?"

"No, none at all." Nick walked back to the door, picked up the carrier bag and emptied it onto the bed.

Anne glanced at it but said nothing as she pulled back the bed covers.

"Well, do you usually dress up for drinks at the flat?" He said with a little edge to his voice.

"Oh! For God's sake Nick stop trying to act like some latter day Sherlock Holmes." she spat, "They've been in the car for ages, I just keep forgetting to bring them in…"

"They were worn last night! Huh! Last night! More like a couple of hours ago, they still reek of smoke and drink.. Have you really got to lie to me?!" He said in a raised voice.

"Okay Nick if you must know they belong to Pam!" she shouted back, her beautiful features twisted in fury. "She went on to a club last night, Jack is due at the flat this morning and she didn't want him to find them. You see, she's also married to an idle, suspicious man who thinks he's a *detective*…Go on! Check the shoe size! She's a good two sizes larger than mine.. I'm a five and she's a seven! Go on damn you! Check!"

"You still lied to me!" He was now shouting, "Pam goes off shagging all night and little goodie two shoes just curls up with a book…. Oh yeh!"

"Well it would be a little more interesting than curling up with you!" she screamed back, "You boring, idle bastard! While I'm out paying for all of this, you just hang around the pub with your cronies and count that as looking for work! Yes! I like a break sometimes, to go out and have some fun sometimes.. Yes, even without you, but I don't go shagging around! Got it?! Now just bugger off for the day and leave me in peace!"

Nick had gone to say something but had changed his mind and left. He looked up and old friend, got steaming drunk and stayed over.

When he got back she had gone. The note said to her sister's in St Albans. He phoned there and her sister put Anne on. They had talked in a strained subdued way and she said that it would be better if she stayed overnight.

To cap it all when she did return Sunday evening she *was* suffering from a bad cold. She went to work as normal on Monday but JK sent her back home. They had hardly spoken.

Nick had tried in earnest to get a job but to no avail, then he had bumped into an old acquaintance from the Regiment who had left as a Major some years before and set up in the security business. He had put Nick onto Julian, it had never occurred to him why he had not followed Julian's job offer himself instead of handing it over.

He had thanked him for the offer but had pushed it into a far recess in his mind. Hah! Nick Summers mercenary! What a laugh.

Then, when Anne recovered, she said they needed to talk about separation. She was, she had stated, at a vital stage of the contract at work and he needed space to find a job, to emphasise the point she set up in the spare bedroom. After a week of this she announced that she would be staying at the flat for at least a fortnight as she would be working late most nights.

The day she left Nick phoned Julian.

The stop over at Lusaka was a nightmare. The Hastings taxied to a remote part of the airfield for refuelling. Bone cold, tired and hungry they were herded into the corner of an empty hangar with all their luggage, once again Julian disappeared. While he was gone they were subjected to three searches, each time by different people in seedy customs uniforms.

They were questioned at length by an official. At first Nick and Frank had been keen to help and readily complied with the demands made of them and then, after the third time just sat in a group, sullen and silent.

After a few hours Julian appeared with a fat official, he looked chipper, washed and shaved and sharing a joke with his grinning companion. After a final belly laugh the official shook Julian's hand and walked away.

Jim was the first to start, "That's fucking it!" He muttered and started to rise.

"Sit down!" warned Frank.

Then Riff, his face set in an uncharacteristic scowl, let rip. "What's the friggin score Julian? We been here hours, sod all to eat and pushed around by these goons...."

"Shut your face, you Kaffir bastard!" exploded Julian. Before he could continue Riff launched at him but was stopped accidentally by Norrie getting up. Frank and Nick grabbed him as Julian continued ranting, "I've had it up to here dealing with you black bastards..." Nick dropped his hold on Riff and grabbed Julian by his shirtfront.

"Julian! Shut it! Just shut it!" He raged through gritted teeth while slamming him up the side of the hangar.

"Just let me at the bastard! Let me go!" yelled Riff, foam coming from his mouth.

"Go on! Let him go!" screeched Jim, his eyes wide with excitement, "Let him kill the bastard!"

Suddenly a guard in uniform was amongst them, he had a machine pistol at the ready. He looked frightened and confused, his eyes darting from one group to the other.

Nick let go of Julian, "Sort him out and quick!" he said in a casual manner. Julian brushed himself down and smiled at the guard, he spoke in his language as he clapped him on the shoulder and palmed him a wad of notes. The guard looked at the money, took it then walked away.

Nick spoke, "Alright gentlemen, have we all got it out of our systems now?" The group were silent apart from Riff's deep breathing. Frank had let him go and he stood there just staring at Julian who continued to straighten himself up.

Nick looked at Julian and spoke in conversational tones, "Julian, we're at the end of our tether old man. We haven't eaten for almost thirty hours, we've been cold and we've been fucked about. Now, after you apologise to Riff you had better say some words to set things right." Nick made a motion with his arm as if to introduce him to the group.

Julian stepped forward, he cleared his throat, "We are on the last leg..." he began but was interrupted by Nick making a stage cough and shooting him a meaningful glance. Julian caught his gaze then began again, "Like you, I've been under a lot of strain," Jim muttered something in the background but Julian persevered. "And I apologise for my outburst, it wasn't called for... But things are now looking a lot better. First, some food, we have an hour or so before we take off, so we'll go and eat..." He then led them through the hangar to a gate on the perimeter fence. Julian talked to the guard obviously negotiating something. It was just before noon and the sun was warm and pleasant on their stiff bodies.

Riff turned to Frank and Nick while they were waiting, "Sorry," he said with pursed lips, "I snapped back there, promise it won't happen again."

"Nobody can blame you Riff," said Frank.

"The sooner we get on with this the better." added Nick.

After a few minutes a truck pulled up at the gate and Julian said with a smile, "Let's go and eat."

The last part of the journey was much better, as well as eating a hearty meal they had managed to grab a shower at one of the hotels. At the same hotel Norrie procured an armful of bottled beers and they had all glugged them back. "Cost me my fuckin' watch that did!" He exclaimed in mock hurt. Julian had not accompanied them into the hotel but stayed with the truck.

They were prepared for the cold this time and had taken care to put on extra clothing. The food and drink lulled their minds and it wasn't too long into the flight before they all nodded off into a refreshing slumber.

Julian was keyed up when they got to Immigration at Salisbury but they passed through without a problem.

Beforehand Julian had emphasised the need to stick to the cover story no matter what but the officials at immigration had seemed disinterested.

Now that Julian was on familiar territory things began to run more smoothly. He organised a mini bus and not long after they had landed they were heading North in the early morning sun towards Bindura. The mood of the group was good, even Julian was smiling and communicative, pointing out various things on the route.

The countryside rolled past, flat ochre coloured earth covered with small thorny trees. After an hour they turned off the asphalt onto a dirt road, the mini bus slowed and rocked as it went over ruts and holes. They became hot and sweaty, dust got in their eyes and as the road got worse they began to hang on to anything that would steady them.

Another half hour passed, the minibus was totally unsuited for the road and moved at a snails pace the engine revving loudly in low gear. Julian, who sat at the front said something to the driver and he swung off the dirt road onto a track which was long and straight and in good repair, the bus picked up speed and they started to relax a little.

After another hour, Julian turned and said loudly. "Gentlemen! Your home for the next few days." They bobbed around in the back trying to see out of the windows. The minibus stopped outside of a large brick bungalow, outside on the porch two black men in simple clothes stared at them.

They got out of the vehicle stiff and sore and looked around. Opposite the house was a large barn like building made of black corrugated iron sheets, there were other buildings, smaller and further away from the main house, Frank guessed that these were the workers houses.

Julian was engaged in an animated conversation with the older of the two black men. The man opened the door of the house and Julian followed him in. They unloaded the minibus and stacked their belongings on the wide covered porch of the house.

"Hey you speekee de English eh?!" It was Jim speaking to the other black man who smiled in an embarrassed sort of way and came closer to the group.

"What your name?" Persisted Jim in a slow exaggerated way.

"Rex, ma name is Rex." replied the man in a smooth dignified voice. The conversation stopped as Julian and Rex's companion returned. Julian paid the minibus driver and he drove off in a cloud of orange dust.

"Okay gentlemen, I'm glad to say that everything here is in order, this is Albert who was my Father's head servant. He and his son Rex will be taking care of us for the next few days, they both speak English very well. They will show you to your rooms, then we will graze." He made an eating motion, "And then for the remainder of the day and night we rest."

15

Harry Macmillan lay on his bed, eyes closed and mouth agape, a book on ornithology lay open on his chest which rose and fell rhythmically. Suddenly his eyes opened and he became alert, his mouth still hung open as he slowly turned his head toward the open window. He was sure that he had heard a sound outside.

It was late afternoon and he had dozed off after downing a half bottle of cane spirit. His shed door in the garden made a certain creaking noise when opened and he was sure that's what he had heard. He lay there, now fully alert. His home was off the beaten track and his nearest neighbours were a quarter of a mile away, it could be thieves but he had nothing but junk to steal, everybody knew that.

He eased himself up and reached for the .38 revolver that he kept in his bedside drawer. As he clutched the cold metal he heard the squeak of a board on the veranda, he thumbed back the hammer and slid effortlessly off the bed, his heart was starting to pound and adrenaline gave his tired muscles and worn joints new life.

He opened his bedroom door a crack and carefully checked the small passageway outside, it was empty. He strained his ears for any sound at all for three minutes, he was sure after that, that there was nobody in the house. Moving slowly, without a sound, he made his way to the front door. Once there he waited, the door was the only easy way into the house, all the windows were shuttered apart from his bedroom which was barred. He would wait here until the intruder either disappeared or tried to get in. He was too old, he told himself, to go outside and take the buggers head on.

Harry heard a movement behind him but it was too late, the hard cold steel of a gun barrel rammed him into the door, simultaneously a voice shouted "DROP IT HARRY!" Harry sighed, thumbed forward the hammer and dropped the revolver.

"I'm sorry about that Harry," said the voice, "But I wasn't sure what type of reception I would get if I up and knocked at your door."

Harry turned and saw a medium built man in jungle camouflage the pattern of the Karudan Armed forces, the face was completely covered in black camo cream.

Harry recovered, he saw that the Uzi was still pointing at him, "Scared of an old man, Hanlon?" he said sarcastically while wiping the back of his scrawny neck with his handkerchief.

"Harry," said Daryl quietly, "don't try and pull any of your tricks with me, there are some young bucks outside that will…."

"Oh for God's sake Hanlon!" said Harry pushing past him, "I need a drink!" He went to the sideboard in the cluttered gloomy room and reached for a bottle.

"Try this!" Said Hanlon, Harry turned and took the bottle that Daryl was holding by the neck. Harry,

once more pushed passed him into the relative bright-
ness of the hallway.

"Ah! Single Malt!" Harry exclaimed as he examined the label at arms length. "How long had you been
in the house?" he asked, still appraising the bottle.

"Long enough to see that you've ditched the set."

"Drink?"

"After business Harry."

"Well, I hope you don't mind but after all that,
I'll take a libation now chum." He found a glass and
poured himself a generous slug. "Your health sir!" he
offered and downed half of it. "My God," he rasped, "
it's moments like this when I wonder why I never stayed
at home. My father yer know had a major share in a Dis-
tillery. Harry, he said, do five years in the army and it's
all yours." Harry studied the remnants in the glass for a
moment then tossed it down his throat. "Wanted me to
join a Highland regiment........."

"What happened to Gant, Harry?"

"Gant? Drank himself to death."

"Uh uh, Harry, we had a guy look at him on the
way through, he was drugged then given a lethal injec-
tion...What happened to Gant, Harry?"

"How the bloody hell should I know!" snarled
Harry, "The bloody Bureau or that phsyco Vander got
to him, all I know is, we were doing fine, he began to
co-operate. I gave him a camera, he was even enthusiastic about it all but the man drank like a bloody fish,
when they said he had drunk himself to death I believed
them..."

"Believed who Harry? Who said that he had died that way?"

"Oh! People.. People at the hotel, I asked them.."

"Why would someone want to murder him Harry?"

" I…Don't…Bloody…Well….. Know!"

"If they knew or even suspected what he was doing they would have got you too Harry. Besides, they wouldn't have killed him as subtly as that…It stinks Harry."

Harry sat down on the worn settee.

"Why did you kill him Harry? Were you afraid he was going down and would take you with him? Or did he threaten to shop you?"

"What is this? Are you some kind of judge and jury all of a sudden? Come off it Daryl, what's really niggling you?"

"Where's the radio and telephone?"

Harry sat back on the settee and sighed. "You're taking a hell of a risk you know chum, there's been a lot of activity here just lately, have you heard what happened to our friendly gorilla, Juba? Everybody's jumpy, you get caught in that uniform and your dead. The radio's gone and the telephone's gone, shoulda done it a long time ago." Harry paused and looked at the bottle again, a frown lined his brow and he turned to Daryl his mouth half open in a sudden realisation, "You've come to finish me off haven't you?"

16

"Close in on to me!" yelled Norrie to Jim Walker. Jim came sauntering over. "And when you move, you move at the double. Come on! Double in to me!" Jim came running up, like the rest of them he was out of breath and pouring with sweat.

"For fuck's sake Jim, what army was you in? When I put me hand on the top of me head like this, it means close into me...Right? You can't go shoutin' all the bloody while when you're operating in the cuds, you've got to use hand signals. Okay the rest of you, close in!"

They had been exercising in the Bush surrounding the farm complex most of the morning. After their Tea meal the previous evening they had all crashed out dead tired. That morning Julian had taken them to the Barn and with their help had burst open a half dozen boxes containing camouflaged jungle uniforms. Other boxes contained a selection of calf length leather boots, peaked combat caps, socks, cam cream, insect repellent and other items that they would need.

Frank realised the need for them to get in as much training as possible. Julian had not said how much time they had but whatever it was, it wouldn't be long enough, he mused. He put Norrie in charge of minor tactical training because he had done a two month course in the Brecon Beacons a few months before and was current.

They had no weapons yet but nevertheless, since first light, he had refreshed them on camouflage and concealment, taking cover, locating the enemy, theoretically returning fire and finally, what they were in the middle of now, Fire and Movement.

"We're a small team," he said to the assembled group that included Julian, "and if we don't work together when we come under fire, we're dead! Its no use all of us firing at the enemy together and then moving together, 'cos we'll all run out of ammo together and we'll all be shot together...Got it?! We split into two man teams on the assault. F'rinstance, Riff moves forward while I lay down covering fire for him, when he gets in a good position he starts firing and I move, if at any time I have to change mags, I shout, CHANGING MAGS! To let 'im know that I can't cover 'im.. "You've got to talk to each other all the time..."

"But you said you don't talk in the cuds!" Cut in an indignant Jim.

"Are you a dick head or what? You fucking Walley!" savaged Norrie. "You keep fucking *quiet* when you are advancing to contact the enemy but once the first shot is fired what's the frigging use of keepin' quiet then!"

"Okay Norrie," interrupted Frank, "that's enough for this morning, let's get back and get some fluids back in." There was a general hum of approval and they all set off for the house.

Albert was waiting on the porch with a large urn that was full of iced orange squash, they were silent for a couple of minutes while they downed mug after mug of the refreshing liquid. After he lit a cigarette Norrie turned to Frank. "That's it Frank, I've taught them enough, what we need is practice then more practice, but what we need most is weapons, ammo and a place to fire 'em." Julian who stood next to them took up the conversation.

"With a bit of luck, what you asked for should arrive today. I couldn't have them here waiting for us, it would have been too risky.."

"I take it, that it's not completely kosher then? The weapons I mean." said Nick

"No! Not exactly, when they do arrive, I will send Albert and his son away for a few days, the less they see and hear the better.."

"When are we going to find out what's going on Julian?" enquired Frank.

"When I think it's right and not before." He replied abruptly and walked away.

"Okay!" shouted Frank, a little anger in his voice, "Let's go, Norrie, take us from the start again, camouflage and concealment, right the way through!" A groan came from the group as they fell in behind Norrie and doubled back to the training area.

Harry felt a cold sweat oozing out of every pore in his body, the silence from Daryl was electrifying. He just stood there in front of Harry his legs slightly apart, the Uzi still pointing at him.

Finally Harry snapped. "Well if you're going to do it, do it! Damn you!"

"Relax Harry, nobody is going to do anything, why should I harm you? Gant means nothing but he *was* the only means we had of getting any intelligence at all about Vander, now we have nothing."

Daryl relaxed, walked across the room, picked Harry's gun up and tossed it onto the settee beside him. He then picked up the single malt poured a shot into the cap and downed it followed quickly by another, he topped Harry's glass up and sat on a chair opposite him.

"Harry, cast your mind back to the days when those bunch of clowns from England.. Sorry, you know what I mean, when that bunch ran Camp Lagonda."

Harry, gulped back the whisky and wiped his mouth with the back of his hand, "Yes," he replied.

"There was one particular guy.. a Major Pern…. Remember him?"

"Mm, Pern, nasty piece of work. A sadist and probably a homo to boot, met him once at a social function not long after that bunch had arrived. They were unsure about things I guess and wanted to meet us Ex Pats to fill in some gaps. Their CO, Henley or Hemmings, he seemed a decent sort of chap, university, Sandhurst, that sort of thing but as for Pern….. I heard that he used to visit the prison in his own time to teach them new interrogation techniques to use on the terrorists. I pity the poor bastards that he used to train them on…"

"Have you any idea where he is now Harry?"

"Who.. Pern? Good God no! After they were booted out of the Country I heard nothing…What's happening Daryl?"

Daryl ignored the question, "Gant said something about Vander doing an official opening of a camp… Camp Lagonda on the eighteenth of this month."

"Yes, that's right, I remember him saying that and I passed it on to you."

"Harry, I need to know for definite every...."

"No! No!" shouted Harry, leaping off the settee like an athlete, a vein in his temple started to throb, "I'm finished with you Hanlon and the bloody lot of them! No more bloody jobs!"

"Me and my men will be stopping here for a few days, we'll take the back room.."

"What the bloody hell are you talking about man?! You can't stay here, it's far too dangerous!"

"Who for Harry, us or you? Look, get the information I want and you'll get two thousand Sterling or the equivalent in whatever currency you want.

"Ha! Two thousand, two million, twenty million! What does it matter? I'm worn out, I'm finished.."

"Killing Gant really got to you didn't it Harry? Was it the same feeling you got when you stuck that needle in your wife's arm and watched her die.."

"You Bastard! You rotten bastard! She was in agony dying slowly. You can't compare...You can't.." Harry broke off sobbing, he collapsed back on the settee his head in his hands.

Daryl dropped to his knees in front of him, and spoke urgently, "Harry! Let me get you out of this rotting tomb, let me get you back to Rhodesia where you can live in free air. We have places, nice homes in the country or the town. I know you have money in the bank there, we will add to that, come on! Let us help you spend your last few years in comfort and happiness. You've done well for us in the past, let us repay you man...But I need this one last job Harry."

"Frank will you take a look at John Wayne over there, he hasn't a clue man!" Norrie pointed to Jim Walker who was supposed to be taking cover behind a pile of rocks. He was half crouched, exposing his body from the waist up, every now and then he would pick up a loose stone, pull an imaginary pin out of it with his teeth and lob it at the "enemy."

"And Julian is not much better. I thought he said he was ex SAS? He doesn't look ex anything to me, but at least he's putting his heart and soul into it." Norrie shook his head, he had been driving them hard since their brief water stop at lunch time.

Sweat poured from them all, making rivulets through the ochre dust that covered them. Norrie gave them a five minute breather. Frank dusted off his combat cap and wiped the sweat from his eyes, "Just persevere Norrie, they're all we've got..."

There was a noise, Frank stopped speaking and the others stopped what ever they were doing and concentrated. It was a thumping noise like a far off bass drum being beaten quickly and rhythmically. Julian stood up and cupped his ears toward the sound, "It's the chopper!" He shouted and as he did, the thumps turned into the familiar tangible sound of a helicopter. It was flying low and fast then turned and circled the farm complex. Julian shouted above the sound to Norrie at the same time drawing an imaginary knife across his throat, "That's it for today, back to the house!"

They humped the last of the boxes from the chopper to the barn. The chopper was now parked up its pilot stood next to it rolling a cigarette. He was tall about six two, slightly hunched over and in his mid thirties. As he strolled near, Frank noticed that his eyes were dim and faded.

Julian gestured for them to join him and the pilot. "Gentlemen, meet our pilot Lou...Lou is late of the USAF and a Vietnam veteran. Lou Meet Frank, he will introduce you to the rest of the team." Frank did so and Lou shook their hands, no smiles or how do you dos came from his lips he just nodded.

"Lou has bought us the toys we need." said Julian eagerly, "Come on! Let's open the boxes."

Riff levered out the final nails in the coffin like box, then pulled off the lid. Inside, on neat, purpose built rests were four dull black rifles with squat triangular plastic stocks. "M-16 Armalites!" Norrie exclaimed and plucked one from the box, he immediately made sure it wasn't loaded then put it into the aim a couple of times. "These are standard issue for the Yanks." He said to Julian who replied a little sarcastically.

"Oh don't worry, they've got thousands, they won't miss a couple."

They prised open more boxes, to reveal more of the rifles, grenades, and ammunition. Julian opened a small box and took out two semi automatic pistols and two silencers, he handed them to Frank, "Just in case we need to be quiet." He said.

Norrie looked around puzzled, "Have we not got a Gun Julian?"

"A gun? What are these, scotch mist or something?"

"No! I mean a gun, a Machine Gun, like a Jimpy or a Bren....A Gun."

"What the hell do you want for God's sake?! I risk twenty years in prison to get this little lot and you moan because *you* haven't got precisely what *you* want.."

"Take it easy Julian." it was Frank, he sounded and looked serious. "It was a fair question. We should have a Gun, something that can put a weight of fire down to get us out of the shit if need be or suppress the bastards while we move on to 'em. If we haven't got one, well, we'll have to do without, but don't jump down our throats for asking."

Julian sighed and rolled his eyes, "Okay, I haven't got a bloody Gun...Sorry! I'll try harder next time."

"Where can we fire these things?" queried Jim, he held his rifle by the pistol grip and rested it back on his shoulder like an old sweat. Before Julian could answer Norrie snapped, "Get your finger off that trigger you numb skull! You never touch that trigger unless your going to fire the fucking thing.. That's how accidents happen!"

At first, Jim looked shaken, then his face distorted into a mask of hatred and fury, he shouted "I've had enough of you, you bastard!" and using the rifle as a club swung it with all his might at Norrie who dived out of the way but not before the butt caught his arm, they all rushed at Jim. Riff who got there first, kicked the legs from under him, he landed with a splat on his back, and contorted in agony as he tried to get air back in his lungs, then Norrie was on top of him. He managed to land a punch in his face before he was dragged off cursing and shouting.

"You fucking Limeys are crazy!" boomed Lou, "Hell! If you got no-one handy to kill, you start on each other.. Jee Zus!"

Jim rolled and got up wiping a trickle of blood from a nostril looking daggers at Norrie who was still being held.

Frank shouted at both of them, "Right! You two, I'll give you ten minutes to cool off then we'll have it done properly, stripped to the waist and bare knuckle, you can get it out of your systems here and now!"

"Fucking suits me." snarled Norrie

"Me too!" retorted Jim, but already his eyes were losing their fire. As the others began to make a makeshift ring from the packing cases, Jim went to Frank and eased him to one side, "He's been pushing me Frank," he said quietly but excitedly.

"For Christ's sake Jim, that's what I wanted him to do. He's been pushing all of us, he's good at what he knows best, you shouldn't take it personally.."

"Yeh! But he's been needling at me, just me! And I ain't going to stand for it!"

Suddenly, Frank had enough, pressure had been building on him day by day. In his eyes things had been getting worse, instead of becoming a team they were still fragmented. "The reason he's been going at *you* my friend," said Frank savagely, "is because your skills are shite! I know you weren't infantry but an Army Cadet could show a better example of soldiering than you've done for the past day! You know less than a day one soldier in basic training. You'd better level with me now before it's too late. You were never in the Army at all were you?!"

Jim looked like he was going to cry, his face crumpled and he bit his bottom lip.

"Well?!" demanded Frank.

Jim bowed his head and shook it, "I'm….. I'm…." His voice was high pitched and he coughed to clear it, "I'm sorry Frank, I have a lot of respect for you…. Norrie too as it happens. I thought that I would fit in and learn. I was shit scared of getting found out. You're right, I tried the army but I never made it. I failed the medical three times, I'm colour blind, not completely, just can't sort out my blues and greens but it's enough to get rejected."

"Do you know what that means?" Frank had simmered down and spoke normally. "We are few enough in numbers as we are, but now we have a dead weight to drag around with us, in fact, as of this minute you're out Jim…"

"No! Frank, not that! I'll learn! You'll see, I *can* do it Frank, just give me a chance….Please!"

Frank pondered for a moment then said, "Get over there, get it out of your system then we'll see."

Jim looked puzzled for a second then smiled. He walked over to the "ring" where Norrie was waiting and threw the first punch. Norrie, agile as a whippet side stepped it, turned and as Jim twisted to face him landed a crunching blow in his face. Jim lost balance and fell over his nose now pouring blood, he shook his head and stood up, he held his fists like an old pug and once more moved into the waiting Norrie swinging his right hand at Norrie's face. Again Norrie side stepped and landed his fist in the pit of Jim's gut.

Jim doubled up winded and fell to his knees. Norrie knew that Jim was no match for him and went to walk out of the ring.

"Stay where you are ! You bastard!" yelled Jim. "Don't you walk away from me, you yellow scum!"

Norrie turned, a wry smile on his face. "Oh boy! You really are a dick head aren't you? Well come on then, off your knees." Jim got up and rushed at Norrie, he went to swing but stopped himself. Norrie side stepped a blow that never came and walked into a stinging left hand from Jim. Before the other could land Norrie danced back and away then went on the attack, a left to the face, a right to the gut, left to the head right to the gut, finally Jim fell back on his behind, winded and shaken.

Frank stepped in, "Okay! The shows over. You two, clean up, the rest carry on sorting the kit out."

Jim went to walk out with Norrie, as he did so he passed Frank and gave a meaningful look with his bruised and battered face, Frank nodded, "Okay! You've got a stay of execution.. but only for twenty four hours, if we've got that long."

"That was pretty pointless wasn't it? Getting two men to half kill each other just before an operation." It was Julian a smarmy look on his face.

"You don't get it, do you Julian? If it hadn't been settled here, we would have had a festering abscess in our midst ready to explode at any minute. I've seen men snap, it's bad enough at any time but when they've got access to weapons and ammunition you've got a big, big problem."

Julian sneered and walked away.

Norrie got to the pump at the side of the house first, gave a half dozen yanks on the handle and sloshed some water over his face and arms which were dashed with blood, mostly Jim's.

Jim came up, he said nothing but waited for Norrie to finish. He then stuck his head under the pump and tried to yank the handle at the same time, it was awkward and hardly any water came out. He was about to stand up and figure out a new way to do it when Norrie started pumping it for him, Jim shot him a glance and then started to sluice the water over himself.

"Always fire single shots if you can instead of long bursts!" Explained Norrie. "Aimed, single shots are more accurate and you conserve ammunition, but if you are in the shit and need to lay down a heavy weight of fire then by all means use longer bursts and remember, no Gung Ho firing from the hip stuff, always aimed shots or bursts! And Jim, don't forget to change mags, twice I've seen you drop the hammer on an empty chamber!"

Julian had taken them a few kilometres from the house to a hilly area to practise firing their rifles with live ammunition. Norrie had chosen a long valley that was wide enough for six men abreast to advance up. As they trod their way warily up the twisting, stone and tree strewn paths Norrie who was a few paces behind would fire a few shots in the air to signal that they were under fire. Once they had taken cover he would indicate a target such as a prominent boulder to them so they could fire and manoeuvre their way toward it.

They had done this a half dozen times and were coming to the head of the valley, this time Norrie would give them something else to think about.

He called Frank over and said a few words to him, Frank then disappeared up the rocky valley.

Frank, unseen by the rest climbed further up the valley until he was about a hundred metres ahead and above the resting men. He found a split in a huge boulder from which he had a panoramic view of the valley below and took up a good position. He didn't have long to wait, he saw Jim first dodging and weaving toward him, moving expertly from cover to cover, he had knuckled down and had worked hard all morning.

Next came Riff then Julian and Nick. Finally, Norrie appeared bringing up the rear. Frank took careful aim at a point just above Julian's head and let rip with ten single but quickly fired shots, he then peppered single shots over all the places where he had seen them taking cover .

This put a whole new slant on things, every time someone stuck their head up to try and locate the "enemy" Frank would put a couple of shots over it. They seemed at stalemate, confused, static and afraid to move. Then all at once Norrie was among them, "Come on! Up! Up! Get your fire and manoeuvre working! Riff took the initiative, he loosed off a couple of shots then shouted to his partner,

"Julian ! Move it !"

Slowly they got the ball rolling and worked their way towards Frank's position. He had long since disappeared further up to another vantage point.

They repeated this type of exercise twice more before Norrie called a halt. Frank had reached the head of the valley with nowhere else to run. They all gathered together totally exhausted and all drank heavily from their third and last water bottles.

Norrie lit up two cigarettes and offered one to Nick. They were all in good spirits, they had all worked hard and at last each man felt as if he had achieved something, getting fitter and working as a team. Frank had partnered up with Jim, Riff with Julian and Norrie with Nick.

They walked back down the valley relaxed and chatting until they reached the truck. Frank and Norrie walked over to Julian, he seemed to be in some difficulty but straightened up when they approached. "That's as much as we can do Julian," Frank said, "We're as ready as we'll ever be, its now over to you."

Julian nodded, he looked yellow and seemed to be fighting some pain. Probably the exertion Frank thought, for once he didn't come back with a rude or surly remark. "Very well, tonight after supper I'll let everyone know what's happening." He lurched off to the other side of the truck.

Frank stood every man down when they got back at mid afternoon and all without exception sluiced off at the pump then fell into a weary doze. Nick who had been appointed chef in the absence of Albert and his son roused himself at sundown and started cooking each man a huge steak.

The smell of the frying onions woke most and they were all seated and waiting long before the meal was ready. The only man missing was Lou the Chopper pilot although his craft was still tethered outside.

When the meal had finished, Julian who had scarcely eaten a thing stood and announced, "Gentlemen, the time has come for me to tell you what all this is about. I will give you the general outline tonight and tomorrow Frank will give us a detailed brief on the conduct of the Operation." He paused and looked around the table, all were quiet and expectant, "Follow me, Gentlemen!"

Julian rose and they all stood and followed him out to the barn, instead of entering through the usual door Julian unlocked another at the end of the building. They filed into a square room with a space in the middle of the floor covered with a large white sheet covering something uneven on the floor. He ushered them to chairs that surrounded the sheet and when they were all seated he began in a halting unsteady way as if part of him was still unwilling to let go of the information he had kept to himself for so long.

"A few years ago, I was stationed at a camp in the centre of Karuda not far from the Capital City of Laka.

Unbeknown to me a few unscrupulous Officers and men under my command looted and hid in the camp where I was, a fortune in gold, US Dollars and precious stones." There was a slight murmur from the team, Julian paused until it went quiet again. "Our job is to go in and get it, bring it back here, divi it up and go our separate ways."

"We can't just go waltzing through customs with bars of gold and bags full of diamonds Julian." said Nick.

"Believe me, there is enough cash dollars involved to make us all happy and further to that I will buy each of you out of your share of gold etc with Stirling or cash equivalent, I can have it transferred to a bank in the UK wherever..."

"Yeh, Okay, but what if you get knocked off ?" Threw in Norrie, "What then?" A murmur rose from the group.

"Well my dear friend, you'll just have to keep me alive won't you? Look, up to now this is a totally secure Operation. You were all moaning because I was tight lipped about the whole thing..."

"What about Lou the pilot?" asked Frank, "And by the way, where is he?"

Julian answered the first part of the question with, "He too, was kept in the dark."

"What's the split?" challenged Jim, his bruised face a mask of concentration.

"The split?"

"Yeh! the split, even Stevens or what?"

"I said to Nick that it would be split.... Twenty per cent to you..."

"You must be fuckin' joking Julian," shouted Norrie.

"I ain't riskin' my skin for twenty per cent of fuck all!" chimed in Jim.

"But even if this haul is half of what I was told it was, twenty will be more than enough.." blurted Julian, angry and confused by the tide of unrest and aggression.

"Julian." It was Frank, he stood up and fixed Julian with a serious look. "We know that you've had expenses and risk, and no-one would expect you to take an equal share but twenty is not enough for the risk we're taking, entering a foreign country, a police state with a relatively alert Army…."

"Very well! Very well!" shouted Julian irritably. His eye started twitching, his arm and shoulder jumped spasmodically. "You.. t…t…take Fif.. Fifty percent and that's my f.. Final offer!"

"Yeh! But we still don't know what we're getting fifty percent of do we?!" insisted Jim. Julian looked drained, his face had become white, he tottered slightly and gripped the back of a chair, he seemed to be fighting for breath.

Nick stood up and made a motion with his arms, "Look!" he said, "It's been a long hectic day and we're all tired. Frank and Julian are going to have a lot to discuss and I'm sure the answers to all our questions and problems will be given tomorrow…. Frank?"

"Yes," said Frank standing up, "Julian, unless there is anything else to discuss I will stand the rest down."

"Yes, just you and I, that's all." He said wearily.

They all filed out except Frank and Julian. Julian seemed to recover somewhat but still looked pale. He flipped the sheet off the floor to reveal a model of a camp complete with perimeter fence, huts, roads, tracks and a parade square.

"Welcome to Camp Lagonda." He said dryly.

17

Two hours later Frank emerged from the room with Julian, the sky was clear and star filled, a couple of crickets called to each other. They set off for the house but were stopped by Norrie who loomed out of the shadows. "Frank, come and see this!" he said quietly but with a sense of urgency in his voice.

Without waiting for an answer he set off toward one of the shacks at the rear of the barn. When they reached the nearest one Frank could see Nick and Jim at the open door. Jim turned and said to Frank in a dramatic voice, "Please tell me we haven't in any way got to rely on that bastard!" He stood aside and Frank entered the shack.

Lying on his side snoring was Lou, he was still in his flying gear which was covered in vomit. A trail of thick mucous bonded his lips to the pillow and made little bubbles when he breathed out, the little room stank of sour booze, three empty bottles lay on the floor.

Frank picked up an empty bottle and sniffed, "It's Bourbon!" Shouted Jim, "And look here! There's a bleedin' suitcase full!" Jim had opened the lid of battered brown case to reveal a neat stack of "Old Grandad" Bourbon.

Frank gave a look to Julian who was at his side.

Julian gave a shrug. "So!? He's had a drink, what's the big deal? Don't tell me you're all teetotal!"

"This isn't exactly having a night cap before he turns in." It was Frank's turn to lay on the sarcasm. "He's a piss head, an alky. I've seen guys like him before. He's downed three bottles of spirits in what? A day and a half! Come on, where did you dig him up from?"

"Okay, he's got a drink problem, that's why I got him cheap! Do you think chopper pilots and choppers grow on bloody trees! When he's working he's dry.."

"I presume," intervened Nick in his casual manner, "that this guy is to be our *taxi* driver to get us in and out of Karuda?"

Julian said nothing and after a moment turned on his heel and walked away.

Frank went to shout something after him but changed his mind and turned back to the others. "Jim, Norrie, put him in a coma position. Nick let's get this booze out of here."

"Frank, what's the score mate?" asked Jim with an edge to his voice.

"We'll sleep on it, okay, now come on, move it!"

They assembled for breakfast just after sun up. Lou was still absent. Frank had checked on him, he hadn't moved an inch from the position they had left him in the night before. The atmosphere was taught. Frank had tried to talk to Julian after he had left the scene but there was no answer from behind his locked door. He appeared, looking ill and sheepish at breakfast.

As they sat and drank coffee Frank began. "Someone last night asked if Lou was to be our ..*Taxi driver* in this operation. Well the answer to that is yes, he is an

integral part...Our lives will depend on a fucking alky."
He paused and looked around the faces at the table one
by one before he carried on.

"I, for one am in favour of disbanding this team
and getting out of it now while we can."

"Wait!" intervened Julian, "You can't pull out now!
We've come a long way...You, yourself said that we are
ready..."

"We *are* ready Julian. We have fulfilled our part of
the bargain up till now. And then *you* import a fucking
drunk to take charge of our lives..."

The door to the dining room opened and Lou
came in, he looked washed and shaven, his long hair
sleeked back. He had changed his flying suit for a fresh
one and when he spoke his voice was steady.

"I heard what Frank was saying and because my
booze is gone I guess that you saw me sometime yesterday. You'd be right to pull the plug on me as your pilot. I'm a lush, that's why they kicked me outa Nam and
that's why they kicked me out of the Airforce over here,
but I'm a damn good pilot..."

"Yeh!" sneered Jim, "When yer fucking sober no
doubt! But how often's that?"

"I can control it! Yesterday was the first time a
drink had touched my lips for weeks. Honest, yesterday
was just a blow out. I *can* control it, but I guess it's up to
you."

"Okay," said Frank, "Julian, I am giving every man
here an option to drop out here and now..."

"But they could compromise those who wanted to
carry on with the Op." blustered Julian.

"Nevertheless, I am saying to you all, think about it carefully. Anyone who wants to back out now, can do so, and…they will get paid a fair wage for their time already spent.."

"I will up the percentage that the team gets to sixty percent!" shot Julian. "And to answer a question from last night, that will be sixty percent of something like two million pounds Sterling…. Guaranteed."

"And Lou comes out of your cut Julian?" asked Jim.

Julian hesitated and then said, "And Lou comes out of my cut."

"Then I'm in!"

There was a general nod of consent and agreement from the rest except Frank. Nick looked at him and said, "Well Frank? We're all in agreement…. Will you lead us?"

"The plan is simple, we move from here by Chopper to a landing zone or LZ twenty kilometres away from this camp." Frank pointed to the model of Camp Lagonda. "We move from the LZ to a point near the camp lay up and put the camp under surveillance for a couple of days, then if all's well we locate the haul and move it to an LZ, call in Lou and get flown back to here. We will study maps and discuss routes etc. a little later. The critical thing is time because on March the eighteenth there will be a ceremony at the camp. All the top brass and probably the President himself will be there. In the following days, from what we can gather, a whole Commando moves into the Camp so we've got to be in and out well before that lot takes place. It's the tenth today that gives us six clear days. For the rest of this day we check and pack our kit, eat and then rest. At 0300 tomorrow morning Lou will lift us out...Any questions?"

Harry Macmillan pushed his Morris Cowley up to thirty five miles per hour on the tarmac road that led into Laka. The engine purred and Harry felt strangely at ease. The sudden and dramatic appearance of Daryl and his team had shaken him badly at first. He had been certain that Daryl had come to kill him. When he had broken contact and threw his communication systems away he had become a loose end that needed tying up and Daryl he knew, was good at tying up loose ends.

In those moments when he was sure that he faced death Harry had felt a calmness that he never knew he possessed. His life had become worthless over the last few years, a slow rotting existence with only memories to ease the way. Then he had killed...No, he had made himself face up to it, and then he had *murdered,* a young innocent person just to prolong that rottenness. It was the most evil thing he had done in his life. Ironically Daryl had been more angry because he'd thrown a bloody radio away.

He would do this *one last job* for Daryl. If he pulled it off he thought, Daryl may still bump him off or he may end up on a smallholding in Salisbury or Bulawayo to spend his last years, he didn't care. Harry tried hard to re-generate his old fears and insecurities but he couldn't, he felt like a man sleep walking.

He parked the car and walked the last few yards to the tall brick building. A large ferocious stone eagle

stared down at him with BUREAU OF INTERNAL SE-
CURITY on a faded sign below it. Harry had on his best
white linen suit and Panama hat.

He went up to the sentry. After removing his hat
he said in his perfected doddering old fool manner "Er,
excuse me old man, I have an appointment with your
big chief...Colonel...Oh what's his blasted name?...Potts
or Potter.. something or other.. I made it by phone this
morning." The disinterested guard checked a list then
spoke briefly into a phone.

After some delay another soldier appeared and escorted the frail old gentleman to a waiting room. Harry
missed nothing. Even though most of the offices were
behind closed doors he heard the clatter of a typing
pool from one, the hum of a conference from another.

The fact that no-one wore side arms inside the
building, that all the corridors were freshly painted and
those police he saw all had good quality, well fitting uniforms gave the impression that this was a secure, well
budgeted, efficient organisation.

The minutes ticked away. Harry sat patiently staring at the plain white emulsion wall in front of him, his
hands resting on the silver handled walking cane that
had been presented to him an age before. After twenty
minutes a female police officer arrived and beckoned
to him, he stood stiffly and tottered along the corridor
after her.

She paused at a door and knocked before entering half way through then turned and ushered Harry
into a large office. Harry entered exaggerating the effected limp even more. He came to a desk behind which

sat a white officer with the insignia of a full Colonel on his resplendent black uniform. However, the face in the uniform was far from resplendent thought Harry who at once took in the weak chin and look of sheer arrogance on the face that was somehow callow and yet had born the brunt of some hard knocks.

He knew a little about Colonel Terrence Potter of course. Local gossip and scratching around in the right places had given Harry a fair idea of what he was up against. The face fitted his mental picture of Potter. He saw at his side and slightly bending over the desk a black, strikingly beautiful woman with perfect almond shaped eyes. This, he thought would be his new wife Tula, now a Major and assistant to Potter.

The escort at Harry's side simply stated, "Colonel Harro Maxmillon, MC, Sir." and left the room.

"Er...Harry Macmillan actually Sir." said Harry smiling and offering his hand. Harry received a limp hand shake and an enquiring look.

Before he could continue, Tula spoke sharply. "The Colonel is a busy man and can spare you only a short time." Harry acknowledged her with a nod and a smile then turned his attention to Tex.

"It's about the reopening of Camp Lagonda Sir. We, er.. that is the club that I belong to are quite interested in this and would like to be there at the opening ceremony." He paused and changed his stick from one hand to the other, a slight grimace on his face as if trying to relieve some pain.

"You see, quite a few of us were at Lagonda in the good old days of the Karudan African Rifles of which I was pleased to be prominent member just after World War Two. And may I say, what a very fine Regiment they were," he paused and saw the look of boredom creep unfettered over Tex's face. Good, he thought and continued.

"You see Sir, I thought it would be quite fitting if some of the old Guard, as it were, was there on the day that it's re- christened, sort of old and new, that sort of thing." Harry trailed off and stood expectantly.

"How did you know about the ceremony?" shot Tex sitting back in the chair his hands clasped behind his head.

"Oh! Ahem!" spluttered Harry, "Excuse me, damn chest infection, can't shake it orf! The ceremony? Quite common knowledge actually sir...."

"How many is there of you?"

"Oh!...Around fifteen I suppose..."

"And you want to watch the ceremony?"

"Well yes, or take part if yer like.... You know, march past with the old banners, that sort of thing.."

"Well, I don't know about marching past and I'll have to check on whether we can allow you lot to be there at all.."

"Just one thing sir, the date is the nineteenth of this month, is it not sir?" Harry fumbled with a small pocket diary and pencil.

"Ha!" laughed Tex contemptuously, "You are really losing it Grandad. Turn up on the nineteenth and it will all be over! It's the eighteenth."

"Oh my God ! Thank you for that!"

Now, if that's all..."

"Yes, yes...Thank you er.. Colonel." Harry turned to go but paused and asked, "Just one other thing Sir."

"Yeh, what is it?"

"If we can't actually be given permission to be in the camp, we could be on the route to wave little flags at the President as he passes. A lot of people would turn out for that."

Tex thought for a few seconds, the President and Paul would like that. There would be a send off as usual on the streets outside of the Palace with hundreds of cheering people, the Bureau would see to that, using off duty soldiers and all the people they could coerce in the immediate vicinity, but having a group en route cheering would be novel...And white people at that. It would be a feather in his cap, the more he thought about it the more he warmed to it.

"How many people did you say you could turn out? For the flag waving bit."

"Oh! Let me think, there would be the Andersons, the Fitzgeralds and their guests and family, the P..."

"Just roughly how many?" Demanded Tex impatiently.

"A round figure would be fifty I suppose.... We could get even more.."

"Okay Grandad, you're on! You get as many as you can to be at the gates of Lagonda.."

"At the gates?!" Oh deary me." Harry looked crestfallen.

"Yeh! Whatsamatta with that?" Tex's mouth hung open.

"Well you see, it's nothing really but in Fifty Two, a mine took out a truck just outside of those gates. Ten killed, awful mess, a lot of our comrades were among them. You've been in war sir, you know what it's like, unpleasant memories and all that...Look, I was thinking, we could be literally en route, you know a total surprise for the old boy as he comes past, some of us have even got our old uniforms and...."

"Yeh, yeh," said Tex irritably, he walked to a table where, what looked to be a map was spread out. Tex studied it for a few seconds and Tula who had remained in the background, dutifully moved an ash tray and other objects off it so Tex could see it better. "Have your crowd then, at the Mangini crossroads at ten sharp on the eighteenth."

"The Mangini crossroads?" queried Harry in his croaky, faltering voice.

"Oh for fucks sake! Don't tell me you been here since Nineteen plonk and don't know the Mangini Crossroads.. Jeesus!"

"They.... They change so many names maybe I do know it but..."

"Look here!" Commanded Tex and pointed to the large sheet on the table. Harry hobbled over looking very sheepish as he put on some gold rimmed spectacles. He saw at once that it wasn't a conventional Ordnance Survey map but a very good quality hand drawn one on a scale much larger than normal.

"Here! This is the Mangini Crossroad. The President and the Field Marshal will be travelling along this route from the City and will turn in toward Lagonda at the Crossroad. It will be an ideal spot, you'd better get as many people as you can there."

"Which side of the car will the President be in? Wouldn't do to be all waving on the side the Field Martial is on, all due respect to him of course sir, but you know what I mean.."

"Look! They'll be in separate cars with separate timings. Besides, can't you use what grey matter you've got left and get the crowd on both sides of the road?" He looked at Tula and raised his eyes to heaven.

She immediately broke in taking Harry by the arm. "You must go now! The Colonel has already given you too much time."

Tula handed Harry to the escort outside of the door and looked at Tex who burst out laughing, "What a stupid old bastard!" He chortled.

Harry burst into his bungalow and strode into the living room where Daryl and Stone Face sat. Daryl was not alarmed his sentries had already alerted him to Harry's return.

"A map quick!" Said Harry putting on his spectacles. Daryl quickly pulled a map from his pack and spread it on the coffee table. Harry knelt down and orientated himself with it. Using a grease pencil he marked the map and spoke clearly and concisely. "Confirmed, the eighteenth of this month, this route here! From the City, through the Mangini Crossroads and on through this way to Lagonda. There is no obvious guard actually on the route but in depth apparently. Lining most of the route they have standing patrols, here, here, here, and here!" Harry quickly drew tactical signs on the map.

"Thank God who ever made the map I saw was trained by us. I understood all the symbols. There is a platoon here, and a headquarters set up of some kind here, possibly to control the whole lot, plus something near the old airfield, but it was just out of my peripheral vision so I can't be sure, maybe another Platoon of soldiers. They will travel separately, Vander first no doubt.

Daryl studied the marked map, he was impressed with the amount of detail that Harry had procured. "This is almost too good to be true Harry, it confirms exactly the info I already have."

"You mean you sent me there when you already had that information?"

"Must have confirmation old boy, how did you get it? Break into Bureau Headquarters or something?"

Harry made an irritable "Huh!" before turning away. He could hardly believe it himself how easily that arrogant pup Potter had given him the precise information he had wanted. He had hoped for a date confirmation for the opening ceremony or a pointer to what route they were taking but to be shown the actual map that it was all planned on was unbelievable.

Harry felt his old self again, he seemed to have shed fifteen years. He poured himself a Scotch and returned to where Daryl was still studying the map. "What are you going to do, knock the bugger off?"

Daryl said nothing at first then looked up, "Pour me one of those would you." Harry nodded and a few moments later returned with a tumbler and handed it to him.

"Look Daryl, what ever you are planning, that oaf Potter in the Bureau will get suspicious when yours truly doesn't turn up with thousands of flag waving ex Pats at Mangini Crossroads."

Daryl looked confused for a second then put two and two together, "Ha! You conned Potter into seeing his operational map! Jesus Harry, you're a bloody star! An absolute marvel!" Harry looked a little embarrassed at the sudden gush of genuine praise, even Stone Face smiled a little and put his hands together in a slow, silent clap.

"Don't worry Harry when my job is complete, you'll come back with us.."

"What is the job Daryl?"

"Come on Harry, the less you know, the better it is for all concerned."

"Is it Vander or the President?" persisted Harry. Daryl sighed and said simply,

"Vander."

18

Five men sat silently in the back of the Huey Chopper. The thump of the rotors and noise of the engine made any conversation impossible, not that any of them would find much to say. Each was lost in his own thoughts about the Operation.

After preparing their kit the evening before Frank had put them all on enforced rest, none had been able to sleep properly. Jim had lain awake fighting battle after battle, imagining what it was like to see a man disintegrate in front of him after being hit with a shower of high velocity bullets.

Riff thought of his family. His mother thought he was taking a hiking trip in Europe. His wife and small son probably didn't even know he was out of the country. Their separation had been quick and deep, he had travelled south from Birmingham to find work and she had returned to Northern Ireland. He felt sad at not doing more for his boy and promised himself that if he became rich after this he would make amends.

Nick thought of Anne but only fleetingly, it hurt too much. Nick was no coward, but wished that he was back in England with her and a small family. He blamed himself for their break up and wished he had worked harder at their relationship.

For the hundredth time Norrie wondered how Brad North had died after he and Frank had "visited"

him. Did the crow bar crush something in his throat?
Or did his heart just give up with the shock and fear. He
was curious to know if he was a wanted man in Britain,
his face on police posters, the army he knew would certainly be looking for him.

Julian tried to focus on getting the riches buried in
the old CO's garden but as usual the thought of all those
riches was pushed aside by the image of Paul Vander
laughing at him and saying over and over, *You stupid bastard, I got the better of you and now you are going to prison!*

The dream had come back to him when he at last
had dozed, being chased through the dark corridors of
Laka prison, unable to get his legs to work properly, feeling hands groping for him. The stench of warm breath
on the back of his neck, black men sniggering as they at
last caught him, then Vander had appeared, urging and
egging them on as they tore his clothes off. Vander had
lunged at his groin with the knife and he had woken
covered in sweat his body aching.

Frank sat next to Lou who was flying the craft fast
and low through the darkness, he looked at his watch,
they had been flying now for fifteen minutes. According
to Lou it would take twenty five minutes in all to get to
the LZ. When they had boarded the chopper Julian had
gone for the seat next to Lou but Frank had stopped
him, "It's my show now Julian." he had said.

Frank was more worried about Lou than anything
else. He would be left back at the farm by himself, they
had hidden the bourbon but a determined man could
overcome a small thing like getting a drink. Lou was to
keep a listening watch on the radio for a call to come

and extract them. It could be anything from one to five days. Would he keep off the drink for that long? All it would take was one little sip and it would sound a death knell for all of them.

He had confronted Lou with his misgivings as he had prepared the chopper just before take off. Lou had assured him that he would keep off the bottle. "Hell! I wanna be rich and die old like everyone else!" He had blurted.

The first few streaks of dawn lit up the panorama below them, they could make out stunted trees dotted over the rock and boulder strewn plain, then they flew down valleys with steep sides and for a time flew over lush jungle canopy with rivers like silvery, green snakes meandering through it.

Lou's voice crackled in Frank's ear piece, "That's the valley you're after, it's right on the nose now." Frank could see a steep ridge line in front of him and straight ahead a narrow gap in it.

"That looks a bit small Lou."

"Bin up smaller than that.. Wanna change you're mind?"

"No! But let's have a closer look!" The gap didn't get much bigger then all of a sudden they were passing through it. Lou banked the chopper steeply to take the almost right angled bend just after the entrance, the sides of the valley closed right in as they flew deeper into the range, then Lou raised the nose of the chopper and came to a hover.

"That's it skipper! There's your L Zee. Good luck and don't worry eh?!"

Frank didn't reply, he ripped off the headset and opened the door. As he felt the skids making contact with the ground, he leapt out and saw that the others were doing the same, he grabbed his Bergen rucksack off Norrie. They ducked the swirling blades and ran clear of the chopper. Frank counted five others each with a Bergen and rifle then gave a thumbs up to Lou who immediately lifted the chopper and continued up the valley until they could no longer hear him.

Frank saw that the team were in all round defence just as they had practised. He wrapped his knuckle on the butt off his rifle to gain attention and then made a signal for them all to move off. He led them in single file at a fairly fast rate up the valley. He wanted to get away from the LZ as soon as possible just in case they had been seen or heard.

"Frank! Frank! It's Julian!" whispered Riff loudly between gulping in huge lungs full of air. They had been slogging now for fifteen minutes and had just about reached the head of the valley. As Frank had slowed to negotiate a large boulder in his path Riff had caught up with him and told him about Julian.

Frank made his way back down the narrow path. He saw Nick and Norrie around Julian who was sitting propped up by his Bergen, his rifle lay unattended on the ground near him. Julian looked ghastly, his face although streaming with sweat was ashen white, as he fought for breath he was overcome with coughing fits.

Nick turned to Frank, "I suggest we rest here old boy, he looks in a bad way."

"What is it?" enquired Frank.

"Haven't a clue, saw him go the same way on one of our training days back at the ranch, he recovered quickly though, maybe asthma or something.

"That's all we friggin' need! A fucking cripple to hump around!" sneered Jim.

"Just shut it!" snapped Frank, "Look at all of you! Norrie, get them in all round defence! What are you doing just standing there gawping?! Move it!" He knelt by Julian who had stopped coughing and was breathing normal if a little hoarsely.

"Julian, what is it? What's wrong?"

"Just got too hot, it effects me badly, just give me a minute."

"I can give you a minute this time Julian, but next time there may not be a minute to give.... If you start to go down again let someone know quicker so we can maybe do something about it. We're nearly at the top now, once there we can rest properly." Julian nodded and with an effort got to his feet.

"Camp Lagonda is eighteen kilometres that way as the crow flies." Frank extended his arm. They all automatically looked in that direction across the seemingly endless plain.

"We will move off from here at last light and try to reach the high ground by Lagonda before sun up." Frank finished talking and put his map and compass away. He looked at Julian who seemed back to normal. They were in a boulder covered shallow hole at the top of the ridge, each man was on alert crouching, rifle in hand, Bergen off and at their sides.

"Okay, we will have one sentry the rest of us sleep, eat, whatever but there is to be no cooking and no movement, we all stay put. Norrie, organise the stag list, one hour each on sentry, I will go first."

"How long will it take us tonight Frank?" Jim asked.

"If all goes well, maybe five hours max."

"Wouldn't it be easier to move in daylight, there's nobody around, it's bloody deserted!" Jim persisted.

"It's tempting but we can't take the risk."

Norrie came up and reported that he'd organised the stag list, then he and Jim crawled away. Frank opened his Bergen and from the top took a green coloured compact radio. He assembled the collapsible antenna and clipped it to the set. After checking his watch he switched it on, immediately the hiss of white noise emanated from the telephone shaped handset. He adjusted it until it was just audible then spoke in a clear, concise, yet quiet voice.

"Hello Old Grandad, hello Old Grandad, this is Heron, radio check over." When choosing what call signs they would use, Frank had chosen Lou's by the brand of his bourbon and his own by the pub in which he did the initial interviews.

There was a delay of a few seconds then Lou's unmistakable drawl cut through the ether. "Old Grandad hearing you good, over."

A relieved Frank replied, "All is okay this end... Out." He paused for a moment then switched the set off to conserve the battery. Unless there was an emergency he would only test the communications twice a day, once in the morning and at night.

Frank looked at his watch, a half hour to go then he would wake Riff. Already he could hear a small chorus of soft snoring in the hollow behind him.

Daryl sat hunched over his map that was spread over the kitchen table. Harry's bungalow was looking somewhat tidier since Daryl had his men re-arrange things. Harry loafed on the settee, he now accepted the presence of Daryl and his men. He reckoned that Daryl had at least three others with him, but suspected there were many more nearby watching approaches to the house and briefed to keep out of Harry's sight. He didn't mind, he would have done it the same way himself.

Stone Face came in and beckoned to Daryl who rose and followed him out to the garden shed. The work surface in the shed had been cleared and a large radio had been set up on it. Stone Face closed the door then spoke in low tones to Daryl.

"Pern and his men were dropped off at first light this morning, here in this valley leading up to Kangi Ridge," he pointed to a position on his map circled in red grease pencil. "The last thing heard was that they were all okay."

"First light? Six hours ago? They could be half way to anywhere by now."

"That's if they'll risk moving by daylight."

"That's the problem, we know nothing of the make up of the team, except for Pern and the fact that they have a black guy with them. They should have listened to me and had them pulled in on some pretext at Salisbury so we could at least get a good look at them. Anyway, that's bygones. If they are professional they will lie up till nightfall before moving, let's work on *that* assumption...And if they *are* some sloppy amateurs they'll tip their hand soon enough.

"Have you thought about what their objective is?"

"My guess is an assassination attempt on Vander, there could be no other reason why Pern would risk his life to re-enter Karuda."

"I still think our friend the pilot knows more but is holding out." said Stone Face putting his map away.

"Well, that could be true, but he says that Pern only told him enough information so that he could carry out a job of dropping them off and picking them up."

"Offer him more money, that's what bastards like him thrive on isn't it?"

"I've tried, he's a strange bird to deal with, can be very stubborn. At the moment I am quite happy that he keeps tabs on them for us. We have till the eighteenth before Van De Borgh and the President come on the scene and if we need to know more by then...Well, I'm sure we would be able to get it from him." Daryl gave a wry smile then returned to the bungalow.

Lou Bristow was bored. At first, being left alone at the farm had suited him. The presence of Pern and the others had rattled him, he had always deplored violence and violent people, that was mostly why he had hit the bottle in Vietnam.

He had flown mission after countless mission dropping troops off on to LZs that were often "hot," picking

up wounded, waiting patiently as they loaded the bloodied men, hearing the "tick, tick" of Viet Cong bullets as
they struck the hull of the chopper. On one occasion
his co-pilot had been decapitated with a heavy calibre
round, spraying him in bone and brains. Through all of
it he had kept his nerve earning him great respect.

Sleep however, would not come unless accompanied by dreams, they were mostly variations of the same
theme. He was always standing on the ground looking
at his Huey a short distance away, which was crammed
with writhing, screaming, wounded soldiers begging
him to take off as the battle continued to rage around
them. He could hear them but could not get his legs to
move toward the craft. He found that the dream did not
come during a booze induced sleep and that had been
the start.

He pondered his position again. After being Court
Martialled and busted for rendering himself unfit for
operational duty he had taken leave and ended up after
a while in Rhodesia where he joined the Air Force. They
had suspected him almost immediately and discharged
him before he could take to the sky.

He had come to the attention of Military Intelligence and under the guidance of Daryl had flown a
couple of covert missions over the border. It was clean,
easy and the pay was good. Lou had contacted Daryl after Pern had approached him. Daryl had instructed him
to play along and report back. When Lou found out that
there was a lot of money at stake he had regretted telling Daryl and now had to try and play it down, he had

omitted to tell Daryl everything, especially about Camp Lagonda and the money.

Lou had found his suitcase full of Bourbon hidden in the locked part of the barn where the model of Lagonda had been. He had broken in to see if he could learn more about the Operation but apart from the suitcase, the room had been cleared.

He tossed a bottle from one hand to the other then stood it on the table next to his bed.

19

Field Marshal Paul Vander sat alone at the huge teak table in the Conference room at the palace. He glanced at his watch, Tex was already ten minutes late. Paul was irritated. Ever since Tex had been appointed as head of the Bureau he had seemed to break away from Paul's influence, no longer did he seem to want the special protection that being bosom buddies with Paul had given him.

Paul knew that Tex had already abused his new found power to settle a few old scores with people that had crossed him. Then there was his wife Tula. The fact that Tex had not only forgiven her for what she had done against him but had married her, completely mystified Paul. Now it was apparent that *she* was the power and influence behind Tex. He rarely made a move, Paul was informed, without him at least talking it over with her.

Paul knew that Tula hated him almost as much as she hated Tex. She had tried to 'come on' to him once, the full works. She was beautiful and he had been tempted somewhat but had enjoyed the astonished look on her face when he had rebuffed her, much more than if he had taken her.

Oh! She was very careful at concealing her hate, saying the right things at the right time and the warm smile that never left her face.

Almost as soon as he realised that Tex was intending to marry Tula he had summoned the part Asian detective Inspector Kompe, whose integrity Paul trusted and told him to have a twenty four hour watch put on her. The matter is very delicate Paul had told him. Use only men you trust and be extremely careful. Paul had studied with great interest the reports that came in weekly.

The high oaken doors at the far end of the conference room opened with much creaking and Tex entered. He walked toward Paul his jackboots clomping down on the wooden floor and echoing in the empty chamber. He looked every inch like a Nazi officer, black uniform with silver insignia and a black leather Sam Browne complete with Luger pistol.

He smiled as he neared Paul and sat in the seat that Paul had pulled out for him.

"Sorry I'm late old man."

Paul was slightly amused at the affected British officer accent that Tex had seemed to acquire over the last month or two. He had also let it be known that he didn't want to be known as "Tex" any more but rather "Terry," not that many would call him by his first name. Those of equal or senior rank preferred to call him simply "Colonel." Paul, on principal, would continue to use the name he had always known him by. Tex's social life had been virtually non existent before he married Tula but she had tried slowly to change that, hence the name change and probably the accent too.

"That's okay Tex." said Paul with a dismissive gesture. "Did you manage to get anything?"

"Not really old man, the meeting was behind closed doors, four men with just the President and Tasi. All I know is that the meeting lasted about two hours and they drank a lot of whisky. There were no minutes taken and whenever my guy entered the room they all stopped talking. There was a large map pinned on the wall showing the Eastern part of the country and its border with Rhodesia and Zambia. My man recovered it after, there were no marks on it, it was clean. The delegation left the country about four hours ago destination unknown after spending the night here at the Palace.

"Was anyone recognised?"

"Not as such, but they weren't Karudans...Sorry but that's all I've got old man."

"What are your thoughts on this Tex?"

"My thoughts? Neither here or there, he gets visitors all the time: black, white, Chinese, Russian, Yanks, the lot, what's so different about this lot?"

Paul stood up, turned and walked a few paces across the room. Tex's indifferent, cocky manner of speaking irritated him more than they ever had.

"Very well Tex, thanks for coming.... How are things shaping up for the re opening of Lagonda?"

"Oh! Lagonda? Done and dusted, security on the route and in the camp.."

"Good, I'd like to check them over sometime, the arrangements that is."

"Oh! Sure thing. I'll get them over to you.."

"I'd like to go through them with *you*, personally Tex."

"Yeh! Yeh, no problem….. I'll give you a call then old man." Tex looked awkward and embarrassed for a second then stood up. "Well, if that's all…"

"Yes, and thank you again."

Paul watched Tex clomping to the large doors, they creaked open and he disappeared. So that was that, thought Paul with a little bitterness and anger. Tex had failed to get any information and had not even batted an eyelid when saying so. He mused for a moment about what would have happened if Tex's predecessor Janka had given such a negative report in such a flippant manner to Juba.

Paul had given him two days warning that the meeting was to take place. Enough time to plant bugs have people followed, any manner of things to gain information but Tex had relied on a butler, now all he had was a map and the fact that the people at the meeting weren't Karudans. He involuntary bought his fist down hard on the huge table.

Paul knew that M'Punga had been very nervous about the meeting with these people. He tried to work out why he had not at least consulted him about it as he had done on many other occasions about all kinds of matters. M'Punga had completely blanked him out, adding to Paul's curiosity and apprehension.

Tex dismissed his chauffeur and walked the few steps to the front door of his luxury villa, he was happy to see one of his patrol cars pass by as he inserted the key. Music was playing loudly. As usual he went in search of Tula immediately. He always made sure that she finished well before him so that she could always be at home when he arrived.

He had implored her to give up work but she had insisted in carrying on and Tex had found that having her around at the office made things go so much easier.

"Tula! My Tulip! Where are you?" Sang Tex as he went from room to room. There was no answer. He turned the Hi Fi system off and shouted again, this time he heard an answer from upstairs. He bounded up them three at a time and barged through the half open bedroom door, there, kneeling on the bed with her bum in the air facing him was a semi naked Tula. Tex started to tear his uniform off but Tula stopped him.

"Come on!" she urged, "There isn't time for that, just open your flies."

They lay in each others arms. Sex always made Tex sleepy afterwards and he drifted in and out of wakefulness. Tula prised herself gently away from him and padded to the shower. Tex woke up, he was still in his uniform, he laughed and stripped off to join Tula.

Tex gave a final "Ooh!" and rolled off Tula. She lay there on the bed her hair still soaking wet.

"Terry baby, Tula's gonna have to shower again." she said with a mock whine in her tone. He turned and stoked her pretty face.

"How did your meeting go with Paul?"

"Oh! You know…He's funny these days…."

"Funny?"

Mick Cotton

"Yeh, you know, *funny* as opposed to funny, ha ha."

"No, I don't understand."

Tex, sat up in the bed. "You know he's never the most talkative of people at the best of times but he phones me up and says he wants a meeting listened in to! What am I s'posed to do? It's in the Palace for a start and M'Punga himself is chairing it, if I got caught at that, he'd have my balls!"

"You didn't do as he bid then?"

"Not really, how could I?"

"You should have come to me."

"He wanted it close to the chest, you know, in strictest confidence and all that."

"Who was at the meeting?"

"Well that's it! No fucker knows...Only M'Punga and Tasi and they're not gonna come out and tell me are they?"

"Be careful of that pig devil darling."

Tex winced, he hated her calling Paul that. He knew she hated and mistrusted him but had implored her to keep her feelings to herself.

"Oh! Tula baby, don't go on so! He's alright, just different that's all."

"I know he is your friend, but he is cold like a lizard..."

"Tula! I'm not getting dragged down this road again, drop it!"

Tula sighed and went back to the shower. Tex lay there and drifted, he saw himself and Paul in Camp Lagonda, raw recruits against the system. Paul smashing his fist into his face, then inexplicably the next day, going out of his way to help him. The formidable Staff Sergeant Reeves, bellowing, threatening, mad staring eyes and flecks of foam on his lips, the ride to the palace in the ambulance with Pern, his own imprisonment when things had started to go wrong. Tula lashing at him with a pistol as he writhed, tied to a steel chair. This last image made him sit up, his heart thumping.

Tula was at the mirror a towel wound round her head a dark moody look on her face. Here we go, thought Tex, every time Paul comes into the conversation, it ends up with her not speaking.

She looked in the mirror at Tex staring at her. "You had better get changed," she said sharply, "We are due at the Palace tonight.."

"Oh Jeez!" cried out Tex, "Do we have to?!"

Tula widened her beautiful almond eyes and shrieked, "Yes! We damn well do! You have known for weeks. It's the President's wife, she's having a party to show off her new jewellery…"

"Which wife?" said Tex sarcastically.

"That's just the kind of thing that will get you shot one day!" Screamed Tula. "And I'm liable to get dragged out in front of the firing squad with you!" She turned and threw her hair brush with all her might at Tex who just managed to roll out of the way in time. "You should watch your big mouth! You.. You.." Tula broke into a language that Tex didn't understand and grabbed a china vase ready to throw it.

Tex leapt from the bed his hands up in complete surrender. "Tula! Okay, okay, calm down love, I'm getting ready!"

Tex was bored. He had been at the party for more than an hour now. Following Tula's instructions he had only one drink to be sociable and for twenty minutes had been nursing a near empty glass.

The plush room was full of chattering black women, grouping around the President's wife Lara who was dripping with diamonds and other precious stones. A few other men were in attendance but Tex found it almost impossible to strike up a conversation with them, they either politely avoided him or dried up with nervousness the minute he started to chat.

Tula had been talking with Lara for some minutes now, gushing and attentive, she now pulled away and closed up to Tex. "Terrence darling," she said loudly in a false, warm manner, "I'll be gone for a little while. Lara wants me to appraise some clothes and things in her apartments."

"Tula, please love, don't be too long." whined Tex. Tula kissed her finger and placed it on Tex's lips. He watched her drift out of the room.

Tula walked down the corridor with determination in her step. She came to the bottom of a narrow staircase with an armed, uniformed man at the bottom. She gave him an arrogant glare and swished past him. At the top of the stairs she came to a thick carpeted passageway with a large oak door at the side and waited. After a few seconds it was opened by Jokko, their eyes locked for a moment and she stood there while he ran a metal detector over her. When he had finished he stood back, no words were exchanged. She carried on through another door, closing it behind her.

Prince Tasi was excited. Ever since he had been informed that Eva had entered the Palace, he knew it would just be a matter of time before she made her way to him. This would be their third secret meeting and he could hardly wait. He stood naked in front of the mirror and sucked in his burgeoning belly. It doesn't matter, he thought, after all she said she found it very, very sexy.

He snorted a line of white powder from the top of his dressing table and grinned as the red warning light in the ceiling clicked on and off. Seconds later his bedroom door opened and she stood there.

"Eva! Eva my darling come to me!" he pleaded with outstretched arms. She said nothing but kept a fixed arrogant stare on him as she stepped out of her clothes to her underwear. "Please Eva, come to your Prince." he again pleaded. She ignored him and went to the large bed. "No!" shouted Tasi, "In here first you bitch!" He ran to her, and pinioning her arms behind her back frog marched her to the bathroom ranting about all the things that he was going to do to her.

"You seem so busy these days my Prince," she whispered as she stroked his hair. "So, so busy." Tasi lay on the bed with his head on her bosom.

"Yes, matters of state, one day I will be king and I need to.. Any way.." he trailed off. The session on the bed had lasted only a minute or so, but it had left him drained.

"My Prince, I tried to call you yesterday but they said you were in conference and couldn't be disturbed.."

"Yesterday?.. Oh some really boring people.. No, not just boring, but nasty and boring." he said sleepily.

"Well tell me about these nasty, boring people then my Prince." She urged gently.

20

After stumbling for what seemed the fiftieth time Frank began to think that maybe after all they should have moved by day. It was a moonless night, they had been on the march now for about an hour.

Getting down the scree slope from their lie up position to the plain had proved dangerous. It had looked quite simple during daylight, but when they tried to climb down it the whole thing seemed to move causing mini land slides as each man fought to keep his balance.

The plain was better but not much, stones from pebble to football size were everywhere causing them to trip and curse every few paces. To add to their misery they now come up against thorny scrub trees that they had to meander around carefully.

The weight they were carrying soon began to tell. Water and ammunition were priority loads and just happened to be the heaviest items of their kit. Frank had now slowed to a snail's pace in order to negotiate a safer route and to prevent someone lagging and getting left behind.

After another hour he called a rest, he urged them not to drink until they had cooled down a little. They all flopped in a circle. Norrie moved up to Frank.

"How's Julian?" whispered Frank.

"I've put him in front of me, he seems to sleep walk, wandering everywhere. I think he's knackered."

"And the others?"

"No problem."

"Good, we'll stop every fifteen minutes or so now that we've made good headway."

After ten more minutes they all struggled to their feet and with difficulty swung the bulging rucksacks back into position, once more they set off. The ground was more clearer now and there were not so many thorn bushes. They skirted through scattered hillocks and negotiated some shallow ravines that were basically dry river beds.

On and on they went through the dark night, each man losing his alertness slowly by degrees and reduced to just putting one foot in front of the other and keeping the man in front in sight. Jim actually slept for an indeterminate length of time and was smacked back to consciousness suddenly as he walked into the back of Riff who had stopped for a few seconds.

Then in the far distance they saw light, weak orange pinpricks on the horizon. Frank halted them and he, Julian and Nick studied them with their binoculars. After some minutes of whispered talks Frank called them all into the centre.

"Those lights we can see could well be our objective Camp Lagonda. By our reckoning it could be around ten kilometres away. Between us and the camp there is an airfield which we'll skirt around. We have just over three hours to first light by which time we need to be in position overlooking Lagonda. Take five minutes more rest here and when we set off, be on maximum alert."

Each man, as tired and stiff as he was watched the fiery rim of the sun rise in the East. They had been on the hill overlooking Lagonda for ten minutes now and had been feverishly preparing camouflaged shell scrapes for them to lie up during the day. They had arrived without incident the airfield they noticed as they passed had been deserted.

They would lie up on the side of the hill facing away from Lagonda. Frank and Julian had gone round the other side to find the best location to observe the Camp.

Frank dropped the binoculars from his eyes and inwardly marvelled how accurate Julian's model of Lagonda had been. They had a perfect view of the main gate, square, accommodation blocks and most importantly the house that Colonel Hennings had resided in.

"There you are Frank...It's all there for the taking, right there in the grounds of that house." It was the first time that Julian had ever used his first name and Frank was surprised that it sent a chill down his spine. "I'm very pleased actually," continued Julian, "they've flattened some buildings but old Hennings' house and grounds are still intact. It was a gamble you know whether or not the whole place had been torn down."

Frank focused onto the main gate, there was a red and white pole on a counter weight and a small sentry box manned by a single soldier. A few yards up the road from the gate was the guard room. The square had a few vehicles parked on it mainly trucks and a couple of Landrovers, a bulldozer and some small piles of what looked like building materials.

"You mean," replied Frank casually while still observing, "that there was a chance that this was all for nothing?"

"Everything's a chance Frank, this one was worth taking. How do you envisage getting the loot out?"

"Well, first things first Julian, let's find a way *in*, any suggestions?"

"Yes, if you come left from the main gate along the road some three hundred metres, you can just make out a rusting double gate almost overgrown with vegetation. It was an emergency exit, it looks as if it hasn't been maintained, it could be useful to us."

"How are you feeling now Julian?"

"Me? Couldn't be better old man.. I'm fine."

"Good, you can take the first stag here. Write all your observations down, they may come in useful later." With that, Frank eased himself back into cover and made his way back to the others.

Stone Face sat across the table from Daryl in Harry's Living room. Harry had gone into Laka to get some groceries. "How do you envisage getting to Vander without involving the President?"

"We now know that Vander will be travelling separately to Camp Lagonda around one hour before the President. M'Punga will have the main bodyguard leaving our friend Paul with hardly any cover for his trip to the camp, he will be relying on the standing patrols he has had positioned for his main security. That is the one and only opportunity we have got, it will still be very risky, our friend didn't get where he is today by acting like an idiot."

Daryl put on some rimless spectacles and looked again at his map, using a match he pointed to a spot on it that was ringed in red pencil.

"Here, is the only weak point in his journey, just as the main road leaves Laka and turns into a dirt road. There are no patrols assigned to that area, they probably think it's too near the city for any rebel activity, we will have to make our move there."

"And the old goat?" queried Stone Face.

Daryl didn't answer at first, he seemed to be mulling something over as he carefully folded his map away. "Harry Macmillan," he began slowly, "was routinely popping people off when you and I my friend, were still swimming around in a bag. He's still ruthless, and as I've told you before never underestimate him, never turn your back on him.."

"I'm sorry Sir, I meant…"

"Just don't underestimate *the old goat*…In answer to your question, he is coming with us as promised. Quite how I can justify this when we get him back I don't know yet. Only our department knows he exists but I'm sure I'll think of something."

Another soldier entered the living room, he was black and powerfully built.

"Another message from the yank Sir, Pern is in position overlooking Lagonda, since first light Sir."

Daryl nodded and the soldier disappeared. "Well, well, they moved quickly. It looks like they are going to chop him outside of the main gate. They've got a nerve, but I'll bet they don't know about all the patrols that will move into that area soon. I almost feel sorry for them."

At midday Frank woke everyone up and got them in a circle. Sleep had bought on stiffness and most felt drowsy. "Tonight," began Frank, "we find a way into Lagonda and set up a forward OP. From there we locate the goodies and decide how to get them out of the camp. We move off at last light…"

"Here we go again!" Jim sneered irritably, "Everything done in the dark. Why can't we move into Lagonda today while it's light? Move in an hour or something. By all accounts the place is like a graveyard.. ..Why not Frank?"

"Nick?" Asked Frank.

"Well, it *is* quiet, we could risk moving, cover's good, it's all green stuff down to the road and green stuff the other side in the camp. Crossing the road would be the only problem."

"Norrie?"

"Let's fucking go for it!"

"Okay, we move in an hour. Rucksacks will be stashed at the side of the road. From there we move to the camp in light order, ammo and water with only the food you can stuff in your pockets."

The move was done quickly, they found a track at the back of the hill and used it. It bought them around the front of the hill and parallel to the main road. They moved along it until they were opposite the rusted gate of the emergency exit, there, they stashed the rucksacks after quickly transferring what they needed to their belt order. The road was quiet, they had heard only one vehicle use it during the last hour.

"We will cross the road in a oner." hissed Frank. They gathered in a group and on Frank's signal dashed across into the lush cover the other side, it took a couple of seconds. In a pre arranged move Norrie went to the gate checked it then came back to Frank. "It's a hacksaw job, rusty padlock, the path the other side hasn't been used in years."

Riff fished about in his equipment and came up with a small hacksaw, Norrie snatched it and made his way back to the gate and hurriedly set to work.

Frank tried to peer through the chain link fence but could see nothing but dense green undergrowth. Norrie was back sweating, "Another blade! This uns broke!"

Riff once again dug into his equipment and came up with a blade. "Take it easy Noz," warned Riff, "That's the only one we got!"

"Well ye shoulda bought more shouldn't ya?!" snapped back Norrie.

"Okay! Let's just take it easy," urged Frank, "just slow it down!" Norrie grunted and moved back to the gate. After a couple of minutes they heard some grating as Norrie attempted to pull open the gates.

Riff and Nick went forward to help clear the debris, soon they had one side open enough for them to pass through.

They worked for a few minutes more to cover the ground disturbance, then carefully closed the gate and replaced the sawn through lock.

Very slowly, they made their way up the narrow, overgrown track. Branches hung over it in profusion. When they stopped for a moment Nick made his way to Frank.

"We're going to be pushed to get a vehicle down here old boy."

"I agree, get Julian up here, we're coming to the end of it." Through the trees about five metres away the vegetation finished and they could see the open spaces of the camp.

With Julian guiding, they moved slowly and with some difficulty through the thick vegetation and parallel to the fence until Julian stopped them and pointed. Frank looked across an open space into a clump of fir trees and made out the red tiled roof of a house.

"That's it!" said Julian, an edge to his voice, "That's Hennings' house."

"What's this?!" asked Harry, a frown on his weathered face. He was holding up a camouflaged smock and trousers that Daryl had just thrown to him.

"They're for you Harry, you're coming with us remember."

"Woe! Woe! Just hang on there a minute partner, coming with you I may be, but putting this stuff on? Never!"

"Look Harry, we've got business to take care of first which means we've got to go from here tomorrow, on foot for a few miles." Daryl had a slight plea in his voice.

"Daryl! You've got to be joking chum! There's no way, absolutely no way I'm trekking through any bloody Ulu for you or anyone and if it means that you've got to leave me behind, well so be it." Harry threw the clothes back at a dumbfounded Daryl and marched out of the room.

"Jesus jumping Christ!" raged Daryl.

"Tomorrow is the seventeenth Frank," whispered Nick, "We need to be well clear by the following day. If the President and Vander are going to be here on that date the place is liable to be crawling with security." He saw an impatient look flash across Frank's blackened face. "Sorry old man, I know that you are aware of that, but…"

"No, not at all Nick. At last light me and Julian go over and try to locate exactly where it's stashed and play it from there." A period of silence passed as the two men looked to their front across the open space to the house and grounds.

"Can you believe that we're here, doing this Nick? This time last year, we were…What *were* we doing?"

"Oh! March, probably on beat up training for Northern Ireland…God! Ulster seems like a million years ago, pity how it all ended. As old Ronnie Gittins would have said, *they done you up like a kipper Frank.*"

"Yeh! It still burns. It's just the thought of that bastard Orchard strutting about squeaky clean. He caused

Pinky's death you know, why couldn't you lot see through him? See the bastard for what he was…Sorry Nick, that was out of order."

"No! You're right of course." It was the first time the subject had ever come up between them and Nick had unleashed some feelings that he had pent up over the months.

"I could see that he was not quite right. Frank, I've always regretted that I didn't do more for you, you know. Talk is cheap and all that but looking back I think that all I was worried about was myself, ending *my* career with the army, trying to patch up *my* marriage.. I just couldn't see further than that."

"What's done is done Nick.. .. No regrets eh?"

"For what it's worth, Alan Briggs fought for you he thought a lot of you…I know it sounds like patronising crap, but he did. Wouldn't have Orchard back in his Company even though he and Orchard's father were big buddies way back."

"Yes, I liked old Briggs he was a good sort."

There was a rustle of dry leaves as Julian crawled up to them. "Ready when you are Frank." he whispered. "We need to locate the rockery."

"Okay, we'll give it a few minutes then go in the twilight."

They crossed the open area to the hedge that surrounded the house and carefully skirted it until they found a gap.

"Shit!" Cursed Frank, "It's occupied." Through the gap they could see the front of the house, there was a

Landrover parked in the driveway and they could hear music playing. As they watched a downstairs light was switched on and they heard a woman's shrill voice calling someone.

"Any idea where this rockery is?" asked Frank grimly.

"Over to the left of the house, there used to be a small shed next to it."

They moved in the direction that Julian had indicated, walking erect in the blanket of sudden darkness that had descended.

"This is it Frank, what's left of the shed is there!" Although Frank couldn't see where he was pointing he was aware that he was next to a small hillock of boulders and stones with various plants growing over them.

"Go and get the rest of them Julian." Ordered Frank. When Julian was swallowed up in the ink Frank tried to get a feel for the size of the rockery. He carefully climbed over, then round it. It was roughly the size and dimensions of two saloon cars parked side by side. Frank's mind raced, this could take for ever he thought. They would have to work slowly and quietly and they would have to use light, fortunately they were at the side of the house that had no windows to overlook them.

Julian came back wheezing, "They're here!" he gasped. Frank broke them up into their pairs and allocated them a start point, leaving one man to keep watch.

Jim and Norrie immediately set to work on a large flat stone that was almost upright like a tombstone and set into the bank, they couldn't budge it so set to work clearing the earth and roots from its sides.

Frank moved closer to the house and took a look through the un-curtained windows, he saw a large woman in her thirties doing something in what looked like the kitchen, he circled the house to look for phone lines.

Norrie got his hands around the back of the stone and heaved back with all his might but it didn't move, using their small digging tools, they dug deeper into the surrounding earth until using his shovel as a lever he was able to rock it slightly back and forth. Jim jammed his pick into the other side and in unison they heaved until the ground at last released the slab.

Pulling it forward they eased it to the ground and went back to the cavity to begin work on it. Jim carefully shone a light and at once let out a cry that froze them all to the spot. They gathered round and saw sticking out of the wall of earth that was behind the slab, a polythene bag tightly filled with wads of paper. Norrie scraped the dirt surrounding it and then eased it out. With his knife he slit the bag and fingered the slit open, "Bingo!" he exclaimed.

"Giz a look!" said Jim snatching the bag. Frank returned from his recce and in the light of someone's torch saw Jim's hands holding a large wad of US bills of one hundred Dollar denomination. "We've cracked it Frank! We've fucking cracked it mate, this lot alone would do us, just think about the rest!"

Frank too was mesmerised for a few seconds, there before him was the very thing that had motivated them all for the past weeks. Jim dug deeper in the bag and pulled out more, his face feverish with excitement.

Frank snapped out of it. "Just keep the noise down and get that light out! Put the money back in the bag, Norrie you control the light, Jim continue to dig....Carefully!"

It was soon evident that Hennings in his haste had emptied the Tea chests by the side of the rockery and piled more earth and stones on top of it leaving the big slab as a marker. One by one Jim retrieved more cash filled bags and then pulled out leather bags. Julian checked inside them and stated with no emotion "Diamonds." and when another was passed he simply said, "Emeralds."

As they were piling the loot Frank called Nick over. "The next thing is getting it out. I reckon we'll use that Landrover parked outside the house."

"Have you thought where we can go with it to wait for the chopper?" asked Nick.

Frank sighed. "To be honest, this has all come a bit quick, I never really thought that we'd get this far and that's the truth."

"What about the old airfield? It was deserted, and it would be easy for Lou to find quickly."

Frank was about to answer when he heard a gasp from the Diggers. They went over and Riff handed Frank a small oblong object that was heavy. "Gold!" He said hoarsely.

Frank checked out the Landrover in the drive. It had a canvas canopy, the doors were unlocked but there were no keys in it.

He got back to the rockery and saw the mound of loot. Riff was now digging and Julian holding the light.

"Can anyone hot wire that Landrover?" He asked. No-one responded.

"Norrie, Jim, there's no alternative, enter the house and get the keys."

"Don't you think we should wait Frank," interjected Nick.

"Wait? What for? We have what we've come for, now is the time to get out.."

"I agree!" threw in Julian.

"Look Frank," persisted Nick, "They're not exactly going to hand over those keys willingly and we're going to tip our hand to the fact that we exist and then we've lost half the battle."

"We were going have to break eggs somewhere along the line! We tie them up if necessary, that will give us a good few hours start..."

"Why not just waste 'em, that'll give us all the time we want." Jim threw in savagely.

"No unnecessary killing!" said Frank equally as savage, "In fact, I will go in myself, to ensure that!" He was angry now.

Norrie clapped him on the shoulder, "Frank, there's no problem, me and Jim'll handle it alright." With that Norrie led off and Jim started to follow him. As Frank turned away to speak to Nick, Julian stopped Jim and passed him two metal objects.

"Here, you might need these." he whispered. Jim took the cold metal objects and realised that they were the two silenced automatic pistols. He caught up with Norrie at the side of the house and handed him one, Norrie looked surprised for a second then shrugged his shoulders. Both men laid their rifles against the wall and Norrie proceeded carefully around the back of the house.

Music was still playing and most of the lights were on. Norrie looked back and whispered to Jim, "The woman will be the most trouble, we must try and get to the bloke first so's he can control her." Jim nodded, his heart was pounding with fear and excitement in equal measures, he gripped the pistol tightly and curved his finger around the trigger.

Norrie eased open the back door and slid inside. He found himself in a short hallway with the kitchen door on the right, he checked it out it was empty. With Jim following he checked the door on the left which was open. The music seemed to be coming from this room. He slowly moved his head until he could see most of the room. On an armchair with a newspaper lying on his chest snoozed the man.

As far as he could see there was no-one else in the room, the man was still in his uniform trousers with braces hanging down and a vest. Norrie moved quickly, simultaneously he clamped his hand over his mouth and jammed the pistol against the bridge of his nose. The man woke violently at first trying to push Norrie off, then after a couple of seconds realised the predicament he was in and slumped.

Slowly, Norrie took the pressure off the man's mouth. His eyes were wide with fear. "Do you understand English?!" He whispered urgently. The man nodded and managed a "Yes".

"Where is your wife?"

"She upstairs, please, what do you want?" whimpered the man.

"I want you to call your wife down and when she arrives you are to keep her quiet, we want your Landrover keys…"

"Here! They are here! Please take them and leave us!" The man fished in his trouser pocket and produced a single key on a ring.

"Don't speak so loud! We need to tie you and your wife up…"

"Please! Leave my wife. I will say nothing, just take the vehicle I will say nothing.. Just leave us!" he pleaded.

Jim walked over and cracked the man on the side of his head with his pistol, "Do as the man asked! Call your bleedin' wife Godammit!" he raged through clenched teeth.

Norrie turned on Jim and pushed him to one side, "I'll fucking handle this!" He yelled. The man seeing a gap, leapt from the armchair and ran through the door. Jim who was nearest, followed. The man was yelling in Karudan at the top of his voice. He reached the stairs and was about to go up when Jim levelled his pistol and fired. He pumped three shots at the man, the pistol made a small noise but the sound of the bullets hitting him made a horrible thwack.

The man fell against the wall blood starting to ooze from his wounds, the woman appeared at the top of the stairs her mouth open wide in horror. Before Norrie could stop him Jim put a shot through her head, she slammed against the wall behind her and slumped to the floor.

The man on the stair stopped writing and lay still. The front door burst open and Frank came in rifle at the ready. He saw the body of the man. "What the fuck's going on?!" He said in shock.

"You said we had to break eggs sometime Frank." Jim said with wild staring eyes, "And I've just broke two of 'em."

"You dick head!" shouted Norrie, "If you had left things to me none of this would have happened!"

"If I'd left it to you Norrie we'd still be..."

"Just shut up everybody!" urged Frank, "Let's contain this, Riff see if there's a cellar or something where we can put them in. Nick keep an eye on things outside, there's been enough noise, Norrie check if she's still alive."

Norrie ascended the stairs. He saw the dull lifeless eyes and felt sick to his stomach, he was aware that Jim had followed him, "Come to check on your handy work?" he snarled.

Jim went to answer but something behind Norrie caught his attention, his eyes widened and he shouted a warning to Norrie. "Behind you!"

Norrie swung round pointing his pistol, it jumped in his hand as his finger tightened on the hair trigger, the bullet smacked into the small figure standing by a bedroom door..

Norrie stood there open mouthed with the pistol hanging down, it fell from his hands and clattered on the bare floor. Jim who was still behind him muttered, "Jesus" as Frank pushed past him to see Norrie slowly walking towards a bundle lying motionless. He reached it then fell on his knees, let out a huge cry of anguish and tried to cradle the body of a boy about eleven years old.

Frank went up to him, "Norrie, Norrie, let's have a look at him."

"I killed him Frank," he sobbed, "I murdered a child."

"Norrie! Come on! Let me look at him man!" He gently pulled the child from Norrie. The small body was floppy and lifeless.

"We've just come in here," said Norrie in a strained emotional voice, "And wiped out an entire family. Here Frank," he passed him the Landrover key, "That's what we were after wasn't it? Well we've got it...Mission accomplished."

"Come on Norrie, get up. Get up man!" Frank shouted as he yanked him to his feet.

They placed the bodies in a cupboard beneath the stairs. Norrie didn't assist, he just sat at the side of the house. They managed to back the Landrover to within a few feet of the pile of loot, then formed a chain and piled it all into the back. After they had finished Frank called them all together but Norrie just sat where he was. Frank walked over to him and sat beside him.

"Norrie, what's done is done. I know, you know and God knows that you didn't mean to.... Do what you did, it was a reflex, it just happened."

"Frank, did I ever tell you about my life at home?" Norrie spoke softly in a detached sort of way, "My dad worked at the pit...Still does. He was a bastard to me mum...To all of us. Used to get paid on a Friday and not get home till late, pissed out of his skull of course…. Every Friday night as long back as I can remember. One night he came back and complained that his dinner was not warm enough, he lined us all up and then threw the plate at me mum and then made her get on her hands and knees to clean it up…In front of us. We were petrified of him, mum went to an early grave, cancer they said but it was much more than that." Norrie lit a cigarette and continued.

"I made a promise to myself that as long as I lived I would never subject a child to any form of physical or mental torture like what me and me brothers and sister had.. Ever! Some promise eh Frank?" Tears wore rivulets in the black cam cream on his face.

"I can only guess what you are going through mate, but you've got to come through it and quick! We can't drag any baggage around with us Norrie. We need you. Now come on!" Norrie rose to his feet and shouldered his rifle he followed Frank to where the others were, they fell silent.

Frank checked his watch. "It's now just on three a.m. I want you all to make sure you've got water, there's tinned food in the kitchen, get it down you. Riff, the bloke was a major in the unit here, his shirt and beret are in the living room, get them on. You will be driving the truck out of here with Julian, there's no room for anyone else, so we will exit the way we come in and meet you on the road. We move in ten minutes.

Riff started the engine and said to Frank through the window, "What if they start something at the gate Frank?"

"There is only one sentry and they don't expect trouble, you should be alright, if not you know what to do."

Riff gunned the engine and pulled away. The rest of them filed off after Frank. Riff turned by the square and started on the long straight road to the gate.

"Put your lights on!" Julian ordered, "If you get any hassle off the bastard, I'll plug him with this!" He levelled his rifle at the window.

"Hadn't we best try and bluff our way first?"

"Huh!" He uttered and sat back in the seat. As they neared the gate a soldier emerged from the small sentry box quickly putting on his white helmet. He went straight to the red and white pole and pushed down on the counter balance, he managed to salute as they sailed by.

Frank reached the road they immediately found the rucksack stash and broke them out, hardly had they done it when they heard the Landrover leaving the camp and coming toward them. They all automatically got into cover. Riff killed his lights and pulled up by Frank who had emerged from the bush.

They jammed their Rucksacks into the back. Frank sat in the front, the rest clung to wherever they could and the vehicle set off again into the night.

21

Paul's Adjutant came in to the office, "Sir, Colonel Potter is waiting to see you."

"Good, show him in." Paul answered and continued to read a document. He heard Tex come in.

"Good morning Paul, I have come to discuss the plans for the opening of Lagonda or should I say, *Vander,* tomorrow." He laid out an operational map on the table and opened his briefcase. Paul said nothing, he stood and walked to the laid out map.

He looked at Tex and something on his uniform caught his eye. "That medal ribbon, what is it? I've not seen you wear it before."

Tex looked a little flustered, "Oh that?! It's the Royal Cross for the Liberation of Karuda. M'punga's going to present the medal to me next month. I was going to tell you…"

"Fine Tex, you deserve it," said Paul dryly, "Okay, show me what's happening tomorrow."

Tex, using the map, detailed the security arrangements and finished up by saying, "All patrols will be in position by zero seven hundred tomorrow morning. Your car and an escort leave for Lagonda at zero nine hundred and the President's convoy at eleven hundred, then you all leave Lagonda together at thirteen thirty after a lunch in the Officer's Mess. Paul I would be happier if you left later in the morning with the Presidential convoy."

"I need to be there before him to ensure that everything is on the ball…"

"Hah! It's a pity, I had a special surprise lined up for *you*. Now, just M'Punga will get it."

"Surprise? I don't like surprises very much Tex, what is it?"

"Oh! Just a load of old duffers want to wave the flag as you passed Mangini Cross roads, thought it might be a nice touch.. Ah well, hope M'Punga appreciates it."

"Who exactly are these *old duffers* Tex?"

"You know, the Ex Pats what live around Laka. Toffee nosed ex officers on their last legs, supposed to be about sixty turning up. Some old git named Macmillan pitched up here, doddering old bastard………"

"I thought the route we were taking was classified information?"

"Yeh? It is Paul, what's the big problem?" retorted Tex a little haughtily.

"Mangini Crossroads, they know we are to go through Mangini cross roads!"

"Well, yeh okay! Practically every route you care to choose goes through there." said Tex awkwardly."

"Very well Tex, I am satisfied with the arrangements and will inform the President accordingly."

Tex took this as his dismissal and turned on his heel as Paul resumed his interest in some paperwork.

"Harry, we're moving out in an hour, can I ask you one more time to come with us." Daryl sat at the table with Stone Face and Harry, they had just finished break-fast.

"My bones wouldn't stand it chum, I'm much too old for all of that."

"Okay Harry, if all goes well on our little mission and I mean *if* all goes well, I will call back here and collect you."

"I'm still not going to stroll through that bloody Ulu for anyone chum!"

"Jesus Harry! Give me a break!" Daryl sighed and stood up. He looked as if he was wrestling with a problem for a few seconds, twice he went to speak and stopped, finally he blurted, "Look, we have a chopper, be ready this afternoon…And that's it! No other offers!"

"This afternoon then." Harry stated simply.

The Landrover reached the airfield. Driving carefully Riff came off the concrete and into the thick scrub. The sun was up. Fear, anxiety, tension and just lack of sleep were now beginning to tell. They flopped off the vehicle and lay around. Norrie made no attempt to get them into any kind of order so Frank gave Nick the nod, he sparked and got them into all round defence.

Frank pulled the radio from his rucksack and fired it up, he pressed the switch and cut the mush out. "Hello Old Grandad, hello Old Grandad, this is Heron, radio check over." He released the switch and the mush cut in again, there was no reply. Trying to keep calm, Frank tried twice more, he could feel panic rising up in his gut as a picture of Lou lying covered in vomit in a drink induced coma flashed before his eyes.

He tried again and this time Lou's voice cut through the ether, "This is Old Grandad, hearing you good. Over."

Frank breathed a sigh of relief and replied. "Mission accomplished, come and get us, co-ordinates nine seven three, one eight six. Over."

There were a few seconds silence then Lou replied. "Negative, I say again, negative. Talk to Jay. Over."

A puzzled Frank repeated his request, but received the same reply. He then sought out Julian who he thought must be the "J" that Lou had referred to. Julian was awake, lying back against the rear wheel over the Rover.

"Julian, there's a problem with Lou, I've told him to come and get us but he keeps saying negative and to see you. What's it all about?"

Julian smiled, "Call the troops together Frank, I want to speak to them."

"What's it about Julian?" repeated Frank sharply.

"Just get them together Frank, there's a good boy, now do it! Unless you want to stay in this shit hole of a country and die."

Steaming with anger and confusion Frank called everyone in. When they had sat in a semi circle around him Julian began. "You see this?" He pulled out a flat metal box with a syringe in it plus a length of elasticated cord. "This my comrades is what has kept me going." He pulled out some squat brown bottles and lay them in line on the ground. "I'm dying you see, day by day, bit by bit. Not long left, maybe a week, maybe a month…. I really couldn't give a shit."

Everyone exchanged glances, Jim spoke, "Why are you telling us this now Julian?"

"Our dear friend Lou," he began again, "is waiting to come and pick us up but he won't even take off until *I*, yes, me personally gives him the correct code word. Just a little thing I discussed with him before we left, he knows he won't receive a penny if he disobeys me and I told him that I just may test him out."

"So why don't you give the code word then old boy?" asked Nick in a relaxed and casual manner.

"Oh! But I will Nick old buddy, old chap, but first I want something doing.."

"You'll be the one who's fucking done you bastard!" screamed Jim, "I'll fucking do you myself!" He tried to scramble up but Riff and Nick held on to him.

Unruffled, Julian continued, "Be my guest, here!" Julian tossed over his silenced pistol which Jim grabbed, "You've already proved that you're good at shooting defenceless people, go ahead! Do me a big favour!"

Jim aimed it at Julian who gave a dismissive laugh, "Even an overgrown schoolboy like you knows that would be rather a stupid thing to do." Jim dropped the pistol out of the aim and gave a shout of frustration.

"What do you want doing Julian?" asked Nick, "We have everything we've come here for.."

"You!" shouted Julian, "You have got everything you want! But *I haven't!*" What use is all this shit to me?!" He jerked his thumb back at the treasures on the back of the Landrover. "Nothing, absolutely nothing! I have made you all rich men, each and every one of you a rich man who will want for nothing! But before you can realise that, you will bloody well earn it!" He yelled out the last few words then slumped back against the wheel looking exhausted.

Nick rummaged in his kit then offered Julian his water bottle. Julian looked up in surprise then took a swig. He coughed and said "How the hell did you get mixed up with this lot?"

"Just tell us what you want Julian, so we can all go home eh?" said Nick gently.

"I once told you that I was incarcerated in the Prison here. Have any of you any idea what that means? On the first day they tried to cut my mouth off, on the first night in the prison hospital they buggered me, and on and on it went every day and every night. Do you know that if it were possible for me to turn a switch that would send everyone of these bastards," he pointed to Riff, "to a slow, screaming death, I would do it with great pleasure!" He stared at Riff who sat there unmoving.

"But, I am a realist and therefore know that sadly this will never come about, so I will settle for the next best thing." He looked around at all the faces and saw that he had unwavering attention.

"The man responsible for imprisoning me will be visiting Camp Lagonda tomorrow and quite simply I want to have a few words with him then put a slug through his head. That's it troops! That's all I want."

"Who is this man?" Jim asked, his face twisted with loathing for Julian.

"He is Paul Vander, last I heard he was a Brigadier or General, maybe he's President by now." replied Julian with disgust in his voice.

"You want us to rock up to Lagonda, knock off a General and just swan out of here? You're fucking nuts Julian!" glared Riff.

"No!" He yelled back, "Not nuts you Kaffir, dying! That's what I am!" Julian struggled to his feet, "Well, what's it to be?"

"We've got a Rover with three quarters of a tank, we could have a go at getting to the border Frank." Threw in Riff.

"Let's go for it," urged Jim, "Let's go and get this bastard General! It'll be worth it!"

"Let's just take his medicine off him." It was Norrie, everyone fell silent. It was the first words he had spoken since leaving the camp. "How long could you last without another fix Julian? I been watching you, it's about every six hours isn't it? When you have to sneak away. You gave Jim those silenced pistols knowing that the mad bastard would use his for the slightest reason. You're sick and you've turned me into a child murderer. Just take his medicines away Frank."

"Julian, take a walk!" It was Frank, "I said, take a walk!" Julian shrugged and sauntered off into the scrub.

Frank continued. "Well, we've had some options. One, we take the Rover and make a run for the border. What's wrong with that? We have limited fuel, we have not got sufficient maps, we will draw attention to ourselves and then we will face problems at the border itself, and once over the border, what then? Time is running out, it won't be long before they discover the bodies and realise the Rover was stolen, so they'll be on alert. Two, we do as we are bid, we ambush the road and take the bastard out when he appears. If we do that, we will only have surprise on our side and nothing else, maybe we could make it back to an LZ for Lou to pick us up and maybe not…Our third option is to torture the code word out of him by depriving him of his medicine or using other methods.. If anyone has the stomach for that..”

“I'll do it!” said Jim eagerly, then immediately looked awkward.

“There's no guarantee that it will work,” said Nick, “He's psychotic. I believe him when he says that he doesn't give a shit about the money, he's got a death wish. As distasteful as it seems I think our only option is to plan it extremely carefully and help him to assassinate this character. We're in it much deeper than I suspect any of us thought we would be. Luck, although it may not seem like it right now, is still with us. We have the loot and we're all intact, let me go and talk to Julian first and then Frank if I fail, I suggest a vote.”

Frank nodded and Nick walked off, Jim blurted out, “Just when we had it all, the demons of shit get involved! Bloody typical!”

Riff kicked at a stone and walked off.

Norrie looked up, his face a mask of despair, “We've had it Frank, who the hell did we think we were? Just swanning into someone else's country, wiping a family out and taking something that doesn't belong to us. I don't want a penny of it Frank. If by a soddin' miracle I get out of this lot I'm turning myself in for Brad North's murder. I hope they bang me up for thirty years.. Oh!

God help me!" Norrie buckled and let out a howl of remorse.

Frank gripped his arms and held them. "Come on Norrie, I need you mate."

"No wonder everyone hates us Frank, we're just killers. Aden, who the fuck was interested in a dump like that? But they sent us there, we killed people and we revelled in it, then they sent us to Ireland. Did you ever see anyone hate you so much as those people? Five year old kids throwing stones and cursing. Women, old men.. Hate, hate, hate! But do you know what? Their hatred is nothing compared with what I think of myself at this moment."

Nick closed up to Julian who was resting against the trunk of a tree, he turned and gave a little smile, "So, you're the one elected to talk me round? Good choice, you're perhaps the only one I'd listen to."

"No, as a matter of fact I'm here on my own accord. I'm puzzled, you show me a certain warmth and yet it was you who cast the deciding vote in that pub in London that ousted me as leader."

"Ha! Divide and rule old boy, it didn't quite come off though did it? Frank, although it grieves me to say, has handled things well and you've given admirable support."

"You speak as if you had wished the whole operation had collapsed from the start.."

"Mmm, You're right, that was my sane side coming through, although I'm happy to report that it's almost totally subdued now. Well, what's the decision? Are you putting me on cold turkey until I scream out the code word?"

Nick laughed, it was a genuine laugh, bought on by the completely surreal circumstances he found himself in. "No, I don't think so, it's just that it's all a bit sudden you know. Look, what if I donate my cut into putting a proper team together, working with a properly thought out plan to nail this man Vander?"

"No deal Nick, I'll never get this close again and remember, *I*, am the one who is to kill him."

"Very well, take me and Jim with you but get the rest back, their hearts are not in it..."

"No deal again, we all go.. All or nothing."

Frank got Lou back on the radio, he explained that Julian had flipped and wasn't responsible for his actions any more but Lou would have none of it. "Just let me speak to him." Was all that he would say in reply.

"Frank!" it was Nick, "No deal, we need to have a vote." Apart from Norrie who said nothing the vote was unanimous, they would go for Vander. Frank cobbled together a plan. They would camouflage the vehicle and leave it in a small ravine near the airfield. It would take them an hour to reach Lagonda on foot approaching warily, a lot less time to get back. Julian agreed to give the code word as soon as the deed was done so Lou could get under way, he insisted on carrying the radio, grudgingly Frank handed it over.

Frank suggested to Norrie that he stay behind to guard the Landrover but he refused point blank. Finally, Julian gave a detailed description of Paul Vander, so as to be sure that no-one shot him before he got to him.

At four pm after a couple of hours rest they stashed their rucksacks with the Rover and set off once more toward Lagonda.

22

Paul sat in the trophy room of his house in Camp Royal, he had retained this residence even though he had sumptuous apartments within the Palace. The house was void of servants and quiet. He poured himself a stiff drink and relaxed on the huge settee.

Things were not right. An alarm bell was sounding somewhere in the far distant recesses of his mind. It centred on Tex and that crafty bitch Tula he thought. She was manipulating him toward some purpose. The bond between the two men had loosened and Paul thought that she had been instrumental in that.

Paul also realised that Tex was the wrong man to be his head of Bureau. He needed a Karudan in the job, someone who knew the people, someone who would work hard to please him. Tex would have to go, he would have to create another job for him. He would promote him he mused, Brigadier Terrence Potter, Inspector of the Royal Army, despite himself Paul laughed aloud.

He pulled a blue sleeved file off the coffee table in front of him, it was titled "Jakaranda", the operational name for the surveillance on Eva "Tula" Potter. Starting at page one he resigned himself to reading it again from start to finish.

Daryl halted his men and they immediately went to ground in the belt of greenery that they had been moving through. There were thirty in all, fully armed and dressed in the camouflage of the Karudan Armed Forces. It was late afternoon and the light was beginning to fade.

He called Stone Face forward with a hand signal. "That is the point where we will set up the road block." He whispered, "Right there where the tarmac road turns into dirt." He pointed to the spot which was about thirty metres away.

"When you have got the men in position, bring the Karudan speakers to me I want to give them a final briefing before dark."

They reached the road by Lagonda. Frank chose an ambush site and they rehearsed an exit route back through the way they had come, back to the airfield and the Landrover. They would head in the opposite direction for a Kilometre or so to mislead any would be followers then turn toward their destination.

To fulfil Julian's wish to personally kill Vander, Frank had to run through various scenarios depending on the size of the escort that Vander would have. They had no idea how he would travel or at what time, most things would have to be played by ear, if there was an armoured car with a gun their problems would increase.

Frank tried to pull Norrie out of his trance like state but to no avail. Jim had now started to assert himself in the vacuum left by him. He seemed to gain more confidence after the kills at the house. At first light Frank would position Riff further up the road to give them advanced warning of anything approaching.

Julian now completely devoid of any pretence openly injected himself, lit up and lay back seemingly oblivious of what was going on around him. Nick talked tactics with Frank at length trying hard to be positive and objective although he felt exactly the opposite. Riff stripped his rifle and cleaned it, he checked his magazines for the nth time.

Jim imagined himself moving forward under intense fire, blazing away and dropping everyone in sight, reaching Vander and dragging him in front of Julian to be summarily executed. To him, at this moment, the money and riches were secondary, *this*, was the life.

The sun went down and they all settled in for a long night.

23

Paul was up early, he had travelled back to his apartments at the Palace the evening before. His man servant had laid out his best uniform barnacled in gold braid and insignia, he ignored it preferring to travel in his jungle fatigues then dress later at Lagonda.

His transport waited for him outside, it was a stripped down Landrover. The driver doused his cigarette quickly and gave a sloppy exaggerated salute. The escort Landrover with a comma seven machine gun and four soldiers roared up and pulled in front in readiness to move.

Paul walked up to one of the soldiers on the back of the escort vehicle, he took his AK47 assault rifle off him and looked it over. It was slightly damp with oil without a sign of rust. It had a spare mag taped to the one on the rifle Paul nodded approval and tossed it back to the soldier. If there had been a speck of rust or dirt the soldier would have been thrown in Laka Prison for a month and kicked out of the elite bodyguards.

He checked with the driver of the escort vehicle to ensure that he knew the route that they were using then climbed in his own vehicle, they sped through the gates at exactly zero nine hundred hours.

Daryl had a final word with his Karudan speakers, there were four of them all black. One was a Karudan who had joined the Rhodesian African Rifles some years before. Daryl knew that his delicate plan would depend a lot on them. He checked his watch, five after nine, it wouldn't be long now.

Paul would be glad to see this day over. As they sped along he mulled over and over the course of action he would take against Tex and his wife. Direct? *Look here Tex, this is a file all about your beautiful Tula, and by the way you are no longer my head of the Bureau.* Subtle? *Tex, you are overworked, take yourself and your wife to Capetown for a long vacation.* A very long vacation.

The driver said something and began applying his brakes, Paul looked up sharply. There was a group of six soldiers ahead on the road and were waving down the escort vehicle.

Paul reached down picked up an Uzi sub machine gun and flicked off the safety, "Don't get too close to the escort vehicle!" He barked.

His vehicle stopped, Paul dived out of the Rover and into the bush, all was quiet. He stepped back onto the road. One of the soldiers that had stopped the lead vehicle came sauntering toward him as if he had all the time in the world, another followed a little way behind, he too looked totally bored and out of it.

The soldier came to within a couple of paces of Paul, his rifle slung and out of his grip. He saluted smartly and smiled at Paul. "Field Marshal Sir," he said in a relaxed voice, "There may be a problem ahead, Colonel Potter has just radioed us to halt you, he want's to speak to you urgently sir, my captain is just over there speaking to him now Sir..."

"Fetch the radio here at once!" said Paul sternly.

"I'm afraid we can't move the radio Sir, it is set up just in there sir!" said the soldier and disappeared in the bushes at the side of the road, he emerged a few seconds later. "Sir, the Colonel Potter wants to speak to you urgently sir."

Paul's guard dropped, if it was to be an attempt on his life it would have probably happened by now. He followed the man a little way down the road then turned into the bush, he saw a group of soldiers with their backs to him, as they turned four others sprang out of the earth and covered him with their automatic weapons. Paul's blood ran cold. He looked at the man facing him. He was white with a ginger moustache, he carried no weapon and grinned at Paul as if he was an old buddy from way back.

"Field Marshal Paul Vander? We meet at last Sir. Please make us all feel better and put the Uzi on the ground for now. I don't want any accidents...Thank you. Come! Take a seat this won't take long." He made a gesture and the armed men disappeared into the bush. Paul sat on a makeshift seat of logs and stones.

Daryl offered a cheroot to Paul who accepted. When he was lit, Daryl continued. "I've been looking forward to this meeting for some time now.."

"And you are?"

"Shall we just say a concerned Rhodesian for now, my rank is Colonel if you want to use that."

"What do you want of me.. *Colonel*?"

"In December last, hardly three months ago, the homestead of a tobacco farmer was attacked in Centenary in the North of my country, he was lucky, they didn't press home the attack and he and his family escaped relatively unscathed. They were terrorist of course.. ZANLA." Daryl paused.

"Around nineteen sixty eight we hammered Nkomo's ZIPRA terrorist infiltration..... Heavily I might add. Since then I'm afraid there has been an air of complacency in my government. Attacks, well organised well led attacks like the one on that farm are now becoming the norm in parts of my country. The Troopies on the ground know it but at the moment nobody is listening. My government, shall come to their senses and we will defeat them, of that, there is no doubt. These terrorists have safe havens in Mozambique and Zambia. Botswana has refused and we hear that Zambia is about to do so, that leaves just Mozambique and Karuda, places where they can rest, train, treat their wounded, amass arms and ammunition and places to plan and lead their attacks from. Your President has already been approached by this scum and he, although perhaps reluctantly, has agreed to accommodate them."

Paul's mind flashed back to M'Punga's meeting with those unknown people, the map of the border to Rhodesia on display. They would have insisted that he was not informed at all, they wouldn't have trusted or tolerated a white man being present.

"Why don't you make proper representations to my President. Why all this?"

"That's a political activity.. Me? I'm a realist." Replied Daryl. "If I want a job done on my car I speak to a mechanic, not get my wife to talk to the clerk behind the desk. Let me put my cards on the table Mister Paul Maas." He paused to see if there was any reaction to using Paul's proper name, there wasn't.

"I have followed your career with great interest, what ever else you may or may not be, you are a good soldier. You halted the rebel activity in Karuda with speed and great professionalism..."

They were interrupted by some loud talking by the road, a soldier came on the scene, It's your bodyguard Sir, they are worried.."

Paul nodded he went back to the road and spoke to them, re-assured, they walked back to their Rover. Paul returned and Daryl continued.

"I want you to turn this situation around for us, by refusing to let them enter Karuda and to turn on them if they do. I have a feeling that they have already infiltrated to some extent, part of their agreement with M'Punga will be to let him know exactly where their bases are, that information would be very handy to us."

Paul studied the man talking to him, he could make out a faint row of stitching on his uniform where a certain type of wings were once sewn, at a guess he thought that he was Rhodesian SAS or a former soldier of that force now mixed up with intelligence.

"And so," began Paul, "I am supposed to walk up to my President, tell him he's wrong, then contradict his policy.."

"You are not a fool Paul. I have the greatest respect for the way you have handled yourself since you've been in Karuda. If there is a way I am confident you will find it...That is of course if you have the will to do it. I don't suppose the old country conjures up many good memories for you."

"And what if I just can't be bothered with all this, what if I was to go my own sweet way? What then?"

"Let us not dwell on negative aspects, let's dwell on the positive. There are two warrants out for your arrest, both murder and a string of others. They will disappear overnight just in case you would like to visit the old country again, also the Brit police are interested in your whereabouts, we can arrange for a death certificate to be sent to them. We also have certain funds at our disposal..."

"I will never leave this country alive," stated Paul simply, "thank you for all that, but warrants? They mean nothing to me Colonel and as for money, I don't need it."

"What else can I offer? "

Paul pondered the unique position he was in. He knew that if he refused to co-operate which was his initial gut reaction, he would be chopped sooner or later. He could turn the situation, he didn't know how far he could trust this Colonel but something told him that he must.

"If I am to co-operate there are certain things I must know."

"Yes?"

"Who are your people in my organisation who supplies you with information?"

"Ha! You start with the hard questions! My intelligence comes second hand, I don't know the source."

"Very well, we have nothing more to say to each other, I will take my chances." With that Paul picked up his Uzi and started to walk off, he almost reached the road when Daryl called him back.

Daryl knew that by being asked an almost impossible question to answer he was being tested on his commitment to the situation, tearing up arrest warrants and manufacturing phoney death warrants were routine even substantial pay offs were possible but exposing an agent? This was a different ball game.

He thought of Eva Saputo or Tula Potter as she now was. She had been a brilliant find, the months and months they had spent training her. First she had got to Juba and when he went, she had hung on to Potter, now she was virtually running the Bureau with an ear inside the Palace through that overgrown spoilt brat of a Prince who was infatuated with her. No he couldn't betray her, she was a jewel, but he had an alternative.

"Please stay, we can do business…"

"And the names?"

"I'll come to that I promise, is there anything else?"

Paul pondered and then spoke, "If by chance the rebels wiped out the President and his Son, then I would automatically, as head of the Armed forces assume control of the country."

"Shit! That's heavy, that's not my line of work. Knocking off heads of state tends to attract a little bit of world attention.. But perhaps a tragic accident…"

"Well, let us say that when this *tragic accident* takes place you will have my full co-operation. I can supply you with intelligence on M'Punga's movements. In the mean time I will look very carefully and sympathetically at this safe haven issue." Paul looked expectantly at Daryl, it was time to go.

"Make me a promise Paul, man to man. This agent, there is only one…Make it quick eh, he's old and past it, this was a one off job for him finding out your movements today and I put him under a lot of pressure to do it.."

"You're giving me crumbs man, I want the meal."

"No, I promise you that's it! This guy was a top man for Brit Military Intelligence in his day, he's damn good! He infiltrated your own Bureau just a few days ago."

"Then how did you find out about the terrorists meeting with the President and what they talked about?"

Daryl had to think quickly, "We have a man, several in fact, inside the Zanla organisation….."

"You have men inside their organisation, yet you want *me* to give you co-ordinates of terrorist camps in my country?"

"Just confirmation that's all, must have confirmation. The man you want is Harry Macmillan, he lives just outside of Laka to the North."

Paul stared at him for what seemed like an eternity then nodded and turned to go.

"It's a deal then Paul?"

"Ya! It's a deal."

"Just one other thing Paul."

"Yes?"

"There's a team of six men in the country led by a man called Pern, an old associate of yours I believe. As we speak they are hanging around outside of Lagonda. I think Pern might want a chat with you about something, thought you'd like to know that...Bye."

24

Nick was worried, he looked across to where Frank was lying but could only see his vague outline of camouflage in the surrounding vegetation. It had gone midday and nothing had moved down the road, then suddenly all hell had broken loose in Lagonda at eleven forty five. They could hear people balling and shouting, vehicles were revving and moving around. They could see nothing in the camp from their ambush position which was near to the road.

Nick decided to break from his position and speak to Frank, as he crawled close he saw Riff loping towards them from his lookout position further down the road, his eyes were wide. "Frank man!" he shouted gasping for breath, "There's a bloody army moving up the road towards us! Armoured cars, troop carriers the lot…"

Just then a familiar noise hammered their eardrums and an Alouette helicopter flew over their heads and started circling in a large loop.

"They've rumbled us!" shouted Jim his eyes wide with excitement.

"Just steady on!" shouted Frank getting up, "It may be part of the security for the President.. Routine stuff."

"What do *you* think Julian?" Nick shot.

"How many vehicles exactly, Kaffir?" he snapped at Riff who ignored the insult.

"At least three Saladin type armoured vehicles with guns, six armoured personnel carriers and truckloads of soldiers, they're about five minutes away..." The chopper over flew again causing them to duck into cover.

Frank got up and with Riff leading went up to the lookout position. He saw the convoy clearly and could hear the engine noise. The lead vehicles stopped and three trucks disgorged their load, soldiers deployed quickly and with determination to both sides of the road, urged on by screaming NCOs. The convoy started moving again.

Riff jabbed Frank's arm and pointed to the main gate of Lagonda, troops were swarming out across the road and straight into the bush threatening to encircle them. Frank had seen enough, he clapped Riff on the shoulder and ran back to the others. "Come on! Let's go! They're looking for us!"

Julian faced up to Frank, "What are you doing?"

"We're going Julian, the game's up!" he yelled.

"You lily livered coward! For God's sake man, Vander will be passing in a moment.. Wait!" raved Julian his white face taut with anger.

"Come with me!" Frank shouted and grabbed hold of Julian's equipment. He dragged him a few yards to a space where they could see a good length of road, the slow moving convoy had moved closer, troops were still exploding from the backs of troop carriers and deploying straight into the bush.

"You stay here and wait for Vander! We're off!"

Julian went to say something but Frank paid no heed, he turned and led the rest off down the pre determined exit route.

The trail was narrow and wound through thick green vegetation between two small hills. They came to a small clearing, just as they were about to cross it three Karudan soldiers entered it from the other side, the two parties saw each other at the same time but Frank reacted first, dropping to his knee he squeezed a long burst at the centre figure they all dropped and a long gurgling scream welled up.

"On! On! Keep going!" screamed Norrie who ran passed Frank in the direction that the Karudans had come from, as he passed them he fired two short bursts and the screaming stopped.

Frank and the rest followed Norrie running at speed. Norrie fired again to his front and Frank passed two wounded Karudans writhing and screaming. The lush green vegetation gave out to the flat stony ground heavily dotted with small scrub trees.

As planned they headed East away from the airfield. The pace slowed and finally Frank gave the order to halt. They flopped on the ground heaving and panting, dragging in huge lungs full of air. There was something wrong, Frank got to his feet, "There's only five of us, Julian's missing!" he yelled. Just at that moment there was a long burst of automatic fire, followed by the short bursts of fire of a different sort.

Riff jumped up, "He's my partner, I'll get him!" Before Frank or anyone could react, Riff ran back.

He had covered about one hundred and fifty metres when he heard a laugh and a curse and another burst of fire. He saw Julian lying at the base of a tree his back to him, he then saw two soldiers off to the right trying to out flank him. Riff took careful aim and loosed off three short bursts of fire, both men dropped. One tried to crawl away but Riff put another burst in him. Julian half turned saw Riff and sank to the ground. He picked up his rifle it had been hit and was shattered. He laughed loudly.

Warily Riff crawled up to him, he could hear shouting from many soldiers to his front.

"Riff!" gasped Julian, "My legs! Finish me off! Don't let them bastards get me alive!" Riff looked down and saw blood oozing from both of Julian's legs.

" Ha! Ha!" Julian laughed again. "My worst nightmare.. Begging a kaffir to kill me. Finish me off you Kaffir bastard!" he screamed.

"Come on!" yelled Riff who then fired off his full magazine into the general direction of the voices. He bent down and hauled up Julian into a fireman's lift and ran back down the track. On the point of collapse, he reached the others who helped Julian to the ground.

Julian suppressed a scream, "Frank!" he shouted. Frank leaned over him, "I'm finished, here I die.."

"Don't say that, Nick is stopping the bleeding, we can make it!"

"Please, fetch Riff, I want to thank him and give him the code word...Hurry I'm slipping!"

Riff came over, he was still panting and covered in sweat. Frank shouted for everyone to be ready to move out. Julian grabbed Riff by the straps of his equipment and with a supreme effort struggled to his feet. He renewed his grip and smiled then showed Riff his fist, in it was a grenade with the pin out. Before he could react Julian let the handle fly off but still held the grenade tight in his hand, "See you in hell Kaffir!" he snarled.

Riff shouted, "Grenade! Get down!" he grabbed Julian's fist with the grenade still in it and with all his strength pulled it between them. The blast blew both of them in half from the waist.

The rest of them, on Riff's warning had hit the ground, because of that and the fact that the main blast had been muffled by the two bodies, none of them were hit.

"Holy Mary, mother of God!" exclaimed Norrie. For two seconds they all gazed at the black smoking bundles of bloody meat.

"Bollocks!" shouted Jim, "The radio, that bastard Julian had it!" Nick found what was left of Julian's equipment a few metres away, the radio was blasted apart. Shots cracked over their heads as a group of Karudans spotted them and opened up. They all returned fire emptying a couple of mags each into the group.

Then Frank was up and they all followed, running for their lives.

Paul sat in his mobile Headquarters just outside Camp Lagonda, his signaller tore off one of his earphones turned to Paul and exclaimed, "They have killed two of the enemy Sir!" They had been listening to the exchange of shots for some minutes now and had heard the explosion.

"Find out the exact position of the bodies."

After a few seconds the signaller handed Paul a piece of paper with co-ordinates on it. He then slid a small hatch open and gave the co-driver the same co-ordinates. "Get me there now!" he ordered.

As they bounced along he studied the map, he looked at the plots on it that he had made. From the position of their first contact with the "mercenaries" as he had dubbed them, he deduced that they had been waiting for him just down the road from the main gates of the camp. They seemed to be running to the East, this would eventually bring them to a wide valley, by radio he ordered the helicopter to dump troops on the route and set up ambushes. He sent vehicle borne troops to block both ends of the Valley.

He sat back and smiled inwardly. Daryl had got his respect, he was professional and well informed. He had no doubt that if he had refused to co-operate with him Daryl would have let him drive to his death in Pern's ambush.

He had acted swiftly after his meeting with Daryl. Returning immediately to the Palace and summoning his Battalion Commanders. He issued quick orders to encircle the area where, he informed them, foreign mercenaries were waiting to ambush the President. He then ordered Tex to have Macmillan taken alive.

Within a couple of hours he had over two thousand troops in the field setting up ambushes and searching.

The hatch slid open and the vehicle Commander gave a thumbs up to Paul. The vehicle stopped and Paul got out. There was a large group of soldiers milling around staring at some black bundles.

"Who is in charge here?" he asked. A tall officer come forward and saluted.

"Which direction did they go in?" asked Paul in Karudan. The officer pointed to the East.

"How many?"

The officer shrugged and asked if anyone had seen them, no-one answered so he again shrugged.

Paul inspected the cadavers. Riff's remains were totally unrecognisable. He looked at the other,

"Find the head of this one!" He boomed and every-one started looking around, he didn't hold much hope of finding it but after a minute there was a shout and a young soldier came up gingerly carrying a round hairy object. Paul ordered it put on the ground and then told them to clean it with water. This done, he knelt in the muddied soil and inspected the face which was intact. He was sure who it was but peeled back the moustache to reveal thick scar tissue around the mouth.

"Pern." he whispered and smiled, "Welcome back to Karuda old boy."

25

At midday, Harry shaved off his goatee beard, brushed back his thinning grey hair then pulled the old chest from the spare room. He hoped that dampness or termites had not penetrated the polished teak. On opening the faint smell of naptha whiffed into his nostrils. He carefully pulled out the folded uniform and laid it on his bed. Wrapped in tissue paper in a box was a dark green Light Infantry beret, which he held aloft and looked at proudly.

At twelve thirty he walked smartly down his drive, the studded brown Brogues clicking neatly on the crazy paving. His hands were clasped behind his back and his swagger stick thrust under his arm. He stopped to look at some vegetation that was over growing the path as if inspecting a soldier in the ranks. Using his swagger stick he deftly pushed it to one side and continued his inspection.

The noise of a speeding Landrover followed by another caught his attention, he heard the slamming of doors and heard someone barking orders in Karudan.

Harry calmly reached down and took his .38 Pistol from the holster, he broke it and checked that the chamber was full.

Two soldiers appeared at the gate and stood open mouthed, staring at Harry who stood in full dress uniform with feet apart and a pistol pointing at them.

"Well come on then! You're making this too easy for me." He shot the left hand soldier between the eyes, the other came into the aim but too late. Harry's shot hit him in the throat. Three others came up behind them and opened fire. Harry dropped like a stone and the continuous weight of automatic fire bounced him back down the path like a high pressure hose washing away an old dry stick.

The four men almost totally exhausted tottered to a halt on Frank's order. They dropped and faced the way they had come wheezing and trying to wipe the stinging sweat from their eyes.

"We've come over a kilometre Frank." panted Nick

"Yeh! We'll turn for the airfield now."

They heard the noise of the chopper and dropped flat, it sped over their head and headed East.

Paul listened in vain for contact reports to come in from the ambushes that he had flown to points in front of the mercenaries advance. He had ordered other troops to close in onto the flanks of their line of advance, he had been waiting for two hours and had heard nothing.

A man handed Paul a signal, it was from Tex and told him that the spy Macmillan had resisted arrest and was dead. Paul threw it to one side. He was disappointed, he would have taken a leading roll in Macmillan's interrogation. He knew that Daryl had thrown him but a crumb by naming just him, he knew there must be other informers more highly placed in the state machinery.

Frank reckoned that they were within one kilometre of the Landrover that was hidden at the side of the airfield. They halted and lay in all round defence, feet almost touching. They were all exhausted and covered in sweat mixed with the orange dust of the plain. Frank spoke just loud enough for them to hear.

"Nick, Norrie, go forward carefully and locate the Rover. Don't move it but return on foot, we will wait here for your return, try and make it back before last light." After a few seconds he heard them scrambling to their feet and moving off, "Good luck!" he whispered loudly but doubted if they had heard him.

"Terrence! Are these rumours true? Is there a mercenary force invading the country?" Tula's eyes were wide with fear and excitement. Tex looked up from his desk, he was flanked by officers from the Bureau, they had been studying a map. He had not seen Tula since coming to work that morning.

"Take it easy love, some mercenaries tried to top the President. Paul found out and the shit's hit the fan, they've got two of the bastards, just a matter of time before they nail the others." he smiled but it dissolved when Tula made an angry face.

"I need to speak to you now! At once!" she snapped. The officers left without being told. Once alone, she approached the desk and sank to her knees in front of Tex with a worried look.

"Your men shot dead an old man today," she stated staring at Tex.

"Yeh! So what? He shot dead two of mine, he was a spy by all accounts. Paul said that he…"

"Terrence!" interrupted Tula, "I have just seen the body, it was that dirty scruffy old man who was in this very office only a couple of days ago! The one that *you* showed the operational map to! My God! He was in a foreign uniform, he must be involved with those mercenaries!" she broke down, large tears ran down her cheeks and her voice bordered on hysteria, "If Paul finds out we gave him information he will have us shot or worse. Terry, he must not find out!"

She came round the desk and clung onto Tex, he patted her back, stared ahead and thought about his conversation with Paul about the ex pats being at Mangini Crossroads, then said woodenly, "He already knows…At least, he's got enough information to put two and two together…"

Tula broke away from him, "He knows?! Oh! My God how did he find out?"

"What does it matter?" said Tex angrily, "He won't do anything, he needs me…"

"He needs nobody!" Screamed Tula, her face a mask of fear.

"Shush Tula, calm down! It will all be okay."

"Terry, you live in a dream world, first you don't get him the information he wants about that ZANLA meeting, then you let a spy, a foreign mercenary see the security arrangements that directly endangers the pig and the President. Then you have the spy killed when he ordered him taken alive! How many mistakes can you make before he turns on you? He may even believe now, that you are working against him!"

Tex went white, he went to get up but then rested his head in his hands and let out a strangled cry, he then beat the desk with his fists, tears welled up in his eyes.

"I will go and see him!" he croaked, "He'll believe me, we've been through a lot, me and Paul.."

"Don't you understand anything Terry? My love, he will have us both put to death, me and your child!" she sobbed holding her stomach, "You don't care...Oh! You just don't care!"

Tula collapsed on the floor, Tex ran to her and propped her up, "Terry," she said sleepily, "You must act first, you must save us!"

"What can *I* do?" he whined.

"Kill the pig! Kill him! Kill him!"

Despite the situation he was in Frank dozed. He allowed his head to rest on his rifle butt and his aching, heavy eyes to close. Norrie was almost on top of him before he woke with a start. He was closely followed by Nick, they dropped down to speak to him, the remaining light was just beginning to fade.

"It's not good mate," he warned, "There are loads of them starting to deploy between here and the Rover and on the actual airstrip there are hundreds more. We got in and out just in time. Looks like a headquarters set up, tents, loads of antennas, the only good news is that somehow they haven't yet found the Rover, it's still intact and undisturbed in that ravine."

Norrie rummaged in his gear pulled out some cigarettes and lit up, "Managed to get some of the water off the Rover 'fore we left." he offered some to Jim and Frank, "Go on! Have a good pull." He urged.

"What the hell went wrong back there? How in hell's name did they know we were there?" Norrie asked in amazement.

"They must have found the bodies and put two and two together." Frank suggested.

"We was bubbled!" shouted Jim, "How could they known it was us?! And why did they reason that we were still hanging about outside the camp?!"

"Well then, who bubbled us?!" Norrie snapped.

Jim spat and looked away.

"Options?" Asked Frank.

"There are only two main options now," Offered Nick, "Option one, we try to recover the Rover and the loot and get away, or two, we forget the Rover and try and make it out of here as we are."

"We can't leave here without the money!" shot Jim, "All this way for fuck all? No way, youse lot do what you want, I want my money!"

"You know how I feel about the money." said Norrie.

"If that's how you feel, fine!" said Jim sarcastically, "You can donate your share to a kid's home or something but don't expect me to just walk out of here with nothing!"

"I should have beaten you to a pulp when I had the chance!" Grated Norrie through clenched teeth.

"Yeh! You shoulda done child killer, 'cos you won't get another chance…"

Norrie launched at Jim, but Jim was ready. He rolled out of the way and stood up, pulling the silenced pistol out of his smock and pointing it at Norrie who was halfway to his feet. Frank cocked his rifle and pointed it at Jim, "Don't make me do it Jim!" he said savagely.

Nick stood between the two men and pushed the pistol out of the aim. "I think we should all just calm down and try and think our way out of this situation," he said quietly but with an edge to his voice.

Nick continued, "My guess is they will sooner or later rumble our little mis- direction ruse and intensify the search in other directions at first light. Having all their soldiers around us might be a blessing in disguise, they may think that we'd be anywhere else but here… Maybe. This has given us a breathing space but no more, if that chopper locks on to us tomorrow, we've had it."

Nick paused for a few seconds then went on. "I propose strongly, that we try and recover the vehicle tonight and drive it out of here. When we were near the airfield we heard vehicles moving all the time so it won't stand out that much. If we leave things till first light, we'll lose our only advantages, darkness and surprise. Forget the money for a moment, we need the vehicle for mobility, water, ammo and food but most of all, for the spare radio. Without that we stand no chance of getting out of here."

Nick's calm reasoning had an effect on all of them, tensions eased and they began to think.

"You said the radio was important Nick," ventured Jim, "But if we ain't got a code word, what's the use?"

"We'll just have to convince Lou that's all." he answered, "It's a chance we are better taking, than not taking."

"Okay," said Frank, "This is the deal, we do as Nick suggests and recover the vehicle tonight. We get an hours rest and then we go. We drive north to Kangi ridge, if we can't get Lou to pick us up we then go on foot to the other side of the Ridge. At least there is green vegetation for cover and that means water, I saw a river from the chopper..... Any problems?"

Nobody spoke, they were all in.

"Then, that's final."

Paul ordered his driver to head back to the Palace. He had just briefed his commanders at the airfield on their moves at first light. He was now convinced that the mercenaries were not heading East anymore, he had saturated that area with troops, either they had been frightened off or they had deliberately misled him.

He had placed most of his remaining troops in two large circles, an inner and outer cordon with its centre based on the disused airfield, anyone breaking out would have to negotiate these lines at some stage.

The rest he had stood by at the airfield ready to mount two Wessex helicopters that would lift them for either back up or cut off duties. He hoped that the mercenaries were stupid enough to stay put for the night but he doubted it.

Again he dwelt on how Daryl had got his information about the mercenaries. Maybe, he thought, just maybe his information came from an external source, but what if someone in my own organisation had known about them, he mused. Someone who wanted him killed and used Pern's hatred to set it all up? He thought of Macmillan and an image of Tex flashed behind his eyes and then faded. He thought about the reports on Tula and the sheer incompetence displayed by Tex that had almost cost him his life "Dealing with you my dear friend Tex is not going to be as difficult as I first thought." He said almost aloud

26

Daryl shook Stone Face's hand and thanked him for his support. They had just landed on the chopper pad at Salisbury Airport reserved for military use. Daryl jumped in the waiting staff car and drove to his Ops room at Special Operations Headquarters in a dull grey building next to Meikles Hotel. While relaxing on the back seat he thought for a moment about Harry and hoped he went quick but he doubted it.

The duty officer immediately approached him as he entered the Operations suite in the basement. "Colonel, Impala's controller has sent a Red Flash emergency signal. Impala wants out, she says that her death is imminent." He handed Daryl the signal.

Impala was the cover name for Eva (Tula) Potter. "Can I speak direct?"

"She is at the safe house now, I can have her linked up in a few seconds."

The duty Officer spoke into a telephone and then handed it to Daryl. "Impala?"

A high pitched voice distorted with emotion crackled in his ear. "Get me out of here! That was part of the deal! Get me out now!"

"Calm down!" barked Daryl. "Calm down and report correctly. Now what is the exact problem?"

"The Pig thinks we are plotting against him, we will be arrested soon!"

"Who is *we?*"

"Me and my husband!"

"Start from the beginning, I don't care how long you take, but nothing is going to happen unless I get the true and full story, now go ahead and don't shout!"

Daryl listened intently as Tula told of how Vander knew of Harry's visit to the Bureau and seeing the map and then how Tex had failed to take him alive. She then told of Tex's failure to secure information on the President's meeting with the ZANLA people. She finally stated how much Paul hated her and would be bound to kill her along with Tex, for he was bound to think now, that they were mixed up in a plot to kill him.

"You are assuming that is how Vander is thinking, you may be and probably are, wrong...Tough it out, I will keep abreast of all developments. I promise that if things get any worse I will personally get you out."

"Worse? Well I can assure you that they will get worse and soon!" she shrieked.

"What makes you say that?"

"Well, my big brave husband is waiting for Paul in his office and is about to kill him, but knowing *my man,* he will fuck that up just like he's fucked everything up he's ever touched."

Daryl felt a stab of frustration through his gut, all his hard work in getting to meet Van Der Borgh and then getting him to co-operate, wasted because of a hysterical bitch and a swaggering incompetent.

"You are right!" he retorted with fire in his voice, "Put your controller on now, and don't worry, we'll have you out in no time!"

There was silence the other end then a rich deep voice came on the line.

"Listen," said Daryl, "Can she hear me?"

"No! She is out of the room."

"Good, first you must locate Vander immediately and relay a message to him by any means at your disposal and tell him it came from the *Colonel*, got that?"

Paul's vehicle pulled up at the Palace gates and after a check by the sentry was allowed to enter. As soon as he got out the sergeant of the guard saluted nervously. "Sir, I have two messages for you!" he said breathlessly. "The first is from a person saying that you must call him, it's a matter of life and death, he said to tell you it was from the *Colonel*, Sir!"

"The Colonel? No name?"

"No Sir! But he said that it was a matter of..."

"Yes, yes, have you a number.. You know, a telephone number?" The sergeant smiled and handed Paul a piece of paper. Paul was about to leave for his apartments but then a realisation came over him and he went to the phone in the guardroom and dialled the number. It was answered immediately by a man with a rich baritone voice.

"Vander here." said Paul.

"The Colonel has given me the following message for you.... I quote." Paul heard the crinkling of paper. "Colonel Terrence Potter is waiting in his office at Bureau Headquarters for you, he intends to kill you...Did you get that?"

"Yes."

"The message further reads, Eva Saputo known also as Tula or Eva Potter, is at this address: Fifteen Widilla Street. She is a spy for the ZANU PF movement and has engineered the attempt on your life by the foreign force headed by Pern. When this failed, she put her husband Terrence Potter up to do same. Signed the Colonel."

"Who are…"

"Did you get that address?"

"Yes but…"

"Repeat it please!" Interrupted the voice sternly.

"Fifteen Widilla street…"

The phone went dead. Paul was deep in thought when the sergeant spoke again. Paul turned and asked him to repeat what he had said.

"The second message sir! From Colonel Potter, he is at Bureau Headquarters and needs to see you there urgently Sir." he said smiling, pleased that at last he had discharged his responsibility.

Tula had calmed down a little. Things had seemed to be happening at last. After she had spoken to Daryl, her controller had taken her to another address. From there he said she would be picked up and taken across the border to Rhodesia. She fingered the small glass phial of lemon coloured liquid that the Controller had given her. *Standard procedure, always issued when agents are bugging out,* he had said. *Break it in your mouth and you are instantly dead, you won't need it, just standard procedure.*

She placed it back in her uniform pocket lit a cigarette and looked at her watch. Darkness had just descended, she wondered whether Terrence had killed the pig yet. She only realised after goading him into killing Paul that it would probably backfire. She had thought of going to Prince Tasi for protection but the thought of being under the direct control of that disgusting pervert had sent a shiver down her spine, so she had run.

She tried to think of other things to cheer herself a little. She thought about starting a new, different life. It had been years since she was Salisbury. Oh! The parties, she mused, a little smile crept over her tear stained, puffy, yet still beautiful face.

Tex was not aware that Paul was in his doorway, he was not even aware that Paul was in the building. The guard had been persuaded not to report Paul's arrival. He studied his old friend for a few seconds slumped on the desk muttering something over and over, the half empty bottle of scotch, the long barrelled .44 Magnum revolver lying next to it, the picture of the smiling, beautiful Tula in front of him.

"Tex! You wanted to see me."

Tex yelled and stood up looking terrified, the picture of Tula sent spinning to smash on the floor.

"Paul!" Was all he could manage.

Paul acted as if everything was normal, "The message said that it was urgent."

"W.. What?" Tex was still open mouthed.

"The message? It must be important."

Tex looked down at the gun on his desk, Paul let the knife slip down his sleeve until the handle nestled between his curled fingers.

"Paul, you know I've always been loyal to you, done everything you asked without question..." He started blubbing and covered his eyes with his hands. Paul said nothing.

"Paul, it's Tula, she's flipped, she's gone in the head mate, she thinks you're going to kill me.... I've been sitting here trying to think why." His last words only just managing to get out. "Here!" He reached down for the gun, Paul's brain did a million calculations on distance from his outstretched hand to one of Tex's shirt buttons resting on the Solar Plexus, he gripped the handle of the knife and cleared it from the cloth of his sleeve.

Lucky for Tex, he lifted the gun by the barrel and not the butt, it saved his life. The gun thudded on the carpet just in front of Paul. "There's one round in there mate and I couldn't find the guts to put it through my head. I've been a bloody fool." He slumped back in his chair head down.

Paul walked over to the desk and took a swig from the whisky bottle then nudged Tex with it. He looked up and took the bottle. "You were saying Tex, Tula has flipped."

"I knew all along," began Tex in a monotone, "I knew all along she was no good for me. She once wanted me dead and when the tables turned said she was having our baby. I knew, I knew, but I went along with it all. A bloody sham, you and the rest must have laughed your cocks off at me. But ye know I didn't care. I think I loved her, still do, she had a way you know...She was well in at the Palace. I even fancied that M'Punga his self was doin' the business with her at one time, she certainly knew about that meeting you wanted me to bug. ZANLA she said to me not two hours ago in this very office. How did she know that and not me or you? Paul, she wanted me to kill you, lure you here and gun you down!" He took a swig from the bottle.

"And why didn't you?"

"I could never do that. As soon as I realised that that was the point and reason behind all her amateur dramatics...I knew then, that it was a choice between me and her. You didn't come into the equation. Well, as you can see, good old Tex has chosen her. She's probably at home but I would prefer it if you didn't do anything there, perhaps I could get her to come here......I don't suppose there's any other way is there?" Tex's eyes flashed a pitiful plea for a moment and then hardened. "Do it Paul! But do it quick!"

Paul went back to the open door and picked up a parcel lying just outside. He returned to the desk and using his knife, cut the bindings. He fished out the blue file titled "Jackaranda" and threw it on the desk in front of Tex.

"Read it! Read how your sow has given herself to at least seven different people since you were married, three of them from your staff here and mostly in your bed. There's also some voice recordings here!" Paul threw a cassette on the desk, "They disgust me to my core, her laughter is the shrillest when they talk about you, don't spare another thought for her."

Paul walked out of the office and down to the Bureau guard house where his escort lounged. They all got up to move, stopped suddenly and looked up at the building. It had sounded like a single shot from some-where in its depths, "Let's go!" He bawled and they piled into the cars and drove away.

The man watched the house from a phone box in the street. He smoked, cigarette butts were piled around his feet. At last! He thought as two unmarked cars pulled up just away from the house and eight people in civilian clothes got out. They looked up at the house and he could just make out the shape of pistols in the gloom. They walked carefully up to the house and two went around the corner to the back.

He lifted the phone off the cradle and dialled a number.

Tula's nerves jangled when the phone rang, she hes-itated then snatched up the receiver. "Eva?! Eva?! Thank God!" It was the Controller's voice "Things have gone wrong! They' re coming to arrest you! Don't let them take you alive Eva! They will torture you.." She heard no more from him but listened to the thump of feet on the stairs. The handle on the bedroom door went down, it was locked. They started shouldering it in. Tula backed away terrified, the first splinter of wood from the door pointed into the room, followed by another.

Tula put the phial in her mouth and crushed it, she gagged and fell to her knees and that 's how they found her seconds later. "She's dying, quick!" exclaimed the sweat covered man who had battered down the door. They threw her on the bed and started tearing her clothes off.

27

They were blessed with a moonless night, the sweat of the day made them shiver in the coolness. Slowly they made their way to the Rover. They heard the voices of groups of soldiers, huddling together from the dark and cold. At one time, passing so close to one group that they could smell the smoke from their cigarettes and see ruddy faces in the glow.

Yard by yard, they felt their way through the hundreds of short scrubby trees, stopping often, scanning ahead with their senses, knees getting torn open on the rocky floor as they sometimes scrambled on all fours to negotiate obstacles.

Norrie, who was leading stopped and turned to Frank, putting his lips almost on his ear he whispered, "We've come too far, we've missed the ravine that the Rover's in, we've hit the airstrip. I followed the exact bearing on the compass that me and Nick used before, we must have only just missed it, we have no option but to turn around and try to find it."

Using the same method, Frank passed the message on to the others, then they slowly turned and started to back track. After ten minutes or so the ground started falling sharply away and Frank knew they had found the ravine.

At last they were at the Rover. Still moving slowly and quietly they removed the cam nets and branches.

They had decided beforehand to exit through the way they had come because they were more familiar with the ground.

The shallow ravine gradually sloped away and they decided to push the vehicle as far as they could before firing the engine. Straining themselves to the limit they got the wheels turning, Jim being the lightest jumped in to steer, he could see nothing and crunched into a boulder.

They pushed it back and started again, this time they went for a half a minute before the front wheel went into a hole jarring them to a halt. "It's no good!" whispered Jim, "I can't see a friggin' thing!"

Frank called a halt, they were draining themselves and had only travelled thirty or so metres. "Okay!" he whispered to them, "This is it, we fire the engine, turn on the lights and go!"

The engine started immediately, Jim switched on the side lights, that illuminated the ground in front adequately and they were away. Frank sat in the front, Nick and Norrie stood on the steps either side the tail gate.

Jim wove his way through the trees and rocks. Frank kept an eye on his compass and kept Jim driving in the right direction. After ten minutes Jim relaxed slightly and slowed the vehicle to find easier routes.

They came upon a wide open track that led roughly North. Jim turned on to it and increased his speed with a shout of glee, "This is like the M1!"

"Turn off it Jim! Get back into the bush!" ordered Frank.

"Come off it!" Jim retorted in surprise, "We're making good time!"

Before Frank could reply Jim automatically trod on the brakes and let out a shout. Ahead was a Saladin armoured car lying across their path, the barrel of its gun pointing down the track at them. A half dozen or so soldiers stood around, one of them waving them down with a red torch. The others had their weapons slung and didn't look alert.

"Slow down, stop short and stick your main beam on! I'll try and take them out." shouted Frank. As soon as they pulled up Frank opened his door to jump out but Norrie and Nick had already started shooting, the main beam went on and Frank joined in. Immediately unseen soldiers started shooting at them from the flank. Rounds snapped over their head and some slammed into the Rover. Frank and Nick emptied their mags into the direction of the shots and it went silent for a moment.

Frank ordered them back on the Rover and Jim skirted around the Saladin and into the bush, an explosion by Frank's door made Jim ram into a tree, he grated the gears and screamed backwards in reverse. Norrie and Nick did their best to return fire and hang on at the same time.

He then lurched forward and went at ever increasing speed through the scrub, they heard another explosion but it was well behind them, some blue tracer cut through the trees to their left, then there was nothing.

Frank checked his compass they were heading East now, he decided to leave it on that course for now. After ten minutes he ordered Jim to stop. He pulled up and switched the lights off.

They gathered at the back of the Rover. "Is everyone okay?" asked Frank. Nick was holding his side.

"Think I got a bit of something off that first explosion." he said casually. Norrie pulled out his torch and pulled Nick's clothing apart, he saw five small puncture wounds in his side just above the hip trickling a small amount of blood. Norrie stuck a shell dressing on it.

Jim, who had gone round the front of the Rover came back. "I thought I could smell petrol! They got the left hand tank!"

Frank checked it out, a neat hole went through the bottom of his door and into the tank beneath the seat, the ground was damp with petrol.

"Nick! Get in the front seat, we've got to keep moving." Norrie took over driving, they headed North again, much slower this time, with no lights at all. Jim managed to find a space in the back and dropped into a doze.

The engine coughed then gave up. In spite of his precarious position hanging on the back Frank must have dozed also. He snapped awake as Norrie came around the back, "That's it Frank, no more juice."

Frank checked his watch, it was two thirty. They had been going for around four hours. He arranged all round defence, put Jim on first stag and broke out the spare radio. He called Lou, there was no answer but he really wasn't expecting one at that time of the morning. He left instructions to be woken at six and fell into the instant deep sleep that only the exhausted can achieve.

Paul was back at the tented Ops room on the airfield an hour before first light. He was told about the contact and studied the position marked by a coloured pin on the map. "These arrows," he stabbed the map, "I presume that was the direction of the vehicle?"

"Yes Sir." said a Colonel at his side.

"They were travelling North and then broke East, looks like they were making for the Kangi Ridge. Have the choppers ready to take off at first light, I will go in the Huey…Have we any idea where they got the vehicle?" shot Paul.

The duty officer looked awkward for a moment then said, "It was stolen from Lagonda the day before yesterday sir."

"The seventeenth?!" queried Paul in an incredulous voice, "They risked compromising themselves before setting their ambush up? I have been giving these amateurs too much credit. Is there anything else I should know?"

"Well Sir, they killed the camp Commandant, Major Namba, his wife and son…"

"Jesus, thundering Christ!" raved Paul, "Why wasn't I informed immediately of this? Get my car now!"

The sky had just started to lighten when Paul arrived at the house. He ordered the locked door to be opened, turned on the lights and looked around. He saw the bloodstains. He stopped at the child's bedroom door and saw the deep purple almost black stain on the bare floor. "They must be desperate men to do this," he said to no-one in particular, "Desperate, frightened, ruthless, but I still can't see them as being stupid, how and when did they get the vehicle out?"

The Lieutenant told him.

It just didn't make sense to Paul, why they would risk exposing their presence *before* putting in the ambush and why did they want a vehicle? Surely they must have made proper arrangements to ex-filtrate the Country.

He strode outside, it was light, he decided to go back to the airfield and get on the Huey, then changed his mind. "Tell the pilot on the radio to pick me up here!" he ordered.

While he waited he paced around the garden deep in thought, then he saw tyre marks where a vehicle had been driven over the grass and through some bushes to a pile of rocks. Curious, he followed them to the rocks and looked around, he spotted something among some plants and picked it up, it was a torch, not a normal issue torch but a powerful penlight type.

Further inspection revealed that all the vegetation in a five metre circle had been crushed and fresh earth scattered around. He looked at the pile of rocks, one huge slab had been hastily thrown back to cover a cavity, using all his strength, he rolled it to the side and knelt in the cavity.

With his hands he clawed away at the dirt until he felt something, it was a small leather bag, he opened it and his eyes widened, he poured out the sparkling contents and gripped them in his fist, everything was now becoming clear.

28

Frank was woken at first light. He had been in a dead sleep, he could hardly remember arriving and he had difficulty in orientating himself.

Nick, who had woken him offered water which he took. "It's been very quiet." he said.

"How's your side?" asked Frank.

"Bloody painful, if you must know," he said grinning and then in unison they said, "but only when I larf sir!"

Frank laughed then turned to the radio, there was still no answer. He gave up after a dozen attempts.

The other two were roused. Frank laid out his map on the ground. "Decision time," he began solemnly, "This is as far as the Rover and therefore the bulk of the loot goes,"

He looked around and then pointed to the map, "We are approximately here, I said approximate because we did some wild ducking and diving last night. We can now see Kangi Ridge which is about five clicks that way. If we get to the ridge and over it to the other side, there is a green valley with water..."

"Have you called Lou?" asked Jim.

"I was coming to that, yes I've called there was no reply.... But that doesn't mean anything yet, he may still be in his pit..."

"Yeh! Pissed out of his skull." Jim spat disgustedly.

Frank ignored him and continued, "We can wait here and continue to try and reach him on the radio, or each man can stuff himself with as much loot as he can carry and then we can move further out of this area. You've seen how barren this place is, carrying all the water we could, would give us a couple of good days at the most.

"Let's go on the attack and nick another vehicle!" urged Jim.

"Where do we start this attack Jim?" asked Nick, "And what do we do with the fifty odd blokes that's going to be around that vehicle? And how do we shake the chopper off? Because as soon as we show our hand it will home in on us."

"Well, we got to do something!" Jim retorted in disgust, "Just sittin' here waitin' for the bastards to come and get us. I'm going to take my chances, take some of the cash and go for it! Norrie, you with me?"

"If I'm going to die, I'll die with my comrades thanks."

"Suit your bleedin' self mate….." They all froze, it was the beat of a chopper, it was sweeping over to the East of them but getting nearer.

"Cam the vehicle!" Ordered Frank and they all set to work, glad more than anything, that there was something positive to do.

Frank looked in the passenger side of the Rover and saw crumpled up, the Major's shirt and beret that Riff had worn to get out of Lagonda. He pulled them out and dusted them off.

Paul now ordered the two large cordons of troops to redeploy and form a long extended line. This line would push northwards starting from the incident by the Saladin. He knew that a vehicle could go no further than the ridge. He reasoned that they must be trying to make a rendezvous with someone. He could not understand why they were not getting lifted out with a chopper or light aircraft. He had placed observers on the ridge to look for such things and was racing to deploy anti aircraft weapons up there.

"I've got him! I've got him! He's on the air!" screamed Norrie. While they had been finishing off the cam he explained that he had accidentally knocked the radio over, to make sure it was not damaged he had given Lou a call, he had answered immediately.

Frank grabbed the handset, he didn't bother with call signs, "Lou, come and get us, we're in shit street up to our necks. Over"

"Hey!" came the reply, "You boys know the score, no code word, no pick up. Stop playing games fellas put Julian on, come on! Let's get this show on the road!"

Frank fought down the frustration and panic he felt gushing to his head. "Lou, listen, this is no duff. Julian and Riff are dead, we are on our last legs. The Kruds are closing on us, we have all the money intact. You can have Julian's and Riff's share, that I promise in front of the rest here, but you need to get airborne now! Over."

A few seconds of silence ensued, the noise of the chopper was much louder now.

"Give me the co-ordinates." Lou said in a resigned tone. Frank sagged with relief. He sent them and told him to watch for orange smoke. Frank then took a deep breath and said, "Lou, you must be aware that there is at least one hostile chopper in the vicinity and probably troops too."

"You fucking dick head!" screamed Jim, "He'll never come out now!"

"Thanks for the warning," cut in Lou's drawl, "much appreciated, with you in two zero minutes. Out."

Norrie snapped and punched Jim full in the face, he dropped to the ground soundlessly, "Sorry Frank, I know it's stupid under these circumstances but I had to."

"Welcome back." said Frank.

Paul sat next to the pilot of the Huey and spoke to him on the intercom. The pilot informed him that his colleague in the Wessex was already sweeping the designated area ahead.

They passed over lines of soldiers walking toward the ridge. The lines extended as far as he could see in either direction. Paul ordered him to fly up to the ridge and when they over flew it he could see trucks with the anti aircraft weapons on the back labouring up the steep gradient.

He then ordered the pilot to sweep from the ridge down to the line of soldiers.

"It's a Huey! It can't be Lou's, it's too early!" shouted Frank.

"It's got Krud markings on the side." said Jim. He had recovered from Norrie's blow and had sat there wiping the blood from his nose.

"Frank, I think you'd better take a look at Nick." said Norrie quietly. Frank found Nick on his side doubled up in the foetal position under the cam net. His eyes were closed tightly and his lips pursed.

"Nick, Are you in much pain?"

Nick didn't open his eyes but nodded. "It's pierced my gut, I'm shitting blood, lots of it."

"Hang on! You know Lou's on the way, I'll give you a shot."

Nick grimaced a smile as Frank dug out the morphine.

"That Huey will come straight over us on his next sweep Frank." shouted Norrie.

He finished with Nick and said, "Get me all the black cam cream you can and hurry!" He tore off his shirt and put on the Major's, before he put on the beret he covered his face with the black cream that was being offered. Norrie and Jim understood and helped covering his forearms and patches that he had left on his face. Finally, he put on the beret, in spite of their desperate situation Norrie burst out laughing.

"Anything to play for time, get in the trees, if it doesn't work knock the bastard out of the sky, but only on my order! Now go!"

The Huey nosed closer then stopped, it then turned sideways, showing a gunner in the door. Frank strode out and waved.

Paul saw the partly camouflaged vehicle and alerted the pilot. They saw the black soldier waving to them. Paul raised his binoculars and smiled. He got on the intercom to the gunner and told him to wave back at him.

"He bought it!" said Frank a surprised look on his black face, "I can't believe it, did you see the gunner waving back!"

Paul gave instructions for the ground forces to close in, then asked the pilot if he had a speaker system on the craft, he nodded. "Then take me to within two hundred yards of that Vehicle but keep out of the line of fire."

The metallic voice boomed over the area, making them all jump, even Nick opened his eyes. "I am addressing the Leader of the mercenary force by the Landrover. This is Field Marshal Vander. You may have heard my next words on a cheap American B movie, but I can assure you that you *are* surrounded. I have gun ships on their way and at least five hundred troops closing in as I speak. I will however take your surrender and guarantee your safety until we can arrange a fair trial. I will land due west of your location. I want to speak to your leader only, come unarmed and come now. If there are any tricks you will be cut to pieces." The chopper rose and went to the West and dropped again.

"How long have we got?" asked Frank

"If he's on time, about twelve minutes." said Jim.

"Gimme some water, to get this shit off my face!"

"You're not going Frank, surely to God?" asked an amazed Norrie, "It's a trap!"

"We need the time, what have we got to lose? One burst from that heavy machine gun on the chopper and we're finished anyway." He wiped his face, checked his compass and walked off putting his own shirt back on.

The chopper dropped Paul off then lifted and hovered as ordered, five hundred yards to the rear. Paul sprinted through the trees then took cover behind a log, he placed his Uzi down and waited.

He saw Frank approaching warily through the trees unarmed, there was something familiar about him. He scanned behind him but could see no-one else. He stood up.

"I gave you my name, and yours?"

Frank inwardly jumped. He saw a well built, tanned man with a shaven head, the hard and somehow familiar face fixing him with a stare.

"Frank, Frank Britton."

"Ah! So we *have* met! I knew it, the Old factory, West Belfast and before that on the street by the riot."

Frank realised through the South African accent more than anything else who he was, "Of course.. Vander...Van Der Borgh!"

"Ten out of ten! I look forward to talking about old times.. I take it you are here to surrender?"

"Will me and my men receive fair treatment?"

"I guarantee it. What happened to Pern? I know my men didn't kill him."

"Grenade, it went off accidentally, took two of them out."

"Was killing me your primary aim or was it part of the deal if and when you got the horde?"

"Look it's complicated, you said we will talk later. I have a wounded man and need to tend to him. How far are your troops away? I need an urgent casevac."

"They will close on you within a few minutes. No tricks Frank Britton, No tricks eh?"

"Just one thing, how did you know we were there by Lagonda?"

Paul laughed contemptuously and simply repeated, "Remember, no tricks!"

Frank turned and walked a few paces, he then stopped and looked back but Van Der Borgh had disappeared.

Frank ran back to the others, Norrie smiled with relief. Frank didn't waste time, "Norrie, me and you will move as far as we can towards the Kruds and hold them off for as long as we can. Jim, Lou can land virtually next to the Rover, get Nick and the loot ready to load on board. As soon as you see Lou, throw the smoke, if that other chopper comes near, do your best to drop it!"

Without waiting for a reply, he and Norrie grabbed extra mags and grenades and set off at the double away from the ridge and into the oncoming forces.

Jim ignored Nick and began stuffing money into every available space in his clothing. Having completed that he opened a leather bag of diamonds, hesitated for a second then swallowed them with a swig of water. He then set about arranging the other stuff in piles that could be managed by a single man. Fearful of the prop blast that would ensue when Lou's chopper came in he placed heavy rocks on the money sacks.

He straightened up sweating and heard the first shots a few hundred metres away.

Frank and Norrie stopped running and approached the unseen, oncoming, lines of soldiers more cautiously. They heard them first, NCOs barking commands and the trample of many boots over the stony ground.

Frank and Norrie turned and looked at each other, they held each others gaze for a second, clasped hands firmly then took up positions a few yards from each other.

Norrie saw the first few soldiers, he put a burst through them, then he and Frank stood up and taking advantage of the shock threw a couple of grenades apiece. Amid the explosions, they moved back twenty five metres and took up new positions.

The air became alive with shouting and screaming that was soon drowned out by an enormous weight of return fire. Even though they had moved back the largely indiscriminate fire crackled over their heads and bounced around them, they hugged the ground.

Frank became aware of movement at his side, they were being outflanked, he loosed off a whole mag in short rapid bursts and lobbed a grenade. Norrie fired to his front, something whizzed passed them and exploded to their rear.

They jumped up again and ran back another twenty metres or so, as they were about to take cover an explosion knocked Norrie off his feet and he lay on his back crying out in agony. Frank ran over and took position by him, he fired at some soldiers on his right and then his left, he changed mags and stole a glance at his comrade, Norrie grabbed onto Frank and heaved himself up, "Come on!" he roared and staggered rather than ran, while Frank covered him walking backwards and loosing off short, rapid bursts

Jim started getting jumpy, the shooting was getting progressively closer. Nick under his own steam, had got himself into a kneeling position, his rifle at the ready and a dozen grenades spread out in front of him, stray rounds and overshoots started cracking over their heads.

A vicious snarl spread over Paul's face as he reached his chopper and heard the fire fight going on. "Damn them! Damn the bastards!" he roared, his voice inaudible even to himself above the roar of the rotors.

He ordered the pilot airborne, then to over fly the action, the pilot blanched but thought better of arguing.

Norrie collapsed and Frank ran to him, a round hit the ground and sent a shower of stone chips over them. Blood poured from a dozen rents and gashes in Frank's head he ignored them and checked his friend out. Blood saturated his shirt in the small of his back. He tore the shirt open, there was a savage gash in the region of his left kidney, he ripped a shell dressing off his equipment and plugged the wound the best he could.

As he helped him to his feet Paul's chopper whipped overhead and started to turn. The Karudans, now recovered from the initial shock started concentrating their efforts. "We've got to keep going Norrie! They're starting to out flank us." Frank shouted.

Norrie rose, with a final effort he screamed out in agony but started to trot back in the direction of the Rover.

Jim, because of the noise of battle saw the chopper before he heard it. Lou was to the North of them flying in a straight line, he pulled the pin from a canister shaped grenade and threw it. Orange smoke billowed from it as it hit the ground. Rounds were still zipping over head and the explosions were getting closer.

He saw Frank backing towards his position laying down burst after burst covering for Norrie who by now was crawling. Jim looked across at Nick who was overcome with pain from his wounds and doubled over.

A murderous, savage smile crossed Jim's face. He checked that the magazine on his rifle was full and took careful aim at Frank's back, suddenly, from his side a bullet smashed into the stock of his rifle taking a piece of his thumb with it. He ducked and whirled round in terror and surprise, his rifle lying some yards away.

Nick lay against the Landrover trying to get another shot off at him, he swayed and tried to track Jim as he rolled over and over to get away. Nick twisted to follow him and a searing pain tore at his guts, he buckled. Jim saw his chance and pulled the pistol from inside his smock, he ran toward Nick and pumped three rounds into his head.

Paul's chopper hovered and the gunner trained the heavy machine gun on the rover and started pumping burst after burst into the area.

Jim grabbed Nick's rifle and dived for cover as the large calibre rounds started exploding around the Rover, he ran to a position that was still partially masked by the orange smoke and loosed off a whole mag at the chopper, it lurched and pulled away.

A half dozen of Jim's rounds drilled through the pilots window narrowly missing the pilot. Paul lost his cool and went insane with anger at the pilot for pulling away, the gunner, who had been thrown off balance by the sudden movement lay in a struggling heap in the back of the craft.

Norrie and Frank made it back to the Rover as Lou plummeted and landed with a thump right by them. Frank half walked, half dragged Norrie and heaved him on board. Jim started throwing sacks of loot on as Frank went to Nick. He saw at once he was dead. Shouting with grief he went back toward the advancing troops and fired off a couple of mags. He ran back to Nick, hoisted him effortlessly in a fireman's lift and ran back to the chopper, Jim was squatting on board.

Frank threw Nick's body on board and Jim loosed off a long burst over his head. As Frank climbed on the chopper, he felt the round hit him in the back. It was as if a someone had walloped him with a cricket bat, he started to lose consciousness as he felt the chopper lift.

His adrenaline pumping, Lou gunned the chopper just above tree height, he headed for the ridge, then veered off as he saw vehicles on top, his trained eye immediately identified them as anti aircraft batteries. He followed a shallow ravine and when he came out hugged a ridge of small hills. He saw a Wessex way over to his right and flying away from them.

Paul's pilot had gone to pieces, the fact that he had actually been fired at and that he was sure Paul would shoot him as soon as they landed took their toll. He lost Lou after the first minute of trying to follow him. A fuming Paul ordered him back to the site of the Rover in case anyone had been left behind.

The first troops to reach the Rover some twenty seconds after the chopper had lifted were greeted with a snow of falling Dollar bills, working feverishly with much excited shouting they dropped their weapons and started gathering the rich harvest falling on the ground and trees.

Frank recovered, he felt no pain, just an aching sensation in his back. As far as he could tell, he was not bleeding. Norrie was at his side holding on to him. Jim was sat next to Nick's body. Sacks of money and loot lay everywhere, now and again Jim would scramble and reposition some wayward sack that was in danger of falling out.

Lou turned and pointed to his own head and then to a spare headset that hung next to Frank. Frank put on the headset and Lou's voice came through immediately.

"Will be landing in ten minutes skipper, can you all hold on?"

"Yeh! Just get us there Lou!" Frank said tensely.

"Tell me," asked Lou, "is the dead guy on board, Nick?"

"Yes, it is," Frank replied, "he got it in the last minute, it was heavy down there."

"You need to know this skipper," said Lou, his voice grave, "as I was coming in I saw Jim shoot him, I didn't know it was Nick until I saw you pick him up and put him aboard. What in hell is going on with you guys?!"

Frank went cold, he looked across at Jim. By the look on Frank's face Jim realised what the conversation with Lou must have been about. He sprang across to the numbed Frank and snatched his rifle away, flinging it out of the side of the chopper. Before the wounded Norrie could make sense of the situation, his rifle too, was snatched and flung away.

Jim started to shout something inaudible, drowned by the noise of the chopper. They saw his eyes widen and face contort with range as his jaws worked up and down. He pointed his rifle at Frank. A look of surprise replaced the rage as he pulled the trigger and realised that he hadn't replaced his empty mag. Frank, his legs stretched out with sacks on them, couldn't react quickly enough.

Jim threw the rifle to one side and went for the pistol in his smock, as he grabbed the butt and pulled it out, Norrie launched at him. He grabbed hold of Jim who toppled backwards. Norrie rained punch after punch into Jim's face but then collapsed in agony as the searing white heat of pain from his wounds lanced through his back. Jim pushed him out of the way, again he went for the pistol but screamed in agony as Frank's combat knife sliced through his thigh muscle. Frank lunged again and caught him in the lower gut but not deep enough. Jim danced back, the automatic now in his hand, he levelled it at Frank but again Norrie was on him from behind, for a second they struggled on their knees. Norrie had the gun hand but Jim was breaking it free. With an almighty heave Norrie pushed himself backwards, they both tumbled out of the open side and were gone.

Paul finished giving his report to President M'Punga. He had told how a team of over two hundred foreign mercenaries led by Pern had set up an ambush to kill the President and start a revolution to install himself as leader. He told how he had mobilised the Royal forces and shot them to pieces as they ran for the border. He told of how Major Eva Saputo was involved in the plot and how his good friend Colonel Terence Potter had discovered this and told Paul, then, overcome with grief and shame over Eva had killed himself.

It wasn't lost on Paul when Prince Tasi who was present at the debrief, dropped his head and covered his eyes at the mention of Eva Saputo.

The grateful President grabbed Paul's hands and with tears in his eyes sobbed his thanks. Tasi too, walked over and held his shoulder, his grimaced face nodding.

Lou finished checking Frank out. He was lying on a bench in the farm. "The bullet hit a back pouch stuffed with ammo, how that lot didn't go off I'll never know, but it saved ye fellah. You've just got a big purple bruise at the base of your spine."

Frank lay there and said nothing, he had hardly spoken at all since they had landed.

"I should lie up for a while Frank, let old Albert look after you. You're in shock man. I've seen it before. After combat some guys just take a while to come out of it. Me, I've got to get that chopper back to the owners and try and explain away those bullet holes."

Lou helped Frank to sit up then squatted in front of him to gain his full attention. "Look Frank, I've divided it all up, its all in the barn. I was going to do it fifty- fifty but reckon you deserved a lot more. Come on! Let's go across to the barn I've got to go soon and I want you to agree with how I split it."

Frank stood up aching and stiff. Lou held his arm as they went outside.

"It would help you know, if you talked about it. Tell me what went wrong back there Frank. What makes it all so damn important that you've got to kill each other?"

The sun made Frank shudder slightly as the warmth enveloped him. He thought of Riff and Julian smoking, bloodied bundles of meat, of Norrie lying broken with Jim somewhere in the Bush and of Nick being buried by Albert behind the barn.

"You, you were the only one outside of our group who knew where we were and what we were doing." Rasped Frank.

"Yeh! So what?"

"How did you get the message to Vander?"

"Vander? What message? You're in a bad way fellah you're rambling, come on, the money, let's get this over with."

"I've got to know Lou, how did they find out?"

Lou stopped and looked at Frank for a few seconds, "Okay, you want to know? Your mission has been monitored since you entered Rhodesia. A guy in Military Intelligence, a Colonel Daryl Hanlon, a guy who thinks he's the only person between good old white Rhodesia and the black, communist hordes of oppression. If anyone set you up, he did."

"You told him we were at Lagonda? I report our position to you and you reported it to him? Was that it?"

"Where is this getting us Frank?"

"We could have made it damn you! We could have made it! Norrie, Nick…." Frank trailed off and sank to his knees.

The chopper took off and made a low circuit of the farm before heading off. Some of the ochre dust blew up and made Frank blink.

END

Made in the USA
Lexington, KY
30 November 2011